IMPRINTS
(On a Healing Heart)

by

Dick Gibson

Bloomington, IN
authorHOUSE
Milton Keynes, UK

AuthorHouse™
1663 Liberty Drive, Suite 200
Bloomington, IN 47403
www.authorhouse.com
Phone: 1-800-839-8640

AuthorHouse™ UK Ltd.
500 Avebury Boulevard
Central Milton Keynes, MK9 2BE
www.authorhouse.co.uk
Phone: 08001974150

The names of persons and companies, other than those that have national recognition, and events that are a matter of historical record, all dialogue, opinions expressed, and most locations, towns, and street names used are solely the product of the author's imagination and are not in any way to be construed as real. Any resemblance to actual persons or names is entirely coincidental.

First published by AuthorHouse 12/04/06

ISBN: 1-4259-6531-8 (sc)
ISBN: 1-4259-6532-6 (dj)

Printed in the United States of America
Bloomington, Indiana

This book is printed on acid-free paper.

Other Books

by

Dick Gibson

Deliberate Steps (Along a Familiar Path)

It Isn't Easy Being a Lion

To Ross and Margaret Gibson for their steady guidance as a youngster, their ever-present support as a young adult, and, above all else, their unconditional love. I was fortunate to have had them as parents.

And to my wife, Sandra, for her day by day encouragement and invaluable counsel over the two years it took to complete the trilogy. Few husbands have had a more supportive, more loving partner than she.

Prologue

The funeral was over. Rob Grant's fiancée, Marianne Marzano, was now at rest in the place she would spend all eternity—never to be a part of the loving home the two of them would have shared beginning late in the year. Barely twenty-five, she'd been taken quickly by acute leukemia and had died on the first day of summer 1970. This warm and compassionate young woman, one who would long be remembered for her captivating smile, was now little more than a collection of glorious memories, ones that Rob would forever cherish.

As he made the heartbreaking drive home to Sheffield in suburban Connecticut, what kept crossing Rob's mind were the last words Marianne had spoken some forty-eight hours before she died: "'member your Mari…." Etched in his memory, those three words would give him reason to grieve for weeks to come about what might have been but would never be. The path that his life would follow was now permanently altered, and he was understandably angry that Providence had denied them the future they had planned out just weeks earlier.

Slow moving traffic gave Rob time to reflect on the three-plus years that he and Marianne had known each other. She'd been his executive secretary at Sentry Oil beginning in April 1967. They'd been a good team and had grown close. Then, as the company became the target of an acquisition, they discovered in those last weeks before the takeover was completed that they were in love. When Sentry became corporate history, they each went to new companies—and in separate directions. Rob remained in New York with IMMCorp, a basic metals company with headquarters on Wall Street. Marianne was offered the opportunity to move into an administrative role with the U.S. subsidiary of an Australian company that was located outside Washington. Painful as it was, they made a complete break and got on with their lives. Marianne's long-term aim was to have a family. Rob had been surgically decommissioned years earlier and couldn't father the children she wanted. But as fate would decree, it was by pure chance that they met again in Sydney while they were both there on company business. They discovered that their love had lost none of its intensity, and they became lovers once again as 1969 drew to a close. Into the new year, their love deepened and Marianne soon decided that Rob was more important than having her own family. During the first days of spring 1970, they set a date to marry in late December.

But their circumstances, and the future they'd hoped for, would change dramatically at the end of April. Rob had been to London on a business trip and flew back through Washington to spend the weekend with Marianne—and also to celebrate his upcoming fortieth birthday with her. Something was very wrong he believed, and he suspected a serious health problem. A distant relative had had the same symptoms, so he insisted that she see her doctor. A battery of tests determined that she had acute leukemia, and she was hospitalized immediately. The disease progressed rapidly, and when her doctors concluded that she was beyond help, she was moved to her parent's home in the Bronx. Less than four weeks later, Marianne left behind all those who loved her. And there were many. They included Rob Grant and his two sons, Mike and Greg.

With a heart that would need time to mend, it was fortunate that Rob had been introduced to Kim Rossi the preceding fall. She was a Sheffield native, legally separated from her husband, and, like Rob, had two sons, Chris and Ian. Although she got financial support from her ex, Vince, she supplemented his payments by working as office manager at Prentiss Insurance, the largest agency in the area. Over a period of several months, she and Rob became good friends. They eventually found that a caring relationship had evolved and they became lovers. When Rob's younger son, Greg, nearly died of a drug overdose, Kim was there to offer her unselfish support. It strengthened their bond. And then during the course of Marianne's brief illness, and subsequent death, she was on hand once again to help Rob through another emotionally difficult time. Kim clearly understood her motivation. She was there to be comforting. Equally important, she was in love with Rob Grant.

But unlike the Marzano family, Rob's personal support system was lean. There weren't but three other people in his life that he could depend on if he felt the need to be consoled. Apart from Kim, they were his former boss at Sentry Oil, RD Borger, Rob's IMMCorp office partner, Helen O'Brien, and Justine Siegel, an amiable young woman he'd dated occasionally—and someone who, over time, had become a good friend. Then, after having lost his management job when IMMCorp downsized, Rob was confronted with yet another setback. In some ways, his life was starting over again at age forty. With a son in drug rehab, his fiancée dead, and his professional life in shambles, he was apprehensive. Small wonder.

Chapter One

When Rob got home from the funeral, his older son, Mike, was waiting for him. "You don't look too good, Dad."

"Yeah, probably not. It's been awfully hard watching a sweetheart like Marianne die. She meant everything to me—so my hopes died with her. Guess I'm not doing a very good job of hiding how much I hurt inside."

"I know. She was real nice and would've been good for us."

"We'd have had a very loving home. But much as I wanted everything to work out, I've known for quite a while that the dream wasn't going to come true. It's been a rough three months, and these last four days have been especially hard to deal with. But life goes on and I've got other dragons to fight. Not the least of them is to find a job. Up to now there hasn't been a whole lot of interest in somebody with my experience. And it doesn't help that I haven't been at my best. I need time, which I really don't have, to get myself straightened out and back on my feet again."

"You had two calls. One was from Greg just a few minutes ago. He wanted us to know that he got to camp OK on Monday. Says he loves it up there and thinks he'll have a great summer. The other one was from Kim. She's stopping by for a little while before she goes home from work. Said she wanted to check up on you. She's being a real good friend."

"She is, but her feelings run deeper than that."

"Well, if she likes you, that's good isn't it? I think you need somebody like her now."

"I won't be able to meet her half way for a while. It's never easy accepting the fact that death is forever, but when it involves your fiancée, a woman you loved dearly, and someone you've been close to going back more than three years, you feel pain all over. Marianne doesn't have any. It's all of us she's left behind who do. I'll get on top of mine, but there isn't any way I'll ever forget her and what we meant to each other. Thing is, the pages that will one day tell the story of my life have just been rewritten, so maybe it's Kim and maybe it isn't. For sure, I'm not getting any younger, and without a job I don't have a whole lot to offer."

Before Mike could say anything other than, "You'll be OK," Kim was at their door.

"Hi, guy. You probably know it already, but I gotta say it anyway. You look terrible." Having called a spade a spade, she gave Rob a hug and held on. It was something he badly needed.

"You buried your mother not too long ago, so you know what's going on inside. Marianne wasn't a wife, or a blood relative, but she mattered. You know how much. Enough said on the subject. I have to begin the process of putting her in a little compartment and storing the memories away. You're here. She isn't. I'll do my best not to be an eternal drag on the good things we have going for us."

"Sounds like a good start. You know I'll help." Mike liked what he was hearing.

After they'd talked for a while, Kim left for home to feed Chris and Ian. Rob asked Mike if he'd like to go have a burger. "I'm in no frame of mind to share our kitchen with a ghost. At least not tonight. On the other hand, there aren't many restaurants we know that don't have at least a couple of 'em. How about if we go back to the Castle? There's plenty of misery left behind from the time Sentry Oil was being gutted like a fish. It couldn't be much worse."

After they'd eaten, and were home again, Rob got out of the suit he'd been wearing. Before he hung it up, he went through all of the pockets and found the note that Helen had given him at the funeral. She'd written down most of what Doyle Strasser at IMMCorp–Australasia had asked. The essentials were that his family had a young friend in Sydney who'd be flying to London and would be stopping in the U.S. for a visit. Would Rob be willing to show her New York and any other sites of interest that were nearby? The friend's name was Susan Bouvier.

On Thursday afternoon, Rob called Helen and asked her to telex Strasser for further details. "Be useful to have her itinerary, and then I'll know if I can handle what he's asked. If it's within the next couple of weeks, forget it."

"I'll get to it right away. Is there anything else I can do? I know you'll have some rough days ahead before the memory of these last few months, and yesterday, especially, won't hurt so much."

"You're a sweetheart, Helen, and I appreciate it that you're worrying about me. But if it means keeping me company overnight, something that's been on your mind for some time now, I won't be worth much for a while. It would be a waste of your time. There may come a day when I'll say, sure, let's find out about each other. Maybe a night or two, but you shouldn't count on that happening anytime soon. And just so you don't misunderstand, you've always been very special to me."

"Those are sweet and honest words, Rob. But I've been lost since you stopped coming into the office every day. It's an altogether different place when you aren't here."

"Now you're getting to *me*, and I've been through plenty of that. Seeing my girl draw her last breath is just about the hardest thing I've ever had to face. But enough of this. Let me know what Strasser says."

"If you're coming in next week, I should have his answer by then. Take care of yourself, Rob. You mean more to me than you know."

"Thanks, Helen. Words like those are a big help. I will be in sometime next week—if only so I can give you a hug. It'll be my way of showing you how much I appreciate having your support."

"I'll be ready. Always have been. Bye, Rob."

"Have a good weekend, gal."

Kim spent Saturday night with Rob and made small but measurable progress toward turning him back into a whole man. During the evening hours, and then into Sunday morning, they slept nestled together. Over breakfast, Rob smiled and in so doing showed the first signs of healing his broken heart.

"Given time, I think you'll live. *Ohhh*. Sorry. Terrible choice of words. I just want to see the Rob I knew back when we had that weekend together up in Sturbridge. You're important to me. You know that."

"Just stay close, Kim. And be patient. I'll get there. You'll see."

"I will. But there's something I want to mention before I close the book, at least mine, on everything that's happened lately. I ran into my good friend, and your old flame, Lu, late on Friday afternoon. While we were talking, I thought she'd want to know about Marianne. She shivered, you could see it, and then her face turned white as a sheet. She never said a word, but it was obvious that it hit her real hard. I remember her saying early last year, that she really liked the girl, even though she suspected that the two of you had something going on. End of story."

"Thanks for telling me. They got along well when Lu came in to tour our building back in December of sixty-eight. Italian bloodlines. Marianne also supplied the potent red wine Lu drank that afternoon, about a month earlier, when we met in the laundry room. You know the story. We wound up in bed while our clothes were drying." Rob smiled at the memory. "It was potent stuff. Remember? You had some of it, too. It came from Marianne's grandfather. I still have some of it—but a much later vintage."

Just before mid-day, Kim left for home. Shortly afterwards, Rob took Mike to JFK. He'd be boarding a TWA flight to Los Angeles and then spending the summer there with Rob's first ex-wife. Before good-byes and hugs, Mike said, "I'll tell Mother it wasn't your fault that Greg had drug problems. I don't think she understands. I'll try to set her straight."

"Thanks, Mike, but what she chooses to believe isn't important. The state of Connecticut and I made every reasonable effort to keep him pointed in the right direction. That's what really matters. Have a great summer, stay out of trouble yourself, and I'll see you on August 30."

Rob was now alone for the first time since the end of August last year. How sweet it would have been to spend these two months with Marianne. Had she lived. "Those words again—the ones Carlo Marzano had spoken just minutes after Marianne died. They'll always be there," he thought.

The following Tuesday, Rob went back to his office to start taking his personal effects home. That included the two oils that another former sweetheart, Sharon Kerner, had painted for him. Helen was glad to see her partner and the hug they shared confirmed it.

"I got an answer from Strasser yesterday. He says their friend won't be here until the last week in July. She's stopping on the West Coast first, and then coming into Kennedy on Sunday afternoon, the twenty-sixth. Her flight to London goes out on Friday evening, the thirty-first. There are details about how to recognize her. Sounds like she's good looking. Strasser says she reminds him some of Candice Bergen."

"Late July will be OK. I'm not ready for much of anything else at the moment." While Rob was in the office, he called RD and asked if they could have an early dinner on Friday. Because it was the long Fourth of July weekend, RD said he'd be up at Long Pond on the Cape. They agreed to talk after the holiday. Then before he left for home, Rob phoned Justine Siegel, the very likable mid-thirties woman he'd met last fall and had dated occasionally. She was someone he was sure he could count on to be a part of his support team.

"Hello, stranger," she said. "I thought you'd abandoned me."

"No, dear heart. I've been watching a young woman important to me die of leukemia. I've been pretty much out of circulation since mid-April. I made a trip to London, and since then it's all been down hill. Sorry. I'm still a ways from being decent company. We'll get together sometime soon, if you'd like."

"I would—whenever you're ready. In the meantime, if you just want to talk, I'm here. Sounds like you were serious about her."

"We'd started making plans to marry in late December. She was Marianne Marzano, the name I mentioned to you on that memorable night last November when you and I first met. If you remember, I pointed out a building diagonally across the street from yours where she'd lived. I also told you why it was that we'd gone separate ways after Sentry was taken over by Argus Oil and British O&G. By sheer chance she and I met in Sydney during my last trip down in December. The love was still there, and we decided that we ought to put our future back in order. There isn't one now. She's dead."

"I *do* remember. What comes to mind about that night was that you looked across the street at her building and I could see from your expression that she'd been important to you. And then Cindy told me, maybe three or four months ago, that she was with RD and had met the girl before the four of you had dinner together. She thought your fiancée was a lovely young woman. I'm sorry for you, Rob. I know what you must be going through, and I understand completely. Call me when you're ready and we'll set a date. I've missed not seeing you once in a while."

"I will. Promise. Just give me a little time."

"Sure. Be good to share dinner and an overnight with you again."

Rob did make progress. Still, the healing process was slow. Marianne was in his thoughts, but the pain associated with her memory did eventually ease some. Kim was great therapy, so by the third week of July Rob's biological needs got the better of him. He phoned Kim and asked if she could come by after work.

"Problem?"

"Not really. Well, sort of. I discovered this morning that I'm still alive, and I'll guess that you understand what I'm referring to."

"I do, and you don't have to ask me twice. It's been a while. I'll be up right after work."

Rob *was* very much alive, and in a spirited session they took each other to high places in a relatively short time. It was electrifying!

"You don't know how badly I needed that," Kim said. "I guess you did, too."

"It's taken time, and I *was* long overdue."

"Tell me about it. I have lots of evidence."

"If you'll come back on Saturday, maybe we can pick up where we left off."

"After a performance like that, I'll come back every afternoon this week if you want. I'm very ready, very willing, and very able," Kim said.

"Why not? The way we seem to be worked up, it shouldn't take long, and you won't be too late getting home."

"You're the one with the full head of steam. I've been ready for quite a while, but I understood the reasons why your mind was somewhere else. You're back, in a manner of speaking. That's good news for me. I've needed you."

Rob and Kim had their late Saturday afternoon and night together. When she went home after brunch on Sunday, Rob drove to JFK to meet Susan Bouvier coming in from Los Angeles. Given the description Doyle Strasser had sent by telex, he had no trouble spotting her among the arriving passengers. Helen had guessed right. She *was* an attractive young woman.

"You're Susan?"

"Right you are. And you're Robin Grant?"

"See? We're both good at guessing." She had a sweet laugh and used it to charm Rob.

"Not knowing what the arrangements would be, I have a reservation at the Roosevelt Hotel. Do you know where that is?"

Rob smiled. "Yes. I know it very well. A tunnel into and out of the rail station begins, or ends, at the Roosevelt entrance. But after tonight, you're welcome to stay with me. You can have my bed; I'll sleep on the sofa."

"That won't be necessary. I'm not a virgin, and I assume there will be an exchange of favors. You'll be my host, and for a few days I'll be your mistress. I'm delighted that Doyle didn't make arrangements for me with some portly, on in years gentleman. I guess he knows you and assumed I'd be pleased. I am. Shall we collect my luggage?"

Rob got Susan's bags, drove into Manhattan, dropped her at the hotel, and then went on to park in a nearby garage at Madison and Forty-sixth. After Susan had checked in, they went off to find dinner.

"Let me suggest a place on Forty-eighth Street very near the building I used to work in. It's a hangout of sorts after five o'clock, so lots of new acquaintances get started around the bar. I call it a boy-girl place. I've only eaten there two or three times, but that was before I went down to Wall Street a year ago April. Food was good, at least then. That all right with you?"

"This is your domain, so I'll follow your lead."

At that point, they were close to his old building.

"I used to work in a big corner office on seven. There." Rob pointed. "Right where the setback is for the upper floors."

"Must have been huge. It has two sets of big windows. Does that mean you had an important job?"

"I thought so. Sad part is that the company was sold to two other oil companies and I was forced to look for another job. I'm in the same boat all over again. IMMCorp has just wiped out my unit—and lots of others."

"What a shame. And I mean that."

"OK. Here we are. Charlie's. After you."

"We would say of you at home that you've been made redundant. Not a pleasant experience. Doyle told me a little bit about what's been going on. Any prospects?"

"Very few. It's a tight job market, especially for administrative people like me. But if I'd already found something, I wouldn't have been able to spend the next few days with you."

"I'm really pleased that you can, although not under the present circumstances. I hope my stopover won't interfere with your search."

"No, no. I've talked with several prospective employers, but I've been fighting something else and haven't been at my best."

"You've been ill?"

"In a sense, maybe. It would be mental, if anything. I lost my fiancée to leukemia about five weeks ago, and it's taking time for me to adjust to life without her. The future isn't what I had hoped it would be, but it's not much different from anything else that's happened over the past seventeen years. But enough. It's not your cross to bear."

"I'm awfully sorry to hear about your intended."

Drinks came, and dinner orders were placed.

"Appreciate it, but let's move on. I have to. No need to dwell on something that can't be changed, now or ever. Tell me about you."

"It's a fairly short story. I'm Sydney born, educated in the local school system, had a bit of university at Macquarie, a school recently founded in northwest Sydney, but I ran out of money and went to work for Brownhurst. I've put away a fair amount in savings and am taking the break I've planned on for quite some time now. London is my final destination, and I'll be there for several months.

"You're taking a sabbatical awfully early in life, it seems to me."

"Like you, I'm older than I look. I judge you to be nearing forty, based on your comment about 'seventeen years', and that means I'm not all that much younger than you."

"I turned forty at the end of April."

"I wouldn't have guessed it otherwise. A woman shouldn't talk about her age, so let's leave it at the fact that there isn't much difference in our numbers."

"Anyone ever tell you that you bear a strong resemblance to Candice Bergen?"

"There's hardly a week when it doesn't come up. Maybe I should be her stand-in."

"And you're not married?"

"No, and I have no plans to be. It isn't that I don't like men, because I do, but I've yet to meet someone I'd want to have around every day. Being that deliberate, I'll at some point be wrinkled, unattractive, and unwanted. That means I could end up a spinster."

"But one with some spicy memories, I should imagine."

Susan laughed sweetly. "You might say that."

When they got back to the hotel, Susan wasn't at all shy about undressing in front of Rob. He liked what he saw. She was maybe an inch taller, trim and nicely proportioned. Long blonde hair added to an exquisite picture of a *very* sensuous woman.

"You may have ideas of loving me tonight. But, how to say it . . . it just isn't done. We have twin beds so we'll each have our own. Tomorrow night will be different, and we'll get better acquainted then. Sorry, but that's the way it will have to be."

"This may be my realm, but those are your rules so I'll abide by them. I've been patient for more than forty years. One more night won't matter."

"Thank you for seeing things my way. Now, I'm tired and would like to call it a day. Part of my body is still on Sydney time."

"I know the feeling well. Night, Susan."

"G'night, Rob. Thank you for meeting me and for a pleasant dinner."

Susan was up at a fairly early hour. Rob shouldn't have been too surprised. She intended to cover a lot of ground in the next few days. From the bed he was lying in this morning, he couldn't know just how far her plans would take him, geographically, during the next few days.

"I have two things I'd like to do before we leave Manhattan. One is the UN Building; the other is Greenwich Village. From my guide, I think we can also see the new twin towers. They seem to be close by."

"They are. The first building should be finished at about the end of the year. It'll give you an idea, if you use your imagination, what they'll look like when they're both completed. The second tower has a ways to go yet. To do what you want, we should check your luggage and leave the car in the garage until later on. We can walk to the UN Building, and then we'll take the subway down to Bleecker Street. That's a good place to start, I think. We'll have lunch down there and do a walkabout, as you'd call it."

They got themselves over to the UN and then toured the General Assembly Building. Susan was mesmerized by the Foucault Pendulum and stood watching it for several minutes. It was a warm and pleasant day, so before they started back toward Lexington Avenue, and the subway ride down to The Village, she took loads of pictures of the Plaza and all the flags along First Avenue that were rippling in the summer breeze.

When they got off at Bleecker Street, Rob didn't have a plan. It wasn't his part of town, so they started walking until their appetites said it was time to stop. Picking a restaurant at random, they wound up in a place where two streets came together at angles so that the building was shaped rather like an isosceles triangle. The food was good, the beer was tasty, and they were then fortified to continue their tour of streets running off in all directions with low-rise townhouses, bistros, shops, and most anything else an outsider might equate with the Bohemia it is. Susan was fascinated. "Reminds me of Paris. At least some of it does. Be fun to live here. Artists, musicians. writers, and all sorts of interesting people who aren't exactly mainstream America."

"I've been a corporate animal too long. And having two teenagers to raise doesn't allow me to think about this kind of alternative. If I were to run away, it would be somewhere on Viti Levu. I loved Fiji."

"I know. It has its own kind of special appeal, but here you can feel the creativity. I wouldn't have expected to find something like this in the U.S., even though the tourist guides describe it very much as we've seen it. The Village is quite unique."

"Same thing in San Francisco. If you're taken with this, then you need to make a stopover in the Bay Area on your way back. That assumes you can book your return that way instead of through Los Angeles."

"That's a long way off. I haven't decided yet. But it's getting late. Shouldn't we be getting on to your place? My feet are telling me we've done a fair amount of walking."

"Fine with me. I'm ready to go, too."

They made their way back to the Roosevelt via Grand Central—and the tunnel. Rob got the car and then picked up Susan and her luggage. Her bags stowed, they headed for Sheffield. Rob had told Kim that he'd have a busy week, but she didn't ask questions. They'd had a very active several days, would be together again on Saturday, and that was all that mattered.

On Monday evening, the first night requirement of "it just isn't done" had been satisfied, and their evening, after dinner out, turned into pleasure time. Susan wasn't the most exciting woman in bed, but she seemed pleased with the event of the evening and said it had been good for her. Neither a woman who hit high peaks, nor one interested in a morning encore, they got an early start on Tuesday morning. It was a good thing they did. She had big plans.

"One of the places I want to visit is Plymouth Rock and the plantation nearby, but you've told me about the old village near some property you have. That sounds interesting, too. Can we do all of that in one day?"

"Sure, if we spend fifteen minutes at each place." Susan charmed Rob again with that sweet laugh.

"I've built a buffer day into my schedule. Could we go to your old village and either stay nearby, or go on to Plymouth this evening?"

"Sturbridge Village is a half day—if we do it right. We'll stop at my land first. That'll only take a few minutes. It's on the way. After we've seen The Village, we can decide then where we'll stay. I figure the drive home from Plymouth will take somewhere around three hours."

"Capital! I'd like us to be on our way as soon as we can get started."

Rob was beginning to see that Susan Bouvier was going to be an expensive guest. And the week had only begun.

They made the drive to Rob's land in just about record time, even with a stop for photos at a rest area along I-86. He pushed his Mustang, so it also tested his ability to avoid a speeding ticket. He did a lot of checking to see who was in his rear view mirror.

Susan loved the land. Everyone did. She had fantasies about coming back and spending a weekend in his new cottage. It was highly unlikely that a trip up here again, at least with her, would ever happen.

The Village tour, and lunch on the grounds, took another five hours. She was fascinated by the early 1800's buildings and took dozens of pictures.

Late in the afternoon, Rob suggested that they go on to Plymouth. "It's a couple of hours, or close to it, so I'd rather not add that to what we're doing tomorrow—plus the drive home."

As it turned out, it pleased Susan because they lucked out and were able to find a comfortable little motel overlooking Cape Cod Bay.

"A better idea, Rob. Very romantic. Just for that I'll give you a better performance than I did last night." That struck him as marginally strange. And for the first time that he could ever remember, he really didn't care one way or the other—that is, until they got involved and she was able to show him exactly what she meant. The sound of the waves must have reminded her of home or another bed on another night. Didn't matter. He had good cause to smile.

Wednesday began with a good breakfast, which was followed by Plymouth Rock, the Mayflower II, and the Plantation. Rob hadn't seen any of them before, so he didn't object to behaving like a tourist. Being aboard the replica Mayflower was fun, although it wouldn't have been for the passengers back in 1620. Both he and Susan were taken with the Plantation and the people who were the "interpreters". Ask them a question about something after their time, and they would say that there wasn't any way they could know. They knew their settlement, but not the future. Interesting, he thought. Susan took more pictures, and Rob was glad he wouldn't have to pay for having all of them developed.

At mid-afternoon, Rob said it was time to start back to Sheffield. "Another night's lodging isn't in my budget," he said. Susan didn't object, so they started the drive back to Sheffield. After they drove west on U.S. 44 to get on I-95, Rob realized it was a mistake to drive past Mystic Seaport. If she saw the signs, she'd want to stop, and he was dead. He kept her eyes looking in other directions and checking the map and mileage home until they were past the Mystic exit.

Back in Sheffield, they went out for a simple meal and settled in for the evening. He put Susan in front of American TV and went to his bedroom to call Kim.

"Hi, babe. How are you?" Rob asked.

"Good, sweetheart. Tried to call you last night, but there was no answer."

"I went up to Massachusetts to see Alan Wilcox, the real estate guy," he lied. "He's not ready for me yet—in spite of what he's said all along. He's got a guy named Davies managing his business, but he's going into sales with a GM dealership and is finished after the season's over at the end of October. Alan would still like me to work for him anytime after that." Pretty good story he'd made up, Rob thought as he hung up.

"So that means you'd leave me behind, I guess. That's not the kind of news I want to hear. It's good for you, maybe, since you're out of work and don't have any income, but I feel lonely already."

"Don't even think about it. I don't have a place to live up there, and it would only be on weekends as it stands now."

"There go our Saturday nights."

"Wilcox has bedrooms upstairs in that big house he uses for his office. Maybe we could spend the weekend there once in a while. We'd go up early on Saturday morning and come back on Sunday evening. Because of your guys, it couldn't be very often. Be a treat, though."

"Not for me. What would I do while you're working?"

"Lots of crossword puzzles? I don't know, we'd figure out something."

"Oh, whoopee doo!"

"Not a good idea, sounds like. Well, nothing will happen anytime soon. In the meantime, it may be that I'll find a good spot either here or in Manhattan."

"I'd like that. Then I'd have you close."

"See you Saturday afternoon?"

"*Yesss*, and I'll be ready for more of that spoons treatment after dark, but only after a good loving. And I have to say that you sound the best you have in months. You don't know how much that pleases me. I know it's been a hard spring and summer, but it says that you're in control and that time is healing the wounds. See you on Saturday, love. Night."

"G'night, babe."

After he hung up, Rob rejoined Susan, and TV, in the living room.

"Someone special, I presume?" She asked.

"Yep. Kim was the one who kept me propped up when Marianne died. Before and after. Don't know what I'd have done without her."

"I'm very much enjoying my visit with you, and our satisfying nighttime activity, but it appears that I shouldn't plan on extending my stay, appealing as it's getting to be."

"Might get a little crowded on Saturday evening."

"Without question, you've taken steps to repair the injuries that your Marianne caused. I wouldn't have wanted to deal with what you just did. At her young age? Dreadful. I'm a guest and am very grateful you're willing to do what you've done so soon after her death. But I feel it's best not to impose on you beyond Friday, much as I think I'd like to. You have your agenda, and therapy of your own making to help you along. Perhaps I've helped a little, too."

"You have, and you can further support the cause through Friday morning, if you're so disposed. I'll put myself in your care until then."

"Won't your Saturday night be a little less interesting?"

"No, I recover well."

"I'm not much of a morning person, but you do know something about female anatomy, and how to satisfy a woman. Your contribution, let's call it, would give me a proper sendoff. If it can be arranged, I'd like to come back through New York. Having you love me when you aren't in mourning should be an even more memorable event."

"Your being here, and getting me out and around, has really helped. I'd never been to Plymouth or the Plantation. I should thank you, too, because you've been a part of the rehabilitation process. If you were to stay on, it could be that I'd start to think we might have the future that died five weeks ago."

"Don't look to me for a long-term arrangement. If you feel the beginnings of a romance, then it *is* best that I go on to London on Friday. I don't want to sustain any false hopes."

"That says it like it is, and I appreciate it that you're being honest with me. For sure, I have an empty space called Marianne that I want to fill, so I'm probably inclined to be too hasty, too aggressive."

"We can talk about it tomorrow on our way to the Roosevelt home over in Hyde Park—assuming you're willing to take me there."

"So far, I've done everything you've asked. Sure, we'll do it. I've never been there either. More therapy. Now, shall we love?"

"I'm your mistress for a few days, like I said. The difference with you is the time you take to get me ready, and then to bring me along. You're patient, and I get far more pleasure from what you do than I'm accustomed to."

"You're giving me higher marks for proficiency than I deserve. But, shall we have at it?"

"Lead the way. I'm yours, completely."

Rob paid special attention to the preliminaries and brought Susan to the highest level of stimulation he could. She might never have known a roaring climax, but there couldn't be any doubt that she was satisfied. Without getting too analytical about it, he assumed that when her sensual needs were met, that was sufficient for her to call a union, at least with Rob, especially enjoyable. A different kind of woman, he thought, one who maybe placed more emphasis on psychological satisfaction.

"That was lovely," she said afterwards. "That you care about a woman's needs is obvious. Not often I feel sorry that I can't purr."

"I call it a mirror reaction. When I sense that my partner is really enjoying herself, the more of a stimulus that is for me. I simply respond in kind. You take a little more time to reach the point where you *want* to be loved—and then to reach the place that satisfies you. When you get there, that turns me on. From start to finish, it's better for both of us."

"You're considerate of other's feelings. I was the beneficiary just now. I'm *very* contented."

"Maybe when you've reached the spinster stage, you'll remember me."

"Not much doubt." She took the initiative, and gave him a wet kiss. "It's unfortunate that I can't stay on. I could use more attention of the sort you provide. I'm very pleased that Doyle contacted you, and that I made the stopover. But he couldn't have known this much about you."

"He doesn't, but it could be he somehow got some feedback from Simone Dekker."

"Of the wool family? They're big money! Did you bed her?"

"No. I didn't meet her until the day before I left Sydney. She might have been interested in getting better acquainted, but you know that 'it just isn't done', as someone once put it."

Susan laughed. "Touché, Rob. She'd have been quite a catch. You wouldn't have had to worry about your future."

"There wasn't time, and it would have taken that. For one thing, it was the wrong time of the month. It's a shame that I won't be going back. Now, dear lady, we need to get some rest. Big day tomorrow if we're going to Hyde Park and see the home of our thirty-second president."

"You're positively right, especially if we're to have a quickie before we leave."

"Not a morning person? Ahhh. Something new has been added to Susan Bouvier's repertoire, it seems."

"It's as I just said, I'm pleased to have made the stop." She gave him a hug and sleep they did.

Rob and Susan spent her penultimate day in the States, as she called it, at the Franklin D. Roosevelt Historical Site. She couldn't explain her fascination with the late president, but she was impressed with the grounds and the Roosevelt home. Rob had to agree that it was well worth the trip, even though his parents disliked FDR and had voted for Willkie in 1940, and then Dewey four years later. Political differences aside, Roosevelt could hardly be ignored as an effective president, the architect of programs that helped America recover from the great depression and an effective leader during World War II. An interesting and informative excursion.

On Susan's last day in Rob's care, he had to face up to the fact that he'd gotten rather attached to this attractive and proper young lady from Australia. He didn't look forward to seeing her go on to London. Over breakfast, she asked, "Could we just drive around to places nearby? I want to take photos so that I can remember where you live. This is a lovely region, your New England, and I love it. Given time, I might love you as well, but I must go on. There are compelling reasons to do so."

They had their drive, and then late in the afternoon Rob drove Susan to JFK to see her off on BOAC's Flight 500 that left at eight o'clock. It would be hard for him to say good-bye. She'd begun to mean something to him and, once again, he was at a place of departure and trying to avoid the vacant feeling that would almost surely follow. He thought, as they were parking, "Guess the fundamental problem is that I don't like to see something end—unless it's distasteful. There's Kim in my life, so why do I still feel lonely? I'm going to miss Susan, though. Maybe I should see a shrink and have him find out why I don't like being left behind." As they made their way to the BOAC counter, Susan interrupted his reverie.

"Don't look so glum, Rob. I'll write and will very likely come this way next summer if you're here and unattached. Before I go, let me thank you for all of the interesting places you took me. It's been a wonderful stopover, and you've been an absolutely splendid host. One other thing. I want you to know that you taught me something new. In just a few days, I've learned that morning sex can be just as satisfying as a loving at bedtime. At my age I should have discovered that by now, but I had to come to America for a tutorial. It was delightful."

"You're welcome—for both the tours, and the lesson learned. About next summer, it's hard to know where I'll be, but I'll stay in touch. I'd like it if you'd do the same. Have a smooth trip and a good visit in the UK." They held each other for a moment and then Susan boarded. "A very sweet and attractive young woman," Rob said quietly. "Too bad they don't stick around, or live long enough, to become a member of the family. *Damn*!"

Friday night traffic was heavy and getting back to Sheffield was slow going. People were starting their weekend, or their vacations. Many of them were probably headed for parts of New England. The Hutchinson River Parkway was one way to get started in that direction. Rob thought about Susan as he sat in stop and go traffic. She never was specific about why she was going to spend nearly a year in London. In fact, she avoided the subject. He had all kinds of wild ideas, not a one of them pleasant.

When Kim showed up early on Saturday afternoon, she asked, "Why do you look so down? Maybe I should go out and come back in again. Hello. It's me, Kim, the gal who cares about you. I thought that after a week, you'd be glad to see me."

"Sorry, love. I am glad to see you. Let me try that hug all over again."

"That's better. And so was the kiss. You haven't forgotten how to do that after all."

"My mind is sort of drifting. It's August, and this is the last month I'll get any money out of IMMCorp. I've spent two months trying to find a job. Thing is, the memories of Marianne linger, so it's unlikely that anyone will hire me until I can put them to rest and then shape up. But the fact remains, I'm still unemployed, there are no really good prospects, and my finances are starting to run a little thin. Had too much fun, I guess. My bank account shows it. But you don't need all this. Looks like I'm going to be forced into talking with Newcombe again about getting into the executive search business. Not exactly my cup of tea, but it would help keep us from starving during the winter months. I'm beginning to feel a little bit like the grasshopper that did."

"Then I've come by on the right day with the right idea. If you come down to the car with me, you'll find a picnic basket on the back seat. We're going over to the park on the Sound and dine out."

"*Great*—and just what I need. You're somethin' else, Kim Rossi."

"This is live bait, you know. After we picnic, I want you to bring me back here and love me passionately before you take me to the movies. By then we'll be hungry again, so we'll stop at The Diner for a bite. I'll treat. Then you can love me again. After a week alone, I'm among the needy."

"Sounds that way. Well, pretty lady, you have a deal. I like your plan. All of it."

Rob and Kim's Saturday was nothing short of terrific. The picnic brightened his day, and it was good to have some fire back in his bed. She *was* in need! Then the Eastwood–MacLaine film, "*Two Mules for Sister Sara*", was OK, even if the massacre at the end was a little too much. A snack after the movie, and a spirited loving before they slept restored Rob's outlook on life. He was neither alone, nor empty. Kim's attention was the kind of cure he needed and just what the doctor ordered.

Over breakfast, Rob said, "Thanks for pulling me out of the dumps yesterday. You don't know how well timed your planned day was. It helped that you built a fire, and then showed me that mountaintop. Twice."

"You did your part, you know. Takes two to tango you once said. And you do that verrry well!"

During the week that followed, Rob kept interview appointments, few as they were, and came up empty. "The market is dead, at least for people like me," he concluded. "Companies aren't looking to hire anyone. They're tightening their belts." He did have an interview with a company in Sheffield, and was hopeful, but he wasn't called back. Younger people with less but similar experience, and lower salary requirements, were getting what few offers were being made. It went back to the point that someone made about him a couple of years ago. It was that he didn't have fourteen year's experience, but one year of experience fourteen times. That wasn't quite accurate in his case, but it might be said that he fell into the two times seven category. At any rate, being forty and having been very well paid was more than most companies wanted to deal with.

Late on Wednesday afternoon, Rob went to his now mostly empty office, visited with Helen, and showed her pictures of Susan that he'd gotten done at a one-day developing shop.

"She's very attractive, Rob. Any hope that it'll go further?"

"With her spending a year in England, and maybe coming through New York on her way back to Sydney, not very likely. And besides, she isn't as good in bed as you are."

"How would you know *that*! You never let me prove it to you, and now maybe it's too late. I've met a neat guy, and it would be hard for me to cheat on him. Still, you could be the exception. I remember how you always had something going on the side. Would depend."

"I'm happy for you, Helen. You deserve better than what you got. Your marriage ruined a good, long-time friendship with Danny. Now, I'm going to make a couple of phone calls. The first to RD to see about a drink, and the second to Justine to see if she'd like some company. Both boys are gone, so I'm alone. Just about like you are on this floor now. Sure is spooky."

"Tell me about it. It's just awful, and I miss you like crazy. I hope everything works out for you, Rob. You've had a year that would test most anyone's character. I still feel terrible about Marianne and think about her more than I probably should. But I'll get out of your office so you can make your calls."

"Hi, RD. Any chance I could buy you a drink at The Watering Hole at about five o'clock or so?"

"No. But I'll buy *you* a drink. You're unemployed. See you at a quarter after five. OK?"

"Sold. See you there."

"Justine? It's a voice from your distant past."

"*Rob*! Funny, I was just thinking about you and wondering how you're doing. We must be on the same frequency."

"I was wondering if you'd be interested in dinner and maybe some company afterwards."

"Be wonderful to see you again. I'd love it. What time?"

"You remember RD from last November. I'm meeting him for a drink first. You name it. I'm the one who's unemployed, you know."

"Why don't you come up to East Eighty-third when you're finished. We can figure out where to go from there."

"See you at home, then. Probably be somewhere around six thirty."

Rob got to TWH ahead of RD and found a small table with a second chair that someone tried to steal almost immediately. "Got someone coming in a few minutes. Leave it, please." RD saw the exchange and confirmed that the "someone" was real.

"How are you, Rob? Maybe it was just as well we didn't get together sooner. Now I can say in all honesty that you look better."

"Been six weeks, today in fact, since we said good-bye to Marianne. Been tough to deal with the hardest hit I've ever taken, but I'm on the mend. Kim, the gal in Sheffield, has been great support, and I'm seeing Justine tonight for the first time in months. She seems pleased with the idea. Me, too. But there isn't much news. I'm still job hunting. It's a tight market. Awful. So, I've about decided to try executive search, not because I want to especially, but Newcombe has shown serious interest in having me join him. We go back to my early days at Sentry. He's something of a nut, more artist than businessman, but he's been effective in the past. I'm damned stuffy in comparison. Too bad you don't have an opening. Be great to work with you again."

"It would, but I don't have requirements of any kind in my department. If you and Newcombe get together, I'll want you to be a source for the few needs that come up. It can't be on a retainer basis, but you'll have an even chance at making placements."

"I'm sure Doug would like it if I could bring in at least one prospect. Be a plus. How's the new job going?"

"Much better than the retail business—even though I was well paid. But I'm enjoying working for a media company. Interesting being in a place where whatever is going on in the world is gathered and then turned into a first rate weekly news magazine. Lots of deadlines to be met, breaking stories to be dealt with. Light years apart from retailing. It's a good environment. I plan to stay on. At least for a while."

Rob and RD talked on about what else was going on their lives, and then walked to Grand Central together. RD got off at his Seventy-seventh Street stop; Rob went on to Eighty-sixth. They promised to stay in touch and have a drink or dinner once in while just to stay current on their news. Rob was happy to have his former boss as a close friend.

At 201 East Eighty-third, Rob buzzed to be let in. "Yes?" Justine asked.

"It's that voice from your past. May I enter?"

"You may, but be careful how you phrase questions." They laughed.

At Justine's door, they held each other. Rob appreciated the warm welcome.

"Thanks for letting me come back," Rob said. "I thought you might tell me to bug off."

"Why on earth would I do that? You didn't offend me. I was just curious about the long silence. But when you explained it to me, I understood. And before we go any further, I want you to know how sorry I am that you lost someone so important to you. The way it happened has to have been terribly painful."

"Still is."

"Would you like a drink?"

"A glass of red wine," Rob said. "That is, if you have any."

"I do, and we'll make it two. I'll join you."

They had their drink, and then went to dinner. Justine was interested in Marianne, and wanted to hear more about how they knew each other. It took a while because some of it was painful to talk about, but Rob needed to empty his mind of at least some of the memories. It was the first time he'd done it verbally, and it helped him in the same way a confession would, he supposed.

When Rob had finished, he said, "You've been kind to listen to all of this, Justine. I appreciate it, and I feel a little better now that my memory and my soul have been purged to some extent. I'll never forget her, but it's out of me now and I've been unshackled—at least partly so."

"It really isn't my place to suggest it, but maybe later on I could help you take your deliverance a step further. I hope you're not offended by my suggestion."

"Not at all. Our nights together have never been anything less than, well, uhh, memorable." Rob grinned.

"That's the face I remember from last fall. You'll survive, and I'll be the beneficiary, very much so, whenever it is we can get together."

When they got back to East Eighty-third Street and were behind a locked door, Rob and Justine ignited a brand new fire, one that took them to lofty peaks and then ultimately to a shared finale. Afterwards, they slept well, but all they had left in the morning were warm smiles.

"I guess we did it all last night," Justine said. "I don't seem to have any reserve to draw on. We should've saved something for this morning."

"There'll be another morning. The best I can do is give you a hug. That was quite a performance, gal."

"You stirred the fire. And you were at the top of your form, so to speak. Spectacular! I'd like you to share my bed once in a while. You give me a lot to remember afterwards. Keeps me humming for days."

"I'll come back. Promise. But it's getting late."

"Don't worry. I'll call my secretary and let her know I'll be a little late. I'm mid-level management now, so it gives me some flexibility. I'll make it up at the end of the day if there's something that won't wait. And now that I've thought about it, maybe I will have a little more of you."

"Strange. I was thinking the same thing."

They joined and took each other to a noisy and growling climax.

"You've made my day," Justine said. "I won't have to explain my smile at the office. It'll be obvious. You haven't skipped a beat, and you're still good at putting out my fire."

Justine went off to shower and Rob called Doug Newcombe.

"Doug. Rob Grant. I'm in town and wondered if I might come see you this morning."

"Should I ask you why you're in this early, or will you let me guess?"

"I'll take your question right out of the dark and put some light on it. I was here to get my ashes hauled. Now that the fire is out, we're cleaning up the mess." Newcombe roared with laughter.

"I thought as much. Sure, come on over. I'll buy you a coffee, and we can talk business—assuming you're ready."

"I'm ready, even though my orientation is still corporate rather than search. But that well is bone dry at the moment. I've never seen it like this, either here or on the West Coast."

"We're busy, but it's generally for people at the upper management level. We'll talk about it when you get here. Where are you?"

"On East Eighty-third. Soon as I scrub off the animal scents that have accumulated, I'll be right along. Probably be close to an hour. Since you're straight across from where I am, I'll take a cab to save time. It's 429 West End Avenue. Right?"

"That's it. See you after the animal has bathed."

Chapter Two

The West End Avenue address for Doug Newcombe was permanent, but for Doug Newcombe Associates, it was temporary. He was operating from his home until office space on Lexington Avenue was readied. Spacious though his apartment was, the location and facilities were far from ideal—even though each of the three other search associates had their own room, a desk, and a phone. The space Rob would occupy had probably been a nursery at one time. After having had big offices, secretaries and status, he'd be taking a giant step backwards in image and self esteem.

"It's time to talk," Rob said. "If I'm to be a part of the team, how would you use me, and what would the salary arrangements be?"

"You'd be given search assignments and would be expected to find candidates who could fill the openings companies have. We don't very often work on retainer, so we have to scratch a little harder to make money. I'd sit beside you for a time just to make sure you're using the people data we have in the best possible way. We use a couple of firms that do nothing but dig up names—people we can approach to find out if they know of anyone who might be interested in a specific opening. It's common for them to ask you if you're asking them if they'd like to be considered for the job. Often they will be, At other times, they may be able to recommend someone. It's a massive spider web. One call leads to others, and then others. In the end, if we do our job we get paid."

"And if we do get paid?"

"Our fee is usually one-third of the annual salary, plus our expenses. I'd put you on a draw against fees, at least until you begin to see some income from placements. Your cut would be 50 percent of what we collect, excluding expenses, and some or all of the draw you've been paid."

"What would the draw amount to?"

"You're coming in with a bunch of experience, so I could manage $250 a week."

"I'd like $300 better."

"How about $275?"

"Done. When do you want me to start?"

"Soon as you're able. Like I said earlier, we're busy with senior level openings. By the way, I make all the first contact calls for new business and do most of the interviews with candidates that we think we're likely to submit. You can sit in with me on anyone you've turned up, but your primary job is to find top quality prospects."

"They'll know who I am. I'll expect to be a part of the interview process."

"I thought as much."

"There are a couple of things I should mention," Rob said. "No, three. First, I can deliver *TWN* as a new client. My former boss at Sentry is their VP of personnel. No retainer arrangements, but he'll give us man specs and will consider our candidates. And when we're finished, I'm going from here to see Stan Baird at IMMCorp about making some kind of an arrangement with them. As a part of the same subject, I'll approach people who interviewed me to see if we can't reel in their companies."

"I'd normally make those kinds of solicitation calls, but they know you, so, by all means, go ahead. Good thinking. You're already an asset with business development ideas like that."

"Second, I can start on Monday. That's the tenth. I'll need to figure out how to get here from Grand Central. It's a detail. Only take a minute or two to sort it out. Third, my final check from IMMCorp comes at the end of the month, so I'll waive the draw until we get into September. I know there'll be a fair amount of lead-time before I make my first placement and see a part of the fee. I'll let you know when things start getting snug. OK?"

"I like the way you look at things. It may be that you're one of the better hires I've made in quite a while. To meet you more than way, maybe, any placements you make with clients you've brought in, I'll sweeten the pot just a little when the fee is split. We'll talk about that when it happens. It'll depend on the total amount we're paid. But getting here from Grand Central is easy. Take the Number Seven train across Forty-second Street to Times Square and then any one of the three lines up to Seventy-ninth and Broadway. You know your way from there."

"Sure. I may be a country boy," Rob said, "but I've been here for a while and can find my may around town."

"Just so you'll know what a good guy I am to work for, I'm not fussy about everyone being here at 9:00 a.m. on the dot. I resisted that when I was a corporate creature, so I understand. If you're sleeping in a little late with someone in the neighborhood, you may need additional time to make sure you leave each other with a smile. I also understand that. Something else. I make a twice-weekly run over to Zabar's. It's to make sure there's plenty of stuff around so you can put your own lunch together. That'll change some when were down at Lexington and Thirty-sixth. It's smaller, and the kitchen is tiny, but we'll still have something around to nibble on."

"Got the picture about the trains and lunch. How soon will the new space at Thirty-sixth and Lex be ready?"

"About ninety days, so you won't have the two extra trains to ride for too long."

"Easy walk and a chance to get some exercise. I can use it."

"It's good to have you aboard, Rob. If you have any questions between now and Monday, you know how to reach me."

"Plan on seeing me at a little after nine. I'll be able to keep at it through lunch, so you'll get what you expect from me."

"Don't go getting hung up on a forty hour week. What we're after are placements. If it can be done in less time, fine. If not, you're a pro and you'll know what you have to do to get the job done. See you on Monday morning."

Rob had to take three trains, but he still made good time getting down to Wall Street. Helen was surprised to see him.

"You didn't go home last night. Same clothes you had on yesterday."

"Man can't wear the same things two days in a row?"

"You never have, so don't give me that hand in the cookie jar look. Justine was it?"

"That was last night. It was someone else this morning."

"Not one bit funny, Rob. Marianne hasn't been in the ground two months, and already you're up to your old tricks. You sure don't believe in mourning very long. What you're saying bothers me. A lot."

"Sorry, Helen. I was just kidding about this morning. I did spend the night with Justine—a name I'd mentioned to Marianne. She also knew that Justine and I had dated. I hadn't seen her in months, especially when my girl was going downhill. But I have a life, and if you had any idea how badly I was ripped up inside, you might be pleased to see that I *didn't* blow my brains out at the end of June."

"I know. I didn't have to go through what you did. Sure. It's your life, but I still think it's a little early."

"Let it go, Helen. Knowing Marianne the way I did, she'd want me to get on with my life. Now, if Stan's in I need to see him for a few minutes."

"He spends most of his time in Canada now, but he's here for part of the week. Let me find out if he's free."

When Helen came back, she said Stan was pleased to know that Rob was in the building and that she was to bring him right in.

"Rob! Good to see you," Stan said. "The loss of your fiancée had to be hard to take, but you look as if you're healing all right. I'm glad you came in. But what brings you down to Wall Street?"

"Doug Newcombe and I have come to terms and I'll be a part of his team starting on Monday. There isn't a thing out there otherwise. Working for a search firm isn't my first choice, but it'll keep me off the poor farm. Hopefully. So, two things. First is, I'd like your agreement that we can work together. And as a part of that, I'll want you to give us specifics about whatever openings you might have."

"Be glad to, Rob. Newcombe approached us some time ago, but I never agreed to any kind of working arrangement with him. With you there, that changes things. Sure. Be happy to see what you can do. You know executive management has a couple of firms on retainer, but we have other openings at a lower level that you could work on. There's hardly anyone in personnel now—as you know. Concerning fees, we've capped them at 25 percent of the annual salary. If we're to add anything for your expenses, we'll talk about it when the time comes. What else?"

"Second item is, since it's likely to be a while before I see any income from placements, I was wondering if I might be able to lean on you to continue the equivalent of my salary for another month."

"That's odd, because when Helen said you were here it was the main reason I wanted to see you. I assumed that with your personal loss, problems with your son, and a tight job market that you'd be having a hard time making ends meet. So, it was just last week that I took your situation up with senior management and they agreed to extend your separation allowance for another month, meaning through the end of September. It's the best I could do. I went for more, but they turned me down. I hope the extra month helps a little."

"It does that, and I'm grateful. More than you know. It has been a tough five months, or nearly that. I'll have to dig in and get some placements made before I can smile and mean it."

"You'll be all right, and we'll do our best to help you along. It's the least we can do. But hold on a minute." Stan buzzed Helen.

"Yes, Mr. Baird."

"Come in, please. There's someone here I'd like you to meet." Stan chuckled softly.

Puzzled, Helen came to his door, then got the picture and laughed.

"Rob has joined Doug Newcombe Associates, and I've agreed that we'll work with him, and only him, on any openings we have. Since the employment staff has been gutted, and they're down to hiring secretaries, file clerks, and mail boys, I want you to be his contact. What Newcombe does fits perfectly in the niche between executives and non-professionals. Since all the mid-level requests come through me, I'd like you to manage those people requisitions and stay in touch with him. Considering what we did to Rob last spring, I've committed to helping him as much as I can. You agree?"

"Sure do. It'll be a pleasure. That's *great*, and you've saved me in the process."

"Meaning what?"

"There hasn't been much for me to do. You're not here most of the time, so I was just about to start looking around. I'll stay now, at least until we see whether or not this keeps me busy."

"Glad you said what you just did. We need you, and maybe an adjustment to your salary will make you think twice about leaving. At the same time, I'll find other assignments for you to work on."

"That's got my attention, Mr. Baird." Helen showed Rob a pleasant smile.

"Fine. Then we understand each other. Now, I've got to get upstairs for a meeting. I'll leave the two of you to work out the details. Take care, Rob. I'm delighted to be working with you again."

"No more than I am. And thanks very much for your positive answers to both of my questions."

Helen and Rob went back to his old office to arrange how they could best work together. But the first words out of Helen's mouth had nothing to do with business.

"You always told me that if one of us left the company…."

"Yesterday you told me you wouldn't cheat on your guy. Something change overnight?"

"You don't count in the cheating thing, I decided. We've known each other for way over a year, and I've already made love to you lots of times," Helen confessed.

"Ahhh, secrets."

"And here I was criticizing you about last night, and it turns out that I'm no better than you. I should be ashamed of myself."

"Don't be. Life goes on. Who knows? Our situation now may not be ideal, but there may come a day…."

"You're turning me on, Rob Grant. Don't you do that unless you're serious."

"Well, I just found out that my severance pay is being extended through the end of September. Stan's doing. Can you wait that long to see what might be out there for ex IMMCorp partners, Helen and Rob?"

"Have to, I guess. Your extension is a good news, bad news thing."

"The extra money is a lifesaver. It's good news for me because it'll be weeks before I see a fee from my first placement."

"We have an opening for a senior cost accountant. Stan hasn't seen the requisition yet. I'll make a copy for you. It'll give you a head start."

"Thanks, Helen. You're still a sweetheart."

"Let me suggest something. You make your first placement with us, and you and I will have our own little celebration. Never mind if you're on or off the payroll. Will you agree to that?"

"OK, it's a deal."

"And now that it's done thing, I should tell you that at the end of the month I'm moving into a little apartment up on East Thirty-second Street. I'll give you my phone number when they tell me what it is. Living at home out on Long Island, and making the long commute every day, have gotten to be a pain you-know-where."

"I know about commutes, but it's time you were on your own again. Being in Manhattan will give you a chance to spread your wings."

"And maybe other parts of my anatomy."

"Easy does it, Helen."

"*Ahhh*, that got your attention." She offered Rob a cute giggle.

"I'm not admitting a thing. But, I've got to be on my way. My first day with Newcombe is on Monday, and I have a bunch of things I need to get sorted out—plus some people to see or call before then."

After Rob and Helen sorted out how they could best work together, he gave her the Newcombe phone number and got ready to go. Before he left, she gave him a hug that confirmed she was eager to see that first placement completed and to let the celebratory evening begin. Rob thought, "I must be crazy to have agreed to Helen's proposition. I'll own her after that."

On Thursday and Friday, Rob used his time to contact some of the people who had interviewed him over the past two months. He was pleased that most of them remembered their having met. All were receptive to the idea of working with him on a non-retainer basis now that he was with a small but well regarded search firm. At the outset, there would be no exclusive search agreements, but Doug Newcombe Associates would have position descriptions and they could submit candidates in much the same way an employment agency would. If they proved they could do the job, other arrangements might well follow. There was no risk for any of the companies. Fees weren't due until something happened. Four of his contacts wanted to meet with him to make sure they understood all the details. He made appointments with them for the following week.

Saturday came and Kim was at Rob's door. "Hi, sweet. You look the best you have in months. New girlfriend?" Rob gave her a loving hug.

"No, although my Helen at IMMCorp is still putting moves on me. The news of the day is that on Monday I'll be starting a new career of sorts. I'm going to be a headhunter."

"A *what*!"

"Executive search. I mentioned it to you before. I've always been a consumer—that is, looking to search firms, and others, to find people who might fill our openings. Now I'll be on the supply side and working with a guy I've known for quite a while. We cut a deal on Wednesday. I'd have called, but I wanted to tell you in person. Besides, I've spent the last two days trying to develop new business. I may be able to deliver a half dozen clients. Two are definite, but I'm working on some others. They're the people who interviewed me but then later on turned me down. Search isn't my first choice; still, it should help keep us afloat. If I'm any good at it, there's a chance I could make fairly decent money. The other news is that IMMCorp is extending my severance allowance, so I'll have income that will take me through the end of September. That's when the well runs dry. But by then I may have made a placement or two. If not, Newcombe, the guy I'm working for, will put me on a weekly draw against fees. The future isn't bright, but it isn't dark either. Want to take me to bed?"

"You're an absolute nut. Yes! Of course—anytime. You *do* have good news, and it shows. I'm glad you've come to terms with the way things are. You've said right along that it's a dead market, but eventually you might find that one of the companies will think again and decide to hire you. Could be lots worse, Rob." Kim gave him a big hug. "I'm happy for you. Now make love to me. It's been a long, barren week."

After a steamy session in bed, Rob proposed that they drive off to Mystic, spend the night, and then tour the Seaport Museum in the morning.

"Great idea! Love to do it. You *are* feeling better about yourself and what's ahead. You don't know how pleased I am to see you upbeat again. You're an entirely different person. Makes me feel good inside. Of course you helped that along a little while ago."

"That was the matinee. You can attend the evening performance if you're interested."

"I already have a ticket. Try to keep me away. What a great outing it'll be."

Rob and Kim had an abbreviated but romantic weekend and they enjoyed each other's company about as much as they ever had. It gave Rob the kind of launch he needed to start a new chapter in his professional life. That Kim was 110 percent behind him, and the decision he'd made, helped enormously.

On Monday, Rob arrived on West End Avenue at a little after nine. Doug took him in tow immediately to show him the various steps necessary to complete a search project successfully. Rob was a quick study and by mid-week he understood most of the essentials involved. There was polishing to do, but that would come along before the month was out.

Rob's schedule settled into a routine of the kind he'd never known before. His day was made up of an infinite string of phone calls, ones that took him all over the US, then making interview appointments for Doug, a small lunch at his little desk, and three trains, most days, in each direction. Rob saw Justine more often, and spent evenings with her after he was finished at West End Avenue. But, on Saturdays, it was laundry, and shopping, and Kim overnight, at least one night, almost every weekend. Her dad and sister were waiting to see where their relationship would go. Kim said she'd already told them they weren't ready for anything permanent. Rob suggested, "They ought to know that even though we may care about each other, we aren't likely to tie the knot. That's been your feeling about marriage from the first day we met. It's no mystery to me. But I have to confess that I do like having you close. It's very agreeable."

"It is for me too, and you know how I feel about you. But we also know where we stand on the subject of rings and vows."

Summer was beginning to wind down and on the last Sunday of August, Rob and Kim went to JFK to meet Mike. He looked tan and healthy. When hugs were done, Rob said, "Your mother's cooking must have agreed with you. You've put a little meat on your scrawny frame."

"Yeah, I ate like a pig, and there were a lot of barbeques down at Huntington Beach. The chicks were even cuter this year. We had some good times."

"We'll talk about that later on—that is, when we aren't in mixed company."

With the beginning of September, a new routine replaced the one that was just barely weeks old. Greg had come back from summer camp, made only a brief stop in Bridgeton, and then was placed in a foundation school in central Massachusetts. Visits with him would now be less frequent. Mike had returned to school, but was around to help with the weekend chores. What did not change were Kim's overnights nearly every Saturday, the occasional evening with Justine, and also Rob's commitment to doing well at Doug Newcombe Associates. He *did* manage to bring in five new clients, with the prospect of there being more. Discussions continued. Newcombe was happy with Rob, and he said so. "You missed your calling. You've taken to search work like you were born to do it. On the other hand, you've been around placement long enough to know how it works on both sides of the fence. It was one of the reasons I was interested in you. One criticism I have, and it's minor, is that at times you seem to be more caught up in the process, that is where the spider web takes you, than in the end results."

"I *am* fascinated by how the links get strung together, but it shouldn't matter if what I do gets results. And I've done that. Helen called this morning to say that IMMCorp has hired the accountant we were high on. Guess they were, too. She asked us to send her an invoice.

"*Damn*, Rob! That's great news. I don't think I ever had anybody new to the business make a placement in just a little over six weeks from start to finish. You're on your way."

"Nice part about it is that I didn't take any draw, so it's all net to me. I like that. My IMMCorp salary arrangement ends next Wednesday, so I'm motivated."

"Just so you'll know my heart's still in the right place, I'll cut you 55 percent of the fee. It's your client, one I couldn't bring in, and the expenses didn't amount to hardly anything since you found the guy locally. I'm *really* pleased. For both of us. Congratulations!"

"There are some other people in the pipeline I think you'll be willing to submit, one of them to TWN. First blood feels good. Expect more of the same, Doug."

"I like your attitude. You'll do well here."

As Rob went back to work, his phone rang. "Hi, it's Helen again. Different subject this time. When do we celebrate?"

"You sure don't waste any time. But to answer your question, next Wednesday night. Your place. Dinner out first, then fireworks of your choosing."

"You're turning me on. Slow down. But there could be two sets of them. One before dinner and then the grand finale after. Maybe even some in the morning."

"Take it easy. I'm forty, remember?"

"That doesn't cut any ice with me. I know about you." Helen gave Rob her new address and phone number. "Rest over the weekend, then next Wednesday come down to East Thirty-second at about six. OK? I look forward to seeing you—all of you. I've waited a year and a half for this."

"I'll try to live up to your expectations. See you on the appointed day, place, and hour. Bye, gal"

Early on Saturday morning, Greg called, collect, and he and Rob had a long conversation. It was the first time they'd had a chance to talk at length, so Greg was full of stories. "I loved summer camp, and I'll be going back next year. Learned how to water ski, do crafts, and all kinds of stuff. It was really neat and the counselors were super. The school where I am doesn't have lots of kids in it like Sheffield did, so we can get help with schoolwork when we need it. It's pretty here, especially now when the leaves are starting to get color in 'em. We're in a small town, kinda out in the country, but we get TV from Boston and can watch the Bruins pre-season games on Channel 38. I like hockey. They've got a new guy named Orr who's great. You should check it out sometime."

"You know I'm too busy with the ladies, Greg."

He broke up with laughter. "Yeah, I know. But while you're resting, you can watch."

"What's the visitation schedule? Nobody's told me anything."

"That's why I'm calling. We have an open house on Columbus Day weekend. That's in two weeks. And I'm supposed to be able to come home for Christmas, December twenty-third to the twenty-seventh, if you'll be around."

"That's good news, Greg. Of course I'll be around. But I imagine I'm to keep an eye on you. I'll do that too, because if you screw up, they won't let you come home again for a while. But about Columbus Day weekend, Mike and I, and maybe Kim, will be there probably sometime after lunch on Saturday. I'll give you the details later."

"I hope Kim can come. I'd really like to see her. Will you tell her I said that?"

"She'll be over this afternoon, and I'll let her know that you want her to come along. She's usually here on Saturday nights, so maybe we could stay overnight someplace nearby and then come back and see you again for a little while on Sunday before we have to start back."

"That'd be great."

"No promises. But give me a number. I'll let you know in a few days what our plans are."

Greg told Rob how he could be reached. They talked on for several more minutes before Greg said he had to go.

"Good to hear from you, finally. Sounds as if you're adjusting."

"It's not like being at home, but I had a good summer and being here is OK. I'll be all right. Gotta go. Love you, Dad,"

"Love you too, Greg. See you in a couple of weeks, but we'll talk before then."

About the time Rob hung up, a body showed up in the living room.

"Who were you talking to at this hour?"

"Your brother. He said to give you a kiss."

"Sure he did. Awww, man! I didn't even get to say hello."

"It's OK. We're going up to see him in two weeks. You're invited, if you can get out of bed in time to go along."

"I'll be ready. Be good to see the little twerp. Been months."

"Where'd you get a word like that?"

"Down on the beach one night. Some chick called me that."

"It's not complimentary."

"Didn't matter. She looked after me anyway." Mike giggled.

"Don't you *ever* get after me about my friends and what we do. Were you protected?"

"Yep. You told me about that. We don't need any more problems."

By the time Kim showed up, Mike had already left to meet friends. The group had plans to be a part of the Sheffield High cheering section at the football game in Northway.

"You're later than usual," Rob said.

"Suppose I should have called. Vince didn't show up until about a half-hour ago. Nobody home but just the two of us?"

"We're it. Mike went off to meet his pals and then the bunch of them are going to the game. How about a drink first, and then dinner out someplace?"

"I'd love it. What do you have in mind?"

"It's been a year since we went to The Filet of Soul. Remember? And it just hit me. I can't believe we've been seeing each other that long. It's just about time that you and I split—if you follow the pattern. A year has been about it. That's the way it was with Lu, and Kate, too, the Las Vegas gal you knew about."

"I'm going to break the string. You'll just have to put up with me. I like having you over at my house, and being here for the overnights is special. You look after me very well. In lots of ways. And to think that I made us wait weeks before we got really friendly with each other."

"The idea of having you around for longer than a year is a feel good thing. I was beginning to think I've been the problem. But I have to say that it would be pretty lonely on weekends if you weren't here. You're easy to be with. I've said that before. It's been an awfully good year. Lots of fond memories. I have to believe there'll be more."

"There will be. Starting with dinner tonight. The place has changed hands, and a guy I work with says the food is much better now. It *was* about the same weekend last year that we went there when we were trying to avoid Lu. Be almost like an anniversary dinner. We'd just met."

"I like the sound of that. Another feel good thing. You're a very special gal, Miss Kim."

While they were digging into baked stuffed shrimp and a grilled salmon filet, Rob told Kim about the open house at Duchene, Greg's school up in Massachusetts. Rob was finally beginning to remember the name of it. "He wants me to come up. It's the long weekend starting on Friday, the ninth. Mike wants to go, for sure, and Greg made a specific request when we talked. He wanted me to ask you to come with us."

"Oh, Rob. That touches me in a place that only a woman, a mother, would understand. You know that I couldn't turn my back on that kind of invitation. Especially after how badly Lu treated him. Just give me the details when you've worked them out."

"What I'd like to do is drive up late on Saturday morning, spend the afternoon with him, the night somewhere nearby, see him again on Sunday morning and then be back here in time for dinner. Question is, can you be gone that long? I'm concerned about your being away from Chris and Ian too much."

"We're a close knit family. I'm with them all week, so one night isn't a big deal. No different than when I'm at your place overnight."

"You're right, and I'd forgotten that I said about the same thing to Greg. Mike may want to ask a friend to come along. Even if not, I'll still have to reserve a second room. When I've put it all together, I'll let you know. Greg will go out of his mind when he sees you. He still needs a substitute mom in his life. By the way, he wanted me to say hello to you."

"It'll be wonderful to see him. Been several months. It was when we told both boys that Marianne had died. I'll never forget that. Those few minutes were so hard for all of us and they still get to me."

"And the other thing I have to tell you is that my search work has paid off and that I made my first placement with Newcombe. Pretty good chunk of money, and there are others coming I think."

"That's wonderful news, Rob. Our anniversary dinner is turning out to be a special event. I'm happy for you, and I'm full of such good feelings. Things are looking better. It's time. Long overdue, in fact."

"What you feel is plain to see. Your glow is very becoming, and it's doing wonders for my frame of mind. Anyone who didn't know my condition might think you were expecting."

"Not a good idea. On the other hand, why do I think I wouldn't mind? Our romantic evening is responsible. My good judgment has gone to hell. I blame you for that. There are times when I want us to be more than what we are. Like the two of us together, and me expecting. Then I come back to reality. Most likely none of it will ever happen. For sure not the part about us having one of our own."

"Starting another family at forty isn't for me, even if it were possible. If we were ten years younger, and just starting out, nothing would please me more than exchanging vows with you, sharing our lives, and being the father of our youngsters. But, there's not much point in trying to reshape the past. We're left with doing the best we can with the circumstances as they are. You're a long way from being ready to marry again. You may never be—like you've said right along. I'm probably closer to thinking you'd be the right person for me than the other way around. But that's my problem."

"Not entirely. I just don't want you to run off anytime soon. We might decide that we *do* have something special going for us that we wouldn't find with anyone else. Greg's counselor, Will Cable, thinks you're a 'keeper', you know, and he might be right. A year later, I'm asking you to be patient. Again. Familiar words?"

"Yep. I was then, and I still am."

Not long after they got home, Mike called.

"I'm at Tom's, and he's invited me to stay overnight. Any reason why you need me to come home?"

"None that I can think of."

"I guess Kim's there."

"No, she ran off with another man."

"*What*!"

"Just kidding. She's here. Anyway, enjoy yourself."

"You too, Dad." Mike chuckled.

Rob and Kim's romantic evening extended into their bedtime hours. Having loved as they did with unmistakable warmth reminded Rob of Marianne and a night like this months back. She'd been gone fourteen weeks now, and he was trying very hard to put her death in perspective—a word she'd used with her papa, Carlo. Memories were less painful, but she would never be far below his conscious level for the rest of his life. If Marianne had lived, she would be sharing his bed this night. But he refused to take anything away from the affectionate loving he and Kim had just shared. She was alive. Marianne wasn't. And life goes on. But he made a mental note to phone Carlo and to finally accept their invitation to visit. He felt that by now he could manage being in the house on Holland Avenue once again. At least he hoped so.

On Monday, Rob kept the promise he made to himself and phoned the Marzano's late in the afternoon. Carlo was at home already.

"Hello, Rob. Good to hear from you. Been almost a month. You OK?"

"I'm doing better and was wondering if I might come up for a little while. Things have settled down, so if you're not busy...."

"Anna and I would like that. What time?"

"I can come up now if that's all right. I'm working near Eightieth and West End, so it shouldn't take too long."

"Remember to get off at Burke Avenue, and then walk away from Bronx Park."

"I remember."

Rob got the Number Two train at Seventy-ninth and Broadway and made the relatively short trip to his stop in the Bronx. Suddenly, a low level ache returned. "How may times had Marianne done this?" Rob asked himself. "Am I going to be all right after all?"

At the Marzano's door, Carlo gave Rob a hug that took the breath out of him.

"Wow, you're strong!"

"I have to be to wrestle the bad guys to the ground."

"Well, I'm not one of 'em. You win." Carlo laughed. Turning to Mrs. Marzano, Rob said, "It's good to see you again, Anna." She gave him a healthy squeeze of her own and a peck on his cheek.

"Sorry I haven't come by sooner, but I needed the time to get settled into a new job and to make sure I was ready to deal with coming back here again."

"Glad you didn't forget about us. We thought when Mari was gone that maybe we wouldn't matter anymore."

"Don't think that for a minute. You'll always matter. It was you who gave me a wonderful partner at Sentry and the one great love of a lifetime. How could I ever forget?"

"What's the new job?"

"It's called executive search. If a company needs a person with special skills, or someone in management, we try to find them. They pay us a fee if we do. It's the opposite of what Marianne and I did at Sentry. We were consumers there. Now I'm on the supplier side."

"Good money?"

"A little early to tell, but it looks like it'll be OK."

"You met up with anybody since Mari died?"

"There's a young woman in Sheffield who was wonderful support back in the spring. She helped me through some tough times. We've gotten to be good friends, but she has two sons and doesn't really need a man in her life. She's been good company though. Name's Kim Rossi."

"Ah, another Italian. That's good. She'll look after you just fine."

"Maiden name was Brunetti. Good people."

"Of course they are."

"What did you do with Marianne's room? Still the same?"

"No, we turned it into another guest room. It was time to let go of all the years she spent in there and the memories that went with them. It's new wallpaper, different furniture. Want to see it?"

"Thanks, no. My need is different. I want to hang onto the memory of those walls and her bed and our last minutes together while she still knew I was there. She knows I still love her, and that we *will* have time together someday. What we had won't ever die. Let's leave it at that."

They talked on for another half-hour, and as Rob got ready to leave Carlo said, "Mari told me you liked my papa's red wine. He's in his eighties, but he's still making it. He likes it himself. Maybe it's why he's still going strong. He remembers you from the funeral, especially when you touched Mari's casket and then nearly passed out. Like us, it told him how much you loved our little girl. As long as he's still living, he wants you to have some of his special red. We got two bottles that he left here a coupla weeks ago. He said that if we saw you again he wanted you to have 'em. There'll be more if you want."

"Thank him for me, will you please? There are lots of fond memories attached to his wine."

"It's a good idea if we don't know about 'em. They were between the two of you and should stay that way. Like Anna and me. There are private times together that we don't talk about with anybody else."

"What we had is still so vivid. It'll always be that way, I suppose."

"I hope you find a good woman, Rob. You deserve better than what happened. You have our blessings, whichever way your life goes. Maybe the Rossi woman will want to think about it some more."

"I doubt it, but she's good company. Now, I've got to get home to my boy and get him fed. At close to 17, he's nearly always hungry."

"Please come see us again, Rob," Anna said.

"I will. Promise. And thanks for the wine. It's good stuff."

Rob said good-bye, headed down to Grand Central and then boarded the 6:05 Express, *The Nathan Hale*, for the ride home. Fond memories of Marianne were on his mind. Suddenly, he felt her presence—and she kept him company all the way to Sheffield Station.

Mike met his dad at the door, and said, "You're later than usual. I was wondering where you were."

"I stopped to see the Marzano's. We've talked since the funeral, but I hadn't been to their place in quite a while. It was hard going back there. They've changed her room, but I didn't want to see it. Leaving my memories of her intact was more important than seeing a new paint job and different furniture. Carlo and Anna have to live there, every day, so I understand their reasons."

"What are we going to do about dinner?"

"How about we go out for a burger or something. After this afternoon, I'm not much into trying to whip up anything at this hour."

"Sure. OK with me."

While they were eating, Rob told Mike that he had overnight plans on Wednesday. "This doesn't happen very often, at least at mid-week, so I'd appreciate it if you'd see what you can arrange." For a moment, Rob's mood turned lighthearted and with a chuckle he added, "If you want me to call Regina, I will. You remember her. A former Mrs. Grant. The second one." He chuckled again. "But if you'd like to stay with Tom, that would have to be your call. He's your pal."

"No problem. I'll call Tom when we get home. I like staying there. We have a great time together. If it doesn't work out, you can call Regina."

When they got back to number 71 Juniper Heights, Mike called the Giordano's. They had no objections, and Tom was delighted to have Mike ask about staying overnight. They were good friends and had been for some time.

On Wednesday afternoon, Helen called Rob to remind him that she would be collecting her commission tonight.

"I don't need reminding. How much of a fee are you looking for?"

"All of it! I'm all worked up and can hardly sit still. See you at about six. Don't forget to bring all your tools with you."

"I only have one, but it'll take care of whatever needs fixing."

"You're already stirring up the fire."

"So are you. See you this evening."

Rob worked through the remainder of the afternoon and got news that he'd made another placement. This one was with one of Doug's long-time clients and was a spin-off of the search he'd done for IMMCorp. Not a big fee, but Rob decided that he couldn't be fussy. It all counted.

Newcombe came by to congratulate Rob on his latest success. "I'm not going to worry anymore about your fascination with the spider web, and the process of getting from here to there. You're doing the job. That's what matters to me. We're getting a better reputation, and with the eight clients you've brought in now, seventy-one should be a banner year for us. So, in the way of making an understatement, let's say I'm happy you're here. So far." Doug Newcombe roared with that robust laugh that was uniquely his.

"Glad you're satisfied that I'm holding up my end. Now, if you'll excuse me, I'm off to East Thirty-second Street to hold up another end. Expect to see me in these same clothes in the morning. They may not fit as well by then." Newcombe roared again."

"Enjoy yourself to the fullest! See you upon the morrow."

Helen was at the intercom within seconds after Rob buzzed, and she had her door open for him when he got to her floor. What she had on was sheer and wouldn't be suitable for dining out, so he got her message inside two seconds. She wanted to collect her commission. Immediately!

With the door closed behind him, Helen said hello and then gave Rob a kiss that said she was ready to make love on the floor if need be.

"Whoa, love. Let me put my attaché case down and take off my jacket. Zippers shred sheer garments and leave nasty marks on bare skin."

"You have forty-eight seconds before I attack."

"In that case, I'll hurry. I don't want to miss out on any of the fun."

"You won't miss a thing. Follow me."

In her bedroom, Helen couldn't seem to decide what to do first. Unbutton his shirt, run his zipper down or unbuckle his belt. She settled on getting Rob's pants off. He was now aroused and it showed.

"Ooooh. *Wow*! Look at that. Tonight, what's yours will be mine. All of it. Finally."

Rob kicked off his shoes, finished unbuttoning his shirt and quickly found himself in bed with an inferno.

"No need for any preliminaries. I had to change undies before I went in this morning. I was ready then. Take me, Rob. I've waited eighteen months for this."

They coupled, and Helen went straight up the mountain to a towering peak. "*Ohhh*. More. Another. Wait."

"How long?"

"About an hour." In the midst of a vigorous physical encounter, they laughed.

"Not possible. You've got five minutes, maybe six, then watch out."

"Whew! I'm up there again."

"You talk too much."

Showing Helen that his limit of five or six minutes was real, Rob gave her sensitive areas the special attention he wanted them to have and the spectacular fireworks show continued. She went to a summit that made her gurgle with joy. Then it was, "Do it with me."

Rob increased the tempo, and they met each other on the moon. Helen inhaled sharply. Rob growled with pleasure. "Now. It's all yours." His words excited her and they brought her back to another peak.

After they'd rested, Helen said, "When you did your thing, I could feel you. I expected good, but *whew*! It was worth the wait. You've probably made it impossible for me to be really satisfied by anyone else. What am I going to do now? Damn you!"

"Your idea right from the beginning, dear heart. But you can start by feeding me some protein so we can have an encore. Thing is, we have to put on clothes to do that."

"Couldn't we have something brought in? Took so long to get you in bed with me, I'd just like to keep you here."

"Let's make a deal. We eat now, and I'll plan on coming back again some evening if you'd like."

"I'd like."

Helen hadn't been in the neighborhood long but she'd found a couple of restaurants, both small, that she could recommend to have dinner.

"You choose," Rob said. "I don't know either one of them. What I'm after is some good beef."

"That makes it easy. The Aberdeen Grill."

When they were seated, Rob said, "It's time we had a serious talk."

"That sounds heavy. But let's order first."

Rob signaled a waiter over and they made their drink and dinner selections.

"Heavy? Not really. But I'm concerned about cutting into your love life. It's a thing called conscience. I'm not a candidate to be your next husband."

"Why not?"

"Age, for one thing. And the same kinds of issues that Marianne and I had. Family being another, I should think. But if you're serious about this guy you've been seeing, then I'm for sure not being fair to him. I wouldn't want someone cutting in on my time if the situation were reversed. Marianne may have had other men, but we didn't talk about it."

"She didn't. I can tell you that. Nearly from the day you started working together at Sentry Oil, there was really never anyone but you. We talked about that. Even in Washington, you were the only man who mattered to her, the only one on her mind. It was good that you met again the way you did in Sydney."

"I'm not sure about that, given what I went through starting right after my birthday. But the memories. Ohh, the memories. They're golden. The ones at the end aren't. Watching leukemia take a life, is, well...."

"Put them to rest, Rob. But you know that she and I are a lot alike. I had the same reaction she did when Walt introduced us early last year. What we just did was something I've wanted almost from the time you came to work at IMMCorp. Maybe even going back to when you came in for your February interview with Stan. Danny liked to play around, and then the unpleasant side of him surfaced. It made my decision about divorcing him easy because all I could think about was you. But then there were times you hurt me with some of the comments you made in the office. You were just playing around, but when you brought up the other women, sometimes it cut pretty deep. It was the way you did it."

"I had no idea, Helen. I knew you cared. But I didn't know until just now how much. You've hidden your feelings well."

"Except that time when I threw the pencil at you. I meant it. And you caught it. That ticked me off even more."

"But what about your latest flame? If you were playing the field, I wouldn't have a problem with ethics, but he matters."

"He does. Some. But tonight, being with you, having you love me, is more important. And I found out on Monday that I'm not the only woman he beds. I thought he was monogamous, but he isn't. It's taken the edge off how I've felt about him. I've been through that already with Danny."

"But I sleep around. Where do you draw the line?"

"The difference is that we've never dated, or talked about a future together. I don't have to explain what you and I have been to each other. I said a month ago that, in a way, you didn't matter. But now you do."

"I need to sit back and think about this. You know something about Kim, I think. She's helped me through some *very* painful days. They go back to Greg's problem, but at that she's not likely to become Mrs. Grant. Still, I'd be kidding myself if I said she wasn't important to me."

"Change of direction. You talked about age differences and family. I don't recall your ever having asked me how old I am."

"Never thought it was necessary, but I've assumed right along that you were younger than Marianne."

"Nope. There was about a six-year age difference between us. I was thirty-one on May 5."

"Good God, you had me fooled. What's your formula?"

"I don't have one. What's yours? You don't look forty."

"Very dry martinis over ice, *and* fiery women."

"Then you've come to the right place for the best treatment in town."

"Think I'll stay the night."

"Good idea. You better. I'm counting on it."

"What about family? You know about my having been fixed, so that has to be a consideration."

"If I marry a man who wants babies, I'll have them. But soon. Danny and I were going to wait, but the more I thought about it, the more sense it made at my age to get it over with. If I marry a man who isn't interested, or can't have them, then that's the way it'll be. I'm not as excited about motherhood as a lot of woman my age—and younger. It's all they can talk about. There are times when it turns me off."

"When I got my notice that our little team was going to be busted up, you talked about finding a job out on Long Island and living at home. What changed your mind?"

"Most of it is that I'll be staying at IMMCorp. Stan's put through a good salary increase, like he promised, and it looks like my job's secure. At thirty-one, living on Long Island cramped my style. I finally decided that I wanted more freedom. I told you about my plans to move here the day you came in to see Stan. Think about it. We sure couldn't have spent a night like this out in Hempstead. Much as I've built you up with my parents, they wouldn't have approved. They think I should try to turn you into a husband, and I don't need that kind of lecture every night over dinner. You understand, I think."

"I've been single now for almost two years, and it's hard for me to think back to when I wasn't. And maybe I won't like the constraints of being married again. No, that's nonsense. Some things in life aren't the same unless you can share them with somebody you really care about. Making love is one of them."

"I know. The real thing is much, much better than the alternative."

"Don't ask me to comment on that."

Helen smiled sweetly and then asked, "How was your filet?"

"Very tasty. You picked a good place. Come back again?"

"Anytime you're willing. Could we go? I'd like to see about that encore you mentioned."

"Good thing you live close by."

It wasn't late, so Rob and Helen slowed their pace and took time to savor the beauty of their union. They went to towering peaks, and after her needs were met he joined her when she asked. Delightfully sensuous. She expressed her total satisfaction with a single word. "*Yessss!*"

"You've made me so happy, Rob. It's a night I'll never forget. Just incredible."

"For me, too. You're verrry good. We'll see if there's anything we can add to the commission in the morning." Helen giggled softly. They then said good night and slept soundly.

Their fires blazed anew in the early morning hours. They loved as if this was their first time together. Fulfilled, Helen said, "You know that I won't have anything but you on my mind for weeks. Like Marianne, I'd like to keep our relationship going."

"I predicted that earlier in the year. We *will* see each other again, and soon, but you know that I'm a long way from wanting to be committed."

"I know. But if we could just go out, and spend a night together once in a while, I'd love to do that. Like I said before, I've been attracted to you since that first day you walked into our office a year ago February. All I ask is that you give me a chance. I told you months back that I'm another partner who cares. Remember? I meant it then. I still do."

"I remember. In spite of all the times I teased you, I've always thought you were special. No promises, but now that I understand what's in your heart, it's only fair that I give myself some room to find out how I feel about *you*. You deserve that. It's possible that somewhere in the midst of all my mixed-up emotions, I'll find more affection for you than I've been willing to admit to my inner man. At the same time, I have to consider that my feelings have been covered up with all the other things that have been going on in my life since last spring—including the other women you know about."

"Makes me happy to have you talk about some of these things. You don't know how much. I'd be good for you, Rob, and I'd make a wonderful partner in marriage, too. I'd be a faithful and devoted wife."

"Easy, babe. You're getting way ahead of me on the subject of marriage. Kate did the same thing, and you know how that turned out. I don't have any misgivings about you being a good partner. And we'd almost certainly be happy together. But you've spent a whole lot more time reflecting on us, and marriage, and our future, than I have. There wasn't much reason for me to think about it because, first, we worked together, then you were married, and now you're involved with a guy I thought you were high on. It's your turn to give me some time. Say, four or five minutes?" Helen laughed, and it relieved the pressure of having to address a subject of this weight at an early morning hour. "By the way, according to my rules, what we're doing is OK now. I went off the payroll at midnight. It's October 1, and I'm history."

"Is there time for a quickie then?"

"*Helen*! You've done me in. I have reasonably good endurance, but there's a limit to what a guy can do. Save some of me for next time. All right?"

"You went way beyond what I expected. Guess I'm still hungry. Maybe greedy is a better word for it."

"Could you handle a mid-week overnight in Sheffield?"

"Oh, yes! Anytime. You've got what I call a clean commute. On in Sheffield, and then off in Midtown. What I've done for years wasn't. The Long Island connections and then the Number Three train to Wall Street. Took hours, or at least it seemed like that. One of the reasons I'm here. A better one is that you're here, too."

"Remember, I had a subway ride just like you did—the one down to Wall Street from Grand Central. More complicated now that I have to go up to Seventy-ninth and Broadway. It's a giant pain. But that'll change before long. We'll be at Thirty-sixth and Lexington."

"If you're serious about a weeknight at your place, it'll take less time for me to get to work than it did coming in from Long Island. Not a problem. Be great. I'd love it. Any idea when?"

Maybe next week. But if I can get Mike situated, it's a lot easier for me to stay in town. Let me see what I can do."

"We need to make another placement so I can get another big commission. Collecting this one was just wonderful. No. Better than that."

"Yeah. No argument there. You're just about what I imagined. Enjoyable doesn't quite say it all. But before I decide that I really can handle your quickie, I've got to go make some money, or at least try to. Hate to break up the party, but it's time."

Back in harness at Doug Newcombe Associates, Rob's search efforts continued. The phone calls ran into the hundreds, and he couldn't have been in touch with more people than if he'd been making a telephone survey on some issue of general interest. His efforts produced good candidates, but no placements.

Early on the Saturday of Columbus Day weekend, Rob got Mike on his feet, picked up Kim, and they drove to central Massachusetts to see Greg. He was right. The school *was* in a small town, and the Duchene campus wasn't all that big. It suggested that students did get the kind of personal attention, both academically and emotionally, that was needed. When Greg saw them coming, he flew across the grounds and nearly knocked the three of them over.

"Wow, that's some welcome!" Kim said. Greg hugged his dad, shook hands with Mike in a way kids thought was cool, and then nearly squeezed the breath out of Kim.

"Not so hard, Greg. I'd like to live until dinnertime," she said.

"Sorry. It's just that I'm real glad you could come along. It's super."

"Well, Mike, I guess we can go."

"No, Dad. I love you, too. But you know I like having a mom, even if she isn't really mine. I'm getting all mixed up. You know what I mean."

"Yes, Greg. We all understand. Now, take us on a tour. You don't have to tell us about the leaves. We've seen them. They're beautiful."

"Pretty place, isn't it?"

"We came up near where our lots are down near Sturbridge. Same thing. I've just got to figure out a way to get that little place built. Can you imagine what it would be like? Especially now."

"I can," Kim said. "A very romantic retreat with the pretty leaves, a crisp fall night, and the fireplace going. Am I invited?"

"You bet. But, it's for all of us. It'll happen. Makes me want to work that much harder. I like the picture you just painted." He smiled at Kim.

The four of them had a Saturday afternoon and Sunday morning visit that could best be characterized as quality time. Each one of them got something out of the hours they spent together. As they got ready to leave, Greg reminded them that he'd be home for Christmas.

"You have to make all my favorite meals. That's what I miss more than anything."

"That's over two months off. When can I pick you up?"

"Anytime on the twenty-third, but I have to be back on campus by five o'clock on the twenty-seventh."

"We'll work out the details before then. Take care of yourself. And study!"

"I will. It's super that you could come up. See you at Christmas."

Chapter Three

On a morning less than two weeks earlier, Rob had told Helen that he needed to go off and try to make some money. And try is what he did, but his two relatively early successes were followed by a string of bitter disappointments. He did benefit from the support and comforts offered by Kim, and Helen, and occasionally Justine, but the money well was beginning to run dry. It was time, he thought, to consider Doug's offer of a weekly draw. Before that happened, fortune smiled and he made a placement. The fee was modest, but it was enough to keep him afloat.

Then on the afternoon before Veteran's Day, Rob got a call from a frantic Tom Giordano.

"Mr. Grant. Mike came up after school. He was using my big Jaguar knife to carve some wood and he's cut the palm of his hand open. He can't move his fingers, and he's bled a lot."

"Is your mother home? If not, call an ambulance and get him to the emergency room."

"Mom's here and she's got his hand wrapped in a towel real tight. We're leaving for the hospital now. We wanted you to know what's happened."

"Thanks, Tom. Be out on the first train I can get. Meet you there. If you're gone by then, I'll call you later. Thank your mother for me."

"OK. But I'll wait for you somewhere near the emergency room."

Mike was taken directly to surgery and, as luck would have it, a prominent hand surgeon, a specialist who practiced locally, was called in.

It was after 5:30 by the time Rob got to the hospital. Tom was waiting.

"Hi, guy. What's the story?"

"Mike's still in surgery. Been there quite a while."

"Not a simple procedure if he opened up his palm, like you said."

"He did a good job on it. He couldn't move his two middle fingers."

"Sounds like he got tendons. We'll see what the doctor says."

It wasn't until much later that an aide came to him and asked, "Are you Mr. Grant?"

"I am."

"Your son is out of surgery, and he's been moved to room 428. You can see him now if you'd like."

"Thanks, miss. Tom, you coming along?"

"Yeah. I want to make sure he's OK, and Mom and Dad will want the whole story."

Mike was in a four-bed room and, with visiting hours having begun, it was fairly crowded. He was just coming out from under the general anesthetic he'd been given and was pretty groggy.

"Hi, Dad," a frail voice said.

"There goes my help with the laundry." Mike smiled weakly.

"Guess so. At least for a while."

"Looks like you're wearing a gauze club. And all the way up to your elbow? Where's the damage, and how did it happen?"

"I was trying to carve a piece of wood. Thing is, I was holding it in my right hand and had Tom's big knife in my left—instead of the other way around. I lost my grip on the wood and cut my hand open. Didn't hurt much then, but there was blood. I saw what I'd done and knew I was in trouble. Glad Mrs. Giordano could get me here quick."

"I owe her," Rob said. "But I'll need to talk with the doctor and the people downstairs. We don't have any insurance, and not a lot of money, so I'll have to work out something. But that's a detail. We need to make sure you're OK."

Toward the end of visiting hours, the surgeon came in to see Mike.

"Well, Michael, it could have been worse, but I think you'll be all right. Lots of therapy coming up, and you'll have to do that if you're to get the use of your fingers back." He turned toward Rob. "You're Mr. Grant, I presume?"

"That's right."

"I'm Dr. Moore." They shook hands. "Your boy severed the flexor tendons to his middle fingers, so we've done reconstructive surgery. His prospects for recovery are pretty good, I think we can say. These things are like rubber bands, so once they're cut, they pull away from each other and have to be retrieved. We've done that, and if he doesn't go out and try to play football anytime soon, his fingers should eventually be all right. Young bodies have a way of being able to recover fairly quickly. It's a little different for people like you and me. Now, you'll need to call my office with your insurance details."

"I've been out of work for a while, so we don't have any medical coverage. Things are a little tight at the moment."

"I'll have to look to you for payment, then. Your obligation won't vanish, personal problems or not."

"Understood, doctor. I'm not in the habit of walking away from my responsibilities."

"Expect me to hold you to your word. And about Michael, he can go home on Friday morning. I'll look in on him first, and then he should come see me on Tuesday after school. My office is nearby, so he can walk it. I don't need you there, unless you feel strongly about it."

"I'm trying to find ways to keep us fed, so I better stick with that. I've lost two very good management jobs during the past nineteen months, both for reasons that didn't have a thing to do with me, so the timing for this couldn't be much worse."

"Call my office and let us know what your situation is. Hopefully, it'll improve soon."

"Thanks. It has to. I'm accustomed to a more comfortable lifestyle than the one we have at the moment." Turning toward Mike, "I'll see you tomorrow evening."

When Rob got home, he called Kim.

"Thought you might like to know what's in the next chapter of the Grant saga. Mike sliced his hand open and had to have it rebuilt. He's up at General Hospital recuperating from surgery. Problem is, I don't have any insurance. Are we havin' fun, or what?"

"Dammit, Rob! I don't believe the kind of year you're having. I'm almost afraid to hang around you in case some of whatever's wrong rubs off on me. But, would you like me to come over?" They chuckled at the contradiction.

"Not necessary. I'm OK, other than the fact that the gods are against me, I think."

"Can't imagine why you'd say that."

"Mike comes home on Friday before noon, so I'll stick around here and pick him up. It's the thirteenth. I hope nothing else goes wrong. If it does, maybe I'll OD."

"I remember what you said to Greg about that when he nearly did. If you need a reminder, I'll play it back for you. Word for word."

"Not necessary. I remember what I said."

"Good. I don't need a giant size heartache. If you can hang on until Saturday, I'll come help you out, rub your back, and then be glad to get into whatever else we can stir up."

"You know I'll be ready. Seems like you're always there, Kim, and you know I'm grateful. See you on Saturday."

Rob saw Mike both evenings, and then brought him back to Juniper Heights before lunch on Friday. Since there wasn't much point in his going into West End Avenue, he did some calling from home. Doug had encouraged him to keep a phone log, with names, phone numbers, and a thumbnail sketch of the conversation. Rob soon found that it proved useful. In this case, he'd be able to show Doug what he'd done on Friday afternoon, and also get reimbursed for his calls. The best part of it was that he turned up two excellent candidates for a VP opening that he was working on.

"Mike, your birthday is coming up next week. Any ideas about what you want?"

"Three Dog Night has an album out that I'd like to have."

"*Who*?"

"It's a group. They're good. Their latest one is called *It Ain't Easy,* and it came out about the time Greg got into trouble. I don't have many albums, so anything new by Jethro Tull, or Black Sabbath, or King Crimson would be OK."

"Love the names. Is this the kind of stuff that's intended to drive me even further up the wall?"

"It isn't Mozart. So, yeah, I suppose it would. But I can play it before you get home."

"It's a deal, then"

"But I can always use clothes."

"Let me see how the budget looks. First thing will be to get your doctor and the hospital paid. You heard me say that we don't have any insurance, and I probably don't have enough in savings to cover their bills, at least both of them."

"Just an album would be OK, then."

"We'll see."

Kim came by after work to check out the patient. "Sorry I didn't get to the hospital, Mike. Couldn't get anybody to stay with Chris and Ian. Anyway, how're you doing? That sure is a big club you've got there."

"It's all right, but it hurts. Only good part is that I won't have to take notes in school for a while. I can't write left-handed."

The three of them talked on and then finally got around to the subject of Mike's birthday the following Friday. He asked Kim, "Could you come to my birthday dinner next week? I'd like it if you could be there."

"Looks like I have two families. Sure, Mike, I'll try. I'm pleased that you think enough of me to ask. Will you be eating here or out someplace?"

"Until I know how much the surgery and the rest of it amounts to, I think we'll be eating out a whole lot less. But a birthday dinner is special, so we'll go wherever Mike wants. He and I will talk it over and then decide next week."

"I can't be here tonight or stay over on Friday night," Kim said, "at least that's the way it looks now, but I'll be back tomorrow. Maybe I can help out a little."

"Like I said on Tuesday evening, you're always ready to lend a hand, and I appreciate it. You know that."

"If the situation were the other way around, you'd be there for me."

"You bet I would. I owe ya."

After seeing that Mike got off to school on Monday morning without any problems, Rob went back to the business of trying to complete search assignments. There were interviews that showed promise and it might be that he would be able to sneak another placement in before the holidays. Time would tell.

On the twentieth, Rob took Mike and Kim to Russo's for dinner. It was the birthday boy's choice, and even though the ghost of Marianne was present, more so tonight for some reason, they enjoyed themselves. Mike got his Three Dog Night album and a new shirt. Rob got the bill for all of it. Fortunately, he had a Visa card—one that Chase was glad he kept busy.

Thanksgiving was upon them the following week, and Regina invited Rob and Mike over to her place to share the big turkey she'd bought. Rob appreciated it because he had little interest in putting together a meal for just the two of them. He'd called Justine to see if she wanted to come out, but she'd made other plans. Just as well, he thought. On Monday, Regina personalized her invitation by suggesting that they come over on Thanksgiving Eve. Rob would have had to be simple minded not to know what she had in mind. It was time for Regina's periodic fix. When the time came, the night before, a good rest, the morning after, and the meal itself were all a great success. Mike had a good visit with Kyle and Denny, and everyone got to talk with Greg when they phoned him at school. The call was important to him, and when they hung up he was a much happier kid.

Back at work on Monday, Doug was able to tell Rob that he'd scored again, but it was another small fee. Made no difference. Almost anything would help keep them going. He felt good enough about Doug's news that he called Helen to see if she'd like to have dinner on Wednesday evening, and company overnight."

"*Yesss*!" She said. "Just about the time I think you've run off with somebody else, you lift my spirits. Or my skirt. Or both, I guess." They shared a good laugh. Rob was glad he'd already made arrangements on Thanksgiving for Mike to stay overnight at Regina's.

"I haven't run off with anyone. You're the most eligible young lady around. Nobody else wants this broken down old rascal."

"Ask me, and you'll be taken. In a New York minute, as we say."

"You can take me on Wednesday. Around six be OK?"

"Perfect. And expect me to jump your bones first, like I always do. I'm undernourished, so I'm counting on you to look after me."

"Your wish is, what is it, my command?"

"Let's not get carried away. Save it for Wednesday."

He did just that. And Helen was all smiles on Thursday as they got ready to leave for work. "We need to do this more often. Being with you makes me feel sooo good, and then again later in the evening. Oh, *yes*! But I miss you at the office, too."

"You and I wouldn't be doing this if we were still at IMMCorp. You have to decide what's more important. But about seeing each other more often, it's still a matter of making sure that Mike is looked after, especially with his hand not yet completely healed. But we never did have our overnight in Sheffield. My fault. It's just been easier to stay here. Plan on next Wednesday. That be OK?"

"You name the night and the hour, and I'll be there. You don't seem to understand, Rob. I'm in love with you. Probably have been for longer than I'm willing to admit."

"That's what Marianne thought after the two of you met that first time. But what about the other guy you're seeing?"

"As long as you pay attention to me, there is no other guy."

"I guess that says it like it is. Just about the same way it was with my old flame, Kate. The decision is mine."

"You've known right along where my heart is. It's all yours if you want it."

"Let's talk about it next Wednesday. Lots for me to think about in the meantime. You do have a way about you. I'll call you next week with details about a train out to Sheffield."

They held each other tightly for a few seconds, kissed gently, and then went on their way to work. Rob tried to sort out how he felt. It seemed that he always cared about two women at the same time. "A flaw in my character," he mumbled quietly.

Rob's days were busy, so they passed quickly. Kim was with him on Saturday night and their feelings for each other seemed to have deepened. But their underlying issues remained.

On December 6, Rob made sure he called Greg to wish him a happy birthday. He was pleased with the twenty dollars Rob had sent. Greg talked about his routine and it sounded pretty much unchanged since their visit over the Columbus Day weekend. Rob reminded him that he'd be up on the twenty-third to bring him down to Sheffield for Christmas. His excitement at the prospect of being home was obvious. It was a long conversation, and Greg was pleased that his dad had called.

Helen kept her date with Rob on Wednesday night, of course, and Mike was very taken with her. He cornered his dad in the kitchen as he was mixing drinks, and said, "She's a real doll. How do you find so many of 'em?"

"My talents are *very* well known." Rob laughed. "No. We worked together at IMMCorp. She's been after me for a year and a half. I told her there'd be none of that as long as one of us was still there. I've been seeing her for over two months now. This is the first time she's been here."

"That's what she said. She looks awfully young."

"She'll be thirty-one in early May. Her birthday is exactly one week after mine."

"I was way off on how old she is."

"Hands off. She's mine."

"*Dad*! She's almost twice my age."

"Just kidding. And besides, your hand isn't quite ready for anything as lively as Helen is."

"Don't be too sure of that."

Drinks served, Helen said, "I really like your place. But it's obvious to me that it's just guys living here. I'd add some female touches if I ever became part of your family."

"I don't doubt that for a minute. And you'd move things around so we wouldn't know where to find anything."

Mike went off to watch TV. That gave Helen time to tell Rob that she hoped their relationship might one day be something permanent. "You know how I feel about you, but what we've had so far has been pretty casual. I take it that I'm not at the top of your list."

"I don't have a list, dear heart, so there's no top or bottom. With what's gone on this year, the subject of matrimony isn't something that's gotten much attention. Mike's hand is the latest distraction. But, I do have good feelings for you, that's no secret, and I want to keep on being a part of your routine. It's the only way I'll ever know if the prospect of a bright future is anywhere close to what Marianne and I felt we had. I have to make the comparison. My memories of her are still too vivid for me to ignore, and her shadow will be there for a while. Be patient, if you can."

"I'm not Kate, and like I said weeks ago, just give me a chance."

"And you remember that I said then, in so many words, that it would be wrong not to do that. We've only been seeing each other for a little over two months and there have been other things going on—the new job and Mike's problem being just two of them."

"I know. So I'm really pleased that we've been able to talk as often as we have and that we've gone out. You might not have agreed to do those things at all. I appreciate your openness, and that you've kept the promise you made last week to get into a subject close to my heart."

"We'll see more of each other. But getting settled into search work is taking time and the cash flow has been pretty uneven so far. You understand. It's all fairly new to me."

"Sure, but I also know you. You'll be fine."

"Those are kind words."

"One thing you just said is that we'll see each other more often. You know I want that."

"When we get closer to the holidays, I'll want to figure out when we can get together."

Drinks finished, Rob was finally able to pry Mike away from the TV, and the three of them went out to dinner. They all enjoyed their food and the banter that went with their first meal together. Helen had a great time putting Mike on, and it was fun to watch them go back and forth. She was good at it. Rob knew that from his IMMCorp days. Then after the lights were out, the pleasure continued. On Thursday morning, they both smiled all through breakfast. Mike understood why.

On Saturday morning, Rob got a call from Doctor Moore himself about his bill for surgery.

"Mr. Grant, it's been a month since I operated on your boy's hand, and you still haven't made payment. If you don't take care of your bill for the amount due by year-end, I'll do my best to see that you go to jail."

"Is that your way of wishing me happy holidays, Doctor?"

"Do not be impertinent, Mr. Grant. You acknowledged your obligation and said that I would be paid. I'm still waiting."

"I've exhausted my resources, and in my situation no one will loan me the money. If you put me in jail, you'll certainly never see any of it. You decide. And the state would then have to care for a minor child. I fail to see how that serves anyone's interests. But before you take legal steps, I've gone to my family, specifically my mother, and she's loaned me enough to cover your bill and the amount I owe the hospital. I should have it within a few days. I'm responsible for the delay because I had hoped to solve my problem in some other way. Borrowing from a seventy-two-year-old widow was a last resort, but you'll probably have your money within the next week or so."

"I'll hold you to that and will expect to see you in a few days."

"Hopefully I can conclude the matter directly with the woman who runs your office."

"You're an unpleasant man, Mr. Grant."

"No, dammit, I'm not an unpleasant man, Doctor! Mine are unpleasant circumstances, and if we were to take a look at your net worth versus mine, you'd maybe understand why I'm not happy with your harassment. I won't wiggle out my debts by filing for personal bankruptcy. Whatever happens, you'll get your money. But I would have much preferred if it could've been on a schedule that accommodated me, not you. That you want your wife to have a new Mercedes for Christmas when I'm having trouble putting food on our table is an imbalance in the distribution of wealth and a huge disparity in the hierarchy of needs that you've deliberately chosen to ignore. Completely. I'll probably be in sometime next week, Doctor."

Rob slammed the receiver down and went off to the market in an ugly frame of mind. The truth was that he already had the money but, after the phone call, he decided he'd make the impatient SOB wait until the last hour before the doctor's office closed on the eve of the new year. And despite more harassing calls and a "final" letter from Moore's attorney that demanded payment, that's exactly what Rob Grant did.

Two days before Christmas, Rob made the drive up to central Massachusetts to pick up Greg. "You look like you're glad to see me."

"I am, and I'm ready to be at home even if it's only for three or four days. If you'll make Gram's chili soup, I'll take some back with me."

"You got it. We'll probably need to use one of our bigger Tupperware bowls. I don't store much of anything that way, so you can take it with you as long as I can have it back."

"Guard it with my life." They laughed, and then started their drive back to Sheffield.

By the time they'd stopped for lunch and got to Juniper Heights, it was late afternoon. To their surprise, Kim was waiting with Mike, and it was a reunion on a grand scale for Rob's troubled son. He was all smiles. "Good therapy," Rob thought.

After they'd visited for an hour, Kim said, "I'd love to stay, but I've got to get back to Chris and Ian. And with everybody coming to my house again this year, I'll be busy through Saturday. It might be that I can go with you when you take Greg back on Sunday—that is, if you'd like company."

"*I* would!" Greg said without hesitation.

"Guess that decides it," Rob agreed. "And I'd like company, too."

"Do my best," Kim said. "I'm off next week and that'll finally give us some time together. We've both been busy, so I'm really looking forward to it."

"So am I. Let me know about Sunday."

On Christmas morning, Rob and the boys exchanged gifts at home. This year, they finally had a tree and it was fun to share laughter and open presents at number 710 first. Regina had invited them to have Christmas at her place later in the morning and then have dinner with her, and Kyle and Denny. Rob was glad he didn't have to put together a meal of that scale. Just as they were about ready to leave, the phone rang. Mike answered.

"Dad. It's Gram." Mike looked puzzled because Grandmother Grant hardly ever called.

Rob answered on the living room phone. "Mother? This is a surprise. Am I in trouble?"

"No, Robin," she chuckled gently. "As you know, it's a special day on the Christian calendar, and I wanted to wish all of you a Merry Christmas. I've just come from a special prayer service and felt the need this year to call before you got involved with whatever you're doing later in the day."

"You don't do this very often, so it's a real treat. It's good to hear your voice. And Merry Christmas to you, too. What are your plans for the day?"

"It's good to have close friends. Those that we haven't buried get together, and several of us are having dinner at The Orchard Inn this afternoon. We do a lot of reminiscing. Some are classmates. Most of them still live in town. The others are from our neighborhood. We'll be a fair size group, I expect."

"Please say hello to anyone who might remember me after twenty-two years."

"I will. But there's another reason why I'm calling. You've had a year that would make a preacher cuss, so I wanted to tell you that you don't need to repay the loan. It's better that you have some of your inheritance when you need it, so maybe this will help you out a little."

"Mother, I . . . I don't know what to say. You can't imagine how much it helps. It *has* been a rough year, and to have lost Marianne made it so much harder. That alone was a trial, but she'd have been here to be my pillar and I lost that, too. The brighter side is there's a young woman locally who's been wonderful help. She has two boys of her own at home but, to give you an example, she was here when I came back with Greg late on Wednesday afternoon. He loved it. Her name's Kim. She's sort of adopted the boys, and has been the same kind of shoulder that was always there around home when I was growing up. But about the loan, thank you so much. There should be something more I could add, but you know it comes from the heart."

"I know it does, and you're welcome, Robin. I'll be giving your brother the same amount just to keep the books balanced. I may not always be able to help out, but we had excellent yields right through the fall harvests, so it's been a bountiful year. Now, could I speak with the boys?"

"They're standing right here and about to take the phone away from me."

"Good luck with your new job. Let me know how you do. And you have my prayers for a good new year. I hope it turns out better than what you've gone through since last Christmas."

"Amen to that. I'll keep you posted. Thanks again for your help. And a healthy and happy new year to you, too, Mother. Now, here's Mike."

When the boys finished talking, the three of them got on their way to Regina's.

"Sorry we're a little late," Rob said. "Mother called when we were about to leave, and since she offered me some financial support, I thought it was a good idea to stay and talk."

"Things sure have gone to hell for you this year. I can picture you coming back from Australia last December, tanned, but absolutely dead on your feet. And I also remember the following morning. Want to stay over again and try to bring back some old memories? Since you've had to suspend alimony payments, that's the least you should be willing to do for me."

"The guys are having such a great time, it would be a shame to break up their fun, don't you think? Sure. Let's see if I've lost anything over the past year."

"You mean over the past month. I told you at Thanksgiving that you were still the grand champion."

"Sounds like you intend to enter me into some kind of competition at a county fair. Season's over, so it'll have to be next year. What kind of stud would you have me be?"

"Any kind—but one who's available whenever I needed servicing."

"Looks like I better buy myself a new appointments calendar."

They shared a good laugh. It had been a while since he and Regina had done that.

Dinner and the overnight were a big success. The four boys were together for the first time since early in the year, and they had a great visit with games, and TV, and teenage chatter. Rob guessed they had nearly as much fun as Regina. Her smiles over their late breakfast gave away any secrets she might have tried to conceal. Mike was at an age now where he read signals like that, and he knew what her cheerful mood meant. He, like his dad, was amazed at how much she'd mellowed in the past two years.

The day after Christmas was like most any other Saturday. Both boys were able to help with the laundry. Even some of Greg's clothes, ones that Rob thought were beyond hope, came out looking like they might survive one more school term. Then there was shopping to do. Rob told Greg he wasn't to leave the building and asked Mike to be in charge. "If you run off, I'll take you back to Massachusetts, today, and you'll miss out on the chili soup you wanted."

"I'm not going anywhere, and I won't ask anybody to come over while you're gone."

"You got to that before I did. Good. See both of you in an hour or so."

Chores finished, Rob called Kim. "Hi, babe. How was Christmas?"

"We had a great time. Just family, but we get along really good and always have lots of laughs. What about you?"

"It's been good having Greg here. Regina did the dinner, and with the four guys together again for the first time in almost a year, they had a picnic. But I was glad she took the meal off my hands. I'm not very good at anything beyond meat, potatoes, and a veggie."

"What's your schedule look like tomorrow? I will be able to go with you and stay overnight if that's OK. Gina will take the boys and look after them at her place."

"All of it suits me. Perfectly. Yea, Gina! About tomorrow, I'd like to get away by no later than ten o'clock. Snow's forecast for late afternoon, and the Mustang isn't the best car on the road under those conditions. If we don't run into any snags, we should be back before it gets bad. Maybe we could even fit in an early dinner."

"Always the man with a plan. After the kind of week I've had, the timing is perfect—and I'm also overdue to wake up in your bed."

"I like the way you put that. Mike's going to spend the night with Tom, so we can make as much noise as the floor and the ceiling can accommodate."

Kim chuckled. "Be wonderful for the two of us to be alone. Nearly like a weekend away. Great. I'm in need."

"Got to go do chili soup. It's a special order from Greg. He's even going to take some back with him."

"Sounds yummy. I'd like you to do that for me some weekend when it's cold and nasty out. It really hits the spot."

"Just tell me when. I usually have most of what I need to whip up a batch in case there's an emergency."

"I'll give you fair warning. Now, I've got to go, too. See you at around ten. I'll be ready."

Greg got his fiery soup, and the three Grant boys had a fine evening together. Football was one of the attractions, but there was plenty of chatter, and a dash of King Crimson before it drove Rob nuts.

On Sunday, Rob got to Kim's just before ten, gave her an overdue affectionate hug before Greg got to her, and then they went on their way. East of Hartford, they stopped for lunch; by early afternoon they arrived at the Duchene campus.

Before they started back, Rob asked Greg about something that he'd completely forgotten to bring up earlier. "When's the next time you'll be able to get away?"

"It'll be at Easter, but there won't really be enough time to come home. After that, it won't be until we come back from summer camp. It's ending a week earlier because of the way the dates are this year, so I might have about five days then. You could come up during the spring break though. I don't have the exact dates in my head, but I can tell you about it when you call."

"Enjoy the soup. I'll have to tell Gram that you brought some back to school. She'll get a kick out of that."

"It'll taste good. You don't have to tell me to enjoy it. I will"

Ready to say their good-byes, Greg gave his dad a hug, did a special teenager's routine with Mike, and then hung on to Kim. She had just a show of tears welling up, almost as if Greg were hers. It was obvious that he mattered to her. Greg was holding up fine, and he even had a smile for them as Rob drove away.

"Down deep inside, he's a good kid," Kim said. "It's a shame that he has to spend these years away from family. They're so important. But we understand why it has to be the way it is."

About the time they got past New Haven on the Wilbur Cross, the first flakes were in the air. Onto the Merritt, and getting nearer home, the cars that passed them were leaving snow snakes wriggling on the highway. Rob dropped Mike off at the Giordano's, and then he wasted no time in getting back to the Juniper Heights garage.

When they got to number 710, Rob mixed drinks and they talked about their day. Finally, Rob asked, "What do you think, sweetheart? Want to try to go out for dinner?"

Kim looked out the living room window and said, "Looks like it's let up some. And the streets seem to be mostly OK. Sure. Why not? If we don't sit around for hours, we shouldn't have any problem. Russo's is close. Is that all right with you?"

"Fine. We can always slide downhill. Easier than trying to come up from your direction."

"Before we go, let me call Gina and make sure everything's OK.

"Hi, Sis. Just wanted you to know we're back safe and sound and that we're going up to Russo's for dinner. The streets don't look too bad. Any problems?"

"Not a one. We're home, in for the night, and we all agreed to sleep late in the morning. There's more snow forecast, so it might be a good idea not spend a lot of time over dinner."

"I just said the same thing to Rob. We're leaving now. If you need to reach me, you have the number here, I think. If not, it's 323-3243."

"Don't expect to need it. Have a good time." Gina chuckled softly.

"You don't need to worry about that. Rob knows how to look after me. Especially later." It was Kim's turn to chuckle. "See you tomorrow."

Russo's was quiet, so drinks and dinner were served at the pace Rob and Kim wanted. When they'd finished, Rob said, "It's starting to snow again, so maybe we ought to have our after dinner drinks at home."

"Yeah. The way it's coming down now, we really should go."

Rob paid the bill, and they slid their way home. Good thing it wasn't far. When they were in the garage, Kim said, "You're a good driver. I feel very safe riding with you."

"I'm a pretty good driver after the lights are out, too." They laughed.

"Show me. It's been a while."

"Only eight days, unless my calendar is different than yours."

"Show me anyway."

"Follow me."

They had their liqueurs, got involved in the preliminaries while they sipped, and by the time their drinks were finished, they were more than ready to extract full pleasure from the beauty of their union. Satisfied, they agreed that while there might be differences on various issues, their nighttime hours together left no doubt that they were physically compatible. Extremely so.

After breakfast on Monday, Kim went home to Chris and Ian, and Rob decided he'd go into West End Avenue to see if there was anything he could do to help get ready for the move to Thirty-sixth and Lexington. Starting a week from today, January 4, it would be the new base of operations for Newcombe Associates. The phones were in, and work was finished on the tiny cubicles where each of the associates would spend their days. Doug was glad that someone showed up to help with the tagging and packing.

"Glad you're here, Rob. Between the two of us, I hope we'll be able to get everything boxed and ready for the mover by the end of the day. They're coming on Wednesday morning, so if we don't get it all packed, maybe you'd be willing to come back for a while tomorrow."

"I'd rather stay with it until we're done. Nothing personal, but I'd prefer not having to make the trip up here again."

"I understand. There won't be any search work to do. Years of experience tell me there's nothing going on until after the holidays. We can all pitch in next Monday and do the unpacking. Won't take long with everyone around."

"Do our clients have the new phone number?"

"All taken care of, and New York Tel will give it to anyone who tries to reach us here."

The two of them kept at it and finished before seven o'clock—earlier than either of them thought they would. All the files and records were boxed, and the furniture that would go to the new location was tagged. Doug would be ready for the moving company on Wednesday morning.

"I really appreciate the help, Rob. To show you how much, could I stir you up a martini?"

"Love it. While you're doing that, I'm going to call a young lady down in Murray Hill." To Rob's surprise, she was home.

"Hi, Helen. I thought you might be out on the town."

"No, the latest guy you know about asked me to go out, but I told him I was waiting for an important call. See, I was concentrating, and you were on the same frequency. Not really. I just don't want to see him anymore. I thought if there was any chance that I might fit into your plans over the holidays, I'd rather spend the time with you. Surprised?"

"Not at all. I know how you feel about us. What's on your agenda?"

"My grandparents are having a lot of family and old friends in for New Year's Eve, and my parents really want me to go. I said yes. But I'm free anytime from about noon on Friday."

"How about you jump on a train, say the 3:30, and spend the first night of the new year, with me."

"Oh, sweet. You know I'd absolutely love to come out. I was hoping you'd ask me."

"Consider yourself asked."

"I accept. Should be great fun." Helen was giddy and laughed.

When Rob got home later, he found a note from Mike that said he was staying overnight again with Tom, but that he'd be home tomorrow by noon. With no mouth to feed, other than his own, Rob mixed himself a drink, and then scrounged around in the fridge for something to keep him going until breakfast. When he'd finished eating, he called Kim.

"Hope it's not too late."

"No. In fact I was just sitting here thinking about you and what a good day, and a nice evening, we had yesterday. Any chance we could get together again tomorrow or Wednesday?"

"Guess I got the message that I was on your mind. Either day will be fine. We worked until we got everything ready for the movers, so I don't have to go back into the city again until next Monday. That'll be our first day in the new office setup at Thirty-sixth and Lex."

"Let's plan on Wednesday afternoon, and I'd like to stay the night if that's all right with you."

"Why would you put it that way? I can't recall that you've ever asked if it's all right. Of course it is. What's wrong?"

"I'm starting to worry that I've been too pushy at times and that one of these days you'll meet somebody nice who's ready to marry, or that maybe you'll simply tell me that it's over. When we met, I never thought you'd matter this much, or think that you might walk out on me. In the early months, it didn't matter. Now it does. But I'm not free to go beyond what we have now because Vince and I aren't divorced yet. We're only legally separated, and neither one of us has filed any papers."

"I didn't know that. Good grief! He has every right to make me an accessory and nail me for alienation of affection, or blow my brains out."

"Don't worry about anything like that happening. I'm sure our marriage is finished. And I told you before, he's busy with other women. He wouldn't do anything that would put him at risk of losing what he's got going on. They're more important than I am—or you are."

"I'm glad you told me where things stand. Still, it doesn't change anything with us. You know how much I care about you. But the shoe *is* on the other foot. Question is, how long should I wait for you to divorce or to decide if I might fit into your plans? If ever. In my case, it's generally been the other way around. Meaning, I've been asked the same question. Kate was the best example. She gave up after a year. Lu would have told you about that at least a year ago."

"Wish I had a good answer for you, so I guess that's why, tonight, it's bothering me more than maybe it should. I don't want to lose you, Rob. If it helps you understand, you're the only one I've been in bed with since Vince and I split. That may explain some of it. The rest of it is that I'm in love with you. You're good for me, I think. But you already know most of these things."

"I do, but it isn't very likely that I'd wait five years. On the other hand, I might. But it's best that we talk about this more when we're together. It's no good over the phone."

"You're right. I agree."

"What's the rest of your week look like?"

"The best part of it is Wednesday night with you. On Thursday, the boys and I are going to spend New Year's Eve at Gina's. She's having friends in. We've been invited to stay with her until Sunday. We're doing that, but when we get home, I want to come by for a little while before we both go back to work on Monday."

"Let's take it a step further and have dinner someplace."

"You know I'd love to do that. I'll make arrangements of some kind for Chris and Ian."

"Time for me to call it a day. I'm really tired. See you on Wednesday, then. Anytime."

"I'll call and let you know when I'm on my way. Night, love."

"G'night, sweet."

Rob went to sleep puzzled by Kim's frame of mind. It wasn't like her to be down, or unsure of herself. It worried him some, but he expected that they could sort it out on Wednesday.

Chapter Four

Having learned that Dr. Moore's office would close at mid-day on December 30, Rob arrived just after 11:00 a.m. to settle his account for Mike's surgery.

"Our attorney's letter get your attention did it, Mr. Grant?"

"Now, you're not going to get testy on me, too, are you, Mrs. Kraay? I've had enough of that from the doctor, but I can see that the two of you are only mercenary when it comes to money."

The humor in that made her smile thinly. "It *has* been seven weeks since surgery."

"Fact is, I've had the money for three weeks, but I was so annoyed by the doctor's lack of bedside manners that I put off payment until today. I figured he could look elsewhere for the money to buy his wife's new Mercedes. And, no, your lawyer didn't frighten me in the least. You can't squeeze blood out of an old turnip."

"How did you know about the Mercedes? It straightened him up when you said that."

"I don't know anything about a new car. I used it as an example. I'm neither privy to the doctor's affairs nor, in my situation, do I care to be."

"It was an interesting coincidence. Here's your receipt, Mr. Grant. And thank you."

"You're welcome. Please give the doctor a kiss for me." Rob chuckled. "And a Happy New Year, Mrs. Kraay."

Smiling, finally, Mrs. Kraay said, "And the same to you, Mr. Grant."

Since Rob hadn't heard from Kim, he organized some lunch and was just about to bite down on a sandwich when the doorbell rang. "Yes?"

"Guess who?"

At the door, Rob said, "Hi, babe. Thought you were going to call first."

"I tried twice, but there wasn't any answer. I figured that you were out with one of your other girlfriends and hadn't gotten home yet."

"Enough of that. Stop it! What's gotten into you? But, yes, I was seeing the love of my life, Mrs. Kraay. She's in Dr. Moore's office and she was taking great pleasure in watching me hand over a pile of money. Here's the receipt."

"Sorry. Guess it's called being jealous. Something new."

"No need to be. You're imagining things that don't have any substance. Maybe you're hungry. How about a sandwich? It's ham spread. My mother's recipe, and I just made it."

"Please. Yes. Maybe you're right. I don't want to turn out goofy like Lu. When I'm away from you now, I get all kinds of wild ideas."

"I know. You laid some of that on me the other night. But you said something about being pushy. I didn't agree with that at all. When times were tough earlier this year, you took control. That's being assertive, and it's what the situation demanded. I was grateful for all your support."

"Thanks, Rob. But, all of a sudden, I realize that I can't compete equally if you find somebody else. What I mean is, if you meet a person you like and she's eligible, then I don't stand much of a chance. Like I told you on Monday, I'm not free."

"Let me put it to you this way. Much as I care for you, I'm not close to making any kind of a commitment. We've talked about that. Have you forgotten? Whatever, I won't make any decisions about anyone until you're either divorced or you tell me to wait because I'm the guy you want at your breakfast table every morning."

"And if I don't do either?"

"Not sure I understand the question considering that you've been worrying about me running off with someone else. But if you don't, then that'll tell me what you've decided about us."

"You're right. Dumb question. Guess it's time for me to put myself in position to be a contender. Vince and I will talk about who's going to file. It's like I said on Monday, I don't want to lose you."

"At the moment, you're the only candidate who's been nominated, so you can relax."

"After fifteen months together, you'd think I'd know how to do that. I'll take your advice and try to loosen up a little bit."

"A long time ago, we talked about people in a relationship like ours trying too hard," Rob said. "Now maybe you understand what I meant."

"I remember. It was a Friday night, we were at dinner, and it was just before we made love for the first time. That was over a year ago. Wonder why I'm putting it all together now?"

"Could be that in spite of what you said then, there was something inside telling you that we might get to a day like this—and that it's also an acknowledgment that ours is a pretty damn solid relationship. My best guess is that you and I could make a go of it, long-term."

"There have been times when I've thought the same thing. But if we're to do anything about it someday, I'll need to be single again. Next move is mine. We'll have to get the process started."

"Even if you were unattached, I have the feeling that neither one of us is ready just yet to step up and say 'I do'. But with your divorce behind you, we'd be able to go ahead with our plans if someday we decide exchanging vows would be the best thing for both of us. On the other hand, if another interest should surface, you'd be free to pursue it."

"That's about as far from my mind as anything I can imagine. By the way, where's Mike? I thought he was coming home."

"He was in and out of here in ten minutes. Going off with the guys, he said. Didn't even wait to eat."

"I need to do some shopping so that we'll have enough to get us through until Monday. Want to come along?"

"If you need a chauffer, I'll be glad to drive my horse."

"That's nearly the best offer I've had all day."

"And the other?"

"That you'll not make any decisions until I'm eligible to maybe add 'Grant' to my name."

Rob and Kim did some shopping, enjoyed a quiet afternoon just talking, had a drink later, and then dinner at their favorite place, The Hearthside. It was good to be back again.

They ordered drinks and asked for menus.

"You know this is the same table where I said something about two people can work too hard to make a relationship work."

"I know. It was the Friday night before your first trip to Australia. And I also remember how it ended. Oh, do I! It still gives me the shivers. It also made me worry some, too. I was in the middle of my fruitful period, and I wanted you. Real bad. But I was a nervous afterwards about what might happen."

"Then you found out that it wasn't a problem—and why."

"Yeah. All the pleasures and none of the unwanted results. Reason number twelve why you appeal to me."

"And the other eleven?"

"Sometime when we have the whole weekend together. We don't have time for it now."

Rob laughed. "Sounds as if they're long and involved."

"No. Just detailed. It was worth the time to put it all together."

"You're beginning to make me think I'm important."

"If you only knew how much. You walked into my life and made me whole again. I'm indebted to you for that."

"Works both ways. If Marianne had lived," Rob suggested, "she and I would probably be married by now. But she didn't live and, as I've said many times before, you were there when I needed your support. You showed me what kind of woman you are. I'll never forget it."

"I guess it's the thought of another Marianne coming along that has had me worried. But, you set me straight on that earlier in the day."

"You're the one who's most important to me, Kim. The decision will be yours, unless I feel that our relationship isn't going anywhere. That's what Kate decided a year ago November. And she was right. It was still too soon then for me to think about making a commitment. And even if I had, it wouldn't have lasted. I'm getting close to believing that I'm ready now. If you'd have me, I'm probably yours. A year from now? I don't know."

"I understand, because I'd probably have the same question if we turned things around the other way."

Food was served, a bottle of Chianti opened and glasses filled.

"Salute! To you, Miss Kim."

"And to you, Rob Grant."

"Now, let's eat. We'll need the energy, you know." Kim showed Rob an understanding grin.

After they'd finished, Rob suggested that they have their amaretto at home. Kim knew what that meant, and she got stirred up just thinking about the preliminaries—and later.

"I like your idea, and what I'm sure you have in mind. The only thing that'll ruin it is if Mike has come home."

When they got back to Juniper Heights, Mike had been home and gone again. His note said that Kyle and Denny had asked him to come over and spend the night. He could be reached there.

"Amaretto anyone?" They both laughed, and then got comfortable for what was about to follow. And what was begun ended in as fulfilling a loving as they'd ever known. Then on the last morning of this horrible year that had been 1970, they took each other to towering summits again. This part of their lives left no doubt that Rob Grant and Kim Rossi were made for each other. No other partner on earth could have satisfied either one of them more.

When Kim was ready to go, Rob went with her to the garage. They held each other for a moment, and then Rob said, "No more worries about me being swept away in a fit of passion?"

"No more worries, Rob. I'm all right now. You've made it that way, and I'm your girl."

"And I'm your guy. Drive safely. I'll want you back in one piece."

"It isn't far, but I'll follow your advice. I want to come back to you just as I am now. Whole and with a heart filled with warmth."

They kissed briefly, but with deep feeling, and then Kim went on her way back to Perrin Drive.

As Rob was cleaning up in the kitchen, the phone rang.

"Rob, it's Helen. I have to cancel our date, and right now I hate my body. I've wanted these two days more than life itself, but it won't happen."

"Suppose I should ask why, but you don't sound well."

"I'm down with the flu. My temperature has been close to 102, and I'm in bed. First it's chills, then I burn up. I came out to Hempstead, but I won't be going to the party. Mom's staying home with me. Call me in a day or two, please? I can't see you, but I want to hear your voice. It'll help make me feel better."

"You know I'll do that, dear heart. Maybe in the evening, so you can fall asleep and have horny dreams."

"Hate to say it, but even that doesn't have much appeal. The dreams maybe, but nothing else. That tell you anything?"

"We'll both survive, and I imagine we'll work something out after you're healthy again."

"Thanks for being patient with me, Rob."

"Never mind the thanks. Just get well so we can romp around soon."

"I do like the sound of that after all."

"Get some rest now. I'll call you tomorrow evening."

"Bye, love."

Back to the kitchen, and the phone rang again.

"Hi, Rob."

"Didn't I just kiss you good-bye a few minutes ago?"

"Yeah, but I wanted to say thanks, again, for what you did to my outlook on life over the past twenty hours or so. You've given me peace of mind, and I went away happier and more relaxed than I've been in quite a while. Happy New Year, sweet. See you on Sunday."

"And to you, sweetheart. You didn't have to call, you know."

"Yes I did."

"Glad to know that. It makes *me* feel good. Be careful driving."

"I will. Bye, love."

Rob had an impulse to call Justine, but he knew from their conversation at Thanksgiving that she wouldn't be back from Oklahoma until Saturday evening. But before businesses shut down for the holiday, Rob ordered a small bouquet of flowers to be delivered to Helen by the end of the day. That done, it finally hit him that it would be a tranquil New Year's Eve. And it was. In the quiet of his apartment, he thought about this night two years ago—and Marianne. The fond memories of their hours together brought warm tears to his cheeks. They'd have been married by now. Last Saturday, in fact. The twenty-sixth.

Had she lived.

New Year's afternoon, Kim called.

"This is getting to be a habit, but I just wanted to know that we're OK and to find out how your evening was."

"Quiet. I was here alone. In fact, I drank one more Gibson than I should have. It put me away, and I went to bed before midnight. I guess you can assure me that it's 1971."

"It is, but I feel terrible about your being there by yourself. If I'd known that you didn't have any plans, I'd have asked you to come with me. It was a small group. You and some of the people at the party would have gotten along well, I think."

"Well, it's history now, and I'm into football up to my ears. I'll go for a walk after while and then fix myself something to eat. You'll be back in a couple of days, and if you get here early enough, maybe I can farm Mike out somewhere so we can mess around. We did that once before. Remember?"

"I do. Very well. Easy, though. You're winding me up."

"Save it. I'll see what can be arranged. Put us in a great frame of mind to start back to work, don't you think?"

"Couldn't imagine a more exciting jump-start than that. See you on Sunday afternoon."

"I'll be here. Thanks for calling, babe."

On the night of the first, Rob called Helen to see how she was doing.

"You are absolutely the sweetest man on the planet!" she said. "I loved the flowers. They are so cheerful, and I feel better already."

"Now, seriously, how are you? All the bull aside."

"The medicine is beginning to work. My temperature is down some, but I'm pretty weak. I'll call Stan tomorrow or Sunday and tell him I'll need a few days. And it'll be a while before I'll be ready for the likes of a growling lion."

Rob knew the answer, but asked anyway. "When did I ever do that?"

"Every time you do your thing."

"Hmmm. Guess I better watch myself or somebody will have me in the Bronx zoo if I'm not careful." Helen laughed gently.

"Can't do too much of that. It hurts for some reason."

"I'm not going to keep you but a couple of minutes. I just wanted check in and see how you're doing."

"The flowers help. Thanks so much, Rob. It really was sweet of you, and it got my parent's attention. You made a lot of points with them."

"Wasn't my objective. But thanks for the warning. They're on your side, too, huh?"

"Always have been, love. See you when I'm better."

"Just get well. I need my partner at IMMCorp around so she can collect commissions."

"That'll accelerate my recovery, for sure."

"Call you tomorrow evening, sweetheart. Sleep well. G'night."

"I will. Thanks for calling. Night, Rob."

Kim got back home late on Sunday as planned, and called to say she would be over as soon as her dad arrived to sit with her boys. Mike was staying overnight with Tom again, and Rob was beginning to wonder if he had a son any longer. At least he breezed through and kept his dad posted on his whereabouts.

When Kim arrived, they had a quick drink and then went to Russo's for dinner. Since they had other aims in mind, they wasted little time ordering and finishing their meal. And once home, they headed straight for the bedroom for what turned out to be an energetic and very agreeable loving. Neither of them had any doubts that it would be anything but that.

"That was just what I needed," Kim said. "I'm ready to face tomorrow now. And I begin the new year with positive feelings about you and me."

"I share that with you, and I'd like nothing more than to finally have some hope for the future. Ours. If we get off track somehow, then I guess it'd be a case of starting over all again. If so, whatever happens next would likely be at about the point where a stand-in mom wouldn't figure into the picture any longer. Then it'd be irrelevant if I remarry, or just have someone live in. Greg's gone indefinitely, and Mike graduates next year."

"Why so late? He's eighteen this year."

"The late November birthday does it. That's the way the California school system started them out. Greg's in the same situation because he was born in early December. It's been the right thing for both of them because they're average students. Starting a year earlier would have been a mistake, I think."

"Well, it's time for me to go relieve my dad and get my two in bed. School day tomorrow, and that first morning back is always a struggle for all of us."

Rob went to the garage with Kim to see her off.

"This is getting to be our regular spot to say good-bye. In January, it's better in here than outside. I'm still glad to have the space next to yours. Wish it could be permanent."

"It wouldn't be here, in any case. If we make it to June of '72, your house might be big enough. Time will tell. I'm not completely enamored with what I'm doing, so it's a hang loose year for me. If something else comes along…."

"I know how you feel. But let's stick together," Kim suggested.

"We're stuck, and here's a hug to continue the process. Feels good. A good-bye kiss comes with it."

"Yumm. Liked that. But I've got to go. Love you, Rob."

"And I feel the same thing for you, Kim."

On her way out of the garage, she waved. He returned it.

As Rob was getting ready for bed, Mike called to say that he was going directly to school with Tom, but that he would be home tomorrow night. Finally.

"Be good to get acquainted again, kid," Rob commented.

"I've had a great vacation. Bet you have, too—without me around."

"In part. But I was home alone on New Year's Eve."

"You're slippin', Dad."

"Helen was supposed to be here the following afternoon, but she's down with the flu. We'll make up for it."

"I'd bet money on that."

"I'm off to bed. See you tomorrow night. Be good to have you home."

"Night, Dad."

Before Rob turned in, Kim called.

"Hi, love. Had to tell you that when I came home, Dad noticed the whisker burns on my chin right away. He smiled, but I wasn't sure how he'd take it. Guess I should be amused, too. I suppose he's never had any doubts about what kind of relationship we have, but I certainly confirmed it this evening. He did say I should suggest to you that maybe you'd like to shave a little closer because it wasn't a good idea to advertise what I'd been up to."

Rob laughed. "I shaved early this morning. It doesn't last forever. If it bothers you, I'll go at it again after I get home. I thought it was becoming because it suggests that we were satisfied."

"I don't know about you, but I sure was. It's a big crest to ride back into work in the morning."

"Nicely put. Looks like we'll both smile as we start the week."

"Time for bed. Sweet dreams, love."

"You too, dear heart. We'll talk again later in the week. After your chin has healed up." They were laughing as they hung up. A good omen.

The weeks that followed, and the days within them, fell into a pattern that was almost dull. Rob got an appreciation for the tedium that machine operators faced when they went through repetitive motions. During the day, it was endless calls, sitting in on interviews, a few small placements to keep them afloat, the commute, fixing dinner, cleaning up when he got home, and so it went. The bright spots were Saturday nights with Kim, usually, one night a week with fiery little Helen, and the occasional overnight with an equally appreciative Justine. She enjoyed his company and was always glad to have him stay over.

On the third Saturday in February, Rob took Kim out for her birthday dinner. She wouldn't be thirty-six until Tuesday, the twenty-third, but family had stepped in and said the evening with her was theirs. Rob was invited, but he couldn't be out in time to join the party."

"Sorry about Tuesday evening, but we're interviewing one of my candidates for a job in the paper industry. I've got you all to myself tonight, though."

"Have you ever. Not right to say it, maybe, but this will be a bigger treat than whatever happens next week."

Over cocktails, Rob handed Kim a small box. It was beautifully wrapped.

"There you go again doing nice things for me."

She opened it and found a thin white gold necklace inside. "Ohh, Rob. It's gorgeous. So delicate. You sure know what I like."

"I was looking for something with an amethyst in it, your birthstone, but a really good one was out of reach this year."

"I wouldn't have wanted you to go that expense in any case. If we were married, that would be something else, but I just love the necklace. It's so pretty. Thank you." She reached over, took Rob's hand and squeezed it. "I'll improve on that later." Kim smiled warmly.

They had a fine birthday dinner, good conversation, and a pleasant evening to celebrate Kim's thirty-sixth. Late in the evening, they brought it to a very fulfilling conclusion with a passionate loving.

Afterwards, Kim said, "I've gotten to be terrible. If you don't love me every few days, I get cranky. Glad you gave me a fix. You're good for me. I've said that before, too."

"Do my best to keep you from getting irritable."

They talked for a while and when they were rested, Kim asked, "Would you take me up to cloud nine again? I need more of you."

"Let's see if everything is still working."

"I'll be glad to check you over, and help out if necessary."

"That's what I like. A willing and helpful partner."

Everything worked just fine and they loved again. Then in the morning, they capped Kim's abbreviated birthday weekend with a repeat performance.

"I sure came to the right place to get my horns pruned."

"Gals don't have horns."

"Details, details. You get the message."

“Yep. Come back anytime. The pruning pro is nearly always in.” They chuckled.

After a late breakfast, Kim got ready to leave for Perrin Drive. Mike, who’d come home in the meantime, gave her a hug, and then Rob went with her to the garage.

“Thanks for the nice evening, the necklace and the personal attention. I’m much, much better now. Ash Wednesday is coming up, so if we can’t get together during the week, I’ll see you on Saturday like always.”

They hugged, Kim went home and Rob went back to number 710 with his conscience bothering him again. He made a coffee, stood out on the terrace and reflected on his dilemma. Mike joined him. “I’m playing around with two hearts again,” Rob said. “Problem is, I care, really care, about both of them, but for different reasons. If Helen hadn’t turned out to be what she is, it would be simple. She’s the surprise, and she means more to me now than she ever has. Guess I’m going to do some juggling for a while until I figure out what’s the best thing for us.”

“You mean best for you,” Mike commented. “I like both of them, so it doesn’t matter to me. In another year, just about, I’ll probably be gone anyway.”

“It’ll sort itself out. Could be that it won’t be either of them. It makes me sad to think like that. They’re both wonderful gals, and I’d be happy with either one of them, I think. But after having spent time with Helen, she almost has the edge. I don’t know, Mike.”

“As March came to a close, Rob’s hard work paid off with a major placement at the senior executive level. It was one of Doug’s clients, but it didn’t matter. Rob’s share was substantial, and the first thing he did was call Alan Wilcox to put him on notice that he’d be up on the first of May to put some money down to get a cottage up.

“Good news, Rob. Let me send you some construction figures to look at. They’ll include the cost of various options, like a fireplace, electric heat, and so on—plus a sheet with the building codes and restrictions that apply to your development over in Hampden Park.”

“You’ve got my address in Sheffield. Send everything there, if you would. I should have all my ducks in a row by May 1, so it’ll be a forty-first birthday present to myself—three days late.”

“If you have any questions, call me. And think about coming to work for me. The offer’s still there. I could sure use you now.”

“You’ve waved that carrot in front of me before. Might happen. But about the cottage, when I get all your information I’ll look it over and be ready to talk specifics when I’m up. See you on the first.”

“It’s already on my calendar.”

On the first Wednesday in April, Rob called Kim and said he was coming over if she wasn't busy.

"I'm not, and it'll be a treat to see you at mid week. Come for dinner?"

"We won't finish in time for me to do that. Go ahead and eat. I'll pick up something along the way."

"No. I'll wait. I've got a high school girl I can call on now to sit with the boys. I'll feed them first, and then you and I can go out for a bite. Sounds like you have news of some kind, so I think that's the thing to do. Agreed?"

"Agreed. See you at about seven, or maybe a little after."

When they were seated at their place, The Hearthside, Kim was all eyes and ears. Tell me your news."

"I've made a whopper of a placement, and I've called Wilcox up at Hampden Lake to tell him I'm going to build this spring or summer."

"Oh, Rob, that's wonderful news. I think. The reason I say 'I think' is because it means you'll be spending weekends up there."

"Not in the beginning. But later on, when there's work I can do, I will be up at the site. You could come along, and we could overnight in Sturbridge."

"What would I do while you're working? Fight off that sex fiend, Wilcox?

"I'd protect you, fair maiden. But you could be in charge of the chuck wagon. We will have to eat. Whatever, Wilcox will be sending some stuff down for me to go over. It'll include cost data. Should be here tomorrow, so we can look at it this weekend."

"Can't. It's Easter and the boys and I, and Dad, will be at Gina's for the weekend. I won't be back until late on Sunday. After you called and said you wanted to see me, but that you couldn't make it in time for dinner, it was why I suggested that we go out tonight. I won't be around after I get off work a week from Friday."

"I'll get horny."

"So will I, but we'll work out a rendezvous somehow."

After Rob took Kim home, she invited him in for a quick nightcap. Drinks finished, and as he was getting ready to leave, they held each other as if they wanted their hug to last the entire ten days it would likely be before they could get together again.

"I've gotten spoiled. But we'll survive. See you on the seventeenth?" Rob asked.

"Maybe before then if I can't handle the long break."

"Whatever it is that you dream up, just remember that I don't get home until after seven."

"We'll talk late on Sunday. Maybe I'll have something worked out by then."

"That's my girl. I'll listen to any and all proposals."

They kissed, and Rob went back to Juniper Heights.

"I sort of left you high and dry, Mike. Sorry."

"It isn't very often that you don't show up, but when that happens I feed myself. Don't worry about it. You taught me how to do that. By the way, Helen called."

"That's funny, because I was going to call her. Like now."

"Hi gal. What's on your mind?"

"You."

"That's all?"

"I was hoping we could talk about when we can get together. It's been a whole week, and I thought I'd see you tonight. I missed you."

"I had to come out here. At that I was late getting away. So, your question raises another one. Any interest in spending Friday and Saturday night here to make up for tonight?"

Helen squealed with joy. "*Ohh, Yesss*!"

"We have plans for late on Sunday afternoon, so I'll have to put you on a train back into the city at four o'clock or so."

"That's all right. I'll have had two nights with you. Terrific! I'm really excited by the idea of coming out. Don't suppose you can tell." Helen giggled cutely. "What a treat! Which train on Friday afternoon?"

"I'd like to be on the 4:15, but I'll confirm that on Friday. That OK with you?"

"It's Good Friday, so I can leave almost anytime after lunch. Oh, Rob, this is just what the doctor ordered. I'm so looking forward to it. Don't forget to call on Friday."

"I won't. Now, it's been a long day, so I'm off to bed."

"Day after tomorrow, I'll share it with you. Yumm! Good night, sweet."

"That you will. Night, babe."

Rob put in a long day on Thursday and started early on Friday so he could get away in time to meet Helen and be on the earlier train. Having gotten caught up, Rob called her after lunch and confirmed that he'd be by the big clock on the departure level at a little after four. It was an easy walk up to Grand Central from Thirty-sixth Street, so he was there ahead of her. When Helen came up from the subway, she flew across the open concourse and collided with Rob at the information window.

"Oomph, maybe you should try out with the Giants. *Some* hit."

"Tell you that I'm glad all this is happening, or about to?"

"I guess so. But let's go see if we can't find a seat." On their way, who should they run into but the same nosy dude who was on a morning train nearly two and a half years earlier—the one who'd asked Rob about Kate.

"You're still at it, I see. Whatever happened to that luscious tall one that rode in with you once in a while on the 8:01 from Sheffield?"

"Good memory. This is the same gal. I washed her and she shrunk."

The guy laughed. "Well, you haven't lost your touch. You still know how to pick 'em."

"This one knew the other one. Small world, huh?"

"What really happened?"

"Came back from Sydney through San Francisco and she pulled the plug. That was in sixty-nine, the first week of November. She was in a hurry. I wasn't. You get the picture." Rob looked at Helen and grinned.

"You're a regular Casanova, then," the man suggested. "That it?"

"Whatever."

"Now I understand," Helen said. "He's talking about Kate!"

To the stranger, she added her own comment. "I'm *much* better for him than she was."

He smiled graciously, and said, "I can tell from your voice that you're a local girl."

"You got it. And I won't run back to Vegas—or anyplace else."

"Well, good luck." The man got on one of the rear coaches. Rob and Helen went well forward so they could get on a different car.

Once they were seated, Helen said, "You have to tell me the story behind that little do."

As they headed toward Sheffield Station, Rob did just that, and he also explained how it helped him sort out something about Kate that had been troubling him. He told Helen about that, too. "I couldn't have held onto her. With her ego, someone would have turned her head, and it would have been all over. I didn't need that."

"You wouldn't have to worry about something like that happening with me, you know. I'd be 120 percent yours."

"I know. If I proposed right now, you'd get off in Port Chesterfield and go looking for someone with a Bible in his hand. Am I right?"

Helen laughed. "I don't know. Since you live in Connecticut, I might wait until we get to Greenwood, or even Sheffield." It gave them a chance to smile. They'd kept things light, so their weekend was off to a good start.

As they settled in at home, Rob reflected on their first couple of hours together, "Helen may be nine years younger, but she's all adult and handles herself like one. No following me around or hanging all over me even though it's patently obvious that she cares about preserving our relationship. We've known each other for two years, and I have the distinct feeling that she'd be a very solid partner—and good for me. But do I care for her in the same way that I do Kim?"

It was later that Rob found Helen standing quietly at the big living room window enjoying the view across Sheffield and Long Island Sound. He interrupted her.

"Hey, kiddo, we'll need to do something about food before long. Mike's left a note behind that says he's eating at Phil Cullen's house, but that he'll be home later. So I guess we're on our own. Think we can manage?"

"Let's give it a try. Any ideas about where to go?"

"Several. What do your taste buds tell you?"

"Doesn't matter. It's your town. You pick."

"It's going to be a physical weekend, I imagine," Rob grinned, "so a high protein meal would be a good idea. There's a new place in town that I haven't tried. It's called the Cattle Baron. You game?"

"For anything and everything."

Rob found the place, was taken with the rustic décor, and they both liked what they saw on the menu. They ordered drinks, both had what turned out to be great beef, and a tasty Spanish red wine. The chatter was nonstop, and it turned out to be a delightful evening.

Spring was in the air, so that added to the warm feeling they took with them to Rob's bed. There was no shortage of passion, and they found great pleasure in what each had to offer the other. Satisfactorily loved, and spent, they slept close to each other. Helen was short, and it was pure bliss to be entangled with her petite body. When she awakened, it was with a loving smile, but with tears on her cheeks. "Good morning, sugar," she said.

"The smile tells me that maybe you're in love, so what's with the tears?"

"I dreamed that you walked away from me, that you didn't like me anymore." Then she clutched Rob and cried softly.

"Whoa, girl. That shouldn't be a part of our weekend. I care about you, I'm here, and I'm going to attack you just to prove that I'm the genuine article."

That brought back a smile, and a change of position to accommodate her lover.

"Here, have a tissue first. Predators don't kiss tear stained faces." A grin, a dab at the tears, and then the loving began, and continued, in earnest. At the end, there were soft squeals, the customary growl, and then matching smiles.

"I'm all better now," Helen said. "It was just a dream, but it hurt. It seemed so real."

"Don't worry about it. We're together. Need more proof?"

"Tonight. By then I'll have recovered. Too many trips into orbit. You sure know how to get me there."

"It was all right then?"

"All right? I guess so. Anytime you want to launch an attack like that again, be sure to let me know. Whew!"

Rob and Helen got breakfast together, and, no surprise, it wasn't long before a familiar face showed up. Hungry, of course.

"Well, look who's here. Hi, Helen. Good to see you again. How're you?"

"Looking back over the past eighteen hours, except for a bad dream I had, just great."

"I won't ask for any details." Mike chuckled.

"You wouldn't get 'em anyway. So there."

"What's on your agenda today, young man?"

"The baseball game at school this afternoon, but I'll help with the laundry this morning if you want me to. I could use the allowance. Been having too much fun."

"Do you get any studying done these days?"

"Sure. I'm caught up. My grades won't be all that great, but they're OK this term. I'll be a senior this fall. Don't worry about it."

"All right, I won't. And I can use your help with the laundry, but I don't want any editorial comments to go with it."

"I'll just think about it then and leave it alone."

"Fair enough. Helen and I will get some shopping done and maybe go for a drive this afternoon. The leaves are coming out and there's color beginning to show up here and there. Good to see it again. What're your plans for this evening? "

"Probably go over to see Kyle and Denny. May stay overnight. Let you know."

"OK, but plan on being around late tomorrow afternoon."

"Why?"

"You forgot about the Rossi's." Rob winked at Mike.

"Yeah. I did forget. What time was it for?"

"You should be here no later than six."

"I'll be back way before that."

"Happy laundering. Here's your allowance, and maybe we'll see you later."

"Right. *Maybe*."

After Mike left, Helen asked what Rob meant by not wanting any editorial comment.

'Has to do with the condition of my sheets. If you had a look at ours this morning, you'd know right away what I mean. Mike took great delight in pointing out the evidence. It began with Kate back in the fall of '68. One of these days, I'll check his sheets. If I find what I expect, then it'll be a draw and no more BS about mine."

Helen couldn't resist laughing. "I see." She laughed again.

The two of them did some window-shopping, went to the market, and then stashed the food at home before driving back roads north and east of Sheffield. The forsythia was out and it added splashes of yellow just about everywhere they drove. The afternoon was bright and warm, and Helen was pleased that Rob was showing her the sights and colors of Fairbanks County. Though she had grown up on nearby Long Island, these roads and small towns were all new to her.

Late in the afternoon, it was warm enough to have a drink on Rob's terrace, and it was a treat for her to look across the Sound again and see the north shore of Long Island.

"This is quite a view, Rob. I love it. It's fun to watch the sailboats. Helps that it's so clear. Wouldn't take much to talk me into putting my clothes in your closet. But I don't have to remind you of that."

"I know, sweetheart. You're way ahead of me on that score. But I'll make a small compromise with you. Pack a bag, enough clothes to get you through to Friday morning, and we'll live together under my roof starting Monday evening. If you need help with your luggage, I'll meet you at your place first. If not, I'll see you at Grand Central in time to make the 5:52. Keep in mind that I may have friends call. That may not suit you, but you'll have to put up with it, or them. And on Saturday next week, and the week after, I have plans. If we get along OK, it could be that we'll do it again in May. Leave four or five things here if you want. There's plenty of room for them in my walk-in closet."

"Ohh, Rob. You have to know that what you're saying makes me happy, really happy." Helen gave him a hug and held on for a moment. "You remember my telling you that all I wanted was a chance. You're giving me that. And I can deal with the calls. I understand, and I can guess who it is you're talking about. It doesn't matter. I'll be OK."

"On May 1, I've got to go up to Massachusetts on personal business, so it's possible that we could work out something that first week of the month or the one after. You'll have the chance you wanted, and so will I. It isn't just in my hands, or my decision alone. I have to satisfy you that I really am the guy you think I am. Someone you want around indefinitely."

"I decided that one year, five months and twenty-four days ago." They both laughed at that.

"Sounds pretty specific to me. You recall what day of the week it was?"

"Yeah, I do. It was a Saturday. Four days before you left on your first trip to Sydney. I cheated on Danny that weekend. You told me I looked good. You were the reason I did it. Then you scolded me when you'd figured out what I'd done. What you didn't know was that I made love to you that Saturday night. The guy I was with was just a convenience. He helped me with my fantasy. Now I know first hand how much better you are than he was. He was minor league. Couldn't hold a candle to you. You'd keep me happy for a lifetime."

"Thanks for the rave review. The things you learn long after the fact."

"Could I have another glass of your red wine? That was tasty."

"Now, I'll share a secret with you. That comes from Marianne's grandfather. I still see her folks about once a month, and Carlo always makes sure that he has a couple of bottles for me to bring home. It was the oil that led Marianne to my bed. She wanted to, but was hesitant. Her grandfather's red helped her decide. So, be warned, it has fiery passion built into it."

"Good! Maybe I'll take your measure before we go eat."

"Given what we've accomplished in the past twenty-four hours, I think maybe you should save some of me for later. Wouldn't want you to come up empty at eleven o'clock. On the other hand...."

"Let's see how we feel after another drink. The stuff sure is potent."

"Take it easy. I don't want to lose you to intoxication."

"I feel the fire, so maybe I should skip the second glass. Would you let me proposition you?"

"Lie across my lap, and let's find out where that takes us."

It didn't take long for them to decide that the red wine had done its job. Verrry effectively.

"Not much doubt that I'm ready."

"None at all. Up. Then follow me."

They joined and took each other to warm and high places. Complete satisfaction wasn't long in coming. Afterwards, they both agreed that if they could purr, they would.

"Delicious," Helen said.

"Can't disagree with that. Now, leave me alone until tonight. An encore isn't a good idea."

"The red wine's very effective. You're right. It makes you feel good. Of course you take advantage of that and add to it. Mmmm. Can't wait until Monday night, and all next week."

"If we're to get to work, we'll have to pace ourselves. Maybe not you, but I will."

"It'll feel like a honeymoon. So don't go getting old on me before then."

"Not to worry. I'll send you down to Wall Street with a smile."

"That's all I wanted to hear. I accept your offer to come back on Monday."

Rob and Helen had dinner, loved again, and by mid-morning on Easter Sunday, they had just about burned up all the energy allocated to meeting each other's needs. Helen wore a silly grin nearly the entire day.

"Never been this satisfied in my entire life. You're good for me, Rob Grant. I hope there's a chance we can work something out. You fill my heart to the brim. Maybe overflowing. I don't want to let go, but I know that I have to give you up until tomorrow evening. I'm really keyed up about getting into a daily routine like we were permanent fixtures in each other's lives. Let me believe that next week. Please?"

"Why not. I'll do the same. Make it more realistic. If we have a fight, then that's it." Rob laughed.

"If you want to pick a fight, I won't be your opponent. I care about you too much to be involved in anything that would be painful. I want our week to be perfectly golden."

"It will be. I'll do what I can to make it turn out that way."

Rob took Helen down to the station and put her aboard the 4:24 express. This wasn't a time to be sad that she was leaving because starting tomorrow afternoon the week ahead would give them their first exposure to how life might be if they married. The two of them had been close for six months now and it was time to find out.

"I know what I'm going to pack, so I won't need your help, I think. I'll go home, grab my bag and take a cab."

"Why don't I meet you at about a quarter of six up at the taxi level on Vanderbilt Avenue? If your bag is heavier than you think, I can help you with it."

"That's sweet of you. Good idea. See you tomorrow." They held each other briefly, kissed, and then Helen left for home all but floating on air.

By the time Rob got back to Juniper Heights, Mike was there, thinking his dad really did want him back before six. Kim called not long after and asked if it would be all right to come over in about a half-hour.

"There you go again. Of course it's all right, you silly girl. See you shortly."

"Did you really want me home, or was that for Helen's benefit?"

"Both. First, Kim's on her way over. Don't know how long she'll stay, but maybe you and I can go get a burger or something. Not a Sunday night meal, especially on Easter, so if you insist, I'll upgrade that to a pizza—or better. Any objections if she wants to go along?"

"Why would I do that? I like Kim. She's nice people."

"Second. Helen is coming back out tomorrow evening and will be here through Friday morning. We're going to see how we do together. We'll probably try it again on a fairly regular basis. She's asked that I give her a chance to show us what kind of companion or wife she'd be. She's a sweetheart, and I agreed. I like the girl."

"So do I. She's neat and lots of fun. But you've got almost too much going on again."

"I know, but I'm getting ready to settle down, I think, so I need to see how Helen and I do. The other news is, I earned a big fee at work and have talked with Wilcox about putting up a cottage on our lots. It's something I've wanted to do for a long time, and now it's *finally* going to happen."

"*Wow*! That's super."

"It means that you won't be going to California this year—for two reasons. The first is that I'll want to put that money into the cottage. Second is, I'll want your help with all the odds and ends that'll need to be done. Stuff you and I can do together."

"I'd rather be doing that anyway. Phil and Tom will probably want to help out, too. We've talked about your plans since last fall. I figured you'd do it someday."

"Wilcox sent me a bunch of information that I have to look at in more detail, and Kim and I will be going up on the first of May to get the ball rolling. He wants $1,500 as a deposit, so I'll give it to him when we get the details sorted out. I hope that by fall, we can spend weekends up there. I'm going to put in electric heat, and we'll have a fireplace, too."

"Sounds groovy. Boy, it'll be a lot of fun on the lake. Even in winter."

"Yeah, Mike, I know. It's a dream that's been a long time coming."

Kim was at the door just about the time Rob finished stirring up a drink.

"Hi, sweetheart," she said as she gave Rob and Mike hugs. "How's your Easter been?"

"Relatively quiet. I spent a little time looking over all the material Wilcox sent me. Maybe next Saturday you and I can take a look at it in detail. Be interested in your opinion. I've gone over the essentials, and have some idea what the numbers are, but I hope maybe you'll want to share in the planning."

"I'd love to, and I really appreciate it that you want my input. This ought to be a really fun project. I'm excited about it, too."

"Did you eat? We haven't yet, and I thought we might go get a burger. Like I told Mike, it really isn't an Easter Sunday meal, so we'll probably eat better than that. Thing is, I'm going to be working late much of the week, so I thought we ought to do something together while we have the chance."

"We ate. Huge meal, so I'm not hungry. Anyway, I can't stay long. I just wanted to sit by you for a few minutes and get my arms around you before we start back to work tomorrow. It's probably a good week for you to be working late because the boys have all kinds of school events going on that'll have me involved, too. But before we go much further, I'm in need of a kiss. I've missed you, and we have another week to go. Can't wait to get you cornered, if you understand."

"I do, and I'll cooperate." Then Rob delivered the requested kiss, and the two of them sat for a several minutes just holding each other. Nothing was said. That would have spoiled the feelings they were sharing. What was passing between them pretty much said it all.

"You don't know how good you feel. By Saturday, I'll want more of the same, plus the special attention you know how to supply."

"I get the picture."

"Much as I don't want to leave, I need to get home. If I have a chance to call, I will. Otherwise, I'll see you Saturday afternoon. Go with me to the garage?"

"Of course. Don't I always?"

Before Kim drove off, they held each other tightly and exchanged kisses that expressed what they felt for each other.

"Sleep well, babe."

"You too, Rob. Call me if you can."

"I'll do it. Bye, love."

As Rob went back up in the elevator, he thought that the emotions and feelings he and Kim shared during these last few minutes had more intensity than they did with Helen. "A matter of degree," he said aloud. "They're both important. But one's free. The other isn't."

Chapter Five

When Monday evening came, Rob waited for Helen near the taxi drop-off point at Grand Central. There was uncharacteristic grousing going on inside his head, and he finally recognized it as conscience, or maybe even guilt. He and Kim had come a long way in their relationship over the nearly nineteen months they'd known each other, and he was tampering with it. On the other hand, she still hadn't filed for divorce, and he decided that it would be best to look after his own heart first. It continued to trouble him until Helen's taxi pulled up. She was smiling broadly—and aglow! It was exactly the jolt Rob needed to end his debate. And it did. Instantly.

"Hi, love bunny. Are you ready for a house guest?"

"I am. Are you ready to be one?"

"This is a high point in my life. You can't imagine how ready I am for these next few days. It's bliss gone out of control."

"Sounds serious. Here, let me take your bag."

"Serious? It is for me."

"You must not have too much in here. It isn't very heavy."

"Be lighter on the way back." Helen smiled.

The two of them made the 5:52 with ease, and when they got to Juniper Heights, Helen proceeded to unpack and settle in as if it were her God given and constitutional right to be a member of the Grant household, however brief it might be.

"Make yourself at home," Rob said.

"I have, thank you very much. I'm the lady of the house for the rest of the week. Just call me Mrs. Grant, if you please." They both laughed.

"Nothing bashful about you. Welcome to Grant heaven."

"You might call it that. It is to my way of thinking."

"How about we get Mike and go someplace to eat."

"I'd love to go out. I'm famished. Busy day. Professionally and emotionally." With that, Helen gave Rob a hug that showed him how strong she was for a little gal.

"Wow! Do you work out? No wonder you didn't have a lot of trouble with your bag."

Helen tilted her head up a little and puckered. "I did the hug. Your job is the kiss."

Rob delivered it in a way that made Helen shiver. "Take it easy, or we'll never get to dinner."

"Mike! Save me."

They went out, had their dinner, and then were a family at home for what was left of the evening. It ended with a spirited loving and affectionate words that again confirmed how much Helen cared for this man she would have as her lifelong partner.

Then, beginning at breakfast on Tuesday morning, Helen took over the kitchen. Throughout the week, and without fanfare, she quietly became wife and mother to the two Grant men in her life. She allowed Rob to help with the meals some, but in her competent and efficient way, it was clear that she was in charge of domestic affairs at number 710. Both Rob and Mike were impressed. Gone was the playful little girl who pursued her partner at IMMCorp. This was a mature, self-confident woman who quickly became familiar with the apartment, and never asked a foolish question about how to get something done. Given the way she handled herself, she might well have moved in with them in the summer of 1968. It felt as if she'd always been part of their lives. At the same time, she was bubbly, proved every day that she had a great sense of humor, and then loved her man vigorously after the lights were out. But morning encores during their workweek would be confined to Thirty-second Street. In Sheffield there was no time, and they'd be, she said, mostly weekend treats. Helen made quite an impression, and she was having a definite influence on how Rob looked at his future. It would be a while before he sorted it out, but he concluded that if they were to marry, it would almost certainly thrive. Easily so. Rob suddenly found that his affection for Helen had grown. Was he ready to acknowledge what he was feeling? He *would* give it room to breathe.

As they were on their way into Manhattan on Friday morning, Helen said, "I sure do face today, and the weekend, with mixed emotions. The week was everything I wanted, everything I'd hope for, and more. I'm yours, Rob. That's no secret. Our week together simply confirmed what I've known for a long time. I'm going out to Hempstead until Sunday evening. Hanging around Thirty-second Street doesn't have any appeal unless you could be there, too. And to use your phrase, it's time I pulled the plug on that guy I thought meant something to me. He doesn't call very often now, but the next time he does I'll give it to him straight. You're a 'keeper'. He isn't. I'm putting all my chips on one number. Pick one."

"A number? How about 71, as in 71 Juniper Heights?"

"That's the number. How did you know?"

"Psychic, I guess." They both chuckled. "You may have a winner."

"I think so, too. But let's wait and see if the number comes up."

"You left clothes behind? I didn't look."

"Most of what I brought out."

"Why don't you come out with me on Tuesday afternoon next week? Same thing. Come back in with me next Friday."

"You know I want to do that. Already I feel better about the weekend. But I'll still go see my folks, I think. They'll want to know about our week together. I'll probably glow, like I'm expecting. They'll know right away how happy I am. It's your doing."

"Glad to provide a valuable service, ma'am."

When they got to Grand Central, they held each other tightly. As they were about to go on their way, Rob said, "Six o'clock. Here. Tuesday. Now you won't forget?"

"Only if I suffer total amnesia. And even that might not do it." A quick kiss, and then a wave from Helen as she disappeared into the Lexington Avenue subway.

Thinking out loud, Rob said, "That's some woman, I'm discovering. Took a while for me to see something that's been there right along."

After he got to the office, Rob kept his juggling act alive by calling Kim at the Prentiss Agency.

"Rob, hi. You don't call me at the agency very often. I'm surprised and tickled. What's the occasion?"

"I haven't heard from you, so I was wondering if we're still on for the weekend. I've missed you."

"That's so sweet to hear. Touches a warm spot inside. Of course we are, silly man. I've been busy with the boys, like I told you last weekend. Tonight isn't possible, but Vince has them from tomorrow morning until late Sunday afternoon. I can't talk freely, so you'll just have to guess what's dancing around in my head."

"Something passionate, maybe?"

"How could you have ever guessed that? Yeah! Be prepared. It's been a while, you know."

"Be good to grab onto you and give you a world-class bear hug."

"I'm overdue. For that and other things. But we can't keep talking like this. You know why. The environment's all wrong to get me turned on," Kim whispered.

"See you in time for lunch. Maybe we can whip up something agreeable—including a little fire."

"There you go again. You leave me alone, Rob Grant!" She laughed softly to let him know that she wasn't serious. Rob joined her, and they were still chuckling when they hung up.

Kim showed up on Saturday shortly after mid-day and she and Rob went straight into the bear hug they both needed. They agreed it felt wonderful. A loving kiss added warmth to Rob's welcome.

After Mike came out of his room, said hello, and then went back to his little TV, Kim said, "You don't know how ready I was for that hug. Too bad Mike's here. I'd like some of that fire you mentioned yesterday."

"It'll still be very much alive this evening. To help us get from here to there, let's put some lunch together. Then, if it doesn't turn you off completely, I've got some shopping to do. Hope you don't mind tagging along."

"Not a bit. I've done that before, and you know me: I like giving you shopping advice."

When they got back from their outing, Rob saw that Mike had left a note saying he would be at Giordano's and spending the night with Tom.

"Well, hotshot. It's a long way to dark, but I can't wait. Let's stir up that fire we talked about. I'm in need of a fix and you have all the equipment needed to make it happen."

And that's exactly what he confirmed for her. Not much question that Kim was looking for some lofty peaks—and she found them. Then, "Time for a duet. Do it. *Now*!" It was all the invitation Rob needed and they joined each other on the *fifth* planet from the sun—Jupiter.

"Guess we needed that," Rob commented moments later.

"Needs to be in my diet more often. It still amazes me that you can wait until I've gotten to the place I want to be. We're so good together. I don't know how we could go wrong since we have other things going for us, too." Rob agreed.

When it got to be time for dinner, they went back to the Hearthside, "their place" since September of sixty-nine. They had their usual leisurely and enjoyable dinner together and talked about the two weekends ahead.

"You'll be over next weekend, right?" Rob asked.

"It doesn't look good. Everybody has other plans. I'm still trying, though. But your birthday is coming up. We have to figure out how to celebrate that."

"It's mid-week. With my schedule, and our trip to Hampden Lake coming up on May 1, why don't we move it over a couple of days and spend the whole weekend up there. Could you get away that Friday afternoon?"

"That'll be harder to do. Let me see if I can work it out. Saturday morning to late Sunday afternoon I can do for sure, but I also want to have dinner with you on the twenty-eighth. Can't do anything else, but being with you that evening is important to me."

"It's a date, sweetheart."

The two lovers made the most of their overnight and then had a quiet Sunday simply enjoying each other's company. It was yet another way that confirmed how compatible they were.

Then on Tuesday afternoon, Kim called Rob at the office to tell him that she hadn't been able to work out arrangements for Chris and Ian for Saturday night. "I'm upset, because I really do want to stay over. But the good news is, we can go out on your birthday, a week from tomorrow, and it looks like we can get away on Friday next week. We can be together right through until late Sunday afternoon."

"That's great. I'm almost willing to exchange Saturday night for the whole weekend of the thirtieth to the second. But we did have part of this past weekend together, and I'll make reservations in Sturbridge at the same place we stayed last time, the Liberty Cap. That be OK?"

"Sure is, especially if we get another passionate room like we had before." They laughed.

"You remember the room number?"

"No. But ask for one suitable for passionate lovers."

"Do my best. But, I've got to get back to work. There are lights blinking all over my phone. We have evening interviews every night this week, so we probably won't talk until the weekend. I'll call you on Saturday, for sure, and then probably Sunday, too. Talk to you then. Bye, babe."

"Bye, love."

Helen occupied Rob's home, and bed, and mind for the balance of the week. What they both quickly discovered was that their second week together was every bit as pleasant and compatible as the first. Rob was growing attached to Helen in several different ways. And he really didn't want to let her go when they got to Grand Central on Friday morning, so he asked her to come back on Sunday evening and stay until Wednesday morning. She was clearly disappointed that she couldn't have dinner with Rob to celebrate his birthday, but she seemed to take it in stride and didn't make an issue of it.

"I've had more of you during the past two weeks than I have any right to hope for, so I won't ask questions. But on Wednesday I'll break my Sheffield weekday morning rule and, if you're interested, we might get your birthday off to a fiery start. I'm being selfish and plan on leaving you depleted. That way there won't be a thing left for somebody else."

"I'll answer you now. I'm interested. And you don't need to worry. It's just dinner out and nothing else. It's my ex who's treating me," he lied. "We've become reasonably good friends since we divorced. She looks after Mike when I want her to, so I try to meet her half way when she asks a favor. In this case, she's lonely, wants company, and is buying dinner. Be five of us, including her two guys. Nothing to worry about, my sweet."

"That makes me feel better. But you're going to be away over the May 1 weekend."

"Yep. I'll be driving up to Hampden Lake the afternoon before. You remember that I've got some lots up there, and I'm finally going to build. I'm meeting the real estate guy, who's also the developer. I'll give him a deposit, pick out a floor plan, and decide on what's to be included during the construction stage. We'll go to contract sometime after that."

"Sounds really exciting. Sorry I can't go along."

"It's all business. There'll be a bunch of things to sort out before we come to a final agreement."

"Will you take me up there sometime? I'd love to see it."

"Sure will. But wait until the leaves and the laurel are out and the building is started. Be more to see by then. In the meantime, plan on coming out on the third, that is if you want to spend the whole week here."

"You know my answer to that. I'd really like to bring all my clothes out, hang them in your closet and leave them here. Forever."

"It's beginning to seem like a better idea every time you come out, but I'm not ready for that much of a commitment just yet."

"I know, so I'll be patient—up to a point. As long as I can spend time with you, even if it can't be every week, you'll keep my hopes alive."

"Helen, you've worked your way straight into the middle of my heart. And as I told Mike, you mean more to me now than you ever have. What we have *is* growing."

"But not in my tummy," Helen said, giggling. "Seriously, that makes me feel so good inside. You know how important you are to me, and what I dream about. Nothing would make me happier than to believe that we could have something permanent. Those are positive words." Helen gave Rob a big hug to show him how she felt about what he'd just said.

On Friday evening, Rob called Kim to let her know that he'd gotten home at a reasonable hour. "Why don't you come over for a drink?" she proposed.

"Sure, love to. We've eaten. Mike has gone out, and I'm not doing anything other than sitting here wanting to see you."

They had a good visit, and much later when her boys were sound asleep, they slipped into Kim's bedroom for a treat. Only problem was, Rob suddenly developed an excruciating pain in his lower abdomen and couldn't perform.

"Sorry about that, love. Don't know what it is, but it's a new sensation. And damned if it hasn't got my attention. "

"It must hurt. You've never let me down before so don't worry about it. It's temporary, I'm sure, but your fetal position isn't exactly the way I like to see you. Can I get you anything?

"No. It's easing off a bit. It's almost like a very severe cramp. I agree. It's temporary."

And brief it was. Rob was up to par on Saturday evening when they had another impromptu get together at Kim's house, and he met every last one of her needs.

"That's more like it," she said afterwards. Wonder what it was last night?"

"Have no idea. If it had continued, it might have been that awful bladder infection I had some years ago. Same kind of pain, but it's gone today, so I can eliminate it as a possibility. If it comes back again, I'll go see my plumbing doctor for an exam. The prostate is always suspect when guys get to be my age, and even younger sometimes."

"You pushed Lu to see her doctor when she had pain like that. She didn't, and look what it lead to. So, I'm asking you to follow the advice you gave her and go see your urologist. In a man, it's not something to ignore. You know that better than I do."

"Yes, ma'am. I'm aware of the downside, and I'll call on Monday for an appointment."

On Sunday evening, Helen came out on a local train that got in at 5:44. Mike was in, said hello to Helen, gave her a hug, and then went out with friends. Without another mouth to feed, Rob suggested they go have something to eat.

"Chinese OK for a change?"

"Is there enough energy in it to keep you going on the playground later?"

"I'll have Moo Goo Gai Pan. It has chicken in it—a good source of protein."

"I know the dish and love it. We'll do a double order, and if we can't eat it all, we can have the rest after."

"After what?"

"Just stick around, hotshot, and I'll show you what it is I'm talking about." They shared a gentle laugh and Rob squeezed Helen's hands to show her that he was glad she'd come out.

After they'd eaten, Helen said, "I like the name of the restaurant. Hou Yu Bin. Cute. I wanted to tell the owner that I'm just fine. Be even better later on."

And she was. After the loving, Helen made an attempt to purr.

"You have to be a cat to get that right, but I appreciate the sentiment. Says I did my job."

"Work was it? A job? I hope you're not looking at it that way already. It wouldn't give us a whole lot of hope for a lasting physical relationship."

"I'm good for at least another thirty years, so I take it all back. Bad choice of words. How about if I suggest that you're fully satisfied and I'm pleased to have helped. Better?"

"Yes. Definitely. And yes."

On the morning of the twenty-eighth, Helen broke the weekday morning rule that applied to her Sheffield visits, put a little something extra of herself into it, and took Rob to Mount Everest before their day began. She also succeeded with her plan not to leave anything behind for someone else.

Over breakfast, Helen gave Rob a tie clip and matching cufflinks. He didn't wear them often because most were too gaudy. "Thank you, sweet. These I'll wear. They're unobtrusive and elegant. You have good taste."

On the way into Grand Central, they both smiled a lot. Mostly at each other. It had been an exciting Wednesday morning.

"You're getting to be a habit," Rob said. "A good one, I'm beginning to think."

"Count on those words to get me through the weekend, But I'll be back on Monday evening, you know.'

"Did I invite you to stay over again? I forgot."

"Now you're being like the guy I worked with at IMMCorp, and not the guy I'm in love with. I'll be on the 6:11 just like you. Count on me being there."

"Maybe I'll rattle your cage and take a different train."

"In that case, I'll run off with the first stud that propositions me."

"Unacceptable. I'll be on the 6:11. Good grief. The pressure I have to put up with." They showed each other a smirk.

Before Helen left to get swallowed up by the Lexington Avenue subway, she gave Rob a bear hug and a loving kiss.

"Five days, this time. I'm going to miss you. But we'll talk before you go. And I may have some good news for you about another placement. There'll be a commission to collect, you understand."

"Seems to me that we're pretty well caught up. But you know I always pay my debts. Talk to you on Friday afternoon, for sure. Maybe in between. Call me if you have a minute. If I'm busy, I'll call back."

"Take some pictures while you're at the lake. I'll also want to see what you decide on a floor plan and all that. It might be partly mine, too, someday. At least I'd like to think that way."

"Could be, sweetheart."

"Love you, guy. Tons."

"Love you, too, my freckled nose sprite."

"First time you've ever said that. I like it. Do it again sometime."

"How about now. Love you, Helen."

She had just hint of tears welling up. "That makes me *so* happy, Rob. I'd like to hear more of that on Monday evening."

"You will. See you then, dear heart."

"Bye, love bunny."

After a quick but tender kiss, the morning of Rob's forty-first birthday was history.

When Rob got down to Thirty-sixth Street, he called his former boss.

"RD. How're you? Seems like it's been months since we talked. This morning I was reminded that a year ago you bought me a drink to celebrate my fortieth."

"That's right! Time for me to do it again?"

"Yes, and no. I can't get loose this evening, but I was wondering if we might get together at TWH on Monday, say about five thirty?"

"Most likely. What's the occasion?"

"Someone I'd like you to meet. We worked together at IMMCorp, she chased me for eighteen months, and I finally discovered that she's a love. Not a Marianne, but she's a lot like her in some ways—and good for me."

"If she's that nice, she's probably too good for you. Sure, be glad to have a drink, and then take her away from you." He laughed.

"Good luck. Don't think it'll work. Whatever, that wasn't what I had in mind."

"Just pulling your tibia. I'll put it on my calendar. Five thirty on Monday. TWH. Got it. And, by the way, we like the guy you referred for the editorial department. You may have a placement. I planned to call you about it on Friday. We should know by then. Looks promising."

"Good news, RD. Be good to see you again even if he doesn't fly. Until Monday, then."

Rob and Kim had a pleasant birthday dinner at the Hearthside. They were regulars now and the owner treated them to a glass of champagne as a starter. Obviously he'd been told what the occasion was. Over an amaretto, Kim handed Rob a narrow box with a bright gold ribbon. Inside was a wide, black leather watchband. It was on his wish list.

"You know I've wanted one of these for ages but never got around to shopping for it. Thank you, sweetheart. I'll have it on tomorrow morning."

There could be no loving after dinner, but they did go back to Kim's house and shared their affection as she lay across Rob's lap.

"Sorry we can't go any further, but there will be the two nights up in Massachusetts. I'm really looking forward to that."

When Friday afternoon came, Rob left early, with Doug's blessing, and he was on the 4:15 train to Sheffield. Kim had brought a little overnight bag to the agency, which raised some eyebrows and questions, and they started their drive to Hampden Lake from there.

"I'm so ready for this. It's a dream of yours that's about to take shape, and I'm really pleased that you want me to be a part of it. Just make sure that Wilcox keeps his hands off my backside."

"Just put me between the two of you, or stand out of his line of vision. If nothing else, jump in my horse and go for a ride."

"I'll probably take you up on that."

With Daylight Time now in effect, they arrived in Sturbridge while it was still light, checked in, had dinner, and then loved themselves to sleep. Next morning, they had a full breakfast and afterwards drove to Wilcox Real Estate in the next town over, Hampden Lake.

Alan Wilcox was in his office, and after he greeted Rob and undressed Kim with his eyes, they settled down to the business of putting the contract details together. Unseen to either of them, Kim shuddered from the visual mugging that she felt had just taken place. She took Rob's keys and went for a drive. Her tour would take her by the beautiful white church in Bloomdale that she liked so much. She got back just in time to see the final details and costs being put together. Kim liked what she saw and nodded that she agreed.

What Rob had settled on was a two-bedroom cottage that would be insulated and heated for winter use. The optional items he chose would include an eight by sixteen foot sundeck, kitchen cabinetry, a brick fireplace, solid pine paneling, storm windows and doors, deep draft well, full bath, and a town approved septic system. The latter was mandatory. There would be a fair amount of interior work to be done, but Rob had the skills and experience to finish those kinds of things himself.

At mid-day, Wilcox had another customer, so Kim and Rob went off to find lunch, but first they agreed to meet on the lots at two o'clock to stake out the location of the building.

"He's still doing those things with his eyes."

"Who?"

"Don't give me 'who'. It bothers me, Rob, and it isn't funny."

"Maybe you should have stayed at home."

"No, Please don't say that. I'm glad to be a part of this. Like I said before, it's a pleasure to see your plans and ideas come together. Can't wait to see something tangible. Any idea when the place will be finished, or mostly so?"

"The draft contract says July 15, but I wouldn't bet a whole lot of money on it."

After lunch, they drove to the lots on Colonial Trail and waited. And then waited some more. But it gave Rob and Kim a chance to pick out a location. She had some good ideas, and he agreed with them. Kim didn't know what the plat looked like, but the spot she chose would be a perfect fit for the driveway that would eventually come in from the back. He found the property stakes and showed her how everything would be situated. Next was the matter of positioning the well. It had to be 100 feet from the septic leach field. Since the lots, together, were nearly 165 feet wide, that part was easy. By the time Wilcox showed up, Rob had sprayed the property pins orange, and he was able to show Alan what they had decided about the building site.

"Perfect, Rob. You take to this like you've been at it for a while."

"I grew up on a farm, and plats and surveys and the like aren't exactly new to me. I also learned carpentry and construction. Dad was an excellent teacher. But then you had to master all kinds of trades to keep things going. About the only thing I didn't do much of was electrical work. Other than that, there isn't anything inside the cottage I *can't* do to finish it off."

"If you came to work for me, I'd have you run my construction business, too. You'd come much better equipped to handle it than the city guys I've had working for me. I've had to look after it myself. You'd be a natural."

"Don't press too hard. I might take you up on it someday if the money's right."

"I'd make it worth your while."

"Rob!" Kim showed him a pained expression.

He turned back toward her, mouthed, "Don't worry," and smiled.

She relaxed and said, "That's better."

"Alan, do you have a cottage with my floor plan that I could look at, something finished?"

"Sure. I can show you two of them. One just for summer use and the other one is just being finished as a year-round place for some people from New York."

After seeing both, Kim said, "It's a decent layout, Rob. The eating bar that divides the kitchen and the living room is a good idea. Make a great serving bar, too. Perfect for weekends. But what really gets me is the pine interior. Smells wonderful."

"Those aren't thin four by eight panels, miss," Wilcox said. "They're individual tongue and groove boards and they're solid pine."

"I noticed. My uncle's in the real estate business, too."

"Then you'd both be a perfect asset to the community—and me."

"No. I'm afraid not. My home's in Sheffield. Always has been. Always will be."

Having chilled Wilcox's ardor, they all went back to the real estate office, Alan's big 1813 house, and Rob and Kim took another look at the draft contract. They agreed that it had in it what Rob intended.

"When you have this in final form," Rob said, "send it to me at home. Now, you want an earnest money deposit, I suppose. How much?"

"If you can give me a check for $1,500, that'll let us get started. I can schedule the percolation test for the septic system and if it's OK then I'll want you to sign the contract and return it to me. And, here's a mortgage application. Just fill it out and send it back at the same time. We should have the perc test done within a couple of weeks. With all the underground ledge rock and a high water table at this time of year, they don't always pass. The engineer will let me know how the test turns out. Your lots are high, so I don't expect a problem. You picked one of the best spots in the development."

"Three years ago, I pretty much had my choice. I knew right away what I wanted in the way of elevation, land contour, and orientation toward the lake, so it was mostly a process of elimination."

Rob then wrote out a check for the deposit, Wilcox handed him a receipt, and they shook hands to seal their agreement.

"Thanks, Rob. I was sure I'd see the day when you'd ask me to build you a cottage."

"Well, that day's arrived. Now, we're going back to the lots, take some pictures, have another look around, and then take it easy. Appreciate all your help, and your patience."

"That's what we're here for, Rob. See you next time you're up."

"I'll check in with you when I'm back. Have a good season."

"You've already helped get it off to a good start."

Rob drove back to Colonial Trail, took his pictures, looked at the property and building stakes and decided that the cottage would go up just about where he'd always envisioned.

"Couldn't be better," Kim said. "I'm really looking forward to coming back when there's something to look at."

"We'll do it—sometime late next month, probably."

Chapter Six

Rob and Kim thoroughly enjoyed the rest of their weekend together. Then on Monday afternoon, Helen called to confirm that she was coming back to Sheffield to look after the Grant guys on Juniper Heights. When she was around, Mike spent more time at home. He liked her because she was good fun and it gave him a chance to laugh with adults. Nothing was ever heavy, and if a subject was headed in that direction, she was able to turn it into something light. It was a gift.

On Monday evening, Helen came up from Wall Street and joined Rob and RD at The Watering Hole for a drink. RD was his usual charming self and the two of them hit it off well. When Helen went to the ladies room just before they left, RD said, "She's an absolute sweetheart, Rob. If you were looking for Marianne's replacement, you've found her."

"A couple of things. Walt Knorr hired Helen for me before I got to IMMCorp. The other is, she knew Marianne. And I guess there's a third item. You asked me at Marianne's funeral who she was. Helen and I got together a little over six months ago, and we've hit it off pretty well. There's still a gal in Sheffield who's always been there when times were tough, and I can't ignore how I feel about her. Only issue there is that she's not divorced yet. Even so, it's a dilemma."

"Take my advice and stay close to Helen. She'd be good for you. It's obvious. I can see it in your face."

As they left, RD proposed that they get together for dinner soon. Helen was all for it, and RD made Rob responsible for setting a date.

On their way to Sheffield, Helen said she liked Rob's former boss. "It's obvious that you like and respect each other. Some of him rubbed off on you—like your expressions, and the way you think about things. They're obvious. He wouldn't ever be a romantic interest, but I could surely work for him. It would be like teaming up with you all over again."

And there was good news from both RD and Helen. Rob had made placements with both of their companies. Nothing at the senior executive level, but the total was a good sum of money and most welcome. Doug Newcombe confirmed on Wednesday what Rob had heard over cocktails.

The schedule for the two weeks following was unchanged. Kim spent Saturday night with Rob, and then Helen came out on either Monday or Tuesday evening and stayed on until Friday morning. Rob was burning the candle at both ends, but he was learning something about his own feelings and aims. If Kim were available, it wouldn't be an easy decision.

Then on May 20, Rob got a letter from Alan Wilcox saying that the engineer had done three percolation tests on the fourteenth and his was the only one that passed. The septic system would be installed within the next few days, he said. And he added that it wouldn't be necessary to send the mortgage application back to the bank. They had enough information to check his credit, and they'd said OK to a mortgage in the amount Rob needed. Finally, all the paperwork was in the hands of a local attorney and, as Alan wrote, "Now all we have to do is build your cottage". The final contract and building layout were enclosed, and he was instructed to sign both and return one copy each for Alan's file. Rob's little dream was just about to start coming out of the ground.

During the week of June 7, Rob called Kim and said he'd be going straight up to the building site on Friday and wouldn't be back until Sunday evening. "But next weekend, plan on being here on Saturday night, as usual, and then the weekend of the twenty-sixth, we can go up to see how they're doing with the building, that is if you're interested."

"I'm disappointed that you won't be around on Saturday, but you know I want to see the cottage and how far they've gotten with it. It's exciting. Maybe I can make arrangements so that we can go up on Friday afternoon. That be OK with you?"

"Sure is. I'd love it if you could work it out. But about this coming Saturday, just about the only weekend I *haven't* been there for you since early January was at Easter. I don't leave you by yourself very often. We'll make up for it over the next two weekends. Promise."

"I like the sound of that. Be good to have you back."

Rob wondered if she suspected that he had other interests. Well she might, because she still hadn't done anything about filing for divorce.

"Got to go, sweetheart. We'll talk next week."

"Bye, love. Drive carefully."

On Saturday afternoon, Mike went to spend the remainder of the weekend with Kyle and Denny, and Helen joined Rob on a trip up to the property to see what progress was being made. They arrived too late to see much, so they checked into Rob's motel of choice, the Liberty Cap, had dinner, and then loved to perfection before they fell into a deep and well earned sleep.

The following morning, the two of them replenished their fuel supplies with a hearty breakfast, and then went off in search of Alan Wilcox. He was already with customers, but he stopped long enough to greet Rob, who then introduced Helen. Alan, as was his way, visually undressed Helen without much delay.

A New Yorker, and not at all shy when it came to dealing with guys like this, she said, "It's obvious you like what you see, Mr. Wilcox. Good for my ego, but would you mind putting my clothes back on? Might as well because I'm not into sharing." Helen then curled the fingers of her right hand into what amounted to a loose fist, aimed the exposed thumb at Rob, and added firmly, "What's mine is all his." The attractive college-age daughter of Alan's other customers watched the exchange, looked straight at Helen, and beamed her approval.

In all the time that Rob had known Wilcox, he'd never seen smooth Alan at a loss for words. His slightly reddened face confirmed that Helen had nailed him. Rob loved it. Turning his attention away from her roguish smile, Alan said, "Good to see you, Rob. You going over to see how things are coming along at the cottage?"

"We'll have a look and then head back to Sheffield from there. Helen and I have some serious lovin' to do before the day is out. You understand about those things."

Helen could barely contain herself, but she managed. The little fires dancing in her eyes gave her away.

Wilcox didn't quite know how to handle that either, so he chuckled awkwardly and let it go. "See you next time you're up. Nice to meet you Miss, uhh…."

"Flynn."

"Yes, of course. Flynn."

At the building site, they saw that the foundation was in place, the floor was down and the building was being framed up. It was easy to see now how the rooms were arranged—and how small Rob's bedroom was going to be. The work was coming along nicely, but neither he nor Helen thought the contractors would be finished in a little over four weeks unless they starting paying serious attention to the completion date in the contract. After having spent something less than a half-hour looking around, they started back to Sheffield.

Helen stayed over until the following Friday morning, and Rob felt as if they had actually married at some point and that he'd forgotten about it. They'd been together for a full week, and he'd enjoyed every minute of it. He was finding out that they were very compatible. Equally important, he discovered that if he was upset about something, Helen would back off. By doing that, she'd simply let his anger run its course. Given his fairly short fuse at times, the way she handled him was an important asset.

As they were on their way into the city on Friday, Rob reminded Helen that he was going to Marianne's grave on Sunday. He said that he was meeting the Marzano's there at three o'clock, and that he'd been invited back to their house for coffee afterwards.

"I want you there, dear heart," Rob said. "You knew Marianne and came to her funeral last year. You've also turned out to be her double in more ways than one. Be a year Sunday since I watched her die."

"You know I'll be there. She was a wonderful girl, Rob, and it really isn't fair that I've been able to benefit from your loss."

"Please don't look at it that way. You're a very special gal, too, and she's happy for us. Believe that. When we leave the Marzano's, you might as well come home with me unless you have something else to do on Sunday."

"Only thing on my list is to spend all the time I can with you."

Going their separate ways at Grand Central, Rob said, "I'll see you at the cemetery at about three on Sunday."

When Saturday afternoon came, Rob had to admit that he was glad to see Kim again, and it was clear that the feeling was mutual. There was something special about her that also touched him deep inside. The quandary persisted. A quiet afternoon together gave way to a romantic dinner out. They both missed not being together the previous weekend, but by the time 11:00 p.m. came, they retrieved what they'd missed a week earlier. Kim was especially hungry, and animated, and it took extra time to meet her needs. Rob didn't mind a bit. He wouldn't be fully satisfied if she wasn't. In the end, they were both fulfilled.

"I was beginning to get grumpy because we missed my regular Saturday visit last week, but I'm just fine now. With two days together next weekend, I'll be all caught up."

On Sunday morning, Rob told Kim over breakfast that he would be going into the Bronx at mid-afternoon. When he explained why, she understood.

"She's still inside you, isn't she?"

"Marianne will always have a special place in my heart. She'll never be a ghost that'll damage another relationship, but in a subordinate way she'll live there alongside the woman I marry. It's one of those things that's a given."

"I'm sorry we never met. From the way you've described her, we would have liked each other—except when it came to you."

"It isn't an issue now. But it was a year ago today that we lost her, and I need to be close to her this afternoon. Your mother hasn't been gone that long, so you know the feeling."

Breakfast and a half-hour of chatter at an end, Rob went with Kim to see her off from the garage.

"We'll talk this week. Could be that I'll call you from the office. Depends on the interview schedule. We've gotten fairly busy, and getting home late isn't something I want as a steady diet. Mike's been good about looking after himself, but I suppose at nearly eighteen he should be able to manage that."

"You know that he could always eat with us once in a while."

"I wouldn't want to impose, but it's sweet of you to offer. He has a good many friends now, so he's nearly always able to find a place at someone's table. And sometimes he waits for me. Anyway, if we don't talk before I pick you up on Friday, you'll be on my mind. Every day."

"Same with me, love." They hugged, kissed affectionately, and Kim started for home.

By the time Rob got to the cemetery, the Marzano's and Helen were already there.

"Carlo. Anna. I'd like you to meet Helen Flynn. We worked together at IMMCorp, and she knew Marianne. You might not remember it, but she was at the funeral."

"I thought she looked familiar," Carlo said. "Maybe it's the freckles. We wondered why she was here but didn't have a chance to ask. She showed up right before you did."

"I invited her. Even though they didn't know each other very long, they became friends. Helen wants to remember Marianne and pay her respects, too."

"Any friend of yours and Mari's is family to us. You'll always be welcome, Helen."

Obviously touched, Helen did something that was a little bit out of character—and totally unexpected. She hugged Carlo Marzano and held on for a moment. It surprised him as well, and he was visibly moved by her gesture.

"She was a wonderful girl, Mr. Marzano."

"Call me Carlo."

"Like Rob said, he and I were in the same department at IMMCorp. Before Rob joined the company, Marianne called to tell me about him, what I could expect, what he liked, didn't like, that kind of thing. I thought at the time that she was really a special person. And then when she came up from Washington to visit Rob, she'd come to the office first, and we had time to get acquainted. Those hours together confirmed what I'd thought right from the beginning. I miss her too, Carlo."

"Well, Helen, I don't know if you and Rob are just friends or if it's something more, but if you're the woman who'll take Mari's place in Rob's life, he couldn't do better. I remember now. She told us about you. I just didn't know your name. You're special, too, I think."

"Thank you. Rob and I do see each other, but it's probably too early to know what's ahead for us. But I care for him as much, and in the same way

Marianne did. If Rob and I have a future together, I'll honor Marianne's name by giving him the love and respect she would have."

It was Carlo's turn to surprise those around Marianne's grave. This bear of a man reached out, took Helen in his arms, and hugged her. Tears welled up and it was plain to see that although a year had passed, Carlo Marzano badly missed his only daughter.

Minutes later, Father Crosetti joined the group, not in an official capacity, but simply as a close friend of the family. The Marzano's asked him to remember Marianne, and he readily agreed. His words rang true, and he captured the essence of the young woman, taken before her time, who had been Marianne Marzano. He touched the hearts of those paying respects, and there wasn't a dry eye to be seen.

Before they left for the Marzanos, Rob went to his car, picked up a trowel and two miniature rose bushes—one cream, the other crimson. He planted them carefully, branches touching, next to Marianne's grave marker. They were meant to symbolize the two of them and the love they'd shared. As Rob was finishing up, a tear that wouldn't be denied fell onto a tiny bud that had just begun to open. It seemed fitting. Anna Marzano felt Rob's anguish and wept quietly.

When they got to the Marzano's home on Holland Avenue, the mood was much lighter. Helen stayed close to Rob during most of the hour they spent enjoying both Carlo and Anna's company and the refreshments they served. The only reference to Marianne Rob made was to point out the room down the hall where she'd died. "I've never been inside that door since that day a year ago, and I never will be."

Then just before they were ready to leave for Sheffield, Carlo took Rob by the arm and said, "You won't be able to look after those little roses, so I'll go every week and make sure that Mari and you are OK." The symbolism wasn't lost on him, and Rob was grateful that their love would live on in a figurative way with Carlo looking after them.

"Thank you. Other than the fond memories, they're all we have left. It's important that those two little plants survive."

"They will, Rob. They will. I'll see to it."

Helen said good-bye to Anna and Carlo. Both of them hugged her and wished her well.

"We'll think of you as family, maybe the daughter we don't have anymore, and we'd like to have you visit us if you want to."

"I'd like that, and I'll plan on being with Rob when he comes to see you. I live on East Thirty-second Street near Third Avenue, so it's easy to get here. Thank you for being so kind."

As Rob and Helen drove away, the Marzano's stood outside their front door and waved. When they were out of sight, Carlo said to Anna, "I hope it works out for the two of them. There's something about Helen that reminds me a lot of Mari. Not her heritage, or her looks, but something."

"She's a sweet, down to earth girl, Carlo. Have you forgotten what our Mari was like?"

On their way home, Helen said to Rob, "I'm glad you asked me to come today. It's been emotional, but I feel like I'm part of a new and wonderful family now. I *do* want to go with you the next time you visit. Their strength lifts my spirits. And that they think the world of you says something about Rob Grant that maybe I haven't discovered yet."

"You know me pretty well, but I was there every step of the way. Getting Marianne to see her doctor, finally, offering her support and encouragement, helping move her things up from Georgetown, driving her car back to the Bronx, holding her hand during those last days, being there when she drew her last breath, and then…." Abruptly Rob paused. His face showed pain and he had tears welling up. "I can't handle the memories, Helen. I've got to pull over. Sorry."

"Will you be OK, or would you like me to drive?

"Why don't you take over? Today brought back all the things I've tried so hard to put behind me during the past year. I'll be all right later."

"Not much doubt. When you love somebody, you sure do it 110 percent. Hope I can help you deal with the past and then pray that maybe someday you'd love *me* that much."

"It's just possible that I could. But it isn't easy to be objective about someone when there's still a busted heart involved."

After Rob got control of himself, he needed to change the subject and the first thing he could think of was to ask Helen how she liked driving his Mustang.

"I like it. It's neat. Handles nice and it's really peppy."

"And you're a good driver. I'll relax and let you find our home port."

When they got home, Helen said, "This isn't a night to go out. There are too many things on our minds. I'll put something together. Wonder if Mike will be around?"

They had the answer to that when they came through the door. He was watching a West Coast baseball game.

"Hi, Dad. How'd it go?"

"Almost as hard as it was at the funeral last June 24. But we survived. The Marzano's fell madly in love with this young lady here. Maybe I'll do the same."

Helen smiled at that. "Your attention and your affection are most welcome. Anytime."

"Before we call it a day, I want to call Greg. They'll be on their way to summer camp this week, so he'll be mostly out of touch for a couple of months." When Rob got through to him, they were about to have lights out.

"Greg. Just wanted to wish you a good summer up at Embden, and to give you some news."

"Thanks, Dad. I will. So, what's the news?"

"I'm finally going to build a cottage up on the land not too far from where you are now. There's a good chance we'll have a roof over our heads by the time you finish camp, so maybe we can spend whatever days you have off in sleeping bags at Hampden Lake."

"Wow! That's cool. I'll have a full week off before I have to come back. The lake is less than an hour from here. Too bad we don't have a boat. I was pretty good on water skis last year and probably will be better by the end of the summer."

"One thing at a time, young man. Depending on how I do, we might think about that in a year or so. All the extra money is going into the building, a heating system, a fireplace, things like that. What I'll want you to do is let me know when you're back from camp."

"I already know that. You can pick me up on August 22."

"OK. We'll set the date. I'll see you then, right after you've had lunch."

They talked on for a few minutes, and then Rob heard the call for lights out. "See you in August. Have a great summer. And behave yourself."

"I will. Thanks. Night, Dad."

When Rob and Helen got into bed, they decided that they were carrying too much of an emotional load and feeling too much sadness to be good lovers.

"We have all week," Helen said. "Marianne is a very, very hard person to replace, and I'll not try to do that tonight—or any other time, for that matter. I'm not her and won't ever try to be."

"But there are similarities. She was an absolute sweetheart. So are you. We were very compatible. So are we. She had a melt-your-heart smile. So do you. She never had wide swings in her moods. You don't either. She had a good sense of humor. Yours is even better."

"Sounds as if I'm in the running then."

"Very much so. Let's hold each other like a couple of spoons and sleep our cares away."

And they did exactly that.

As planned, Helen spent the remainder of the week with Rob and Mike. She was comfortable to have around and seemed to be enjoying her status as a semi-permanent fixture. Much as Rob enjoyed having her close, Kim was never far from his conscious thoughts, and he was looking forward to spending the weekend with her at the lake.

On Wednesday evening, Rob said he'd finalized plans with RD for the two of them to join him for dinner the following Monday evening. Helen was pleased that it could be worked in at the start of her vacation. "We go out to the Hamptons every summer. It's been a regular thing ever since I was a kid, and my folks want me to go with them again this year, too. No exceptions. They're leaving on Saturday morning, but we'll have our dinner with RD, you can overnight with me for a change, and then I'll go out early on Tuesday morning."

"Good idea that we take a break. Could be that you'll find some handsome stud out there who'll sweep you off your feet, and I'll never see you again."

"Right! My folks wouldn't let that happen, even if I were available. There'll never be any other man in my life—unless you throw me away."

"Wouldn't spend much time thinking about that either. When will you be back?"

"Mom and Dad are there for another week, but I'm coming back into Manhattan on the fifth, and then on out to Sheffield sometime late that morning. With the Fourth on Sunday, that Monday's a holiday. I go back to work on the sixth. Want company again that week?"

"If you're not tired of me by then. Sure."

"Not ever, Rob Grant."

"I'll be here, so call and let me know when I'm to pick you up at the station."

Rob and Helen ended their week together and were about to follow their usual Friday morning paths. "Don't forget, we're meeting at The Watering Hole at six on Monday. RD is in charge of picking out a place to eat and we'll go to dinner after we've had a drink. I'm off to the lake tonight. You have a good weekend and I'll see you at TWH as planned."

"Think I'll go out with Mom and Dad tomorrow, and then come back in on Monday afternoon. It takes nearly three hours, but it'll be worth it to have dinner with a couple of foxy guys like you two. Like I said before, you can spend the night with me before I have to go back to East Hampton on Tuesday. Be special."

"I'll make arrangements for Mike. Be fun to sleep in your bed for a change."

"Don't plan on a lot of sleep. It'll be a week in between."

"Mike will probably miss you, too. But, I've got to go, love."

"Be sure to give Wilcox a kiss for me." They laughed. "See you on Monday, hon. My train gets into Penn Station at 5:15, so I may be at TWH a little early."

"In that case, I'll leave the office in time to be there before five thirty."

A quick kiss, a bear hug, good-byes, and Helen was down the escalator. Rob headed for Lexington Avenue and Thirty-sixth Street.

The past couple of weeks had involved some long days, so Newcombe wasn't at all bothered by the fact that Rob wanted to leave at around four o'clock. Doug knew that progress at the cottage was on his mind.

"Have a good weekend and take some pictures so we can see how your project is doing."

"I'll do it. Got the camera right here. Looks like a decent weekend, so the blue skies and green trees ought to be vivid. You have a good weekend, too. See you on Monday morning."

Rob and Kim made good time for a Friday afternoon. They checked in at a reasonable hour, found a restaurant with a terrace on the edge of a lake and bedded down early enough to have an extended and very agreeable loving. They both needed each other. And since they had nearly two full days in front of them, they were lazy on Saturday morning and avoided thinking about any kind of schedule.

They finally got to breakfast, but it was at an hour when the restaurant wasn't busy. The place, called Smokey's, was their favorite now. They could always be counted on to serve a generous meal—one that helped replace all the energy they'd burned the night before.

After breakfast, Rob drove straight to the building site and was amazed to see how much progress the builder had made in just two weeks. He was also shocked to see the amount of trash that had accumulated around the building. It was obvious that Mike and his friends would have plenty of cleanup to do before much longer. Kim walked up a ramp that was set up at the entry door in back and came through to the nine foot sliding glass door in the living room. "Be careful, babe. Right in front of you will be a big deck if you remember the plan. When we come back, maybe you can take that next step. Wouldn't try it today."

The roof was on, as was much of the siding. The windows were in, and the fireplace was almost finished. It was beginning to look like a place to live, albeit small. Kim was clearly excited. So was Rob.

"I said it would be good to see something tangible, and it is," Kim said. "It isn't a very big place, but it'll sure be cozy. I want to see it when it's done. Maybe if it's chilly we could get the fireplace going. I'd love to do that."

As they were about ready to leave, Alan Wilcox showed up. Since Kim was in shorts, and she wanted to avoid having him undress her again, she went to the car.

"Hi, Rob. Lookin' good, huh?"

"Coming right along, but I can't see it being finished by the fifteenth. Is there a penalty if it isn't?"

"No. It isn't in the agreement. But I'll take care of you in some other way. All the guys who are working here are local and independent—in more ways than one." He chuckled.

"I'm just pulling your leg. There isn't any rush, although I'd like it to be finished by early August. I'll have my guy and his friends up here to do some of the cleanup and painting."

"Be done by then. Guaranteed. Something wrong with your lady friend?"

"Not really. She's just tired. I wore her out last night and this morning. Ferocious lions like me have big appetites. Look up their mating habits, and you'll see what I mean."

"I know about 'em. That's why you have so many different ones up here, I guess. You're too much for just one woman to handle." Wilcox chuckled again.

"Something like that. We've got to be on our way. I'll be back again one of these days."

"See ya, Rob."

Having seen the cottage and how near it was to completion, Kim asked if they might go back to Sheffield and spend the night in Rob's bed. That suited him. It was cheaper, for sure. But her primary motivation was that her dad was taking Kim, her two boys, and Gina and a new romantic interest of hers to Chatham on Cape Cod for a week starting the following Saturday morning. Tonight would probably be their last night together for about two weeks. Rob had known for nearly a month that this was coming, but Kim didn't have the exact dates until just yesterday.

"I'll be cranky when I get back. Be even worse if we didn't sleep in your bed tonight."

After dinner at The Hearthside, Rob and Kim made good use of their hours together before she had to leave right after Sunday brunch. "We'll certainly start the week with a smile," Rob said, "but twelve to fourteen days seems like a long way off. Expect me to miss you. You *are* important to me, in case you've forgotten."

"I'll send you a card with lots of X's and O's on it. Maybe when we get back we'll be home early enough for me to see you on the eleventh. If not…."

Rob, as always, went with Kim to the garage. They held each other and hung on. When it was time to go, they shared a loving kiss, but it wasn't enough to overcome the emptiness they both felt when Kim drove out of the garage.

On Monday evening, Helen came in from the Hamptons and met Rob at The Watering Hole shortly after five thirty.

"God, that's an awful ride," Helen said. "The place we rent is about 100 miles out, and the train crawls. Takes forever."

"What you need is a drink. And a hug."

"I'll take one drink and two hugs."

"Done, and done. Twice."

RD showed up, and with a smile that said he was glad to see the two of them, he hugged Helen and shook hands with Rob.

"So, have you set the date yet?"

"For?"

"The wedding. I want to be best man."

Rob and Helen looked at each other and smiled.

"No," Helen said. "It sounds like a grand idea, but we aren't into calendars. If it's to happen, we won't know what day it is. But when we figure it out, you'll be the first to know."

"Where's your date, RD?"

"I called too late. Both young ladies I asked were busy. But that means I can enjoy your company tonight. No distractions."

With that as openers, the three of them went to dinner and had a wonderful evening. RD played host, was his usual scintillating self, and he picked up the tab. After they'd eaten, he asked if they wanted to come back to his place up on East Seventy-seventh Street for a nightcap. Helen had the answer. "My family and I are way out on Long Island for the week. I came in from East Hampton, and go back very early in the morning. If I'm to look after this guy, it'll have to be tonight. You understand these things. I'll bet a big chunk money on it."

"I seem to recall how it goes." RD laughed and said, "Enjoy your evening. We'll do it some other time."

Rob thanked RD for dinner, and promised that they'd get together again soon. Helen was quick to second the motion.

On his way home, RD thought Rob was fortunate to have found someone who was Marianne-like in so many ways. He hoped it worked out that Rob and Helen would make it a partnership one day soon. He liked them both and promised himself that he'd stay in close touch.

For her part, Helen thought RD's suggestion about being best man had a good sound to it. "I'd be really pleased if RD could stand up for you. I like him and it would be perfect. And there wouldn't be any need to have a big, expensive ceremony. We've both been through that."

Rob smiled and said. "If it's to happen, you'll know when I'm ready. Tonight, we'll just pretend it's our wedding night and practice some."

She laughed brightly. "I'll settle for that, but only temporarily."

Helen couldn't seem to get enough of Rob and loved him until a late hour. "My train goes back early in the morning, so we've had to do it all tonight."

"I'm guessing that you're fully topped off by now," Rob said. "If not, too bad because I'm deflated and flat like a paper person. You were full of fire. Whooo!"

"You're the guy with the bellows. I just respond. Make sure you have it handy again next Monday."

Before Helen left for Penn Station on Tuesday morning, and the long ride back, they had a good breakfast. And since it was too early to go into the office, Rob said he'd go along and see her off.

"Love it! I was hoping you'd say you wanted to do that."

"Lots of ghosts in that building. You know whose they are. But it's time to do away with them, I guess. Life goes on. You're in it now. That should be enough."

Helen was touched and had just a hint of tears showing. "Those are words that make me very happy, Rob. Not a good time for you to say things like that. It has to do with the lunar spook that just showed up. I'll miss you more than usual because of it. But I'll be fine by next Monday." Helen smiled.

"Spend the week with me then, right through Friday morning?" Rob asked.

"Yes, sweetheart. Something to really look forward to. I'll be in Manhattan in time to be on the 11:20 train to Sheffield. Gets in at 12:32. I checked the schedule."

"My sweetheart, the travel agent. I'll be there."

"See you on Monday, love bunny. Love you so much."

"I feel the same way, dear heart. Have a fun week out on the Island."

With Helen gone, Rob would have a quiet week. That was fine for a change. He wanted to be alone with his thoughts, so he decided to walk back to the office. Thirty-fourth Street was busy, but he succeeded in focusing on where his life seemed to be headed. It was time to settle down. His mind, like a pinball machine, bounced off Kim, then Helen, and even Justine. For a moment, he considered inviting her out for the weekend, but then thought better of it. Maybe he could have a harem, because he loved both women who were a part of his life. Finally, he said aloud, "Stop it! Spend your time on no-nonsense questions and answers."

Once back in the office, and his day had begun, all of the thoughts that had come with him across Thirty-fourth Street and up the two blocks to Lexington Avenue and Thirty-sixth were swallowed up by his search work and the endless phone calls that were an essential part of it. The days were so alike that they all ran together. Rob got acquainted with his son again over dinner on those evenings when Mike wasn't eating somewhere else, so they were bachelors once more. If only temporarily.

Rob thought about driving up to Massachusetts but decided against it. There was plenty to do at home, and they'd be gone enough weekends when the cleanup, staining and interior finish work got underway. There would be busy weekends right into early fall.

On Monday, July 5, Helen was on the 12:32 train, and she greeted Rob with a hug that confirmed that she'd missed him. "I'm *so* glad to be back. You-feel-wonderful!" she said. "Thought I was going to die before the week was over. I woke up at five o'clock to be on the train at a quarter of eight—the one that connects with a train in Jamaica that comes into Penn Station." They had a good laugh about that.

"Not too eager, huh? You feel pretty good yourself. Lunch?"

"Yeah, but let's do it at home. I'd like the peace and quiet."

"Let's hope Mike isn't playing King Crimson or one of those other albums. Nothing quiet about any of 'em."

When they got back to number 710, they found that Mike had gone out, but he didn't leave a note saying where or for how long. "Best we don't trust our luck that he'll be gone all afternoon," Rob said. "He could be in the building or on the grounds somewhere."

"We've waited a week, and we're not exactly starving animals, so we can wait until it's the way it should be. The situation and timing are important. We'd lose our edge if we had to worry about being surprised."

"Well put. You talked me right out of attacking you on the living room floor."

"Let me make lunch," Helen offered. "First time I've been hungry all week. Being away from you does terrible things to my appetite. Now, watch me gain weight."

"And watch me take it off after dark."

"We have a deal, sounds like. I'll eat like a pig. You provide the exercise to keep me trim."

"Good to have you back, sweetheart."

"Glad to be back. Really glad." Helen gave him a squeeze before she put lunch together.

It was a glorious early July day, so they took their plates to the terrace, ate, talked, and watched the sailboats out on Long Island Sound. It couldn't have been more pleasant.

Late in the afternoon, Mike called and said that he was with Tom and that he'd probably stay the night. Helen took that to mean that she and Rob could get in a little pre-bedtime practice. She was right. And it was shamefully enjoyable.

"I'm guessing that you ate out a lot in the Hamptons, but I haven't, so could I interest you in going up to Russo's—or someplace else?"

"We mostly ate in, barbequed a lot, so I'm ready. Whatever you suggest."

They had their dinner out, continued the process of trying to catch up on their loving and then both of them slept better than they had in a week.

Their workweek resumed on Tuesday. For the balance of the week, Helen came home with Rob each evening and stayed on until Friday morning. Part of her job over the weekend, she said, was to reopen the family house in Hempstead and then help her mom and dad unpack the car. After having spent the week with Rob, and now feeling a bit lonely, she was glad to be busy.

Then on Sunday evening, Kim called. "We're home, love. I can't get away, but could you come over? I'm desperate to see you."

"Sure can. I'm on my way."

At the door, Kim nearly squeezed the breath out of Rob and kissed him with the kind of feeling that left no doubt what was on her mind.

"Where are your guys? Gone?"

"No they came back exhausted, took baths and are sound asleep. I need you bad, and we're going to risk it." Kim wasted no time getting into bed, and Rob discovered that she had never been so ready so quickly. "You're fertile."

"I am, and horny beyond words."

"No preliminaries?"

"None. Do me. Now!"

The bed might have been bigger because they were all over it until Kim went into orbit around Venus. It didn't take long, and she brought Rob with her. Not often in his life had he had a nearly out of control woman on his hands. It was exhilarating stuff. But exhausting.

After resting for a few minutes, Kim said, "Your equipment seems to be OK now. No, better than that. *Verrry* OK. Did you see your doctor?"

"It's always been all right, except for that one night. But, yes, I did."

"And?"

"He had some tests run, did an internal exam, which was an adventure, and said that there wasn't anything out of the ordinary. Prostate's slightly enlarged, but that's not unusual for someone my age. His conclusion was that I'd have to look elsewhere for an answer. I got his report just before you went to the Cape, but I wasn't able to call until after you were already on your way."

"Good to know there isn't a problem. I worried about it some while we were away."

"He gave me a quick lecture, and said I ought to have a regular checkup. Something else to add to my list of things to have somebody look after."

"You know better than I do that he's right. Don't ignore his advice."

"Yes, Mother."

"I'd attack you again, but I don't want to take chances that one of the boys might wander in here. You've taken the edge off my needs, but I'll take another installment on Saturday."

"I was going up to the lake, but I'll stick around if there'll be more refreshments this weekend. Sounds appealing."

After Rob got dressed, they hugged and shared a sensuous kiss just as a young voice was heard, "*Mom*?" Kim was needed.

"Wow, we timed that about right. I'll call you later in the week. Night, love. Thanks for getting me down off the ceiling. I'll survive now."

"G'night, sweetheart. Thanks for the unexpected treat."

Chapter Seven

Just after 2:00 a.m. on the morning of July 20, Rob's phone rang.

"H'lo."

"Mr. Grant?

"Yes."

"This is Officer Rubino down at the police station. We have your son here."

"Which one, and why?"

"Michael. And I'll let him tell you why."

A sobbing Mike got on the phone and said, "Dad. I got the keys off your bedroom dresser and took your car out."

"And?"

"I wrecked it." More sobbing.

"You *what*!"

"I was driving too fast down a street that ended in a 'T' and I hit a high curb. It's where the city keeps all their trucks and stuff. I'm sorry, Dad."

"I do *not* need another son giving me a whole new set of problems to deal with and maybe wiping out what reserve we have in the bank. I guess you're all right—other than you're suffering from a bad case of stupidity. OK, hotshot, give me back to the officer who called."

"Yes, Mr. Grant."

"Lock him up. Be good for him. I don't have any way to pick him up at this hour."

"We'll do like you ask. We smell alcohol. He'll spend the night here and someone on the morning shift will run him up to the Heights. You pressing charges?"

"No. At least not now. I'll deal with him tomorrow. Where's what's left of the car?"

"In the pound. What do you want us to do with it?"

"Get it over to the Ford dealer."

"That'll mean another tow charge."

"I'm sure it will, but I've got to see what they say about fixing it."

"The whole front underside is ripped out pretty bad. Be real expensive, I'd guess. You may be better off trading it in."

"It's not quite twenty-seven months old. I love that car. *Damn it*!"

"I know how you feel. We'll keep your boy here. He's broken some laws, and we'll have to write him up for at least driving without a license."

"OK, officer. Thanks, I guess. G'night."

Rob was absolutely fuming, and it took him nearly two hours to get back to sleep.

"Doug. I've got another problem, and I don't know what time I'll be in."

"What now?"

"Mike came into my bedroom during the night, took the keys to my Mustang, went for a joyride and tore it up. The police say they smelled booze on his breath."

"Holy shit, Rob. Won't it ever end?"

"If someone had been here with me, there's a chance one of us might have heard him. First item on my agenda is to see if the beast can be fixed, or if I'll have to spring for another car. It'll be towed over to the Ford dealer this morning. I'll try to be in sometime this afternoon."

"Why don't you take the day? I'll cover for you. I'm at your desk and from the open files I see here, you're pretty much on top of your searches."

"Thanks, Doug. Appreciate it. It may take the whole day. And I have to deal with Mike. The police have had him locked up since two this morning."

"I don't envy you. Any idea what you're going to say to him?"

"Nope. I'm going to let it unfold on its own. Not a good plan, but I'm too upset to have one. I suppose a TV father would have all the right words. I don't have any of 'em."

"Well, take it easy. You still have to live together. See you tomorrow morning."

Rob then called Kim at work to give her the bad news. She was shocked—and *very* disappointed in Mike.

"This is one of the concerns I've had about our being partners. My guys are a problem. Both of 'em. I don't want them to contaminate Chris and Ian."

"Two adults, together, would probably make it work better. But, yeah, you have a point."

"I've got to sit on Mike hard, but I haven't figured out just yet what to say or how to do it. A shouting match won't get it done."

"Just be the guy you were with Greg last year, and you'll be fine."

"OK. I'll give it a try."

"If you need to use my car, let me know."

"Thanks, sweetheart. I may have to. But it looks like I'm going to get familiar with the public transportation system. It's a good thing there's a bus to the station that stops right across the street. I'm so aggravated about this that I see red."

"I'll call you when I get home to see how your day turned out."

"I may be in jail for murder by then."

"Cool off, Rob. That will *not* be the answer. I've got to get busy, but I'll pull up your policy later this morning. I'd forgotten that you've been a customer of ours since before we met. Talk to you later in the day."

Rob then called Helen with the same news.

"This *would* be a week that I didn't stay with you. It might have made the difference. Damn! Guess I'll just have to move in and be a mother to that young man."

"I thought you already had. The way it looks, more than half your clothes are here. We'll talk about it soon."

The intercom buzzed.

"I heard that. Sounds like you have company. I'll let you go. Call me later. Please?"

"Yes?"

"Officer Daniels, Mr. Grant. I have your son."

"Bring him up, please."

When they came through the door, Rob shook hands with Daniels and then, and without saying a single word, glared at Mike. He froze.

"Mr. Grant, I'm going to stick around until I see that we won't have to come back and deal with domestic violence."

"There won't be any. I don't hit people. Most of 'em are bigger or stronger than me."

Daniels smiled.

"Dad, I'm . . . I'm sorry. I'll do whatever you want to make it up to you. I loved that car, too. I know how you feel."

"No you don't. You're not inside here with me. You're OK, that's a blessing, and the car can be replaced. Bodies can't. Same with Greg. But what is it with you two? What were you thinking? You've got a streak of suicide in you. Both of you. And you got into my booze, stole the Mustang, drove without a license and then tore it up. It there anything else destructive you can think of to do? Today's your mother's birthday. When she's out of bed, and before she goes to work, you're going to call her and explain exactly what you did."

"Not a very good birthday present."

"You bet it isn't. And don't sit down. Stand right where you are. I'm not done yet. While you're at it, you might ask her if she wants you back. I'll buy the ticket."

"Oh, *Dad*." Mike broke down.

"Yeah, I'd be afraid and embarrassed, too. What you did, the whole lot, are criminal acts."

"Mr. Grant, we've cited him for driving without a license," Daniels said. "We couldn't prove that he was under the influence because he was able do the basic tests we gave him."

"I hope you've got a bad hangover, Mike. Serve you right. But what do you know about the car, Officer?"

"What do you mean?"

"Where is it?"

"It should have been towed by now. We asked that it be moved to the dealer's back lot first thing this morning. If it isn't there yet, it should be before long."

"Any chance we could ride back downtown with you?"

"Sure. I guess there aren't going to be any problems, so we can go if you're ready."

"You're never ready for something like this."

When Rob saw his Mustang, he couldn't decide if he wanted to scream or cry. "Take a good look at it, Mike. You do excellent work."

"I don't like looking at it, either."

"Well, remember it! For the rest of your life."

Rob got the service department manager and had him come up with a ballpark idea of what the repair costs would amount to. After looking the car over, he said it was impossible to figure it accurately until they could put it up on a lift, but he gave Rob an "at least" number, and he nearly choked on it.

"That's the cost of your joyride, young man."

Mike looked away.

Then Rob went inside to see Ernie, the salesman who'd sold him the car sitting dead on the their lot.

"Ernie, what can you do in the way of a trade-in on the 'horse' I bought from you in April of sixty-nine? I just got rough idea of what it would cost to rebuild it, and I nearly had a heart attack."

"You're not giving us much of a trade-in."

"C'mon, Ernie. Don't start sounding like a car salesman. Work with me on this. I've come back to you instead of talking with Buick or one of the dealers in town."

"What do you have in mind?"

"Another Mustang. I loved this one. And you can see how much my son loved it, too."

"That kind of affection you can do without." He scowled at Rob's son and Michael Grant wanted to crawl into a hole.

"Well, let's see what we have in stock"

They looked at the new seventy-ones, and although Rob thought they'd improved their looks and had also solved the problem with the pointed nose hood that kept getting dents in it, he didn't see anything that turned him on. Ernie showed him the locater of cars available from other New England dealers. A couple of them might do, but he still wasn't really excited about what he saw. Last, they had a look at what was coming in. That did it. Rob checked the color charts again and found what he wanted.

"There! Light pewter metallic coupe with saddle interior and a 351 Cleveland engine. That's the one I want, Ernie."

"It's just come off the line. We won't have it for probably three weeks yet."

"I can live with that, I think. Show me what you can do with the numbers. But be gentle. I'm already busted up." Ernie laughed.

The trade allowance was slim, but the first set of numbers didn't look too bad. Kim's agency had the insurance, so there'd be at least a little bit of help there, Rob assumed.

"Two years ago, I didn't really need a car. This time, you've got me over a barrel. Maybe I should go talk with the Pontiac dealer and see what they can do on a Firebird. I took a couple of Polaroid shots of the dead horse. It'll give them some idea what the trade-in looks like."

"Let me go talk to my manager before you do that. We want your business, Mr. Grant."

"And I'd like to stay with you. Your location is convenient, and you have a pretty good service department."

When Ernie came back, he and his manager had put together a deal Rob thought he could handle. Mike hadn't said a word throughout all this. With the big numbers being tossed around, he was beginning to understand what his nocturnal adventure would wind up costing his dad.

"Only thing is, I don't especially like the interest rate your finance outfit is charging. Let me see what I can do locally, or with Chase in the city. I bank with them."

"Fine. Since the car hasn't even been loaded for shipment yet, you have plenty of time. And I'll make a note that you have first rights to it. We don't very often sell a car that's still at the plant."

When Rob got home, he called Kim at the Prentiss Agency.

"Hi, gal. I may have struck a deal on a new car. It's still at the factory, but the dealer has come up with figures that are manageable, even without knowing what kind of money I'm going to get out of my policy. Big thing is, their finance charge is higher than those I've seen advertised in the Star. Didn't you say you had a cousin with one of the banks in town?"

"Yeah. Len Fortuna. He's in consumer loans with First National. What time's best for you?"

"Not sure. Probably on my way to the station."

"Why don't I pick you up on Friday morning and then drop you off at the station when you're finished."

"That'd be great! What a sweetheart."

"Maybe we could have breakfast someplace first."

"Love it. I'll buy."

"It's a deal."

"See you on Friday. And Saturday night, too," Kim said. "I'm still not caught up on my backlog yet, you know."

"We'll work on it. If I had you Friday night, too, we might be able to balance the books."

"Good idea. I'll work on it."

"Thanks for your help, babe."

At home again, Rob said, "Mike. Time to talk."

"Yeah, I s'pose so."

"First. The liquor supply is locked up and will stay that way. Second. Your allowance is suspended indefinitely. It won't pay for the new car, but you heard what the numbers are. If you want spending money, I suggest you get a job bagging groceries or something like that. I'm not paying your fine, so you'll have to work that out. Third. It'll be a while before you'll get a driver's license. The state may have something to say about it. If not, I will. Any questions?"

"Nope. Guess I better go out tomorrow and start looking around for a job of some kind. The only thing is, I want to help up at the cottage on weekends, so I'll see if there's something I can do just during the week, at least until school starts."

"The hole you dug is a deep one. You figure it out. And if I find out you're into alcohol again, I *will* ship you back to your mother in California. There's plenty of time to get into booze after you're 21, and legal. You follow?"

"Yep."

Kim picked Rob up on Friday morning, they had their breakfast at "The Diner", and then in his meeting at nine o'clock with Fortuna, Rob came away with a much better rate on a car loan. It put the new car buy, and the monthly payments, well within his comfort level. Afterwards, Kim took him to the station, gave him a hug and a quick kiss, just like any commuter's wife or sweetheart might do. Then as he was closing the car door, she gave him the news that, yes, she'd be spending the whole weekend with him. Rob grinned broadly.

"I like seeing that. It says you're pleased with all the good news."

"You bet I am," Rob said. "And you're the reason for it. Thanks for all your help."

"You coming in on the 6:43?"

"If that's OK. But if I can get away earlier I'll call you at work before five. Might be possible for me to be on one of the trains I used to take during my corporate days—the 5:09. Gets in just before six."

"I'll provide taxi service in exchange for dinner."

"You've got yourself another deal. See you tonight. Now, I've got to run. Really." And he sprinted to catch the 9:45.

When Rob got to the office, the first thing he did was call Ernie and tell him that he had his loan from First National and that he should go ahead and write up the agreement. "I'll come down tomorrow with the papers on the dead Mustang, and the insurance information you'll need. I'll be ready to sign the agreement on the new one. Be after lunch, I imagine."

"That'll be fine. See you tomorrow, Mr. Grant."

Helen spent most of the following week with Rob and thoroughly enjoyed her role pretending she was a wife and stand-in mother. And Kim was a Saturday night and sometimes Friday night regular.

On the last Saturday in July, the thirty-first, Kim picked up Rob and Mike at a little after 7:00 a.m. and drove them to the lake. The cottage was finished now, and they all worked like beavers around the place until they were worn out. On the way back, they stopped for something to eat. Then once they were home, they showered and collapsed. Even so, Rob and Kim managed to find just enough energy to take care of each other's needs before they called it a day.

The following Wednesday, Ernie called Rob at Newcombe's to tell him his car had just come in and that it would be ready by Friday evening.

"Given my schedule, I'm not sure I can make it before you close, so it'll have to be Saturday morning. You're all set with the bank and the insurance company, I guess. Figure on ten o'clock or so."

Rob called Kim and gave her the news. He also asked her if she'd like to have dinner and then stay over on Friday night.

"Yeah! I can work out something by then. What time can you be in?"

"We have a late afternoon assessment interview, but I should be able to make the 6:11 if I walk fast. That'll put me at the station at about 7:10. If I'm going to be later than that I'll call you at home. Like always."

"I'll be there. I'm as excited as you are about picking up the car tomorrow."

"In part, I suppose, because I won't be borrowing yours anymore."

"Rob! That has nothing to do with it. Your remark is out of place. Don't take the edge off a fun thing."

"You're right. Sorry. See you on Friday evening."

Rob saw Helen off on Friday morning and told her that after today, there wouldn't be any more bus rides down to the station. "You'll see my new 'horse' on Monday. Think you'll like it. Better looking than the old one. A design change, heavier, a bigger engine, and it's a very different color from the sixty-nine. Call it sexy."

"That's wonderful news, Rob. Can't wait. You have to be excited."

"I am, I guess. Ought to be a fun machine. We'll know soon enough."

They said their good-byes at Grand Central and both went off to finish their week. Rob had trouble concentrating, which told him that he *was* looking forward to taking delivery in the morning.

Then the big day came. Kim saw to it that he started the morning with a smile, not that he needed it, but it very nicely set the tone for the remainder of his day.

At the Ford dealer's lot, they saw the car sitting there all bright and shiny and ready to go. "Oooh, I love the color, Rob. Looks like metallic cinnamon with a chocolate cap."

Kim opened the door and got her first look at the interior.

"It's called saddle. Like it?"

"Perfect match. You sure know how to pick 'em. You'll have girls all over town wanting you to take them for a spin. I better keep an eye on you."

"Let's go find Ernie and get the keys. I'm hot to trot!"

As they started for the door, Ernie spotted them and came out with everything in hand.

"Mr. Grant. I suppose you're looking for these." He handed Rob the keys, some freebies from the dealership and then he gave him a rundown on the changes that had been made in the Mustang over the past two years.

When he'd finished, Ernie said, "Enjoy, Mr. Grant. This is a great car. You'll love it."

Rob opened the door for Kim, and then he sat behind the wheel. "Feels bigger. I like it already."

"Wait'll you find out what kind of power that 351 Cleveland engine delivers," Ernie said. "You'll be impressed—but don't get carried away."

"I won't. Thanks for everything. I'll probably see you when I come down for service. Buy you a coffee or something." Ernie laughed.

"You're on. Take care."

Rob started the engine and liked what he heard. "Oh, boy! Sounds like it means business." Then, in gear, he *could* feel the difference. "Since I'm single, maybe I'll marry this thing. I'm already infatuated with it."

"It won't be as much fun when the lights are out."

"On second thought, maybe I'll hold out for you, assuming you get your divorce."

Kim didn't take the bait. Instead, she suggested, "Let's go for a drive. Could we?"

"Sure. And after we're back, I'll drop you off to pick up your car."

They took their drive, did some shopping, picked up Kim's car, and then went back to number 710 to find that Mike had done the laundry and folded everything. He left a note behind saying he was at Phil's house and would see the new car later.

"Mike seems to have shaped up," Kim said.

"He's got a job now, but he's still on a short tether. If he screws up now, I'll ship him back to California. He knows that, and it is *not* on his list of things he wants to have happen. He'd rather put up with me than do that. He's also excited about the cottage at the lake."

"Whatever you said seems to be working. Guess you handled him like you did Greg when he got into trouble. You'll have to tell me about it sometime."

Rob stirred up drinks and they went to the terrace to enjoy the warmth of an August afternoon. They chatted and watched all the sailboats out on the Sound. Mike came home, and then to the terrace and said, "I came through the garage. That's a neat machine, Dad."

"Thanks. You made it all possible, you know." Mike's smile vanished.

"Yeah. I'm like Greg was last year. Pretty stupid thing I did."

"You might say that. But two things. One, I'll sleep with the keys in my shorts. The other is, you don't get to drive this one. You forfeited that right early on the morning of July 20."

After Mike went inside, Kim said, "I'm not sure I want to handle your keys."

"Considering the kinds of exploring we do after dark, and then what usually comes after the preliminaries, I'm surprised to hear you say that."

"Suppose you're right at that." Kim tilted her head back and laughed.

Toward evening, Mike said that he and the guys would probably go for a burger and then just hang around at somebody's house.

"We're going to have dinner out later on. You be back tonight?"

"Not sure. But I'll leave you a note, or call, and let you know where I am if I'm not coming home."

"Fair enough. Have a good time. But behave yourself."

"I get the message."

Over the weekend, Greg called to say that his week's break from school had been moved down a week to the twenty-ninth. They were giving him most of the long weekend, and he wouldn't have to be back until Labor Day, September 6.

"I'd like to make one of the trips with you," Kim said, "but I know for sure that the sixth is out. We're having our barbeque, like always."

"It's a right powerful stallion I ride now. I might be able to get back in time to eat a hot dog before it gets icicles on it."

"Not much chance of that in this weather. Be great if you could show up, even if you can't be there the whole afternoon. I'll let you know about the twenty-ninth, though."

The two ensuing weeks followed the usual pattern of search work, Helen during at least part of the week and Kim on Saturday night. Over dinner on the evening before Rob left to pick up Greg, Kim said she wouldn't be able to make the trip. The reason was simple. She couldn't get anyone to stay with Chris and Ian. Even her high school age sitter was away on vacation.

On the last Sunday morning in August, Rob and Kim had an early breakfast. The new Mustang was still short of 1,000 miles, so he'd have to drive at slower break-in speeds for a while yet. Mike was at Tom's, so Rob made the drive to Massachusetts alone. He didn't mind. It would give him a chance to think about life in general—and his own in particular.

Rob's drive northeast was easy. The weather was good and traffic was fairly light. When he got to Duchene, father and son were glad to see each other. Greg was still trim but he'd grown, and Rob could see that he was going to need some new clothes.

On their way home, the Mustang crossed 1,000 miles and Rob was able to bump up the speed just a little. It made for good cruising and a faster return. By the time, they got to Juniper Heights, Mike was there to meet Greg, and they had a reunion that began with a bear hug and a goofy handshake.

"Kim's asked me over for a little while. Want to come along?"

"No," they both said. "It's been lotsa months since we've seen each other, and we want to shoot the bull. We'll turn on the music you don't like, make a sandwich and get caught up."

"Fine. But don't eat too much, too late. When I get home, maybe we can go have a pizza or something."

"Yeah!" was the reply to that idea.

Kim told Rob after he got to her house that her dad would come by and look after the boys if she wanted to go say hello to Greg. "I could have saved you the trip over, but when I called Mike said you were already on your way." She was pleased that she'd be able to see Greg, so not more than a few minutes later, she followed Rob back to Juniper Heights.

That Kim wanted to come over made Greg's day. He gave her a hug that said he was glad to see her. They both wore broad smiles and then went for another hug. It made Rob feel good to watch them share a happy moment.

When they went out for pizza, Kim wasn't especially hungry so she had a small salad. They enjoyed each other's company, and the chatter and questions went on non-stop. There was hardly time to eat. Then, from the restaurant, Kim went back home to relieve her dad.

Toward bedtime, Greg said he was glad to be home, and that he was looking forward to sleeping in his own bed.

When Helen came home with Rob on Tuesday evening, she finally got to meet Greg. Mike had already told him how much fun she was so he was primed for it. To no one's surprise, they had a great time sparring. She also got Mike involved in the give and take and by Friday, as she and Rob were ready to leave for the station, Greg was quick to give her a good-bye hug. But the way he did it suggested that he thought she was a fragile little flower. When she nearly squeezed the air out of him, he found out differently.

"Wow! You sure do eat lotsa Wheaties. Or is it spinach? You're strong. Dad have anything to do with it?"

"Some." And they shared a cute giggle. The two of them had become friends, and Greg loved her like the mom she might be someday.

Rob said to Helen on their way to the station, "You haven't said a word about the car. What do you think?"

"Yes I did. It was the Tuesday evening just after you got it. Where were you?"

"Missing in action, I guess."

"All right. Let me try it again. It's great. I love it. And I love you, too."

"I paid attention this time. Both the Mustang and I like what you just said." Helen smiled.

On Friday afternoon, and the start of the Labor Day weekend, Rob came home early so they could load the car with sleeping bags, a cooler, and enough food to keep them going over the weekend. When they'd finished, he wasted no time getting started for Hampden Lake. They would put in two days of hard work before Rob took Greg back to school on Monday. The weather outlook was good, so he was sure they'd get a lot accomplished. If the forecast turned out wrong, which often happened, it wouldn't make any difference because there was plenty to do inside.

Chapter Eight

The fourth of September was a very busy Saturday, but before the day was out Rob would be introduced to a local resident—someone he decided soon afterwards that he might like to know better. He couldn't know it at the time, but that chance meeting would rearrange the relatively fixed pattern of his life, at least as he had known it for well over a year.

At mid afternoon, while Rob was stripped to the waist and perspiring heavily from laying tile on the kitchen floor, Alan Wilcox showed up to say hello and to see how he was getting along with his do-it-yourself projects. Trailing behind him was a rather plain looking young woman with long, stringy brown hair. Upper East Side Manhattan she was not, but there was something about her, and her friendly face, that got his attention. He couldn't quite figure out what it was, and it puzzled him.

"Rob, say hello to Sarah Stuart. She teaches in Bloomdale and lives with two other teachers in the upstairs apartments I have at the office."

"Sarah. A pleasure. I think I've already met your car. Alan pointed it out to me once."

"Hi, Rob. I'm glad to meet you."

"Are the other two teachers guys or gals."

"We're three girls. No guys allowed." Her delightful little laugh amused him.

"For some reason you look familiar. And that's not just eyewash. Have you ever lived outside of this area?"

"Grew up in Worcester. And I went to school at UMass, Amherst."

"Never in New York or that vicinity?"

"Uh, no. Other than to visit. But I haven't been there for probably four or five years."

"I don't know. You must have a twin out there somewhere."

"Well, I recognize you from the times you've been up here before. On one of your trips last spring, you gave Alan your plans for this place."

"Might be that's it. But there are lots of people through his office. How come you'd remember me?"

"Easy." She didn't elaborate. Rob had to settle for a warm smile.

"Maybe we'll see each other again one of these days."

"Could be." Another smile, and Sarah Stuart went back to the office with Wilcox.

Rob mumbled inaudibly, "I'm gonna have me some of that. Wonder if she's part of the horny bastard's private stock? I'll bet one of the three teachers is."

Rob stopped working at noon on Monday. He got cleaned up and then made the short drive with Greg up to Duchene. Before they left, Mike said he'd say good-bye now and keep on working until Rob got back.

"I should be able to finish the outside staining. There isn't all that much left to do."

"I'll be back by two o'clock. It's only about thirty-five miles from here, but it's all minor state roads. If you'll make sandwiches out of what's left of our stuff, we'll munch on 'em on the way back. Either that, or we'll have to throw it away."

Before Rob started back, Greg said, "I forgot to tell you. I brought the Tupperware back last Sunday. It's up in the cabinet where it came from."

"I missed it. Thanks. But, in spite of all the time we spent together, we never did talk about how long you're going to be here."

"The coming school year, for sure. After that, I don't know. You'll have to talk to somebody on the office. Or maybe Mr. Cable would know."

"Good idea. I'll ask him this week or next. Got to go, young man. Great having you at home and at the lake. I really appreciate all your help around the cottage, and here's twenty bucks to hold you over for a little while."

"It was good to be home. Thanks for the new clothes and the money. I'll try to write more because I know we can't always talk."

"Stick with your studies and we'll expect to see you again at the Christmas break."

"Bye, Dad." They hugged and held on for a moment.

Rob returned Greg's wave and then had misty eyes as he pointed his new Mustang in the direction of the cottage at Hampden Lake.

When Rob and Mike were close to Sheffield, they headed for Kim's house and the barbeque—if that part of the holiday celebration was still underway. It was, and after hugs they dug into the food. There was plenty of it left.

"You just missed my dad," Kim said. "You're never going to meet him."

"We'll get lucky, and it'll happen one of these days."

"Glad you're back OK. I thought you might drink too much beer in weather like this."

"I put away my share on Saturday and Sunday. Good thing the toilet works. But I forgot to take something essential with us. Toilet paper." Kim laughed. "But there's a little market on the main road and they had whatever we'd forgotten to take with us. In fact, we could probably do a lot of our shopping right there. They seem to have almost everything we'd ever need—including great cuts of beef *and* live lobsters."

Rob and Mike were the last to leave. "Hate to see the weekend come to an end," Kim said. "I missed not being next to you on Saturday night. If you're going back up to the lake on Friday, would you take me along? I'm not much into sleeping bags, but I'll give it a try."

"Making love on the floor is hard on knees, but maybe we can figure something out. Both bedrooms have doors, so if we're not too noisy, we might be able to get away with some loving."

"I promise not to scream, '*Now*!' when we orbit some planet."

"Good. You pass the mute test. I'll take you with me. If Mike doesn't want to go, you can scream all you like. Thing is, it's deathly quiet between those hills, so you'd probably be heard all over town. Maybe turn some old people on."

"Or off." They laughed.

"Got to go, babe. We have some stuff to clean up before we hit the hay." Rob and Kim held each other for a moment and exchanged tender kisses.

"See you on Friday, love," Kim said. "If we don't talk before then, I'll be ready at a little after five."

"See you then. Night, sweetheart."

With a heavy work schedule, and evening comforts provided by Helen, the short week went by quickly.

When the weekend came, two nights of sleeping on the floor were two too many for Kim. "When you have a bed, or we can stay in Sturbridge, I'll come back."

"I know you weren't comfortable, but you've been good about it."

"The other part has been fun, mostly because it had been two weeks. I didn't mind the floor then. How are your knees?"

"Red, but unpeeled. It helped that we could make some adjustments to our orientation."

"Interesting way to put it." She smiled.

On Sunday morning, Rob worked inside the cottage, while Mike continued the seemingly endless task of cleaning up outside. Shortly after mid-day, they started home. But since their breakfast had been skimpy, they stopped on the way back to have a bite to eat.

"You'll be up there next weekend, I suppose?" Kim asked.

"I got a letter from Wilcox this past week that says the closing is next Friday. The attorney is coming to the bank, so we'll do it there. Since they've scheduled it for nine o'clock, it makes sense for me to go up on Thursday night. And, yes, I'll be there all weekend. There's still a lot to be done inside. Mike's finished with the exterior staining. That part is all set, I'm glad to say. Crummy weather isn't all that far off, so getting that done was a priority."

"If you're back at a reasonable hour on Sunday, I'll come over and make dinner for the two of you. That assumes Mike will be around, too. If not, we'll rearrange the evening some to suit us." A naughty giggle followed. Mike heard none of it. He was sound asleep in the back seat.

"Sold! I'll be back by five or so. What's on the menu?"

"Lasagna, and I'll have garlic bread ready for the oven. You'll need to make sure you have the makings for a salad of some kind."

"The market at the lake is open on Sunday, so I'll pick up what you need before I start back. Like I said, they seem to have anything and everything in that little place."

Helen came out to Sheffield with Rob on Monday evening and stayed with him until they went into the city on Thursday morning. She was such good company, and had he been pressed to make a decision soon between the two women in his life, it would have been impossible to decide. Not really, because neither Kim nor Vince had taken that first step toward filing for divorce. He'd need to talk with her about it again soon. They'd been close for two years, and she was still tied down.

On Thursday evening, Rob made the drive from Sheffield up to the lake, and would sleep on a cot he'd been able to pick up cheap. But as he was about to pass Wilcox's office, he decided on an impulse to see if Sarah Stuart was there. One of the other teachers, Gwen, was at home. She said Sarah and the other member of the trio, Jeanie, were at a place called The Corner House in the next town over. Rob got directions, found it, and walked in on the two of them and a shaggy faced dude who had just joined their little party. Rob asked Sarah if she remembered him. In the dim light it took a split second. Then she saw who it was—and smiled brightly.

"Forgotten about me already? It's only been two weeks. We're off to a wobbly start." They both chuckled.

Rob stood talking with Sarah for a few minutes, and then he asked if she was interested in going someplace else.

"No, but I'm ready to go back to Wilcox's."

"I'll drive you if you'd like."

"I would."

When Sarah got into Rob's new Mustang, she made a fuss over it.

"What a neat car. Smells brand new. Nothing quite like it."

"Be five weeks old on Saturday. And about Saturday, or tomorrow, would you be interested in having dinner with me?"

"Sure. I'd love to. I have plans tomorrow after school, but Saturday would be fine."

When they got back to Wilcox's place, Rob and Sarah talked for several minutes, and then he walked her to the door. When they were just inside, he tried to put a move on her, beginning with a kiss, but Sarah put her hands on his chest, held him off, and said, "Go way, you." It was *not* a convincing rejection. Her warm, teasing smile said that she liked what he had in mind—but not just yet.

"I'll see you on Saturday night. Seven be OK?"

"That'll be fine. Look forward to it. Good night, Rob. Glad you came to get me."

"Me, too. Night, Sarah."

The closing on Rob's little asset got underway shortly after nine o'clock. To his surprise it didn't take long to get everything done. He now owned some real estate again, subject to the lien of course. Opening up a checking and savings account didn't take much time either and he was back in his car at just after 10:00 a.m. There would be lots of time yet to get work done inside.

Late in the afternoon, Rob took some of the scrap wood off the pile of construction rubble that had accumulated and built a little fire. It had gotten chilly and the heat from it felt good. He stirred up a martini, and had a one-man party to celebrate his having added his name to the list of taxpayers in Hampden Lake, Massachusetts. A second martini, made him feel even better about ownership, but not the taxes that went with it.

But as it had begun to get dark, he decided that it would be a smarter idea to eat dinner than to have another drink—much as that was a temptation. He drove into Sturbridge and found the Oxen Pub again. A sirloin strip was what he considered the doctor would order, if there had been one around, so that's what he had. Then afterwards, he stopped at the little market on his way back to the cottage and found what he needed to hold him over until Sunday noon. He was glad to see that they were open until 9:00 p.m. He made a mental note of it.

On Saturday evening, after another productive day of interior work, Rob got himself cleaned up, put on denims and went off to pick up Sarah. She came down wearing a pretty dress and then, seeing how he was dressed, said, "Oh! Guess I better change into something more casual."

Sarah did just that, and they settled on a Chinese restaurant in Sturbridge that wasn't fussy about what people wore. Over dinner, Sarah commented that she expected Rob to show up in a jacket and tie and she'd made reservations at a white tablecloth place not far from the bank in Monroe where he'd been the day before.

"Sorry to disappoint you. I mostly work casual during the week and didn't bring anything other than what you saw me wearing on Thursday night—and what I have on now. Another time maybe?"

"It isn't a problem at all. We just didn't take the time to get our signals straight."

"I'm still a farm kid at heart, so anytime I can get out of a button-down shirt and tie, I'll do it."

Sarah smiled. "I'll remember that next time."

They talked on into the evening and Rob, relaxing, continued to drink and lost count. It was a mistake. When they got back, there was serious kissing as they sat in his car. Rob got to the point where he suggested that it might be a good idea if Sarah invited him in. She agreed.

"Time to go inside and maybe see what develops," he said.

"My bed's pretty small, but let's find out if we both fit."

Small or not, it didn't matter. Rob had put away too many dry Gibsons over ice. The result was that those parts that he was now expecting to perform in their customary fashion had already gone to sleep.

"Guess I need to confess that I'm *very* embarrassed. Can't remember that this has ever happened but once before. Same thing. Too much booze. Sorry that I've let you down."

Sarah laughed. "We've gotten down to bare skin, so I guess it tells us something about our wanting to go further than just hugging and kissing. There'll be another time before long—that is, if you'll come back. But don't worry about it. It isn't a usual thing, I imagine. Problem is, you don't show that you've had that much to drink. But your body is telling you something else." She laughed again. "In a way, it's funny. But we'll get it right in another week or so."

"You're being forgiving. I appreciate it. In a way it *is* funny. It wouldn't be if I thought it was a permanent affliction. Best I can suggest is a little bit of preliminaries-type pleasure."

"No. Let's wait until we can be there together."

"I hadn't planned on it, but maybe I should come back again next weekend and try to put things right. Dinner again?"

"Yes. I'd like that."

"If you're up to a sleeping bag and a hard floor, we'll make a night of it. I'll take it easy on the booze. Promise. I still can't believe it made that much difference."

"Forget it. And sleeping bags aren't new to me. Be fun, or at least different. Never slept in one before when it wasn't outside."

"Time for me to go back to the cottage and pout."

"Oh, stop it!"

"All right. I will. See you next Friday evening. In denims."

"You can take me to the Oxen Pub. We'll fit right in."

"You have a date. Night, Sarah."

They kissed with warmth, and then held onto each other for a moment.

"Good night, Rob. And, no pouting. Please? We'll both be all right."

"OK."

Rob went back to his cot miffed. "A ready and willing partner, and I blew it. Dumb!"

During the night, Rob was revisited by the dream that he hadn't had in almost two years. It was of the young woman's face that he associated with his land, and the same one who showed up with Wilcox at a cottage under construction in that last dream. It awakened him, and he bolted upright.

"*That's it*! She's the mystery woman. Sarah is the one in those dreams. I got some of it partly wrong. Her face isn't exactly the same, but it's remarkably close. That's absolutely incredible. How far back do the dreams go? Nearly three years? And she was the one who always seemed to figure into my future. I wonder if she really does. Not if I have a repeat performance, or lack of it, like earlier tonight. And she hasn't exactly made my heart turn cartwheels. Be curious to see what evolves." Rob thought about it for several minutes, then laid back down and slept peacefully for the rest of the night.

On Sunday, Rob went down to the little market nearby and bought the ingredients Kim wanted for a salad. When he got home, he called to let her know that Mike would be staying overnight with Tom. "Keep some of the lasagna for yourself, love. He won't be here."

"That rearranges our dinner schedule. I told you about that."

Kim came with two servings of lasagna and some garlic bread, as promised. But before they ate, she took Rob by the hand, led him to his bedroom, and became the beneficiary of what he had expected to leave with Sarah.

"You've fixed me right up. I'll be able to get through the week now, especially if we have a little encore in the morning."

"Best we do that, because I have to be back up at the cottage, at least on Saturday. I want to finish putting up some louvered room dividers I built this weekend. But you've got me the first weekend in October. All of it, if you want."

"I do. The cottage has gotten to be your new mistress, and my competition. But I understand, I suppose."

"I'm getting to the point where I have the inside pretty well finished off. It's close now, and you know me. I'm driven. What we have left are the louvers, some staining, wall coverings of some kind in the bedrooms, drapes and curtains, the hardware to hang them on, and carpeting for the living room at some stage. A bare floor needs to be covered, and I'll get to it as soon as I'm able. But let's talk about this over some of your good food. I'm starved."

Over dinner, Kim asked, "Then what are you going to do when it's all done?"

"Invite you up for a long weekend, and spend all of it making love with you in front of a roaring fire. What do you think?"

She smiled warmly. "Oh, yumm. Maybe we can get caught up then. But what about food? We'll have to eat sometime."

"It'll be catered by someone with very bad eyesight." They laughed.

After they'd cleaned up and gotten breakfast set up, Rob and Kim sat on the sofa and held each other, just as they did nearly two years ago at her house. Then hands started searching and finding. Shortly afterwards they joined and then shared the product of their love.

It's always so good, they agreed. They stayed close together, whispered words of love, and then before long they slept. Entangled.

Morning came earlier than either one of them wanted it to, so to brighten their day they took their bodies on a quick trip to a nearby planet. It was worth it. Now they could start their week with a smile. And they did just that.

"Plan on me coming back next Sunday, lover. I need you. Maybe we should make this a full time involvement."

"Ahh, well, there's the small matter of a husband standing between you and me and a commitment like that."

"We disagree on lots of different things, so I've been dragging my feet until I see that we can get it done for the least amount of money possible. I can't afford to put it in the hands of my lawyer and have him charge me for negotiations that might run on for months. We need to work out the settlement first."

"I can relate to that. Regina and I should have done the same thing. It would have made sense. We didn't disagree on all that much, but negotiations went on for over four months. So Jay Silverberg's invoice wasn't exactly petty cash. The problem was her lawyer. In the beginning, he wouldn't bend. We'd have saved a pile of money if he hadn't been such a jerk."

"We want to avoid that. Or more accurately, I have to keep the fee within reason. It's a matter of money."

"Keep me posted. But, I've got to be on my way, I left early on Thursday and took Friday, so I'll have to spend some extra hours getting caught up. It's different from the way you want to get current. That doesn't involve a lot of hours. Just extra energy." They chuckled at Kim's ongoing feeling that her lovemaking was always in a deficit state.

"You promised to bring my account up to date on the weekend of the second."

"We'll do that. Now, I'm off to the garage. You leaving with me?"

"Too early for me to go in. I'll stick around here for another hour, or close to it," Kim said. "Call me this week, will you?"

"I will. Bye, babe."

"Bye, guy."

Helen spent most of the week with Rob, but since he was working longer hours, she was coming up to his place first and they left from Newcombe's when he was ready. On Wednesday evening, everyone had gone and when Rob got ready to leave, Helen stood planted in the middle of the office floor.

"Stay a few minutes. I need you," Helen said.

"Here?"

She grabbed Rob, rubbed her body against his, and then kissed him with passion.

"I've always wanted you to do me in your office," she confessed. Rob chuckled softly.

"You horny thing, you. This is a little bit crazy. But why not?"

The sofa where candidates sat during interviews was turned into a loving platform. Helen was in need and then satisfied. They both were.

"Now I feel better. And you can do that later on at home. It's that time of the month and I've been in bad need all day long. I could hardly wait until everybody left."

"Not much question you were ready. But it's a good thing somebody didn't forget a file or their attaché case. Wouldn't we have been a spectacle? *Ohhh*, boy!"

"They could have learned a lot just by watching." They laughed, dressed, then went up to Grand Central and boarded a train to Sheffield. After the lights were out, Helen needed more attention. Rob hoped she would leave something for him to take up to the lake this weekend.

Rob put in longer hours and it allowed him to get away a little earlier on Friday afternoon. He was off the train in Sheffield at 5:12, and at Sarah Stuart's door just before 7:30.

"Hi, Rob."

"Hi, gal." He gave Sarah a hug.

"I thought you'd forgotten about our date. Guess I didn't know what time you'd be here."

"I'm normally here later than this. But I left earlier than I usually do, and drove like a maniac just so I could give you a hug before half past seven. I made it just in time."

"I'm glad you did. I was beginning to worry a little."

"No need to do that. I worked in my dress denims today, as you can see, so we can go eat anytime you're ready."

"I've been on the edge of the sofa since about seven. Are we still going to the Oxen Pub?"

"You bet. I need a tasty steak and some of that guy's mellow music. What's his name?"

"Skip Rydell."

"Yep. That's him."

The restaurant was nearly full, but Rob and Sarah did manage to find a table in a far corner. To their surprise, they had a good view of the guitarist. It helped that the place wasn't all that big. They ordered drinks, and to be certain that tonight wouldn't be a repeat of last week, they stuck to wine. White wine was Sarah's regular before, during, and after dinner drink, and Rob had a California red that he knew and liked from his days on the west coast. He ordered steak. Sarah had lamb, both of which came with potato and salad. This was the night to get acquainted, so Sarah had lots of questions about Rob, past, present, and future, and he wanted to know about her.

"You teach in Bloomdale, over near the pretty church."

"I'm at the elementary school that's kind of across the street. When you come into town from the east, you turn left at the traffic light, Route 19, and it's a hundred yards, maybe a little more, down on the right."

"So what grade do you teach?"

"Fifth grade. Eleven-year-olds mostly. It's a good age, and I enjoy working with them."

"This is your first school?"

"It is. I'm starting my third year."

"That makes you twenty-four, then?"

"On the first of November."

"I'm well into forty-one. That means you're seventeen years younger than me."

"Seventeen and a half. Almost to the day. I overheard you telling somebody that your birthday is in late April. Is that right?"

"The twenty-eighth. Any problem with the age difference?"

"None at all. First, you don't act like you're forty-plus. Second, you could pass for early thirties. Third, I'm attracted to someone who's more mature than most of the people in my age group. I learned that last year when I went out a few times with a guy in his mid-thirties. And just so you'll know, our relationship was strictly platonic, but the fact that he was older suited me much better than dating people in the mid to late twenties bracket. I'm not sure why. That I was so close to my dad may have had something to do with how I look at the age thing."

"That sounds like past tense."

"It is. He died on the golf course a little over six years ago. He was only fifty-three. I took it pretty hard."

"I didn't mean to pry."

"You're not prying. It's all right. And you're sensitive to that kind of thing. I like it that you are. It's an example of what men your age do that guys in their twenties don't usually think about."

"I understand—in part because I lost my dad not quite four years ago. For a long time we had a love-hate relationship, but during the last ten years of his life, we were close. That he's gone still hurts."

"It takes a while, doesn't it?"

"Sure does. Would you like a nightcap?"

"I love white wine, but it's probably not a good idea. I want tonight to be what we'd hoped for last week. I don't want to lose the edge."

"I'm still sorry about last week. Women don't have the same failure rate as men because there's nearly always a way to bring them around, assuming the guy knows what he's doing. And I'm glad you're thinking ahead. It's beginning to stir me up, so maybe we ought to see what can be done about it."

"There's no one at home, so I'm ready—in more ways than one."

"Shhh, or we'll never get out of the parking lot."

After a sensuous kiss in the car, Rob wasted no time in getting back to the Wilcox building. Then, in the door, they went straight up to Sarah's room and her little bed. Undressed, she had no doubt that Rob would be an especially satisfying lover, so never mind the failure of a week ago. After a few minutes of foreplay, Sarah confirmed that Rob was *very* ready and said, "Mmm, impressive. I want you. Love me."

When they joined, it was electrifying. For both of them.

"You feel *wonderful*," she said. "I'm already near the place I want to go. Wait for me?"

"Yes."

Minutes later, Sarah stiffened as she reached a crest and a gentle climax.

"I'd like another one of those," Rob said. "Exciting stuff."

Shortly afterwards, Sarah murmured, "*Ooooh.*" She'd reached an even higher peak and added a cute little squeak when she arrived. A brand new sound. Rob couldn't help but smile because it pleased him that she was finding total fulfillment.

"One more, then it's my turn," Rob whispered.

Sarah was totally immersed in the passion she felt, so it was only moments later that she said, "I'm way up there. I want you with me." Rob shifted upwards firmly and increased the rhythm of their movements. It wasn't long before Sarah murmured, "Close." Then. "Unnh. *Now*! Do it!" she begged. Rob growled when the pyrotechnics began. She felt his release and squealed, "*Yessss*! Together. Ohhhh!"

They both exhaled hoarsely and went limp.

"Perfectly delightful!" Rob said quietly.

After they'd rested for a few minutes, Sarah commented, "You don't know how happy I am that you know what you're doing. You were able to wait until *I* was ready for my big finale and it made all the difference. This is the first time I've ever felt the excitement, the sensations I thought I should. Mmmm. Wonderful! And very juicy, too."

"Doesn't take a genius to figure out that it was good for both of us. You'll learn that there isn't much in it for me if you aren't satisfied."

"Ohh, I am that. Completely. I don't have that much experience, but I've always been left behind. Now you know part of what I was trying to say when I talked about younger guys. You're one terrific lover, Rob Grant. You know about a woman's needs. At least the kind I have. I was very ready for this, especially after last week when things didn't work out the way we'd planned. It was even better than I expected."

"Should we try to get though the night in your bed or go do sleeping bags?"

"Let's just stay close. We can try your floor tomorrow night."

"No bigger than your bed is, we don't have much choice." They both chuckled softly.

But they made do, and they also made equally passionate love again in the morning. What they quickly discovered was that they were good together. Exceptionally good. It helped that Sarah was younger and that her desires were every bit as robust as Rob's. He had a feeling that there would be more loving before he left on Sunday afternoon. And there was. Rob hadn't had an appetite quite like this in a long time. Apparently Sarah was deprived, as she'd suggested indirectly, or else he *had* turned her on. Whichever, they couldn't get enough of each other.

When Rob was ready to leave for Sheffield, he lingered briefly before finally saying good-bye. Throughout their pleasant weekend, hours when they'd gotten to know each other better, they both sensed that they were on the threshold of a good relationship. And it was more than just the physical aspect of what they'd shared. Sarah seemed to be a really sweet young woman. During the time they spent together, Rob also began to see that she had beauty inside. Knowing how to recognize it was a lesson he'd learned from Justine almost two years ago.

"I'll be back up on the evening of the eighth," Rob said. "Monday is Columbus Day, but I probably ought to go back on Sunday afternoon."

"We have the day off. Any objections if I follow you back? I'd like to see your place, and then spend the night in *your* bed."

"I didn't know that you'd have the holiday, although I might have guessed you would. Great idea. I'd love it One thing about it, it'll be good to get away from your little bed and the sleeping bags. My body is complaining."

"Mine too. Maybe we can find a bed for the cottage. Make weekends much more enjoyable."

"Let me look into it. But, teacher lady, I've got to be on my way. We'll talk before I come up again. You have my numbers, and I guess Alan won't have any problem if I use his office number to call you. What time do you get home from school?"

"Nearly always by five thirty or so. I usually work for a while after the kids are gone."

"OK. We can work it out. I want us to stay in touch. This has been a weekend to remember."

"Sure has. I'm just sorry you don't live closer. Twelve days is a long time between hugs—and other things."

"The idea of working up here is starting to look more interesting all the time. It'd be one huge career change if I did that. But the notion of being near you gives me another reason to think about it seriously."

"It's really sweet of you to say that. Drive carefully, Rob. You've gotten to be kind of important to me during these last two days, and I don't want anything bad to happen."

"I'll be careful, and I'll call you when I get home just to let you know that I'm OK."

"Would you please? It'd give me peace of mind."

Rob and Sarah held each other for a moment, and then kissed in a way that confirmed that they already meant something to each other.

Sarah waved as Rob drove off. He returned it. She felt a little hollow after seeing his car enter a shallow curve and then disappear. "I really like you, Rob Grant," Sarah said quietly as she looked down the empty road he'd just taken.

While Rob was driving back to Sheffield, he thought about Sarah. Most of the way home, in fact. She had reached a soft place inside that made him care about this sweet young woman who was gentle—and also mature beyond her nearly twenty-four years. Thinking about the dreams he'd had, he asked himself if he was trying to turn them into a self-fulfilling prediction. Or was it possible that he could set them aside and feel his warmth for her without help from the love and the peace the apparition had shown him in his dreams? It would most likely be months before he would begin to have an answer.

The first thing Rob did after he got his jacket off at home was to call Sarah.

"I promised, so here I am. All in one piece."

"Glad to know that. It's good to hear your voice again, even though it hasn't been much more than a couple of hours since you left. I've been thinking about you. And it's more than just the passion we shared this weekend. You've left a big imprint. Maybe more than that if the hotter fire we built was because I'm in my productive phase. I can't imagine that with teenage sons you'd be interested in starting another family."

"I don't know. If Bing Crosby can do it, why not me? I'm a lot younger."

"That isn't as funny as I think you'd like it to be. I wasn't paying attention to where I am in my cycle so it probably explains why I put a little more of myself into what we were doing. I'm not short on passion. You turned me on last weekend, and I really wanted you on Friday night. Badly. You gave me all of what I needed. And more. All weekend. I just got careless."

"Don't worry about it, Sarah."

"How can you say that so easily? I'm the one with the problem, maybe."

"Sarah, it's time I explained something to you. I was put out of business years ago. Fifteen to be exact. It's permanent, so there's no need to worry your pretty little head about it. That answer your question?"

"It does. And in that case, you've made my weekend all the more enjoyable. Until you come back, I'll be thinking about our being together again. At the same time, you've given me complete peace of mind."

"It doesn't bother you that we couldn't have a family—that is, if we someday got serious about a long-term relationship? It has been with at least a couple of other people in my past."

"None whatsoever. I have kids all day long. I'm happy to give them up to their owners at half past three every afternoon Monday through Friday. I don't need any of my own to keep me happy."

"If they mattered, our liaison would end if babies did get to be important."

"They aren't. But there's something else that's been on my mind. I want you to know that I really enjoyed spending time with you and that I want to see you again. By that, I mean beyond our Columbus Day weekend together."

"You will. I thought about you all the way back. There are other women in my life, but you've gotten my attention and have also given me such warm feelings during these past two days. And it's more than being in bed together. We'll talk about it when I'm up on the eighth."

"I'd like that. Call me if you can. Please? I want to stay in touch while you're there and I'm here. I'll miss you, I've already discovered. That's either a good sign or a bad sign. I can't decide which, but I do know I'll be glad to see you again."

"You'll have me for three days starting on the eighth. Be fun to have you here."

"I can hardly wait. Maybe you'd dream about me in the meantime?"

"That's been going on for quite a while."

"Meaning?"

"Tell you about it when I come up a week from Friday. Could be you'll think I'm either a psychic or completely nuts. You may have a little trouble believing me."

"I'll give it a try."

"Well, gal, I've got to go see about something for dinner. We'll talk later in the week."

"I hope so. Bye, Rob."

"Take care, Sarah."

Late in the afternoon, Kim was at Rob's door and obviously glad to see him. For a change, Mike was around, so the two of them shared a hug.

"Why don't we go out?" Rob suggested. "I've been eating stuff off a hot plate for two days, and I'm due for something more interesting."

Until they left for dinner, Rob and Kim sat close together, talked, and kissed during pauses in their conversation. His mind was on Sarah part of the time, so those moves were at Kim's initiative. He decided that it was unfair *not* to give her his full attention. She'd been alone all week, and he knew how that felt. And with a new woman in his life, suddenly, his conscience was bothering him some. With all that Kim had given him over the past two years, she deserved better than to have him seem preoccupied. And she did raise the question.

"Your mind seems to be somewhere else. Something wrong?"

"Not really. Just thinking about all the things we've done up at the lake and what still has to be done. I sort of want everything in place before the weather turns really bad. But I'm running out of money to cover the things on my list. The little placements are keeping us afloat. It's the extra stuff that isn't in the budget just yet."

"You don't have to do everything at once, you know."

"Yeah, but I'd like to get to a point where I can sit by the fire with a martini, watch a football game and not be bugged by something I think ought to be done. Immediately. But knowing the kind of guy I am, there'll always be something I can find to do. That comes from having mostly grown up alone on the farm when my brother was away at Purdue, then on submarines during World War II. You learn how to keep busy. There are times when being a self-starter and disciplined drives *me* nuts, though. Anyway, it isn't you, sweetheart. We'll be OK tonight and next weekend. We'll have most of those two days together."

"I know, and I'm ready to have you all to myself from Friday night right through until Monday morning."

"That's news. You worked out Sunday night, too?"

"I did. It'll give us a chance to function like a family starting after work on Friday right up until we get back into our routine on Monday. In two years, we've never done that before, and I'd really like to see how we do together."

"I'm all for it. We ought to plan on dinner out, maybe a movie, some serious loving, and whatever else we can dream up."

"Yumm. Makes me feel good just to think about it. And I especially like the part about the loving."

They enjoyed their dinner out, and a pleasurable session after the lights were out. Rob wondered if there was anything left after the kind of weekend he and Sarah had shared. But he knew that there was always an entirely different feel associated with each physical encounter. And the sensations, too, were unique to that relationship.

And that held true when Helen came out with Rob on Tuesday evening. He liked having her around, and their time together was pure joy. Maybe he should stop procrastinating and marry her, he thought. It would be a good marriage. He was sure of it. "So why the delay?" Rob couldn't answer his own question—other than he still liked variety.

Kim moved in late on Friday afternoon, but the pleasant weekend they had planned took a severe hit when the mail came on Saturday. The property management company in New York advised Rob that they were terminating his lease at the end of the year, and that he was to vacate the apartment no later than the end of the day on Saturday the eighth of January. The reason for the eviction was that his sons, and their behavior, were disturbing other tenants in the building.

"I-do-not-believe-this!" Kim heard him and knew something had gone wrong. "Mike!"

"Yeah."

"Come here a minute. Take a look at a letter I just got."

Mike was rarely profane, but his immediate reaction to the letter was, "Bullshit!"

"Then why do you suppose they're giving kids' behavior as a reason?"

"I don't know. Greg isn't here, I don't have friends in all that much, except for girls once in a while. But whenever anyone's here, we don't run around the grounds or make a lot of noise, so it's got to be something else. We're not it, or the building manager would have talked to you about it by now."

"You know me. I fight stuff like this, but this is one case when I'm not going to. I'm happy in number 710 and would like to stay, but they must think theirs is the only building in town. It isn't, so we've got time to find someplace else to live."

Kim was shocked after she read the letter, and then remarked, "I can't believe this either, but this is my town, and I can help you find another apartment. It won't have this view, probably, but there's no reason to move very far from here. I don't want you to do that. There are places available at Parkside Village, I've heard. It's close. But there have to be other buildings with vacancies. Let's go get the Star and take a look at the ads. I'd ask my dad to help, but he goes into New York every day so he doesn't know as much as I do about the Sheffield market."

"You know I appreciate it. Like always, you're there to help. The timing on this is awful. The holidays are coming up, search income has been spotty, my bank account could use a transfusion, and more to the point, I don't want to be bothered with something like this. *Dammit*!"

Mike went to spend the weekend with Tom. Rob and Kim had dinner out and talked at some length about his imminent move out of Juniper Heights. They'd gotten the paper and decided they'd use most of their Sunday together checking out rental ads and driving around to look at the buildings that had vacancies.

"This isn't how I planned to spend the weekend, love. Sorry to put a damper on our first ever three nights together."

"The positive side of it is that we're having to function like a family that's had something like this come up. Let's say it's a test, or that it builds character. If we're to live together someday, we'll have to go through this anyway. My place won't be big enough, and for sure yours isn't."

The Sunday ad searches underway, the first thing that struck Rob was that rents had gone almost out of reach in the three and a half years since he'd looked around for a place to live. He said as much to Kim.

"My search income doesn't support the kinds of rates I'm seeing in the paper. Hard to believe how they've increased. I'll bet that's why they want me out of number 710. They can get a lot more than what I've been paying. Guess I better be looking for another job, too. Something with a regular income. This is turning out to be more of a pain than I thought."

"You don't have to move right away, so there's time to see what else comes up. And I can make some calls to people I know who're in real estate. If you haven't found anything by Thanksgiving, or maybe a little after, then we can start getting concerned. Let's not get uptight just yet."

"Well, I've got an escape route. It's the cottage. Worse comes to worse, and I can always move up there. The mortgage payments are less than half the rent I'm paying now."

Kim frowned. "I don't want to hear you talk like that, Rob. If you move up there, then you're gone from my life, and I don't want that. Not ever." Tears welled up.

"I don't either, so let's try to find something, make the commitment, and get it behind us. What I have to do is knuckle down and try to get some placements made, or see if I can't move back into corporate life somehow, somewhere. Easier said that done when you're over forty. Looking younger than that doesn't count for much."

Rob and Kim spent part of the afternoon looking at buildings, taking addresses of those with vacancy signs in their windows, and trying hard not to be depressed. It was not the way they had intended to spend this special weekend together and Rob apologized again.

"That's the last time I want to hear you do that. It's not your fault, and if I was looking for a family-type event to be a part of our weekend, we got more than we bargained for. But lots of couples have to deal with something like this, I'm sure. It's all right, Rob. Things will get better."

On Monday morning, Kim promised to make phone calls from the agency, as time would allow, to see what was available and what the rental rates were. Prices really had gone up and it was discouraging. Rob called Helen and told her what had happened on Saturday.

"I've got a meeting to go to late this afternoon," she said. "I can either come out a little later this evening or meet you tomorrow in time to make our usual train. Sounds like you need me tonight, so if you don't mind picking me up at 8:53, we can have an hour or two together before we turn in."

"Yeah, I'd like it if you'd come out tonight—that is, if you don't mind. I'll see you down at the station."

When Rob got home, he called Kim to find out if she had any news.

"It's not very good. All the places that had reasonable rents are already gone. Looks like you have to jump on something the minute it comes on the market. The people who had signs in their windows should take them down. Those rentals are gone, too. It may have something to do with all the big companies that'll eventually be coming in. We're going to have to be really aggressive the way it looks. I'll help all I can."

"I know you will. It's only been two days since I got the notice, so we shouldn't be discouraged. I have to be up at the lake this weekend, but I'll make calls during the week, too. I don't want you to carry the whole load. That's not fair. Something should turn up eventually."

"I'll do my part. You know that. It's easier to contact local people from here. I know some of them, and that should help."

"We'll talk later in the week. Thanks for all your help, love."

"Glad to do it. I want to keep you close by."

'G'night, Kim."

"Night, sweetheart."

Helen looked weary when she came into the light and Rob got a better look at her.

"Hi, sweet. What was the meeting all about? You look tired."

"The guy I had over since five o'clock wore me out. No, it's not nice at all for me to say something like that. That's downright cruel. You're the only man in my life."

"If I find out that's the way things are, you know how I'd feel about our relationship."

"I do, and I'm not taking any chances. But the meeting was about good grammar and how to write concise and effective reports. You could've taught the course."

"Well, let me get you up to the Heights and make you a drink."

"Sounds good. I need one. And if it helps me get some of my energy back, you know how the evening will end up."

"I can make a wild guess."

"What's the story behind the notice you got? I can't imagine that Mike is involved in raising hell around the building."

"As nearly as I can figure out, it's smoke that's covering up the real reason. The rents have skyrocketed in the past three years or so, and I'm guessing that company accountants are behind it."

"No reason to get into a lot of discussion about what if, because if you don't find a place here, or move to the lake, the answer's simple. You move in with me."

"That's a thought. But I'd have to work out something for Mike. Unless you want him to sleep with us."

"Work out some other arrangement."

"If it comes to moving out of Sheffield, I'd probably pick Mike up from wherever he's staying and take him to the lake on weekends. We'd have at least some time together. That way, you could have your other guy in on at least Friday and Saturday nights—and maybe even on Sunday."

"Say, wouldn't I have a lot of fun, though? But if it's all right with you, I'd spend weekends in Hempstead with Mom and Dad, and then have you all to myself for the rest of the week. In fact, I'm already beginning to like the idea of splitting my week that way. The folks have been after me to come out more often. See what you can do about Mike. And stop looking for a place in Sheffield. I know you like this place, so do I, but thinking about having you at home with me all week is a really nifty idea."

"Nifty?" Rob laughed. "That was one of my Aunt Mary's favorite words. But we may be onto something. If Alan Wilcox finds out I'm at the lake on weekends, I'll bet he's going to want me to go to work for him. In fact, I may just do that. It would give me a chance to find out something about the real estate business—at least his version of it. But I'm obliged to see if I can't find an apartment someplace nearby so that Mike has a home he can come back to at night. This is his last year at Sheffield High, and I know he really wants to finish up here."

"I understand. But I'd like you to keep in mind that you have a place with me if you want it. Now, take me to bed. I've found just enough energy to climb one modest size mountain."

It didn't take long before they curled their toes with pleasure and then slept peacefully.

On Tuesday afternoon, Rob made two personal calls that he felt were necessary. The first was to Justine. He'd neglected her, but with everything else afoot, there really hadn't been any way to fit her into his schedule.

"Justine. It's Rob."

"Hello, lover. Where have you been hiding? I've missed you and should probably be cross, but with our loose bond, if I can call it that, I don't have any right to be."

"I'm sorry we haven't been able to build any new fires. My days have been long and spare time has been a scarce commodity. But one of the reasons I'm calling is to tell you that my lease on number 710 won't be renewed."

"Oh, Rob, that's awful news! You know how much I like your place, so it makes me sad to think about it. What are you going to do?"

"There's an even chance that I'll have to move up to the cottage in Massachusetts. The rents in Sheffield have gone out of sight, and I'd be rent poor if I tried to stay there. I'm not making the kind of money I did at IMMCorp."

"I don't like the sound of that. But if that's the way it turns out, I'd like to see you before you move—wherever you go. My guess, then, is that you'll eventually leave Manhattan and that'll leave a gap in my social life. You're special."

"Sweet of you to say something like that. But about New York, you could be right. The real estate guy up at Hampden Lake wants me to run his businesses around the lake, and I'm leaning in that direction. My annual income will take another hit, but the cost of living up there is much lower than in the New York metro area, so we could manage. Mortgage payments won't be a whole lot more than my forty-six ride ticket on the Penn Central."

"I understand what you're up against. These past two years haven't been easy for you."

"You don't have to remind me. Anyway, the reason I'm calling is to bring you up to date and let you know that I want to see you sometime soon. The problem is that I'm working long hours, chasing after apartment listings in Sheffield, and on weekends trying to make the cottage habitable in case it becomes home. Whatever, I'll try to keep you posted. I owe you that."

"It's good to hear your voice again, and I'd like to see you. Work me into your crazy schedule if you can. You know we'd have an enjoyable evening together."

Rob laughed. "Yep, no doubt; I'll stay in touch as best I can."

"Thanks, Rob. I'll be thinking about you."

The second call was to Sarah. He thought she ought to be brought up to date, too—even though he'd be seeing her on Friday evening.

"Hi, dear heart. Rob. When we talked last Thursday, I didn't have any warning that we were going to get a letter telling us that we we're being evicted. But that's what's happened."

She wasn't the least bit sympathetic, and Rob couldn't have guessed that Sarah would react quite the way she did. All she'd shown him since they'd met was her gentle, compassionate nature.

"I imagine you're upset, but I see it as good news. Reason is, I care about you, so I'm glad there's at least a tiny chance that we'll be neighbors and lovers, or maybe more than that someday."

"I understand what you're saying, but it'll take time for me to get all this sorted out. You might tell Alan what's happened and let me know what his reaction is."

"He'll be here during the weekend. I imagine he'll come to the cottage early and want to unzip us out of our sleeping bags. By the way, I was in the storage room upstairs and found a big piece of foam all rolled up. I'm going to steal it. If we put it on the floor over at your cottage, it'll make sleeping and other things lots better. It isn't heavy, so I'll shove it in the car on Friday night. If I had a key, I'd take it over before you get here."

"Great! But about a key, I'll bet Alan has a spare for the contractors who worked on the place. They nearly always come in pairs."

"Let me look on the board that has all the keys on it. Hold on a minute."

Rob could hear the sound of keys rattling as she checked all the hooks. Then, finally. "You're right. Lots 146 and 147 on Colonial Trail?"

"That's it. And while you're there, you can wash the windows and sweep up."

"Listen to you! Only if I'm a permanent fixture someday."

"Not too fast, girl. There are a dozen other women I have to dispose of first."

"One might get the impression that you're the only expert lover in all of New York City. You've got ninety days. By then I'll want your personnel report and the status of all twelve."

"You're not being *too* aggressive."

"I told you when we talked a week ago Sunday that I like you. I want an unobstructed view of where it might lead."

"If I'm living up there, you won't have any competition. And it's beginning to look like there's a chance I *will* be your neighbor. Where are you taking me for dinner on Friday night?"

"A place right here in town. It's called the Lakeside Lodge. The guy in the kitchen makes a great baked stuffed lobster."

"You've got a date, teacher lady. Now, I've got to go. My fan club awaits."

"You're full of it, Rob Grant. But I'll say it again. I like you. Drive safely, please. See you on Friday evening."

"That you will, girl in my dreams."

"I like hearing that. You have to tell me about it over the weekend. Bye, handsome."

"We'll get to it. Bye, cutie."

On the train into New York on Friday morning, Rob said to Helen, "If we don't find an apartment in Sheffield, the suggestion you made on Monday evening could be the way it'll work out."

Helen smiled, and said, "Good news for me. You know how much I like having you around."

"We're good together. In lots of ways. We'll have to see how it goes. In the meantime, I'll be up at the lake until Monday evening. See you on Tuesday?"

"Definitely. I'll come to your office after work."

They hugged and said their good-byes at Grand Central. It was a routine that had been going on for a year now, but for some reason Rob could see it coming to an end. It hurt some to think about that day because he truly liked Helen and what she'd brought into his life.

Then, before his day began in earnest, Rob called Kim to tell her he'd be back late on Monday afternoon and asked if she'd like to come over for a drink after he was back.

"Yes, I'd like that, love. But before you go, I should tell you that I haven't found much that's available in the rental market. I'm shocked. Maybe when we get closer to the end of the month there'll be some new listings."

"I've run into the same thing. Let's talk about it on Monday. If you're free, we might have dinner," Rob suggested.

"Let's do that. I can't talk any longer. Too much going on around me. See you on Monday. Be careful, sweetheart."

"I will. Bye, love."

At mid afternoon, Rob finished his battery of calls, brought his search files current, and headed for the 4:15 train to Sheffield. With a couple of modest-size placements behind him, he could breathe a little easier and decided that the weekend would be brighter, with or without the sun. It was right at seven thirty when he drove up near the back door of Wilcox's combination real estate office and apartment building. Sarah was looking out the window and nearly flew out the door when she saw Rob's Mustang pull in. After he was out of the car, she gave him a bear hug.

"Whoa. Feels like you're glad I showed up."

"*Yes*! I've been looking out the window for half an hour and worrying just a tiny bit."

"You shouldn't. I'm fine. And you look like you could use a kiss."

"I can. Make it memorable, please."

And he did.

"That got very close to delaying dinner, but you're probably hungry. So am I. We don't have far to go. The restaurant is just on the other side of the lake."

Sarah went back inside, got her coat, and they were on their way within a couple of minutes. When they got there, Rob understood now why he'd never paid much attention to the small-ish sign. The place *was* lakeside, and down off the road. Visible, but not conspicuous. Inside, he liked what he saw. Old barn board walls, subdued lighting, a lake view, and a crackling fire going in an oversized native stone fireplace.

"If the food is good, I can tell you now that I'll come back here again. This will be our place. It's a funny thing I have about a new face and a new place."

"But the Chinese restaurant and the Oxen Pub came first."

"The Chinese place didn't have much going for it other than pretty good food. Not a lot of memories could be stored there. And the Oxen Pub wasn't new to me. I'd been there before. With someone else, I should add.

This is you and me. The ambiance is light years away from China. The Lodge is my kind of place."

"Your rules, so it's perfectly all right with me. I love it here."

They had drinks, talked, ordered the well-known baked stuffed lobster, talked some more, and then finally went up to Rob's cottage. Sarah had cleaned up just a little, hung an old sheet over the sliding glass door and also turned up the heat to take the edge off the chilly evening.

"Thanks for thinking about our privacy. Since we won't have an audience, I wonder if it's too late for a little fire."

"Never too late for that. Let me help you get some wood in. I brought some matches just in case you wanted to get one going."

"You're too much, Miss Stuart. Anything else?"

"You have to see the foam slab I brought over yesterday. Let me show you. Here."

"I had visions of some thin little thing. Wonder what they used it for? That has to be five or six inches thick. Already my body is saying thanks."

"Mine, too. Remember, I'm usually the one on the bottom."

"We can change that around, if you'd like. It's different."

"I like the idea. But you're stirring me up. We'd better get the fire going first."

There was plenty of what they needed to start a good fire and even some dry logs to throw warmth back into the room. Sarah had brought a bottle of wine, two in fact, some plastic glasses, and an opener, so they had a little after dinner party to celebrate the beginning of the Columbus Day weekend. Then as the blaze began to die down, and Rob and Sarah's fire began to glow brighter, they slipped out of their clothes, into the sleeping bags, and then took each other to places where passion ruled. Sarah went from crest to crest and finally said, "I want you with me." By then, Rob didn't need to be asked twice. Their pace increased, and abruptly her delightful little squeak signaled that she'd gone to the place she wanted to be. He immediately joined Sarah at her summit. His growl confirmed to her that he'd arrived.

"It's all yours now," he said.

"I'll be pleased to look after it. Mmmm."

"There'll be more."

A moment later, Sarah said quietly, "We're very good together, you know. I'm glad Alan asked me to come over with him on Labor Day weekend. And even more so that I said yes."

"That makes two of us. Suppose you'd told him you had to go buy a hat or something?"

Sarah laughed. "I might have turned him down. But then, I knew it was you he was going to visit."

"Or, suppose I hadn't come to the Corner House?"

"I don't want to think about it. Makes me shudder."

"Like a few minutes ago?"

"No, you silly goose. That was *very* different." She giggled sweetly.

"Only problem with making love in these things is that they're going to get pretty ripe before much longer."

"We have a washer over at the office. When the time comes, I'll take care of them."

"At the rate we're going, that'll be Sunday morning." They shared a gentle laugh. "More fire or more fire?"

"If the latter means you, yes!"

"We might take you off the bottom for a change. I need to check out the foam."

"A new approach, at least for me. Suppose it isn't for you, so I won't ask about it."

"Shall we experiment?"

Sarah discovered that it was not only different to be in charge, but it was also incredibly stimulating. It was a new level of pleasure—and a place she hadn't been before, Rob was certain. As she reached orbit, her soft squeal gave way to a throaty groan that said she'd found the very epicenter of passion. She begged him to join her. Caught up in her excitement, he quickly followed.

Sarah didn't move or say a word for a couple of minutes. As Rob waited for her to recover, he stroked her hair. And then, "You've taught me something new, and I nearly went out of my mind for a few seconds. I've never known sensations like those. There isn't a word for them. Maybe I'll make one up. Let you know what it is."

Feeling playful, Rob said, "OK. But I think we should keep practicing until we get it right." Sarah couldn't contain herself and laughed.

"I can't imagine there's a place beyond where I just went. And I'm way past my productive window. In fact, I'm close to the other end of my cycle. We should be able to sneak Monday in. For sure, I don't want to be wearing an 'Out of Order' sign when I get to your bed."

"Don't worry about it. I have a feeling we'll get another chance to baptize my bed before I have to move."

"If I have anything to say about it, we will."

"Any interest in some sleep?"

"I'm ready. Would you snuggle with me? I'm still up there, so I don't want to fall too hard."

"I'll make sure you don't. But I wonder about the foam. We must have flattened it by a couple of inches."

"You're being silly again. Just hold me, and don't worry about the foam. It'll be just fine."

They whispered good night and slept like a couple of loving rocks.

Chapter Nine

Late on Saturday morning, Alan Wilcox knocked on Rob's door. He and Sarah had loved again energetically, but they were up and dressed.

"Oh, Rob. I completely forgot to tell you that I did speak with Alan, and you were right. He wants to talk to you about working for him starting next spring. I'm sorry. Other things on my mind—like you, and last night." She smiled warmly.

"Not important, dear heart. I figured that's what he'd have in mind.

"Alan. Good morning. You know this young lady. She just stopped by to inspect the cottage."

He chuckled. "Her car is at my place. She walk over?"

"Looks like that's a gotcha." It was Rob's turn to laugh.

"You do all right for yourself, Rob. And that goes back quite a ways."

"What's on your mind?"

"Sarah told me last week that you're being evicted from your apartment down in Sheffield and that there's a chance you might be moving up here."

"Could end up that way. Sounds like Sarah has expressed the hope that I will. Yeah, I may not have a choice. I'm finding that rents have really gotten out of hand. But what I can't do is walk away from the search business anytime soon. I've got too many irons in the fire, so there's the prospect of earned fees. Fairly big ones."

"You might think about coming up here and working for me on weekends starting in April. I'll need somebody like you by then. The guy who's been looking after things is definitely going to work as a salesman for a GM dealership in Springfield. Since the season's just about over here at the lake, we'll be closing down a week from tomorrow. The plan is to open up again on the first of April. That's early, but Easter is on the second and generally there are people out looking around that weekend. I'll want to help you get a license, not for the property I own, but for anything else when I'm the broker. You have to be licensed as a salesman first, and then you can sit for the broker's exam after that. But even if you're still living down there, you could come up on Friday night like you are now, visit with Sarah, have your evenings together, and sell for me during the day."

"Let's talk about the possibility of my having to move up here—if that's how things turn out. For sure, I don't want to pay the kinds of rents landlords are getting these days. What then?"

"I'd have you over at the office full time during the season here at the lake. Normally, that's about mid-April through the end of October. During the winter months, I'd probably have you working for me in Springfield. Another investor and I are negotiating to buy an eight-story office building downtown, and I'd eventually want you to manage it."

"Sounds like you'd put me on salary."

"Here at the lake, you'd have a regular $200 a week draw against commissions. In the office building, my partner, McCallum, and I would have to work out some kind of salary arrangement. I'll talk to him about it next week. Oh, and something else. I'm looking at a small apartment complex down in Florida and would be converting the units to condos if it works out that I eventually go to contract on it. It's likely that I'd want you to keep an eye on the renovation work and then handle sales down there, too. But nothing's firm. We're only at the investigation stage."

Sarah was beaming. She could picture Rob as maybe a permanent neighbor and weekend lover sometime soon. Or maybe he'd ask her to move into the cottage with him once it was furnished.

"I can see absolutely every one of his ideas going through your head, young lady," Rob said. They all laughed.

"Who? Me? I'm just listening." More laughter.

"Lots to think about, Alan. You waved some of this in front of me as far back as three years ago," Rob recalled. "We're a whole lot closer to putting something together that makes sense for both of us. But first, I have to figure out what my permanent address will be, and then how soon I can pull out of the search business. There aren't any firm answers just yet, but what's fairly obvious is that if I can't find a place with an affordable rental rate by early December, then it looks like Colonial Trail will be it."

Sarah was pleased, and the sparkle in her smiling eyes confirmed it.

"The other part of it is that the guy who hired me into the search business is bankrupt and has filed for protection. A new face, in the person of Paul Lenard, has entered the picture. He's a friend of Newcombe's and, like me, has international management experience. So, with his having had years of profit center responsibilities, he's much more of a heavyweight. Paul's a good man. He's forming a new company, of which I'm a part, restructuring how we operate, and we'll be moving into new offices on November 1. The long and the short of it is that I can't walk out on the new company—at least not just yet, since I'm a VP in the new firm."

Sarah, wide-eyed, was taking all this in.

"I understand," Alan said. "Life's a little simpler out here at the lake, so you're a bigger fish in our little pond. But it's those credentials that would help me out with all of the businesses and the projects I have underway. You'd bring years of experience to Wilcox Enterprises."

"I'd be less than honest if I didn't say that it has considerable appeal. I really like the area. Unlike New York, it's very tranquil. And I should probably add that the young lady here is also a part of the attraction."

"It's a good thing I brought her over to look at your place on Labor Day weekend. She may be my best ambassador." Alan grinned impishly.

"I'll keep you up posted on how the pieces are sorting themselves out. All the answers should be in place within about 60 days. The season's over here, so there isn't any rush. But you'll have my decision and a game plan well before Christmas. Fair enough?"

"More than fair. Now, I'll leave you two alone. I've been here long enough."

"No bother at all, Alan. Thanks for coming by. It's good to know that what I can bring to the table would be a good fit with your business plans. I really appreciate it that you've sketched out what you have in mind. It's an interesting proposition."

"You're welcome, Rob. The two of you have a good weekend."

"You, too, Alan."

After Wilcox left, Sarah gave Rob a bright smile and a big hug to go with it.

"I like just about everything you two said. But you haven't been sharing all of your goings-on with me. Lots of things came out into the open during your conversation."

"New as we are to each other, does that surprise you?"

"I suppose not. But I figure that if you can peel away my outer layer and discover the kind of fire I've had bottled up, at least until last night, I thought maybe you'd be willing to share some of what's inside you, too."

"Not the same, dear heart. I exposed my passions just as you did, but all the rest are personal or business matters. As you heard, I'm facing some pivotal decisions fairly soon. You have a pretty good idea, as do I, how things are going to turn out. After having spent some time here, and meeting you, I'm starting to get oriented toward the idea of leaving New York. If there's a way to make money working for Wilcox, *and* a sweet face to look at over breakfast, then hanging up my spurs every night on Colonial Trail sounds like it might be a pretty good idea."

"You probably won't ask me for my reaction, but I'll say it anyway. I think so, too."

"I'm going to gamble on the possibility that I'll be moving up here. Even if I don't, one thing I'll need in this place is a stove and a fridge. Want to go shopping with me?"

"Where?'

"This is your neighborhood. What do you suggest?"

"Auburn, probably. There's a big mall there with a Sears store in it."

"They usually have reasonable prices, and the quality is mostly OK, I guess. Sure. Get yourself together and let's go see what we can find."

As they got started, Rob asked, "Which direction is Auburn?"

"It's side-by-side with Worcester," Sarah explained. "We take the Mass Pike to I-290, and then off it at Exit Nine. It's right there. Easy."

The appliance department had an excellent selection. Rob quickly found what he was looking for—and at good prices. Both items were part of a Columbus Day sale. After he'd paid for them, he worked out the delivery details with the clerk. The driver would be instructed to contact Sarah the following Saturday, and she'd show them where the cottage was.

Then, while they were at it, Rob pulled out the measurements he had for each of the windows. "We're going to blow my budget and get the hardware for the curtains and drapes. If we find something for the slider, you can have your sheet back. The glass is double glazed, but I still want lined drapes or ones with some kind of thermal backing."

"I'm not sure why you need me. You seem to have all this worked out in your head."

"You can be the one to pick out some kind of neutral color. Besides, you're cute to look at."

"Thanks, buds."

Rob was able to find curtain rods and drapery hardware for all seven windows and the nine-foot slider. Sarah looked at what they had in stock, and then picked out drapes for it. They were off-white and called Oatmeal. "They'll match the pine interior perfectly," Rob agreed.

After they had lunch at Friendly's, they went back to the cottage and Rob got busy with measurements, drilling holes, and putting up the drapery rods for the slider. That was the number one priority. Before the end of the day, he'd managed to get most all of the hardware installed, pulled down the sheet that Sarah had worked so hard to hang, and then hung the drape over the nine feet of glass that faced the deck. The living room was no longer a fish bowl.

"It looks *great*, Rob!" Sarah exclaimed.

"You picked out a perfect neutral color, babe. Couldn't be better." Sarah was pleased to be a part of the process. It was as if she was doing her own place, and she was obviously excited to see the first steps being taken to turn the cottage into a home."

"Since you're making me feel like the lady of the house, and you've spent a whole bunch of money today, I'm treating you to dinner," Sarah announced.

"Well, now. That's an offer I can't refuse. Guess I better wash my hands."

"Part of it's a bribe. You were going to tell me all about your dreams, but you haven't yet. So, maybe if I buy you a second martini, you'll open up."

"Not necessary. We simply had our minds on other things last night, *and* there's no rush." They smiled. "So, where are you taking me?"

"We've burned a lot of energy since yesterday. Any objections to going back to the Oxen Pub for some good beef?"

"None at all. We probably have another busy night ahead of us." Rob wore a naughty smile. "I'll have the bigger steak this time."

Over dinner, Rob told Sarah his story about the dreams he'd had. "They began about two years ago, I guess. No. Before that. I was always in a quandary of some kind. In the first one, a young woman with a pleasing face appeared. Nothing more involved than that. A later one that I recall clearly had Wilcox, the land, a cottage going up, and the same young woman in it. I *couldn't* figure out the connection. What made it so interesting is that the apparition had a calming smile, asked me to be patient, and always left me reassured. When you and I met on Labor Day weekend, you remember that I asked if you'd always lived in this area."

"I do."

"That you looked so familiar was confusing. Then, to my surprise, as if it was intended to serve as a cue, I had basically the same dream again last Saturday night when I drank too much and my equipment let me down. The dream woke me up, and the pieces suddenly came together. I knew then, finally, why I thought I recognized you. Your height, and build, and hair weren't an exact match, so that part of the picture was one of the reasons why I hadn't found a quick answer. If I'd paid more attention to your face—that is as a part of the total image, I'd have probably solved the puzzle before last weekend. You're it, Sarah Stuart. I'm firmly convinced of it. What you should also know is that the spirit always interceded in the midst of my dilemma and finally brought peace to my night. At the same time, it seemed to have something to say about my future. I'm very comfortable with the idea that you and the image are one and the same."

"That's absolutely incredible, Rob! But before your dream a week ago, when was the last time the presence came to you?"

"The one I remember vividly was when I stopped in Fiji on my way to Sydney. That was just before Christmas of sixty-nine. There was one after that, but I can't recall exactly when that was. It got tangled up with all the major problems I had last year."

"You don't strike me as the kind of person who's unhinged, so I'd like to believe that you did have the dreams and that I was in them."

"We've been together for a few weeks now, and I have to say that with having gotten to know you better, the similarity between you and the apparition really surprise me. The same smile, your gentle nature, the way you say things, it's remarkable. But it isn't the first time I've had foreshadows that were the portent of something that did happen."

"Other women?"

"No. The messages either preceded something unpleasant or they were involved with an idea for a product that didn't exist—or were about ones that could be improved on. Best example I can think of immediately is the Polaroid camera. I envisioned instant pictures. Problem is, I don't have enough confidence in my dreams to bet any money on them. But I'm fascinated by those that had the likeness of you in them and that you're here. And I'm really pleased that it's all come about."

"So am I, Rob Grant. It'll be interesting to see how the future you pictured turns out. I'm well along with my thinking that I'd like it to unfold the way you saw it."

"We can't get too far ahead of ourselves. There's a big difference in our ages. I'm a bona fide antique now. Remember?"

"Not an issue. I've already commented on that. You don't need to bring it up again."

"OK. At least not during the rest of October."

Back at the cottage, Rob built two fires. One in the fireplace, and the other in Sarah Stuart. Both flourished. As Sarah reached her finale, her measured breathing carried with it the sound of "Mmm. Mmm" when she exhaled. It told Rob that he'd made her happy, and it pleased him no end to know that. She'd said it earlier and was absolutely right. They were very good together.

On Sunday afternoon, the two of them got their things organized and packed. They pulled the new drapes closed, locked the door and were then on their way to Sheffield. Rob led the way in his new Mustang. Sarah followed in her big Ford Galaxie. He was eager to get home, so he drove at the speed limit, and a little more. Even with the slowdown going through Hartford, they made the 115 miles in just a little over two hours. At 71 Juniper Heights, Rob showed Sarah where to put her car in the visitor's parking area. After she'd pulled in, she got her little overnight bag, locked the car, and rode with Rob to his assigned space, number ninety-two, in the underground garage.

"I like this. It has to be great in summer heat, but even better when it's freezing cold."

"Has its benefits, but if I move to the lake, this'll all be over. It's one of the reasons I hate to give up this place."

They went up in the elevator and into number 710. Mike was waiting and wasted no time giving Sarah a hug. He was happy to see her.

"I also like the welcoming committee. How're you, Mike?"

"Good. Glad you could see our place before we move."

"It's a neat apartment. Now, let me see. The sofa can go on the wall facing the big slider, the TV will fit in the corner to the left of the fireplace, your easy chair will…."

"Wait a moment. You've only been here three minutes, don't even have your coat off, and already you're arranging my furniture up at the cottage?"

Mike was in hysterics. "I love it. You're somebody who can outdo my dad."

As Sarah was taking off her coat, she said, "I couldn't resist it, Rob. What I've seen so far is very nice. You have great taste, and most everything would fit. Could I see what else we have to move up to the lake?" Sarah broke into laughter. "I just wanted to see the look on your face. I'm just putting you on. Being aggressive isn't part of my nature at all, but my fantasy got out of hand when I saw your reaction. Seriously, you have a comfy home, and I can see why you don't want to give it up."

"Would you really like to see me move up to Colonial Trail and be a part of the Wilcox empire, or was all of that done in jest?"

The expression on Sarah's face suddenly turned serious. "Yes I would, Rob. I'd like it very much. I assumed you'd have figured that out by now. Guess my routine about arranging furniture and all that was coming from my heart. I saw you running in and out of Alan's office a few times, but we've really only known each other for five weeks. And it was just two weeks ago that we got to know each other even better." The meaning of that wasn't lost on Mike. "Short as it's been, it pleases me no end to look up at the hillside across the lake and see your cottage sitting on lots that were vacant until early last spring. Now I can hope that you might be around, at least on weekends. This time of year, if I saw smoke coming from the chimney, I'd feel good all over just knowing that you're there."

"Are you also telling me there's something going on inside that pretty head of yours?"

"I think it's reasonable to say that. A little early to tell, maybe, but I have some awfully warm feelings inside when you're around."

"Why don't we have a drink and talk about what it means. You like a dry white wine, and I think we can find something you'll like. Mike, there should be a bottle of Sauvignon Blanc somewhere in the fridge. The name on it is Mondavi. If you'll get it out, I'll open it."

"Sounds like you know something about wines."

"Not a whole lot. But there were three or four vintners in California that I thought bottled a pretty good wine, at least at the time I lived out there. They've probably gotten even better at it by now."

Rob made his dry Gibson, and poured the Sauvignon for Sarah. She took one sip and said, "This-is-*wonderful*! But anyone who got started drinking Boone's Farm apple wine would probably think bottled water was terrific." Sarah laughed. "Just kidding. I do know better, and this is something I would try to find at Yankee Spirits. They might just have it. The stuff I've been buying comes in a half-gallon jug. It's something I can afford."

Mike got bored with talk about wines, and went to his room to watch a football game.

"Now, let's get back to what you were saying about your feelings when I'm around. I'm intrigued, considering that we're still not all that well acquainted."

"I don't necessarily agree with that. We've come a long way, especially in the last two weeks. Sure, there are lots of things we haven't talked about, but they'll surface over drinks or dinner, or just lying in bed talking afterwards."

"Afterwards? After what?"

"If you can't figure that out, then I've failed to make a lasting impression. I have a complex, you know, and I may just cry." Sarah laughed.

"Wouldn't want you to do that. Go on."

"You asked me a serious question, and I'm trying to tell you how I feel about you, but you're making fun of me."

"It's a bad habit of mine. My apparition deserves better. I apologize. Really."

"That's better—or it will be if I could have another glass of your good wine."

"That one sure didn't last long. A refill comin' right up."

"You made an impression on me the very first time you came into Alan's office. You never saw me, or even looked in my direction. There was a woman in the car. She waited for you."

"If she had very dark hair, it was probably Kim. I still see her. She lives in town."

"Then you came back again with plans and talked with Alan. That went on for a while. The same woman was with you but took your car and was gone for quite a while."

"You were keeping tabs on me, it sounds like."

"Not really, but it's hard not to see what's going on. And you caught my eye. You're easy to look at—in case you don't know it."

"Kim left because she didn't like Alan undressing her with his eyes."

"You don't have to explain that to me. He's always left me alone, but a new face always gets his attention and I've seen women squirm a little."

"My friend, Helen, took him on and said that if he was finished she'd appreciate it if he'd put her clothes back on. She also told him that he wasn't getting any of her because she was all mine. That's close to what she said. Alan was utterly speechless."

Sarah laughed until her sides hurt. "I love it!"

"Helen's a New Yorker and good at give and take."

"Let's come back to me," Sarah said. "What I saw during your visits was a New York executive, or something like that. I'd never seen one before, at least that I could recall. I think panache is a word I'd like to use in some context to describe how you struck me. You showed me a great deal of it, and I was impressed. I still am. But, you're very human and the kind of lover some women could only hope to find, I imagine. Still, I see you as a complete person. You have a good sense of humor, and you're sensitive to other people's needs. I've seen that already. Just little things you do confirm it. We *are* new to each other, sure, but I've grown very fond of you, and I hope we can spend more time together. Sure, there's a lot I don't know about you. In fact I know practically nothing about your personal history, so I'd like you to give me some time to find out who you are—the guy inside, I mean. Would you do that?"

"If I move up to the lake, you probably wouldn't be able to get rid of me, and in the end I'd bore you to tears."

"Wrong! You're too complex for that to ever happen, at least anytime soon. I'm fascinated by the subject of you, and I want to get inside you and your head."

"Some of what you find won't necessarily be to your liking. I'm not a killer, or a wife beater, or a crook, but I have been married and divorced twice. How do you feel about them apples for openers?

"Big deal. I don't even want to know the reasons why the marriages didn't last. Given time, I'll make up my own mind about who and what you are. But I already have a fairly good idea about some of those things." Sarah smiled warmly.

"One of these days I'll share some of my stories with you. But not between now and when you leave tomorrow. The next twenty-four hours or so are set aside for you to get acquainted with us and the way we live. But first, we need to start thinking about dinner someplace. OK if Mike comes along?"

"I would hope so. He's part of the picture, too. Seems like a nice kid."

"You might not think that way if you'd seen what he did to my other Mustang about three months ago. I'll show you a picture sometime. It isn't pretty."

"Guess I said the wrong thing. He's been friendly and very polite, but I don't live with him every day like you do."

The three of them decided on Italian and went to dinner at La Taniére. It had been a while since they'd eaten there, but Rob found that the quality was still good. Not much change from the times they'd eaten there with Kate, he decided.

And, as was usually the case, it was also a time when Mike could get to know a new friend of his dad's. There wasn't but about a six year age difference between Sarah and Mike, so they had similar interests, up to a point. His music wasn't one of them. The best part of the exchange was that the two of them got along well, and it was unmistakable. That was important to Rob. If ever their relationship went any further, he didn't want there to be any friction between his companion and the boys.

After they'd gotten home, Mike surrendered Sarah to his dad and went to his room to watch what was left of a Sunday night hockey game.

"Nice evening, Rob. Mike sure has a lot of questions, not the least of them about us. I hope you weren't upset that I told him how I'm beginning to feel about you."

"I wasn't at all. He'll ask me later about what I think."

"And how will you answer him?"

"That I like being with you, that I have good feelings about us, but that we'll have to wait and see how things go. That'll take a while. I've been counted out twice, so I'm being cautious."

"I know. But isn't it time that you started telling me about you. My story, as you found out, is a relatively simple one."

Rob tried, as he'd done since the fall of sixty-eight, to make the summary of his forty-one and a half years as concise as possible. He was getting better at it: the rural upbringing on a small east-central Iowa farm, having been in the Navy during the Korean conflict, followed by university years at Iowa State, his professional life with Trident Aviation, Sentry Oil, and IMMCorp, the marriages, and failures, his problems with the boys, and where life stood on this tenth day of October.

Sarah's comment was that the highs and lows of his life, with a little polish, might be the stuff of a good novel. "I read several paperbacks during the summer and at least half of them didn't have that much substance to them," she said.

"Thanks for the idea, but I'm not a writer and wouldn't know where to begin. Probably at the end and work backwards." They chuckled.

But it was time to get comfortable, and that led to touching, and eventually to bed. It was late, and Mike had long ago said good night.

The bigger, comfortable bed made their union ever so much more enjoyable. Sarah, mindful that they weren't alone, softened her little squeak when she reached the summit of her mountain, but there was no doubt that she was entirely fulfilled. Rob's contribution left her nearly purring before they both slept with arms and legs entangled.

Their holiday Monday morning began with loving and then shifted smoothly to further talk about themselves, the weeks ahead, and where Rob saw his life headed.

"Which way do you think it'll go?" Sarah asked.

"In your direction, if you want to know what I feel inside. It isn't anything tangible, but I see a change coming. More hunch than anything else. What Wilcox outlined for me is tempting, even if I don't know much about his business. But I'm not apprehensive about a career change, the challenge that would be there, or being able to perform in a way that would satisfy him. And the fact that you'll be there has appeal of its own."

"To hear you say that I might play a part in your decision pleases me. More than that. I'm touched. It means that I do matter some."

"You do. Not much question about it. I wouldn't have asked you to come down if you didn't. And you'll have guessed correctly that there have been others here before you, but you mean more to me than just an overnight romp in bed. We could have confined our loving to the lake, and I might have asked someone else to keep me company last night. But it was important to me that you see where and how we live. The future? There might very well be something out there for us. Much too early to tell, though. If there is, this is one of the stepping-stones."

"When will I see you again?"

"Halloween weekend. I have to spend at least some of my time here making an effort to see if there's a place we can move to. Mike's in his last year, and it wouldn't be fair to move him into a new school at this stage."

"That's a long time between visits."

"I know. But it's an eighteen day wait for both of us, not just you."

"There isn't anyone else in my life, Rob. Just you. You've already said there are others in yours."

"Be patient, dear heart. Please? My crystal ball is beginning to clear and it's showing me that before long you could very well have things your way. By that, I mean starting in early January. Now, what I want to see is a big smile. It'll tell me that you like the sound of that." Sarah beamed.

Late in the morning, Rob and Sarah teamed up and made a big breakfast that was intended to hold them over until they had dinner. Even Mike was able to eat his fill.

At mid-afternoon, Sarah got everything together and Rob carried the little overnight bag she'd brought with her down to the Galaxie. Both of them looked just a little bit sad, Mike told his dad later in the day.

"I'm going to miss you, Rob Grant. I've enjoyed our weekend together so much. Thank you for having me down. I don't suppose I'll see your place again. It's depressing to think that because it's in a good location and very comfortable."

"It does hurt some. But about our weekend, there's always so much to look forward to at the beginning, and then the contrast at the end of the three days. You go back to your classroom, and I get ready to move from one place to another. Two places, actually. The first is to new offices. We've been kicked out of our Lexington Avenue and Thirty-sixth Street space because Newcombe didn't pay the rent, so we have to vacate during the week that ends with Halloween. And you know the story on the apartment. It's these two things that are keeping me around until the afternoon of the twenty-ninth. I'll be thinking about you, Sarah Stuart, and we will talk. And you'll find this amazing. Letters from Massachusetts *do* get delivered here." Sarah needed to laugh about something. And she did.

They held each other, kissed tenderly, and then Sarah, with a good-bye wave, was on her way back to Hampden Lake, Mass. Rob had that empty feeling inside as she drove off. Given how early it was in their relationship, it was becoming clear that he liked her more than he was willing to admit.

It wasn't until just about dark that Rob stirred up a drink and then phoned Kim.

"I'm glad you're home. Can I come over? I need a hug."

"Sure can. I'm having a drink. Join me."

"I may just do that. I haven't had one all week. Problem is, I can't stay very long. Be wonderful to see you, though. Been too long."

They had their drink, and a good visit with some loving hugs, and the promise of two Friday to Monday weekends together coming up. Kim said she could hardly wait.

On Tuesday morning, and back at work, Paul Lenard made his presence felt by calling a 9:00 a.m. meeting that included everyone who worked with Doug Newcombe.

"We have a new corporation in place and new officers. All of it takes effect on Monday the first of November. You know most of the details already. I'm simply confirming it. The company is called Newcombe Associates, Grant, Engelhardt, Ltd. I'm the president, Rob is executive vice president, and everyone else is a vice president of one sort or another. I'll be overseeing operations so that we don't run aground again, have to file for protection from our creditors and be forced to move again in six months. You get the picture. NAGE, as we're going to call it among ourselves, will be run like a business. The objective is to make money."

Lenard set the tone and the die was cast. Rob liked his style!

Helen spent her partial weeks at number 710, Kim continued to help Rob with his apartment search, and she accompanied him after they got organized on Saturday and Sunday mornings. And then on the last week of the month, NAGE, and the people who were part of the company, all pitched in, packed boxes and helped get situated at 150 East Thirty-fifth Street, also home to William F Buckley's *National Review*. They were good quarters and better suited to the executive search business. There was the feel of professionalism that the old address lacked.

On the twenty-ninth, after having put in some long days, Rob left their new quarters in time to make the 3:30 train to Sheffield. At Eddie's Garage, where his Mustang was parked, he waved at Maurie, the lot attendant, pulled onto I-95, and then headed for his cottage and Sarah Stuart. He was really looking forward to seeing her. Traffic wasn't too heavy yet, so he made good time. It wasn't much after 6:30 when he drove into the parking area behind Wilcox's building. When Sarah heard a car pull up, she looked out the window. Seeing that it was Rob, she smiled broadly, and ran out the door to give him a bear hug.

"I am *so* glad to see you. For the first time in I don't know how long, I remember what it's like to really miss somebody. You feel good. Take me upstairs and love me. Now. Will you please? I'm in my needy phase and very ready for you."

"Nobody here?"

"Nobody here. They're both gone until Sunday evening. And the office is closed for the season, so tonight we can pull out the sofa bed and not get claustrophobia—or sore knees."

"I'm your captive stud. Lead me to your bed and the pleasures that await therein."

And love they did. Sarah went to a towering peak very quickly, and she stayed there until Rob answered her appeal to surrender what he'd saved for her. Round one came to a very satisfactory conclusion. He discovered that her little squeak had matured some during the last eighteen days. Afterwards, they both laughed about the change.

"Your little squeaky thing has taken lessons from somebody. It's an adult now."

"No lessons. No practice. It's just a body that's very glad to be attached to yours."

"That was exciting. Maybe we can try it again before I have to go back on Sunday."

"Why not after we come back from dinner, and tomorrow morning, et cetera, et cetera, et cetera? But tomorrow night we have to get through a party here first. It's to celebrate Halloween. Complete with costumes.

Mostly people from school, but you're invited, of course. Do you have something to wear?"

"I don't do costumes, so you'll have to put up with faded Levis, a jacket to match, and a pair of elegant Lucchese boots. I'll show up as an undersized urban cowboy."

Sarah smiled. "You'll do. There are a couple of people I'll want you to meet. More about that later. I'm famished. Could we go eat?"

"What do you have in mind?"

"Lodge be OK? They also have good baked stuffed shrimp, and a great sirloin strip."

"Fine with me. That's our place, remember?"

They had their drinks and dinner and got caught up on the last two and a half weeks. Rob talked about the new steadying hand at NAGE and how his discipline had already made a difference in the attitudes of everyone involved. Even Newcombe seemed to be glad that someone else was responsible for steering the ship. He'd finally acknowledged that he was more artist than businessman. Lenard was completely the opposite. His broad management experience was serving them extremely well.

Sarah's weekdays at school were routine, she told Rob, other than the fact that she suddenly found herself roped into contract negotiations with the school board. She had some strong feelings about what was fair for the teachers, but the meetings had turned out to be less than cordial. A couple of the board members were parents, and she soon discovered that they were entirely different people than when they came in for their regular parent-teacher conferences. She was getting her first look at the real world of being a teacher in public education. It wasn't all that it appeared to be from the outside looking in. There were long hours during the week, and often times lesson plans and grade reports to put together on weekends. Now in her third year, Sarah didn't want to hear criticism about their summer vacations. Rob agreed. It didn't take long for him to learn that being a conscientious teacher was a very demanding job—one *he* wouldn't want. By the time they got to June, they'd damn well earned the time off.

On Saturday morning, Rob moved the new stove and refrigerator to the spots where he wanted them and then turned them on. They worked! It was a start. They also took time to run back to Sears and find little drapes and curtains for the other windows. The balance of the day was spent putting up the rest of the hardware and then hanging what they'd bought. It was beginning to feel a little bit like home.

"Kind of exciting, isn't it?" Sarah said to Rob. "By the time you put carpet down and move your furniture in, it will be a home." She laughed.

"There you go again. But you're close to the truth, I'm beginning to think. I've got about a month to find out if you're right. I haven't had much success finding something decent in Sheffield that's affordable. I'll know by the week after Thanksgiving what's next. It may be that I'll be forced to move here. But if that's what makes sense, I won't fight it. I've run the numbers, and from a financial standpoint this is the path of least resistance. I'd feel better about it if I had a couple of other options and could choose what I thought was best. The way it's beginning to look, I won't have that luxury. Even my job choices are down to NAGE or Wilcox. But at least I'm keeping busy and making a little money."

At the end of the afternoon, Rob and Sarah got ready for the Halloween party at Wilcox's. Each promised the other before they left that they wouldn't drink too much. Making certain that the after-hours part of their weekend would be completely satisfying had taken on greater meaning since they hadn't seen each other for eighteen days.

Once the party began, Rob saw that people took their costumes seriously. One came in a Colonist's uniform, complete with tricorn. Since the man was tall and had a heavy beard, he looked like the genuine article. Others were dressed as a soapbox, a pirate, a bag of gold coins, a princess, a tramp, a bat, a witch, and so on. Sarah's colleagues, and their spouses or companions, had really gotten into the spirit of the evening. Because of it, both Rob and Sarah felt a little bit out of place. But after drinks were poured once, twice, and maybe a third time, it really didn't matter. That was probably the case right from the start. Then, as they were circulating, Sarah finally came across Derek Erwin and his wife, Julia.

"Rob, these are two of the people I wanted you to meet." Sarah introduced them. Derek looked to be a guy about his age, Rob thought. He also seemed to be full of life. His wife was more reserved. As they got into an extended conversation, the four of them hit it off well. Then as the less than serious drinkers were beginning to drift off and head for home, Rob suggested that they grab a bottle of wine, a six-pack and go over to see his little cottage. They liked the idea and agreed.

"We have a lovely selection of cement blocks to sit on, but before we go let's make sure we have bottle openers and some plastic glasses. My place isn't very well equipped just yet."

At the cottage, Rob got a nice fire going, turned on his portable radio and managed to find a soft music station in Worcester. As it turned out, they enjoyed a little after-Halloween party of their own. The Erwins were fun people to be around, and they apparently liked the idea of getting better acquainted with Sarah and this guy from New York that she had in tow. Julia was the administrative assistant at the elementary school where Sarah taught and Derek was head of the science department at the local high school. He and Sarah hadn't gotten to know each other all that well since his building was regional and several miles distant. They talked on until nearly midnight. While they were at it, they made plans to have dinner together in mid-November. It was an enjoyable evening, and it would continue to be so since neither Rob nor Sarah drank enough to cool their passion *or* diminish the pleasure of their loving after the Erwins left. From nearly any perspective, their weekend was turning out to be a big success.

Early on Sunday afternoon, Rob got his things together, made coffee, and then he and Sarah stood at the serving bar and chatted before he started back to Sheffield.

"I just remembered that we have a teacher's convention coming up," Sarah said. "I have Friday off. Any interest in having some company?"

"Love to. Does that mean you'd come down on Thursday night, or what?"

"I wouldn't drive down. My bright idea is to take the train into New York on Friday morning in time to have lunch with you. What do you think about that?"

"Be great fun! You could meet the people I work with. It'll be our first week in the new offices on East Thirty-fifth. Here. Let me give you my card. It has the new address and phone number on it."

Chatter at an end, and their coffee gone, Rob turned down the heat, and then got ready to lock up. Since Sarah hadn't driven over, he'd drop her off at the Wilcox building before he started home.

"Just one more thing," Rob said. "Your birthday is tomorrow, so I have a little something for you." Rob pulled a brightly wrapped package out from under the bar and handed it to Sarah.

"When I told you it was the first of November, I wasn't hinting that you should buy me a present. But it's sweet of you to remember. Looking at the shape of the package, can I guess what's in it?"

"I don't know if you *can*, but you *may*." Rob chuckled. "No. I'd prefer that you didn't ruin the surprise."

Sarah opened the box and found a bottle of Boone's Farm apple wine in it.

The expression on her face was priceless. "Oh, *no*! Are you serious, Rob?" She was in stitches.

"I thought it was your favorite." He joined in the laughter.

"Not since my college days, when we couldn't afford anything else. I don't believe you."

Then Rob reached under the bar and pulled out another beautifully wrapped box. "Well, just to show you that my heart's in the right place...."

"If it's another bottle of that apple stuff, I'm going to file for divorce."

She opened the second box and pulled up a bottle of 1966 Sauvignon Blanc from the California vintner, Beaulieu Vineyards.

"Ohhh, Rob. You shouldn't have. BV. This is *good* stuff! You and I will share it. When your kitchen is ready for me, I'll do lobsters some night. This will go perfectly with the meal. I'll leave the bottle here. It'll lure you back."

"You have a deal. See? Already you're making a move up here feel like it's the right thing to do."

"My plan wasn't supposed to be that transparent."

They got into Rob's Mustang and drove to the back entrance of the Wilcox building to drop Sarah off. He wasn't ready to leave her behind, but it was time that he started back to Sheffield.

"See you on Friday, dear heart. Let me know what train you'll be on so I'll know when to expect you."

"I'll call Penn Central while you're on your way home and either let you know tonight or tomorrow what time I'll get in.

They hugged, kissed warmly, and Rob was on his way down that same road that Sarah didn't like to see empty when he was out of sight. But there would be the long weekend again. She was already looking forward to it, because this man was beginning to occupy a good many of her thoughts and an even more important place in her heart.

Rob had no sooner walked in the door and said hi to Mike when Kim called and asked if she might come over.

"Absolutely. Let's have a drink and dinner, if you have coverage."

"I don't, but I'll have a glass of wine and a hug if you have one to spare."

"Plenty of them. Just give me your measurements and I'll have one tailor-made for you."

"The biggest available, and I'll see you shortly."

Before she arrived, Rob called Sarah to tell her that he was home OK. He knew she worried some about his trips back and forth.

"Sweet of you to call. And I have some news for you."

"You're pregnant?"

They laughed, and Sarah said, "If you weren't fixed, I sure would be by now. No, that's not even close. I have the train information for Friday. I get into Penn Station at 12:25."

"Take a taxi, and I'll meet you in front of our building shortly after that. We can make lunch by about one o'clock, I figure. See you then."

"I'm already thinking about it—and you. See you on Friday."

Kim was in need of a hug, and she confirmed it by hanging on for a moment to let the warmth sink in.

"I can't stay long, but you've been on my mind, and I just wanted to be close to you for a little while."

"Let me get you that glass of wine."

Sitting close to Rob, Kim said she was getting discouraged about the rental situation. "I haven't gone looking for rentals very often in the past, but when I have I've never seen anything like this. I'm afraid of losing you. With nearly all your weekends at the lake, I already have, sort of."

"Don't get down yet, love. I've got about another five weeks before I have to make a decision. There are times when I feel like you're doing more than I am. That's not right."

"It's my town, and I don't mind at all. What helps you helps me, that is if I can find something for you. But it's like nobody is moving. Either that, or there are a lot of people making better money now. You already know what's happened with the rents. Too bad I don't have any property to lease. It would be good supplementary income."

"Maybe I should be looking in Port Chesterfield, or maybe further east. I haven't done that so far."

"I did it for you, and the rents aren't any better down there than they are here. Going up toward Bridgeton didn't seem to help much either, and your commute would cost more. It's making me depressed. If you go up to the lake, something inside tells me that you won't have just moved, but that you'll be gone from my life."

"Don't give up, sweetheart. Let's hope for the best. You know I want to stay here. It's important to Mike, too."

"I know." They talked on for a while, and then Kim said, "I've got to go, Rob. Dad needs to get home, and I told him I wouldn't be long."

"We're in our new offices starting tomorrow. I'll call you after we've settled in."

Rob went to the garage with Kim. It bothered him to see genuine sadness in her eyes. For some reason, he was beginning to think that he probably looked the same way. It hurt to think about what was happening. Sheffield had gotten to feel like home, and Kim was part of the reason he felt comfortable here.

Helen's busy schedule cut into her evenings, so she spent just three nights with Rob. She was interested in knowing if he'd found a place to rent. If not, she could start getting excited about the possibility of having him move in with her at the start of the new year. But she knew Rob wasn't ready to give up on finding a local rental just yet, so his plans wouldn't be firm for at least another month. Part of Rob's dilemma was that, much as he liked Helen, he'd really prefer to spend his nights with

Kim, but she wasn't divorced yet, and hadn't even filed, so that kind of arrangement was out of the question.

At around a quarter of one on Friday, Rob went down to the front of their building and waited for Sarah. Her taxi pulled up minutes later, and he jumped in.

"Forty-eighth and Fifth, driver," Rob said. Then he gave Sarah a hug. "We're about to have ourselves a little test. The place where we're going to have lunch is P. J. Murphy's and Paddy, the owner, has an incredible memory. I haven't been there in about two years, so we'll see if he's as good as I remember him to be."

He was. When they walked through the door, Paddy said, "Hey! Look who's here. Welcome back, Rob. Where have you been keeping yourself?" They shook hands.

"Here and there. Paddy, meet Sarah from Massachusetts."

"Sarah, my pleasure. You sure do get around, Rob," Paddy said.

"Things in my life have been completely rearranged. You remember Marianne?"

"The pretty Italian girl with the million dollar smile? Sure do."

"She died of leukemia a year ago last June. Only twenty-five. We were engaged, so it took quite a while to rebound. It was rough. Then my company on Wall Street changed direction and I was out job hunting longer than I wanted to be. I'm in the executive search business now with a guy named Newcombe."

"I'm terribly, terribly sorry to hear about your Marianne. She was a lovely young woman, as I remember her. But, Newcombe? I know him. He gets rowdy after a couple of drinks."

Rob laughed. "That's him. See, Sarah, you come back here in five years and this guy will call you by name. And more. I told her about you, Paddy. But this may be close to my last visit. The way it looks, I'm about to move up to Massachusetts. If I do, it'll mean a drastic career change. This young lady may figure in my plans at some point."

"Well, I'll say this for you Rob. You still know how to pick 'em. Now, I need to get you to a table. If I have a couple of minutes, you can bring me up to date."

"Good meeting you, Paddy," Sarah said. "And thank you for the nice compliment."

"You're welcome, Sarah. I meant it."

When things slowed down, Paddy did come by to visit. In fact, he sat at Rob's table and listened to a quick rundown on what had been going on in his life.

"Life's been a bumpy road for you, Rob. The story about your boy is one that no parent wants to hear, but it looks like you're holding up. Maybe this young lady can help keep things on track from now on." Paddy took her hands in his. "This is a good man, Sarah. Look after him. Now, I've got to go back to work. Great to talk with both of you. Rob, your drinks are on me."

"Thanks very much, Paddy. We'll see you on the way out."

"I'm impressed, Rob. In a way, I can see why you hate to give up New York. It's been your business home for almost five years, and you've obviously gotten to know a lot of people during that time. After a while, you get comfortable with your surroundings."

"I suppose so. Hadn't really thought about it quite that way, but you're right. I'll miss some of the people I've gotten to know."

On their way out, Rob and Sarah said good-bye to Paddy and thanked him for the free drinks. "When we're back this way, you know this is the one stop we'll make if we're hungry. Maybe even if we aren't."

"If I don't see you again, good luck with wherever life takes you. You've been a good customer and a special friend. I wish they were all like you. Sarah. Nice meeting you, and if you become partners, I wish you all the best."

"Thanks, Paddy. You're one in a million," Rob said. "Look after yourself."

When they got out on the street, Sarah said, "I've got a lump in my throat. That was a man and a lunch I'll never forget. I'm touched by his sentiments and what you'll be giving up if you come to work for Wilcox. It'll never be the same for you."

Back at the office, Rob introduced Sarah to the people he worked with—and to Diane, who doubled as receptionist and secretary. There wasn't much for Sarah to do while everyone was at work, so from her little overnight bag she pulled out a paperback copy of Stanley Elkin's book, *The Dick Gibson Show*, and continued reading until Diane had a few minutes to chat with her. With dissimilar backgrounds, they had little in common and the end of the day arrived just in time to save them both. As Sarah and Rob got ready to leave for Grand Central, all of the other NAGE principals said good-bye and wished them a good weekend.

On Saturday afternoon, things on Juniper Heights were relatively quiet, so Sarah tackled schoolwork that she'd brought with her. It needed her attention before Monday, so she worked on that for a couple of hours. Mike had gone off with friends, so while Sarah was correcting papers, Rob decided it was time to introduce Sarah to his mother's chili soup. The season for it had begun. She gave it high marks, and said the recipe was a must have. Rob wrote it out for her. Afterwards they went down to the Nova Theatre to see *The French Connection*, which was now in its fourth week and still pulling in big audiences. They agreed it was a good movie.

After a night of loving, and a late breakfast, Rob and Sarah made tentative plans for her to come back on the nineteenth, the eve of Mike's eighteenth birthday. Over a second helping of soft scrambled, Mike asked her, by coincidence, if she'd come down and be a part of his birthday celebration. Sarah said she'd be honored and quickly agreed. Then at mid-afternoon, Rob took her to the station to board the 2:58 train to Springfield. By the time she picked up her car and made the drive east to Hampden Lake, it would be 6:30 or so. "Riding the train will give me time to finish up what I have left to do. I'll be all caught up and ready for my fifth graders in the morning," she said. "The weekends sure go fast when I'm around you."

"It was the schoolwork that helped make it so."

"Ouch! I'll remember that when I come back in two weeks."

"Mike won't let you work on his birthday anyway. And I agree with that."

With hugs and a tender kiss to help sustain her during the trip home, Sarah boarded the train north, this one called *The Senator*. She waved from the window and then was gone. Rob never liked good-byes, and the ones involving Sarah were now getting just a little bit harder to deal with. Something of hers had attached itself inside him. She was bright, lively, passionate, and so much more attractive since she'd cut off her long, stringy hair. No longer a flower child, if ever she'd been one, she now had the appearance of a young, professional woman. Her warmth and her gentle nature, which Rob knew were there right from the beginning, were traits that appealed to him. Very much so. And her beauty within was also easy to recognize. It was too obvious to be missed.

Kim had gotten into the habit of calling late on Sunday afternoon, and today was no exception.

"Just wondering if you have any of that good Marzano red wine left. I could use a glass right about now. The sun has long since gone over the yardarm as we say Down East."

"Bring your body over here, and I'll hug it. At least once."

"With an invitation like that, I'll be right over. I planned ahead and have a sitter to look after the boys for a little while."

Rob and Kim had their hugs, and a glass of wine, and made plans to spend next Saturday night together. They didn't talk much about rentals because there was very little to add to what they'd said a week ago. Then as good fortune would have it, Mike went out for a little while and the two of them made good use of their time alone. The wide smile Kim wore going home replaced the anemic one she'd had when she came in. It warmed Rob's heart to see her spirits improved. Their time alone, she said, was exactly what she needed to help her get through to Saturday.

The week at NAGE went by quickly. But before everyone left on Friday, Paul Lenard called a general meeting to begin at 9:00 a.m. on Monday morning. If he said nine o'clock, that was exactly what he meant.

When Monday came, everyone was there on time.

"Starting on January 7, it's a Friday, we'll start having breakfast here with your primary contacts at client companies. Normally, that'll be one person. The idea will be to have them talk about his or her company, and their anticipated manpower needs. We'll propose ways we can help them meet their requirements more effectively than anyone else they work with. Be prepared to talk about how we can do that. Maybe it's past searches or people you know who can lead us to good candidates. And I'll want whatever other ideas you may have. We have some very capable search people sitting here, and my assessment is that we should have seen better results through October. Parallel with better production with existing clients is the need to develop new ones. The only one of you who has done well in that regard is Rob. He added several companies to our client base when he came aboard, and two of those have regularly turned to us to fill openings. I might add that it's no doubt helped that he knows the young lady at IMMCorp pretty well." That got a soft chuckle from those around the room. Except for Rob. "Seriously, use whatever tools you must to get results." Hearty laughter. "Bad choice of words in this instance, but I expect you to utilize every one of the resources you have at your disposal to find new clients. I'll meet with each of you individually to get your ideas on how we, together, might be able to help expand our list of clients, and ultimately add to our net revenues. If you have questions, we can address them when we meet. The Thanksgiving holiday is coming up, but let's see what we can do to finish off the year in grand style during the approximately five weeks we have left to get it done."

Rob had a few searches underway that showed promise. They were all mid-level, but, if they resulted in placements, the fees would certainly put food on the table *and* pay his moving expenses when the time came. Still, there'd little extra for Christmas. Another less than glowing year-end outlook coming up, he thought. This one was made worse by the eviction notice and the uncertainty of what his address would be in early January.

Helen called at mid-afternoon to say that because of her work schedule, and the Veteran's Day holiday on Thursday, she proposed that they make other arrangements for the coming week.

"If you can work out something for Mike, I'd like you to spend a couple of nights with me for a change. The thought that you may not be up on Juniper Heights, or even in Sheffield, that much longer is beginning to bother me. I love your place, but you'll be dismantling it before long. Sad to think about. Could you stay here Wednesday and Thursday evenings? We'd have the holiday together. I'd really like that."

"We're supposed to work part of the holiday, but I'm pretty well caught up. I should be able to check in and then take off. You're a favorite because of the placements we've made with you, so if you came along we could call it a business meeting." They chuckled at the idea. "And about Mike, he seems to like staying with friends who have a Mom around. This is the same guy who said it didn't matter. Maybe it's because he gets fed better. Whatever, I know he's going to be at Regina's on Wednesday, so I'm sure it won't be a problem if he stays over another night. Usually isn't, but I'll have him ask anyway."

"Be wonderful to spend the day with you in the city. But you know that I'm excepting to have you around full time starting in January."

"Another three to four weeks, and I'll know what's next. As things stand now, you own me, at least on about the same schedule you've been on when you've come out to Sheffield."

"You know I'd like it to be permanent."

"Yep, but I still have two sons, and property in Massachusetts now that I have to think about. Nothing seems to be set in cement, but I think you can expect me to exchange your clothes at my place for some of my stuff to hang in your closet, at least for a while."

"Even that sounds good. But Stan's calling, sweetheart. See you on Wednesday at about six."

"Right around then, I should think. Bye, love."

Chapter Ten

On the Thursday before Mike's birthday, Sarah called Rob to give him details on her arrival at Sheffield Station the following evening.

"I can make the 4:30 train in Springfield, but it goes straight into New York so I have to change in New Haven. No problem. I'll be in at 6:59."

"Since we're going out on Saturday night, I'll feed you at home. I've laid in a supply of white wine, so you can have a sip or two before we eat."

"A sip or two? By Friday night I usually need more than that. You haven't been paying attention to how much I like the kind of wine you pour in my glass."

"Not to worry. I guarantee that you won't run out."

"My kind of guy." Sarah laughed. "See you tomorrow night."

"I'm ready for you."

"And I'm ready for you to have me."

Sarah's train was just about on time, and after a separation of almost two weeks they were happy to see each other.

"Been trying to figure out why it is I missed you so much this time," she said following a big hug. "Guess you're getting to be more than just important. Makes me feel good, both inside and out, when we finally get together again."

"And I'm really glad you're here. There are people I know that Mike could have invited, but he wanted you to make the trip down. Maybe I should pay attention to his reasons. Ask him over dinner tomorrow. We both might be surprised. But to be fair to you, and speaking for myself, I'm delighted that you could make it. Bring any schoolwork with you?"

"No." Sarah laughed softly. "I learned my lesson last time."

"So, teachers have lessons, too." Rob chuckled. "Great. The weekend is ours and I don't have to share you with any fifth graders."

"Not a one, and I think we both like the idea of that. I'm sure we can figure out some way to occupy our time." Sarah showed Rob an impish smile.

"First thing I have to do is get you fed. You liked mother's chili soup so much that I thawed some I'd saved from two weeks ago. Not as good that way, but it still sticks to your ribs."

"Good night for it. I did snack on the train into New Haven, but I'm hungry again."

They ate, talked about the past two weeks and were about ready to start for bed when Mike came in. That extended visiting hours for another forty-five minutes or so because they were pleased to see each other and had things they wanted to talk about. Sarah could always come up with the kinds of questions Rob wouldn't think of, so she was good at getting people to open up. No doubt that it was one of the things Mike liked about her. That he invited Sarah, and not Kim, or Helen, to be a part of his birthday celebration was something Rob couldn't quite figured out. And Mike wasn't much help in that regard. Maybe one day he'd be able explain why.

Rob and Sarah spent part of their Saturday doing some shopping. Afterwards they were contented to just sit and enjoy each other's company. When Mike was finished with the laundry, he went off to visit friends and, as it turned out, collect birthday gifts. He came home with a fair amount of loot.

"Looks like I don't need to give you anything. You did all right out on the street. Stop any cars or carry a sign advertising that you're eighteen today?"

Mike laughed. "Nope. Didn't have to. Look at all this stuff. Tom had a little party and a bunch of people showed up. I was surprised. I've got more friends than I thought."

"Hang on to 'em, Mike," Sarah said. "They can be really important to you as you get older."

"I know. If we move away, it'll be nice to stay in touch and then visit whenever we can. I learned that about the kids I knew in California. Thing is, I don't know where some of them are now. And they were guys, mostly, that I liked a lot."

The drinking age in Connecticut was twenty one. Mike said he'd like to have a beer with his dinner, so Rob agreed, reluctantly, that they'd eat across the state line in New York where eighteen was legal. With driver training, Mike now had his license and could prove that he was of age.

The restaurant someone had recommended for dinner was in Port Chesterfield, so they took I-95 to the Greenwood exit and then drove down U.S. 1 until they found it—a steakhouse called Chuck's. The dark woods and booths or tables with little islands of light suited Rob. Equally important, the steaks they saw on people's plates looked tasty, and the aroma coming from prime grade beef was mouthwatering. All three of them decided that their appetites were ready for what they saw being served.

None of them spent much time with the menu. Steaks of one kind or another, the salad bar, and a baked potato with sour cream and chives were ordered right after they'd told their cute little waitress what they wanted to drink. It was white wine for Sarah, always, a dry Gibson over ice for Rob, always, and a beer for Mike. He got carded, of course. It gave him high pleasure to show the waitress that he was eighteen. She smiled and wished him a happy birthday.

"She's a doll," Mike said.

"Well, you're eighteen now. Maybe you can have her for dessert," Rob suggested. Mike cackled.

"I don't know that she'd agree to that. It's probably a good idea if I don't ask. But she's really neat."

"There are plenty of them around, so stick with your high school girls. This one is older than she looks. Her hands give her away."

When food was served, they all dug in as if they hadn't eaten in days. Still, there was time for chatter and various questions from Sarah about what Mike planned to do after graduation. Like a good many teenagers, he wasn't quite sure. The only thing definite in his mind was that he didn't plan on going to college. He recognized his limitations. A trade school of some kind, or maybe the military, would suit him better, he said. Rob couldn't disagree. He was, after all, the parent who signed his report cards.

The birthday dinner was a big hit! Mike enjoyed having Sarah at the table, and he told her so. Twice. With dessert, Rob handed Mike a birthday card and said, "No gifts this year. I'm out of bright ideas now that you've reached this point in your life, so this will have to do."

Mike opened a silly card with a furry animal on it, and then pulled out a fifty dollar bill. His eyes got as big as saucers, and all he could say was, "Oh, Dad, thank you very much. After what I did to your other Mustang, I, well, awww, you know what I mean."

"I'll not forget it, and neither will you. But life goes on, and at some point we have to stop looking back."

When they got home, Rob called Greg before lights out so he could wish Mike a happy birthday. When the two of them got off the phone, Greg asked Rob what their new address would be starting in January. "Still too early to tell, but it's beginning to look like it'll be Hampden Lake, Mass." They talked for a couple of minutes longer, and then Rob promised to let him know, probably in about two weeks what his decision would be.

The call at an end, Mike thanked Rob and Sarah for a birthday that he expected he'd always remember. Next on his agenda was to call his friends to tell them about his dinner, including the legal beer, and also to thank them again for their gifts.

After hugs and a good night from Mike, Rob and Sarah were left alone to hold each other and to share something that could only be characterized as affection. They soon took their needs to Rob's bed and loved passionately, after which Rob felt for perhaps the first time that what they'd shared had satisfied more than just a physical need. Sarah trusted her instincts and had no doubt that his feelings for her were deepening. But as was her manner, she'd let Rob discover, in his own good time, the true meaning of the growing affection she was certain he now felt.

And they both awakened on Sunday morning knowing they'd crossed a threshold of sorts. The sensation was foreign, at least to Rob, since there were none of the "too much, too soon" thoughts that had troubled him over the past three years. This was entirely new, and there was something genuine about his feelings. At least he was beginning to think that way.

Rob and Sarah put a late breakfast together, and then felt the need to talk about their situation and their relationship. Mike knew they wanted time to themselves and went off to watch an NFL game on TV with his friend Phil.

"We seem to have come a long way in a fairly short time," Rob heard himself saying. He'd used those same words before—specifically with Kate three years ago. But this time they seemed to take on a different kind of meaning. For some reason, it *wasn't* too much, too soon, but the pace at which his fondness for Sarah had evolved made him more curious than apprehensive. There was something at work here that was unique. With his other relationships, he'd felt it was crucial to know someone for at least a year so that he could get his bearings. Marianne was the exception, but they'd worked together. In this case, he considered that maybe the dreams counted. They did go back fully two years. And more.

Sarah responded to Rob's comment by saying, "Not, really. You've convinced me that we've known each other, or at least you've known me, since sixty-nine. We're just filling in the gap."

"I'm assuming we'll have a chance to do more of that soon. I can't see any other conclusion than when we get to January that we'll be moving up to the lake. Unless I come up with a big placement or two soon, I won't be able to handle a first and last month's rent, plus another as a security deposit, the cost of moving, and then the mortgage payment on the cottage, too. Looking back, it may have been the wrong decision to build it. But then, there wasn't any way I could plan on the cost of having to replace the Mustang and then getting the eviction notice. Like it or not, I'm almost forced into moving up to the lake in about six weeks. Not that it's bad, but the timing is wrong. I'll still have to commute into New York for a while. It'll mean working two jobs. Manhattan during the week, and then Hampden Lake on weekends. You won't see much of me—except when I get ready for bed." They both laughed about that. A touch of levity was in order.

"If you'll let me weekend with you, I can help out. Maybe do the shopping and get the laundry done. You know, the little things that need doing. I'd like to think that I'm starting to be a part of your life, or at least your routine. I care about you, a lot, in case you hadn't noticed."

"I've noticed. And it's mutual. But I don't want you to feel like you have to be my domestic and an errand runner."

"You don't seem to understand. I'd love it if I could look after you and share the load. Does that explain how I feel?"

"Doesn't leave much room for doubt or questions. But you're too good for me, and I'm too old for you."

"Promise me something, Rob. Don't make comments like that again. Please? Neither point is valid, and it really bothers me that you're still making an issue of it."

"OK. I'll let it rest for the time being."

"No. Just forget it. I'm asking you in the nicest way I can."

"You're being tough with me—in a very gentle way, that is."

"There isn't any need to put yourself down. I don't like it when you do that. It's out of character."

"Now you're being a teacher. But I guess it's my turn for a lesson."

"I'd like to see us do something with what's off to a good start. I'm willing to be there for you and help out on the cottage end. I could also keep your bed warm on weekends if that's of any interest. In New York, you're on your own, but I won't pry."

"With the cold weather already here, a bed warmer has lots of appeal." They both smiled.

"I don't suppose you'll be coming up next weekend. What about the week after?"

"We're having Thanksgiving with Regina again, but I'll be up on the fourth. Actually I'll drive up on the afternoon of the third. Any interest in dinner?

"You already know my answer, so why ask? It's time to go back to the Oxen Pub, I think."

"Good idea. But you need to get your things together if you're going to make your usual train home."

"You know I really want to stay longer, but I have to get back and work on the school stuff that I didn't bring with me this time. Glad I left it there. We've had a much better weekend. What makes me sad is that this is probably the last time I'll be here before you move. I know you hate to give it up, and I'm going to miss it, too."

At the station, Rob and Sarah held each other and were still hanging on when the train pulled in.

"See you on the third," Rob said.

"I'm spending Thanksgiving with Mom, but we'll probably eat at Gram's house this year. It's a long weekend, and I'll call you from

Worcester while I'm there. Mom's seen your picture and knows who you are now."

"Have a wonderful Thanksgiving, sweetheart. See you a week from Friday."

"You too, my babe. And I'll be ready to give you lots of hugs on the third. Drive carefully. For me?"

"I will. Promise."

A hug, a warm kiss, a wave, and Sarah was gone again. This time, it *really* bothered Rob to see her go. "Maybe moving up to the lake isn't such a bad idea after all," he muttered.

When Rob got home, he was lonely and depressed. He decided it was his turn to call Kim. He needed company. A telling sign of sorts.

"I was just about to call you and see if you and Mike wanted to come over for dinner," Kim said.

"Mike's off at Phil's watching football. I probably ought to stick around to see if he comes home anytime soon."

"Well, if we can't eat together, maybe I could come over after we do."

"I'd like that. Let you know if Mike shows up. I'll call you a little later, in any case."

Mike called and said he would eat at Phil's house but would be home afterwards. Rob fixed himself a drink and than made a sandwich. He wasn't hungry, so it didn't matter what he ate. Kim called, sensed that Rob was in the dumps, and showed up to keep him company.

"Looks like the move's got you down," Kim said. "I don't blame you. And I'm not much help because I don't like what I see out there on the horizon."

"Just stay next to me for a while. That'll help. Maybe it'll work for both of us."

Kim did sit close, and then Mike came home. She didn't ask about his birthday, and it was just as well since it would have been hard to explain. Mike knew that and kept away from the subject. Kim stayed until about 10 o'clock, and when Rob went with her to the garage, they hugged in a way that said they both had a feeling that their days together were numbered. After he waved good-bye, Rob went back to number 710 with misty eyes. Kim had been an integral part of his life for more than two years and seeing their relationship come to an end was something he didn't want to face. Sarah was important, yes, but she didn't yet have the permanent place in his heart that Kim did. With Marianne laying claim to another part of it, he was running out of pieces to share with anyone else. Rob hadn't been this depressed in nearly eighteen months.

It was a short week for most people—other than banks, restaurants, and retail businesses. As had been the case since sixty-eight, Regina suggested that Rob and Mike come for Thanksgiving dinner, and they had no reason to decline. She always turned out a good meal, and their holiday dinners had been pleasant. Rob had told Regina about the possibility of the move to Massachusetts, so once again she suggested that they come over the night before. A little excitement, in addition to the turkey and fixings, seemed like a good idea. He expected the same offer to be there at Christmas. It would be her way of wanting to say good-bye.

Thanksgiving eve, and the day itself were enjoyable. Rob and Regina finally had an adult relationship, but she didn't want him back under her roof any more than he wanted to be there. Late in the afternoon, he thanked her for a great meal. And she thanked him for the treats the night before and again at first light. She showed him her crooked little smile to confirm that she meant it.

Kim filled the rest of Rob's weekend, and they made it a happy time, in spite of the fact they expected that it would be one of the remaining few they'd spend together. When she left on Sunday afternoon, it was hard for both of them, but they held on. There was still a chance that Rob would find a place in town that he could afford, so they hadn't given up hope, slim as it was.

When the week began, Helen spent a couple of days with Rob. As they talked about the weeks ahead, she made it clear that her focus was on getting her apartment ready for a new tenant early in January. He couldn't resist asking her if she had a new lover, but his question didn't go over well. That he might be moving in with her was far too important a matter to joke about.

And then on Friday, as Rob was about ready to leave for Grand Central and Hampden lake, he learned that he'd earned fees for two executive-level placements. They'd come at the right time because his bank account was getting close to what might be called threadbare. If an apartment became available at a rental rate that made sense, he could very easily afford the deposits and the move. If not, he was out of options. By the end of next week, he would have to make the only decision open to him. It would mean a move to central Massachusetts and then, in all likelihood, the launch of a new career.

Sarah was excited when she saw Rob pull up behind the Wilcox building. She was out the door in a flash and delivered a hug that said exactly how she felt about him—and this moment together.

"Guess that means you're glad to see me again. How are you, dear heart?

"I'm *sooo* happy you're back! If you were edible, I'd take a bite."

"Easy. There are probably town laws that prohibit cannibalism and sensuous things like you suggested. Am I right?"

"Sensuous things? Ohh, I get it. You have a naughty mind, Rob Grant." Sarah grinned.

"What's for dinner?"

"Me! Now I'm being naughty, too. But we talked about the Oxen Pub. Is that still all right?"

"Sure is. That way we can eat meat and not get arrested. And I think we ought to change the subject before we get in trouble with the law for our language and the insinuations."

Sarah didn't bother to respond. She gave him another hug instead. That done, Sarah got her coat and they went on to Sturbridge for dinner, shared the events of the past two weeks and very much enjoyed just being back together again.

"Any progress on finding an apartment in Sheffield?" Sarah asked. "Or are you about to become my neighbor?"

"Last I heard, you suggested moving in and keeping house. But, no, there hasn't been anything new turn up. The other news is, I did get paid for a couple of *very* good placements, and I could handle something within reason. Problem is, the rental market seems to have gone beyond what I can afford on a regular basis. Next week is the end of the string, and then I have to decide what's next. A decision isn't quite what it is because I'm down to one choice, and you know what that is."

"I'm sorry, but I'm also glad. That's being selfish, I know. It's just that I really miss you now when you're there and I'm here. Does that tell you anything about how I feel about us?"

"There hasn't been much doubt about that since you were down for Mike's birthday. Up until then, it was mostly a matter of looking after our physical needs, but something happened two weeks ago. It was like we got inside each other, that there was more to us than doing well in bed. You felt the same thing, I think. Still, I'm a long way from committing to something permanent. As much as anything, it'd be the fact that we're almost from different generations. I know you don't want to hear it, and you come across as being older than your twenty-four years, but I have to be aware, as Marianne once put it, that you could be a widow by the time you're fifty."

"At fifty, I'd be in my prime. Then I could have another lover and a second exciting life."

"Not funny, dear heart. I don't want to be your training ground for someone else."

"I apologize, Rob. What I said was in extremely bad taste. Forgive me. Please?"

"Just this once. As punishment, you'll have to surrender your body to a pagan ritual later on this evening."

"Sounds exciting. Just name the time and place. I'll do my penance with pleasure. Sounds like it'll be more fun than anything else. If it's hedonistic, it's supposed to be." They laughed.

And it was pleasure from start to finish. Having loved until they were spent, they slept soundly until the sun was just barely peeking over the hills across the lake. It brought with it the smiles of two contented lovers.

With some extra money in his bank account, and the reasonable certainty that he'd be moving into the cottage soon, Rob invited Sarah to join him on Saturday afternoon to search for carpeting. And where else would they start? Sears, of course. It didn't take long. He found a short-shag carpet in deep gold that was generously sprinkled with medium and dark brown fibers that fit the bill. Sarah agreed. He had the dimensions and since they were having a carpet sale, he went for it. Installation date was January 14, a Friday. Rob told the salesman that he might have a couple of pieces of his own to be installed. That would cost extra, he was told, but since he had an account he'd be billed for the cost of the additional work.

On their way back to the cottage, Sarah said, "I like what you picked out. It'll be perfect with the natural woods and the dark brown cork you put on the fireplace wall. It'll be warm and cozy."

"Well, with the new curtains and drapes, we have privacy. And we can refrigerate food now, cook, and get our feet tickled by new carpet soon. We still don't have a bed, but there's no need to worry about that. Not much doubt that by this time next week, I'll be calling movers to give me estimates on what it'll cost to get our stuff up to Hampden Lake. You'll most likely have that new neighbor you've been hoping for."

"I still have in mind that maybe you'd want a guest on weekends. I can cook and sew on buttons. I'm also sensational with a broom."

"Good grief, it's absolutely everything a man dreams about nearly every night. You're hired."

"Not the kind of a arrangement I had in mind." Sarah giggled and squeezed Rob's arm in a loving way.

"Where are you taking me to eat tonight?"

"The cottage. If you'll stop at Wilcox's, I have a surprise for you."

"What have you been up to, teacher lady?"

"Just you wait. You'll see."

"In that case, I'll drive a little faster."

When they got to the Wilcox building, Sarah took him inside and pulled an old sheet off two new wooden stools. There was also a picnic basket with plastic plates and glasses, utensils, and some food for supper and tomorrow's breakfast. "Now we can sit at the bar and eat like we're halfway civilized. You notice there are two wine glasses and a jug of my favorite white wine. We're having a party tonight to celebrate your decision to be a neighbor—maybe more."

"You're too much, dear heart. This is really sweet of you. If you keep doing things like this, I may just want you around on weekends."

"That's the general idea. But you shouldn't figure it all out this early in the planning stage. Ruins all the other surprises."

"Such as?"

"Like saying I think it's fairly obvious that I'm in love with you."

"You're not supposed to tell me things like that over an old sheet and open picnic basket in a real estate office. That should happen later in the evening with glasses of wine in front of a crackling fire."

"Then let's go over to the cottage and create the proper mood. If you'll be in charge of the fire, I'll look after the wine."

"When was that ever any different?"

Sarah brought a pan and a couple of pots from the Wilcox kitchen, ones that were rarely used. "They'll never miss these. They're yours until the movers arrive with your stuff."

"You've got it all worked out in your pretty little head that I'll be here in about four or five weeks. Is that it?"

"Never any doubt. You see, I have this Haitian voodoo doll with pins stuck in it that's been helping me kill apartment deals in Sheffield. Notice how well it's worked so far?"

"That's hardly fair. I can't compete with witchcraft."

"You know I'm joking. I wouldn't presume to change the direction of your life, at least not that way. But it'll be wonderful having you here on weekends."

"I'm not excited about the long drive every Monday and Friday, if that's the way it works out. And for a time this summer, I'll be working seven days a week. Worse than being a doctor."

"You know I'll be all the help I can to lighten your load. Just see if I don't."

"Is that intended to be a declaration of support, or do I hear something that might be interpreted as having a sensual connotation?"

"Both. You'll probably need lots of attention. Teachers are taught about things like that."

"Not after hours stuff, though, unless the curriculum has changed very dramatically." They laughed at the direction their silly conversation had taken. "Let's get the fire going and the wine poured."

With all the dry scrap wood still around, it didn't take long for there to be a cheerful fire blazing. Sarah had put the food she'd brought with her in the fridge, the new stools were in place at the bar, and the wine was ready. It was a delightful prologue to their first real meal that she'd be getting together shortly on the new stove.

"The stools aren't as comfy as your sofa, but they beat sitting on cement blocks," Sarah commented. "But this is so cozy. The fire. The wine. It's very romantic. Maybe we should make love before we eat."

"Funny. I was thinking the same thing."

And they did.

"Dessert first," Sarah said afterwards.

"And third," Rob added. They laughed.

Rob stirred up the fire, and Sarah made dinner. Another glass of wine or two, and they were feeling very mellow by the time they'd finished eating. The soft music FM station from Worcester, WSRS, added to the mood.

When the fire died back to embers, they took the warmth they felt back to their makeshift bed, loved, and held each other close throughout the night. As Rob was falling asleep, there were emotions at play that he hadn't felt since the days, three years earlier, that he and Marianne had discovered how much they meant to each other. The memory of her and all that she'd been gave him a moment's pain, but he recovered when he realized how she and Sarah had the same asset: exceptional beauty inside. They were otherwise different, but he couldn't ignore that one especially important similarity.

Sarah was up early and had coffee going. Rob went off to the little market nearby and brought back the thick Sunday papers from both Springfield and Worcester.

"I thought it best if we each had our own so we wouldn't get into a fight. Couldn't have that to start the week."

"There won't be one. Worcester was home, so that's always been my paper. I'll have a look at the other one after you're finished with it. But let's have some breakfast."

They ate, read their papers, and then Rob got his things ready for the trip back to what had been home for the past four years, or nearly that long. When they were on their way to Wilcox's, Rob suggested to Sarah, "You might as well have the spare key. With those dandy new stools, maybe you'd like to sit at the bar and do some of your schoolwork, or just check to see how things are. I'll leave the heat at sixty-eight degrees so it won't be freezing. But one thing you might do is call New England Tel and have them hang a phone on a wall in the kitchen. Good place might be opposite the end of the bar. Would you do that for me?"

"You know I will. Any color preference?"

"Oh, red. Why not? Never had a red phone before. Be my private hotline to wherever. And ask them to give me a coiled cord on it that's long enough to sit at the bar and take notes."

"I'll call them this week and make a late afternoon appointment to have it installed. There are phone lines running down Colonial Trail, so it shouldn't be a problem."

"Appreciate your helping out."

"You know I'm glad to do it. Remember, I've already promised that I'll be all the help I can. When will you be back up?"

"The next two weekends, but not Christmas Saturday or New Year's. Be a fair amount of packing to do no matter what my next address is."

"On Friday, come straight to the cottage. I'll wait for you there."

Rob dropped Sarah off at the Wilcox building and said, "See you next weekend, dear heart."

"Bye, Rob. Please drive carefully."

They hugged, kissed softly, and then Rob started his lonely drive back to Sheffield.

Kim joined Rob late in the afternoon and spent Sunday night in his arms. After her depressing report on apartment searches, she now knew what the future held for the two of them. That neither she nor her husband had filed divorce papers was also a contributing factor, so the few plans that she and Rob had made for a life together would never become reality.

Then the week began. Stan Baird had invited Helen to attend a Monday evening dinner meeting with him, so she wouldn't be coming out with Rob until after work on Tuesday. He used the free time to suggest to Mike that they go out for a burger. It was time to talk with him about their situation.

"Unless there's a miracle and we turn up an apartment here this week, it's definite that we'll be moving up to the cottage. It's obvious that I can't afford the rents here any longer. You're not too far from the end of your senior year, so it would be a crime to take you out of school now. Question is, how do we arrange for you to finish at Sheffield High?"

"I know what's going on, so I've already talked to Regina and she'll let me stay with them until I finish in June. She said she'd talk to you about making payments to cover the extra food. If I have to stay here, I'll be OK with them because you know I get along with Kyle and Denny. We always have a good time together. And Regina is a mom now, too. Big change in her."

"I'm pleased that you know what we're up against and then explained that you'd like to finish school here. I'll call her late in the week to work out the details, assuming I don't find a place here in the next few days. If not, I'll ask movers to give me estimates of what it'll cost to haul our stuff up to the lake. Wherever we go, we sure won't have much of a Christmas."

"If there's anything we can pack ourselves, you know I'll help out. I still owe ya, and you know what I mean by that. But what about Greg?"

"Yep, I understand your meaning. About Greg, I'll pick him up on the nineteenth and then run him back after lunch on the thirtieth. He's supposed to back be on campus by five o'clock, I think it is."

"When I talked to Regina about living there until June, she told me she's expecting us to have Christmas with them. She knows what a mess we'll be in by then. After you take Greg back, I'll knock down our beds and then move in with them the Sunday after that. We go back to school the next day, the third. Sure is a lot to think about, isn't there?"

"Yeah, I'd rather not have to be bothered with any of this, but one of these days I'm probably going to pull out of New York and get involved in real estate up at the lake. Wilcox wants me to go to work for him. It's a total change of career, and I'm gettin' too old for that."

"Too old? Baloney! You won't be old even when you're seventy."

"Nice of you to think so, but it would have been simpler if I could've stayed with Sentry or IMMCorp. No choice, though. Those situations were completely out of my hands."

"I know it hasn't been easy, but the ladies have helped, I think."

"You might say that. Allowed me keep my sanity. Helen will be out tomorrow, so the therapy continues." Rob chuckled. "But I'll be going to the lake on Friday afternoon. You haven't been up for a while. Why don't you go with me and see what's been done? Sarah's been wonderful and has helped out every weekend."

"I really like Sarah. Maybe you've finally found somebody you can hang onto. I know she likes you. You can see that. Kim would be good, too, but I know she won't leave Sheffield. That's too bad—for you more than Greg and me. It isn't that important anymore. I know how much you like her. But your friends haven't really been any of our business. Sure has been a lot of 'em. Helen's neat, too. But she's like Kim, I suppose."

"She won't leave New York. And she'd be crazy to walk away from the kind of job she has and the money she makes now. I like her, too, but I'm also discovering that there's something special about Sarah. Maybe things will work out with her. I had dreams about her long before we actually met."

"You had dreams about somebody you didn't even know?"

"Yep. You ready to go?

"Sure."

"Let's do it. I'll tell you about them on the way home. Sarah's the only one who's heard the story so far."

As Rob drove, he talked about his dreams, the first of them going back nearly three years. He started by asking Mike if he remembered when Sarah showed up with Wilcox on Labor Day weekend that he asked her if she'd lived anywhere else.

"I remember, and I thought it was a funny question, like you were trying to put a move on her—or maybe just making conversation."

"No. I had a reason. She looked familiar. Then it was when I went up for the closing in September that I figured it all out. I was sleeping in the cottage, and then sat straight up in the middle of the night with the answer. Her height and build weren't an exact match, but her face, especially, was damned close. Enough so that it wasn't a problem matching Sarah up with the young woman I saw in a repeat of the same vision that night."

Rob told Mike the rest of the story, and how things seemed to be working out pretty much the same way they had in his dreams. "Even our move up there is part of it. And that she would figure into my life is another. I keep trying to break away from the story, if you can call it that, but all that does is put me right back into what the dreams showed me. It's what you might call spooky."

"Guess so. Geez! All you can do is try not to think about it too much."

"But when something pops up, and you say to yourself that you've already been there, or you've done that before, it rattles your cage just a little. Know what I'm saying?"

"Yeah. We just had something about that in school. What was it called? Oh, yeah. Déjà vu. And you're into it. Wow!"

"It isn't the first time it's happened that I've had dreams like this. So I need to pay more attention, I guess. The ones I've had about the person who turns out to be Sarah have been mostly accurate. Well, we'll just have to see where it all winds up."

On Friday morning, Rob reminded Mike to get a sleeping bag out and be ready to go at about four thirty.

"I'll be out on the train that gets in at 4:22 and will come straight home. Meet me in the garage, it'll be warmer there, and we'll leave right away."

"Any problem if I ask Tom to come along? He hasn't seen the place in a long time."

"Nope. Not a bit. His folks have been good to you, and us, so invite him."

"I already did. I thought you'd say yes. We still have Greg's sleeping bag. I'll bring it along."

There was nearly a full day to be put in before Rob and the boys left for Hampden Lake, so he went into Manhattan earlier than usual. When it got to be a little after nine, he took a break from search calls and phoned Justine on her private line.

"Hi, Justine. I haven't done very well keeping you up to date, so if you have a couple of minutes I'll do just that."

"I don't, but for you I'll make time." She chuckled softly.

"Thanks. The big news is, it's official. We're moving up to the lake. I couldn't find an apartment that's within reach, so I really didn't have any choice. The better news, at least for me, is that I'll be getting into real estate up there and will very likely unplug from New York at some point. Part of it is that Newcombe is getting harder to live with, and I don't need that kind of grief."

"Will I see you before you go?"

"Sure. I won't give serious thought about giving up my place in the search business until we get into summer. We'll work it out somehow."

"Just let me know. It'll be good to see you again and to have you share my bed—among other things."

"I'll do it. Now, I've got to run. This is a short day because I'm on my way Down East just after four. I'll stay in touch."

"Thanks for calling. Really sorry about your news, so I hope to hear from you again before long."

"You will. Bye, gal."

Chapter Eleven

Rob and the boys made good time on their trip up to Hampden Lake. It had snowed some, but the roads had been looked after and weren't a problem. Tom was really excited about spending the weekend at the lake and said so. When they got close to the cottage, Sarah saw them from the kitchen window and came out on the deck to wave at Rob and the boys as they drove up. After he'd introduced Tom and Sarah, they went inside.

"I thought you might be disappointed that I brought company," Rob said quietly. "Won't allow us to get friendly before we eat."

"Not a problem, Rob. It's good to see Mike and to meet Tom. There's always tonight, and a little delay will make it that much better—especially after a glass of wine, or two. Or three." Sarah giggled sweetly.

"Any plans for dinner?"

"I was going to suggest that we eat in, but we don't have enough here for the food disposers you brought along. Let's go for pizza. We'll have time enough in the morning to figure out what to do about food. There's enough stuff for breakfast, but we'll have to go to the market after that."

"What? No Sears this weekend? What a disappointment."

"We don't need anything else until you move. I guess that's definite now?"

"It is. I called three moving companies and asked them to give me estimates. They're sending someone out next Saturday morning to take a look at what we have to ship. I'll be coming up here in the afternoon and then going on to pick up Greg on Sunday. We'll drive straight back to Sheffield from Duchene. I won't see you after that until I'm here the first week of January. I've given the movers a pickup date of Wednesday the fifth and expect that I'll be in by the end of the day, or at the latest the following morning. If you don't mind, plan on a weekend here helping get boxes unpacked and making sure the bed is put together properly. We'll need to test it, of course, just to make sure it's OK."

"Of course." They both smiled.

They had their pizza and lots of friendly chatter. Later on, Rob and Sarah extracted total fulfillment from their night together. They'd missed each other. When morning came, and with nothing other than grocery shopping on their agenda, they slept late. Then after they'd all had a good breakfast, Sarah started to fuss about food for the rest of their weekend meals. Rob went a step further and said he couldn't see any reason why they shouldn't begin filling up the refrigerator and kitchen cabinets with what they'd need to live on starting in a couple of weeks. He made up a list of what he could remember they had on hand in Sheffield, and then tried to figure out, as best he could, what they might buy today. He assumed they'd wind up with duplicates of something. It didn't matter. They'd eventually eat it .

"There are bigger markets in Sturbridge, and others in Southbridge that aren't too far from here," Sarah told him. Rob decided that since they didn't have to make their usual run to Sears they might as well get acquainted with them—at least the stores nearby. The guys opted to go off and explore the neighborhood. Grocery shopping wasn't high on their list of ways to spend part of their Saturday.

By the time Rob and Sarah got back from their visit to the two markets in Sturbridge, the explorers had returned and were there to help bring everything in. Sarah got busy putting down shelf paper, and when she'd finished, they'd taken their first steps toward setting up housekeeping at the little cottage on Colonial Trail. Rob had mixed emotions about it. The reality of it was that he could easily afford the mortgage payments, and the cost of living in rural Massachusetts was a far better fit with the kind of money he was earning at the moment.

When evening came, Sarah shared the bright idea she had about what they might do for dinner. Rob quickly understood why she'd picked out some of the things she had while they were shopping. Sarah then went on to explain that they'd need the fire that Rob had just made, and also a few of the saplings that had sprung up from tree stumps that were left behind when the lot was partially cleared.

"My big plan is to have an indoor wienie roast. We'll get started once the fire has died back and we have a bed of deep red coals. Then for dessert, we'll toast marshmallows. What do you think, guys?"

Tom flashed a big grin and said, "All *right*! Way to go, Sarah." Rob and Mike heartily agreed.

Sarah had bought the wieners and marshmallows, of course, as well as chips, and cheese, and olives, and pickles, and buns. She'd also remembered to buy catsup and mustard—and even an onion if anyone wanted to add a little punch to their franks. "We're missing beans in tomato sauce," she said, "but I thought this would be enough. Besides I don't like 'em very much."

Rob said he'd be in charge of getting the saplings. Oak would be best, he thought, and he knew where to find them only about twenty paces from the back door. The bright, outdoor security light he'd had put up recently made it easier for him to find what he wanted. Within five minutes he was back with what they'd need to blacken their hot dogs.

The four of them had a great little indoor picnic, one Tom would talk about for weeks afterwards. Without a TV, their evening was spent talking and watching the flames licking at the back of the fireplace. Rob and Sarah sipped their wine and later went to their temporary bed filled with the warmth the evening and their feelings for each other had fashioned. Mike and Tom decided to put their sleeping bags in front of the fire. In fact they liked it so much, they kept it burning throughout the night. It was a treat to have the scent of burning oak mix with the aroma of Sunday morning coffee. It made the brew taste ever so much better.

They had another late breakfast and shortly afterwards Rob and the boys got ready to start back for Sheffield. Sarah said she'd brought schoolwork with her and would stay on until the fire was out and she could close the damper. "We don't need squirrels in here. And I've had so much fun, love, that I'm losing track of things. I forgot to mention that the phone will be in this week. I made arrangements to meet the installer here on Wednesday afternoon. It's a short day at school, so it'll work out perfectly. If you want, I'll call you at work."

"I'd like that. Be the first to use it." Sarah smiled in a way that said how she felt about this guy from suburban Connecticut and New York who had come into her life on Labor Day weekend.

"With the flurries blowing around, we probably ought to get started. Mike, would you go down and start the car? Be nice to have it warmed up first."

"Sure, Dad."

When they were ready, the boys went to the car and waited until Rob and Sarah had said good-bye. It was a tender moment they shared and it ended with an affectionate hug.

"Please drive carefully, Rob. I worry about your long trip to Sheffield. Even more so with snow in the air."

"You don't have to be worried about it. I promise to come back to you in one piece."

"I'll call you when your phone is in—and then see you sometime on Saturday afternoon."

A quick kiss and they were on their way down Colonial Trail. "At least it isn't the other road," Sarah thought. She waved just before they turned left and were out of sight. She could see Rob wave back. Then the empty feeling set in. It had been a good weekend, and already she missed him. Terribly.

On the way down, it had begun to snow a little more heavily, but they made it back without serious problems or delays. Mike was spending the night with Tom, so he dropped them off and then went home to an empty apartment. It matched the mood he was in, because his life was about to take a sharp left turn into Massachusetts. He would miss number 710. There were a good many stories the walls could recite if they were able to talk. End of an era, he thought. It would never be the same. Then the jangle of his phone interrupted his reverie. It was Sarah.

"I told you I worry about you, especially when the weather's bad. I just wanted to make sure you're OK."

"We didn't have any snags on the way down. It's sweet of you to call, and to worry, but you have to remember that I'll be doing this every week soon. You'll have to figure out how not to be on edge when I drive away."

"I know. Let me work on it. I'll be much better about it when winter's over. But I can't talk long, Rob. I'm on Alan's phone. See you soon. Maybe you'll think about me some in the meantime."

"Once an hour. And I'll be sure to drive carefully. Bye, dear heart."

Rob poured himself a drink, not wine, and sat down for a few minutes to think about what the sequence of events would be over the next four weeks. He didn't get very far into the subject when Kim was at his door.

"Hi, love," she said. "Glad you're back safe and sound."

"How're you doing?" Rob asked.

"Not well. But I'll feel better if you'll let me stay over."

"You don't have to ask twice. Any interest in going out for dinner?"

"I'd like that. Could we go to the Hearthside one more time?"

"Exactly what I had in mind. Like a drink first?"

"Yes, please. I need one. It might help me understand whatever happened to our weekends together. I miss not being here with you."

"There's so much to do to get ready for the move up to the lake. It's definite now. No use kidding ourselves. I have people coming in on Saturday morning to give me estimates on what it'll cost to move. Then I'm going up to get Greg. It won't be much of a holiday for him, but he'll at least be able to come back and say good-bye to his friends."

"I want to see him while he's here."

"Anytime. But you'll want to know about the weekends coming up. Christmas is out, I suppose, so the next one will be the last one. Are we still invited to Gina's for her New Year's Eve party? We could have the whole weekend together."

"We are, and I want the weekend, too. I could maybe spend the day after Christmas with you after I go to mass."

"Plan on it. Time's running out, so I want us to be together whenever we can arrange it. We're out of number 710 on the fifth."

"This is so hard, Rob. We sort of thought that you and I would go on like this without any interruptions. And then after I had my divorce, we could make plans about us. I know we've talked about our future, but there didn't seem to be any urgency. Now it's about over. At least that's the way I see it."

"I'll be pulling out of New York before long and going to work for Wilcox. He's making it worth my while. I can handle the mortgage, and the cost of living up there isn't anything like it is here. I'll be able to make ends meet pretty easily. It's a shame how economic issues can destroy a loving relationship like ours. We've meant so much to each other."

"Couldn't we keep on seeing each other somehow?"

"Not sure how. You know I won't be going into New York much longer, but while I still am I'll be coming down on Monday morning after you're at work. My week will be shorter, so I'll work evenings and then go back to the lake early on Friday afternoon. Guess I might as well start calling it home. That's what it'll be before much longer."

"Doesn't give us much of a chance, then. None at all really."

"We've known each other for over two years, love. If we haven't been able to put our lives in order, or come up with plans that make sense for both of us in all that time, what difference will another few weeks make? I can't afford to stay here, short of moving in with you, and we know that isn't possible. If you'd gotten your divorce, we most likely could have figured out a way to stay together. I want to be here with you, and it hurts to think that I'm headed in a different direction. I'll be jealous of anyone, everyone, who comes after me. Years from now, when I think back about us, and then you and someone else, those kinds of thoughts will bother me. I'll bet serious money on it."

"Let's go eat. And when we get to the restaurant, I'd like to change the subject. This is getting to me, and I don't want to cry. We still have some days left, so we should try to make the rest of our time together something pleasant to remember."

But it was Rob who had tears welling up. "You said it was hard. It's worse than that. I can't seem to make a relationship go anywhere. Kate walked away. Lu went goofy on me and did the same, Marianne's dead, and now you. I wanted what we've had to survive. In the worst way. Not because the others didn't, but because I'm in love with you, Kim Rossi.

"You've never said those words before, Rob—at least not quite the same way. I like it. And it says a lot about what your feelings are for me. You're not making dinner out any easier you know."

"In that case, we have to pretend that we've just left Lu at the hospital and that we're on our way to get acquainted. Let's pretend."

"We can try."

"No, love. It ain't gonna work." A wave of sadness swept over Rob, and he shuddered.

"Oh, sweetheart. Just hold me tight." Kim's eyes filled with tears.

For several minutes, they held each other close until the damage was mostly repaired.

"I'm sorry about that," Rob said. "It's been lurking in the background for probably three or four weeks. Now that it's out of the way, I'll be all right. And I should be able to make the most of the time we have left until I move."

"No need to apologize. Haven't I always been there for you when you needed me?"

"You have. Without fail. But who's going to be there the next time? Don't look too far ahead or we'll never get to dinner."

Finally, they each made peace with their emotions and shared a caring, loving evening at the Hearthside, the place where it all began in late September 1969. Afterwards, they took their love to Rob's bed and assured themselves that the memories they would carry with them through the years would be filled with the warmth they continued to feel for each other.

Early morning was given to looking into each other's eyes, and then holding on tightly for a few minutes before their week began.

As they left for work, Kim said she would call late in the week to confirm that she'd be spending both Friday and Sunday nights with Rob. "That way I'll be sure to see Greg when you come back. More important, is that I can spend a little more time with you than we planned on."

"You're doing a better job of planning than I am. Too much on my mind, I suppose. Be wonderful to have you here while my address is still Juniper Heights."

Rob recovered and in the run-up to the holidays, Helen spent Tuesday and Wednesday night with him. She wasn't sure about the following week, the days just before Christmas. "Coming out to Sheffield depresses me some. I have such good memories of all the wonderful things that we've shared here. I hate to see it all come to an end. So what I'm really looking forward to is getting my present *after* Christmas and New Year's, meaning when you move in. It'll be wonderful having a man around the house kinda permanent like."

"You'll probably get tired of our arrangement and throw me out after about the third week."

"Not a chance. I've waited too long for it to happen. But there aren't any chains to bind you to East Thirty-second Street. If you get tired of me, or you move up to the lake, then I'll try to be understanding about it. I have the feeling that you'll eventually make the cottage your home. That'll hurt, a lot, but whatever direction we go, I'll always remember what we've had.

It's no secret that I want to be Mrs. Grant, or at least Mr. Grant's companion, and keep you around permanently. I'll hang on and hope. I care too much about you, and what we've been to each other, to be angry if it doesn't work out the way I want it to."

"I know that, but you're way ahead of me on what the future looks like. Why don't we just enjoy being together and take what's out there one day at a time. I don't have a roadmap or dates on a calendar that tell me that I have to do thus and such at some point. So I suggest we just relax. We'll get along very nicely and for sure have some good times while we're at it—just like we've had when you've been here. The fun at your place includes nights, too, you know."

"You don't have to remind me. We're good. Verrry good, in fact. Mmmm."

"What are your plans then?" Rob asked. "Should I get the impression that you won't be coming out with me next week?"

"I said I wasn't sure, but I think that with everything else going on, the holidays and all, this is probably my last trip out. Like I said, it's depressing to think about you, and me, and 710 coming to an end. Sure. Let's plan on getting the rest of December behind us. I'm taking a few days off, will spend most of them in Hempstead, and then I'll finish up getting ready for you. On the other hand, I may just get horny and want to come out with you one afternoon next week. That be OK?"

"Very OK. Early in the week would be best. Greg will be home, and I'll probably start boxing up stuff on Thursday. We're basically shutting down the business on Wednesday afternoon, the twenty-second. Then I won't be back until Monday, January 10. Expect to see me that evening."

"Can't wait. Why don't you plan on bringing some of your clothes down one day next week. I think I'm about ready for you to do that. Then maybe you could spend the night with me."

"Let me see what Mike's up to, and I'll let you know. I *will* be bringing some of my things down next Wednesday. That's certain. It's the start of our holiday break, so I can drop them off and then stay the night, assuming I've made arrangements for Mike."

"In that case, this *is* my last trip out with you. Sorry that it's all over for us at number 710."

"Me, too." Kim was very much on his mind when he said that.

On the way into the city, Rob said, "We need to see the Marzano's before Christmas. I know they've liked having us visit, but I'll most likely make this my last one. I've seen them at least once a month since July of last year, so it's time to tell them there's a chance I'll be pulling out of New York. On second thought, I probably ought to stop by until that happens. Assuming it does."

Then, late on Thursday afternoon, Sarah called with Rob's new phone number.

"Hi, handsome. How're you?" she asked.

"Fine, dear heart. Thought you were going to call me yesterday."

"I would have except the phone company changed the appointment. I was lucky to get the message. Anyway, I only have a minute. Your new number is 245-9076. You already know the area code is 413."

"Thanks. I'll make sure they have it here. Hate to cut this short, but I have to get out of here if I'm to make my train. See you on Saturday afternoon. Be ready for a glass of wine and a little fire, in both the fireplace, the one with the chimney, and the other . . . well, you get the picture."

"I understand, and I'll be ready for any and all of it. Take it easy on the drive up. I'll be here, no matter what time you show up. Just get here safe and sound. Bye."

"I'll do it. Bye, sweetheart."

Before Rob left East Thirty-fifth Street on Friday, he had a meeting with Lenard to let him know what his schedule would be until the tenth.

"I'll be in on Monday and will work through until we close for the holidays. I might be able to come in on the third and fourth if I'm needed."

"I don't think it'll be necessary. You have some things working, but you seem to be current. If any of your people wind up being placed, that'll happen now without you around. You've done everything on this end that's necessary. It's up to the companies to decide. Take the week and get yourself settled in. You put in enough hours. No complaints there. And I know that once you're back you'll give it your best. What'll your routine be starting on the tenth?"

"I'll either come down on Sunday evening or early on Monday morning, park in Sheffield and take the train in. I have a place to stay nearby, so I can put in whatever hours are needed to get the job done. There won't be a daily commute from now on—just a five minute walk."

"I won't ask you about your arrangements. They're none of my business. Sounds as if you'll be right here in Murray Hill. Convenient."

"No secret, Paul. I'm staying with Helen. Let me give you her number in case you need me. The plan, as I said, is that I'll either be there by Sunday evening, or I'll come straight down from the lake and into the office on Monday morning. It'll depend on my workload and where I am with my searches."

"You're living proof that a rolling stone doesn't gather any moss, so I have to assume you also have company up at your place."

"Reasonable guess, Paul."

"Well, as long as we're exchanging pieces of paper, we got paid yesterday for one of your lower level placements. Here's a check for $1,800. I may have another one for you before we shut down for the holidays next week. I've been leaning on clients to meet their obligations in a more timely fashion. In the case of IMMCorp, they owe you one, too. You might want to take that up with Helen, since you have an in, so to speak." Paul had to laugh at that. Rob joined him.

"Thanks. I appreciate it. This will help with everything that's going on, not to mention Christmas. If there's another one next week, I'll finally be able to get out the hole I'm in. Lots of expenses associated with moving and getting my place habitable."

"I can imagine. Have a good weekend and drive sanely. We need you back in one piece."

"Sounds like the advice I get on the other end when I start this way."

"So there is someone up there. I thought so. You're too much. Be on your way now so that you don't keep her waiting. My regards, and tell her that she ought to come down and have lunch with us someday. Love to meet her."

"I'll pass your message along. But you've already met Sarah. She was here at the beginning of November. See you on Monday, Paul. And, thanks for the check."

Just before Rob left, Helen called to say that she'd been in touch with the Marzano's. "Since you're staying over on Wednesday evening, we'll see them late that afternoon. They're delighted that we're coming up. And don't forget to bring more of your clothes down with you. There's plenty of room in the closet now."

"I'll swing by your place before we go up to the Bronx. Plan on dinner somewhere on the West Side—just to do something different."

"Good idea. Love it. And you too, Rob Grant. Take it easy on the road, and say hello to the boys for me."

"I'll do it. Gotta run, sweetheart. See you on Wednesday at about four."

By the time Rob got home, he saw Kim's car parked in the space next to his in the garage and found when he got up to number 710 that Mike had let her in.

"Hi, hon," Kim said. "Glad you're home in time for a leisurely drink." She gave Rob a big hug and an affectionate kiss.

"Good to be home. I guess I can still call it that."

"We'll eat in tonight. I brought food. One of your favorites. My Italian sausage concoction."

"Great! That's really sweet of you. But Mike probably won't leave us much. You know what he does to it when you put that casserole in front of him."

"I made extra. There'll be enough for everybody."

And there was.

The two of them made the most of their evening together, loved to perfection, slept like spoons and then Kim was on hand for the walk-through by the representatives from the three moving companies. Her face was long and the sadness in her eyes had returned. The reps left their estimates, and Rob told each of them they'd have his decision by Monday. Mike did the laundry and then took off to see Tom. He'd be there overnight. Rob put together a light lunch, and then after he and Kim did no more than pick at their food, they went down to the garage.

"See you tomorrow afternoon," Rob said. "If you want to come over earlier, call first and see if Mike's gotten home yet. If you aren't here, I'll let you know right away that I'm back."

They hugged, and hung on to each other for a moment. Just as they got ready to go their separate ways, they decided that in the days that remained, they had two options. They could either be miserable, or they could make the best of their circumstances, enjoy each other's company, and by so doing add something positive to all they'd shared.

"We'll have better memories if we get some pleasure from these last few days together," Kim said. "I'd prefer it that way. This isn't the end of life for either of us. What goes around comes around, somebody once said. Who knows, we may wind up together someday in spite of the setback of your moving away. It happens. Let's think positively about it. For sure, it isn't very likely that I'm going to find a replacement for you anytime soon. And we might want to remember what my attitude was two years ago, that is about not wanting a husband, or being married again. I'm right back where I was in the early fall of sixty-nine. You were the exception I'd have made, so maybe there's still something out there for us after all."

"That's quite a pep talk. But you're right. Let's make the best of what we have and believe that we might one day pick up wherever it is we leave off. The thought of that makes me feel better."

Rob and Kim hugged again, kissed softly, and then drove off in different directions.

On his way up to Massachusetts, Rob couldn't shake the feeling that he was exploiting all three of the women in his life. "Maybe it's the way the game is played," he thought. "But it sure as hell isn't how I was brought up. Only problem is, I'm fond of all three of them. But if two of them "walked", I'd most likely be happy with whoever was left. Sarah's a little too new for me to think that way, but I'm growing very attached to her. Yet if I had but one woman in my life, it's likely a couple of others would surface. That seems to be the way things have worked out. Variety and living a little bit on the edge. Problem with Kim is that she's still married, and it'll be next to impossible for me to spend any time with her except by phone. That's no good. Yet she still means a great deal to me. Helen? What a love. But she's a New Yorker, has a good job now, and she'd be foolish to give it up. And the reality is that I can't live with her fulltime, because with all my worldly belongings up at the cottage, which place would I call home? In any case, there are the boys to consider. Sarah? I like what I feel about her. She's there, close by, and like Helen, she's another absolute sweetheart. But leaving East Thirty-second Street and Helen will be very hard for both of us. She'd be a wonderful partner and a devoted wife. I almost wish she lived up at the lake. I'd probably be willing to marry her next week. She'd have me and would try to move the ceremony up to Monday afternoon. *Damn*, Rob Grant! It isn't easy being a lion."

Traffic was heavy, and Rob's reverie was interrupted by some nut trying to make better time than the number of cars on the Merritt Parkway would allow. The idiot nearly sucked Rob into a traffic accident and, considering their speed, it would have been a mess. Finger waves were exchanged and the guy drove off to intimidate someone else. "Looks like that asshole has started his holiday celebration a week early," Rob said aloud. "That was close!"

By the time Rob got to Colonial Trail, an agitated Sarah was keeping watch at the back window. The moment he pulled up she rushed out to greet him.

"I've been worried about you," Sarah said. Then she gave him a hug. It was accompanied by a shiver that confirmed she was alarmed.

"Lots of traffic, dear heart. Some moron down on the Merritt was weaving a basket in traffic and trying his level best to get somebody involved in an accident. He nearly got me, but my Mustang smelled his breath and kept us out of trouble." Sarah laughed softly and gave Rob another hug.

"Now you know why I'm apprehensive. You told me to get it under control, and I'm trying. Just promise me that you'll drive defensively. You're valuable cargo."

"I don't want to get busted up any more than you want to see that happen. But, I'm not here to talk about traffic. How about we go find something to eat."

"We don't have to go anywhere. With my help, you now have a fully functioning kitchen and I've put dinner together. I also got a fire going, your drink is mixed, and it's in the fridge. We're in for the evening. What do you think about that, mister?"

"Sounds like I'm home from the battlefield. Feels good to be taken in tow. I'm ready to put up my feet and relax."

"I'll look after you tonight. In exchange, I want to go with you when you pick up Greg. I know I wasn't invited, but unless I see him tomorrow it'll have to wait until Easter and that's not until the beginning of April."

"Done! It'll be good to have company, and he'll be glad to see you."

Sarah did look after Rob. The food was great, their evening filled with affection, and their night together simply magnificent. After a good breakfast, they got a fairly early start to pick up Greg.

When they got to the Duchene campus, it was crawling with families picking up their youngsters, all of them starting an eleven day vacation. Greg easily spotted the Mustang, one of the smaller cars in the guest lot, and he ran across to greet Rob and Sarah. He gave her a hug first. The need for a mom was still there. Rob didn't mind. It made both of them feel good—for different reasons.

"How are you, Greg?" Sarah asked after he'd hugged his dad.

"I'm OK, and I'm really glad to see you, I mean both of you." They all smiled.

"Well, you're just in time to help pack boxes," Rob said.

"Oh, great. Just what I always wanted to do." He laughed.

"But you'll have time to say good-bye to your friends in Sheffield. This'll be the last time you can call it home. The new one will be just down the road starting on January 5. Could be the counselors here will let you come home on weekends once in a while. But let's get started."

As they drove, Greg said, "I'm not sure about weekends at home yet. There are kids who come from towns lots closer than Hampden Lake, but they can't get off. I'll be there for another year, maybe two, the way it looks. I can ask when I get back."

"It's a team effort, Greg. We'll both ask after I get settled in at the cottage."

It wasn't long before they were back on Colonial Trail. Sarah told Rob that she wanted to be dropped off there, if for no other reason than that was where her car was parked. "But I think I'll go in and just enjoy being in there," pointing toward the cottage, "even if you aren't. It's beginning to feel a little bit like home. Is that bad?"

"That kinda puts me on the spot, young lady. If you're starting to think about rings and vows, it's too early for me to get comfortable with that idea. There isn't anything fundamentally wrong with the notion of having something permanent, but I still need time. If you're saying that you like the three of us, and enjoy sharing our little nest, then I have to admit that it isn't 'bad', as you put it. We have something special going for us, I think it's fair to say, but you know my history and you also know that I'm not likely to do much of anything at an accelerated pace, at least when it comes to a long-term personal relationship. I also have some recent memories to shake."

"I know, and I understand what you're saying. But you also know that I care about you, to the point that I'm *really* worrying about your long drives now. What's most important is that you're letting me be a part of something good, meaning you and your life. It gives me such wonderful feelings inside. The cottage, and being here, is just one piece of it."

"I like what you're telling me. Before long, we'll share much more of what it is that gives both of us a lift. You know you're welcome. Use my extra key. If you like being here, come and go as you please."

"I had hoped you'd say that. You can count on one thing. I'll be here on weekends—that is, if I'm welcome. The ones we've spent together leave me with such warm, furry memories. They cross my mind all day every day after you've gone. I smile a lot during the week."

"It sounds as if you're after a piece of my heart, Miss Stuart. Is that the impression I should get?"

"That isn't anything new, Rob. Just so you don't misunderstand, you've taken over a big part of mine. Nearly all of it."

Greg was taking all this in and not saying a word. Now sixteen, he was old enough to better understand what was going on. He also remembered what his dad had been through when Lu walked away from them and then when Marianne died. He'd been witness to how badly he'd been hurt. Greg had grown up some, and he wanted to see his dad happy.

"You know that you matter to me, too. A lot. So I guess we're both being pretty open about where we stand. Something for me to think about on the way back to Sheffield. On that subject, we probably ought to be on our way. That sky off to the west looks to me like it has snow in it. That's a forecast coming from the farm boy in me. Dad was my mentor. He was good at it."

"We also heard on the Worcester station that snow's in the forecast," Sarah reminded him. "I don't want to see you go, but you already know that I'm a world-class worrier. Much as I don't want to, I have to agree that you ought to get started back."

They hugged, and Greg collected one of his own.

"Have a great Christmas, Sarah, and say hi to your mother. I hope we'll get to meet sometime soon. Before that happens, you remember that I'll be coming through on the thirtieth when I take Greg back. Maybe you could have another fire going. Better yet, have two going." They both grinned, then kissed, and Rob and Greg were on their way toward I-86.

Sarah waved as they were about to turn into Old Town Road and disappear from view. Her eyes showed sadness, but her heart was filled with affection for Rob Grant.

Snow was in the air and then on the ground. Rob drove carefully, but he and Greg did have a chance to talk about school, the imminent move, and his dad's feelings about Sarah.

"Since you're interested, I guess I owe you a rundown on where things stand. It'll be for my benefit, too, in some ways, although I did think about it some on the way up yesterday. If I could somehow continue my relationship with Kim, I'd do it. Longer term, I'd most likely ask her to think about our getting married. Helen? A wonderful gal but, like Kim, she won't leave what's always been home to her. And I can't move back to Sheffield or into New York, so there are real problems to deal with before either one of them could be a permanent fixture in our lives—at least the way my situation is now. It's going to be very, very hard saying good-bye to Kim. We've been so close for over two years, but there isn't any way we can continue a long distance love affair. Another snag is that she hasn't even filed for divorce yet."

"Kim's my favorite," Greg said, "but I know what you're telling me. When she's gone, I won't go wacky like I did when Lu dumped us. I'd get along with her the best, I think. She's a mom and understands boys. I'd mind her."

"Helen senses that I probably won't be around much longer, but she'll get all she can out of whatever time we still have together and then move on. She'll always have a part of me in her heart, and I'll have a part of her in mine. But she has grit, will deal with our separation, and then one day she'll find a good man who'll love her as much as I do. She deserves that."

"She's nice and good fun."

"Sarah? She's young, but a lot more mature that her twenty-four years. And you already know that she's a real sweetheart. We have the start of something awfully solid, I think. Anyway, what it boils down to is that she's about all I'll have left once Hampden Lake is home. I don't mean that quite the way it sounds. Sarah is very good for me. New as we are to each other, I've gotten to like her, a lot, and she tells me I'm important to her. You heard the things she said before we left."

"Glad I'm not the one who has to decide. Sarah's still kinda new, but she's really neat, too. I don't know, Dad. It sounds like when you're at the lake that it'd be real hard to keep anything going with Kim or Helen."

"Well, you understand the problem, then. But a change of subject. Why is it you have to be back on the thirtieth instead of *after* New Year's Day? I never see anybody to ask them the same question."

"They're guessing that parents will be at a party someplace and that the kids will get into trouble. Even if it's at home, there'll be stuff around and nobody paying any attention. Guess it's happened before. They don't know how you do things. Doesn't matter, because they figure it's possible for something to go wrong."

"This year, I *won't* be at home. Kim's sister is having a few people in and it'll be the last time we'll be together socially. I don't like thinking about it. Glad we're almost home. The mom you'd like to have should be there to give you a hug."

"That'll be great. But I'm going to miss her—and not coming back to the place we've lived since I was almost thirteen. I hope I can keep some of my friends. Not the ones with the drugs, but the ones I care about."

The snow had gotten heavier, so pulling into the garage before there were real problems was just about a tie. Kim's car was in *her* spot and dripping melted snow, so it hadn't been there long.

Greg got his bag and they headed for 710. When they went through the door, Greg's reunion with Kim was emotional. Rob had a lump in his throat because things like this would come to an end in a few days. He got control of himself, and they shared a hug of their own. Both of them tensed. It said everything about the sad day coming that neither of them wanted to face. But they recovered and smiled away the blues. At the end of the reception line, but not upset by it, was Mike. He and Greg did their complicated handshake and giggled about it in the process.

Since the snow had let up, Rob proposed dinner out, and although pizza wasn't Sunday night fare, Greg was calling the shots and that was what he wanted. It was about as close as it could be to a family night out without being able to certify it as such. This 'family' would cease to be one within a couple of weeks, but they didn't let it dampen their spirits. When they got back to Juniper Heights, the boys stayed up and talked late into the evening. Rob and Kim went to bed, spoke soft, private words, and shared the depth of their feelings with quiet passion.

There was no reason to hurry on Monday morning. It was just days to Christmas and there was nothing that demanded urgent attention. Rob took a later train, and Kim said over coffee that she'd let the boys know when she was leaving. Since it wasn't likely that she and Rob would see much of each other until Sunday, they hugged and then hung on for a moment before he went down to the garage.

"We'll talk during the week. Maybe we can get together for a drink or something. Aim for Thursday," Rob proposed.

"Perfect. I have Friday off. Maybe I could stay over. I'd really like to do that. Only thing is, it's Christmas Eve, and I'd have to get home fairly early."

"You know that isn't a problem. Plan on it. See you sometime late on Thursday. It's the start of our holiday break, too."

Plans made, Rob left for the station to begin his short week in New York. From Wednesday afternoon on, he'd have nineteen days off, would make the move to Hampden Lake—and know heartbreak again.

After Rob got home on Tuesday, he packed a suitcase with clothes that he could leave at Helen's the next afternoon. They would be only those things he'd need during the week. So, mindful of the fact that home would soon be a Massachusetts address, he tried to be prudent about what he would leave in her closet on East Thirty-second Street and what Allied Van Lines would deliver to his cottage on Colonial Trail the first week in January.

And then late on Wednesday, Rob and Helen kept their date with the Marzano's. Carlo and Anna were glad to see the two of them again and made certain they understood how much they appreciated their visits. Rob told them about what was going on in his life. He also said he'd do his best to stop by whenever it was possible. Before they left, Rob took Carlo aside, explained that he'd be moving to Massachusetts soon and that he'd most likely be leaving New York, permanently, sometime later in the new year. Although saddened by the news, Carlo said he understood, but that he'd want Helen to know that she'd be welcome anytime. He also told him that he was looking after the two little rose bushes that Rob had planted at Marianne's grave last June. And, while he was seeing to it that they were protected against winter's cold, Carlo assured Rob that they were still very healthy and hugging each other. He was sure that Mari was helping keep them alive and well. When it came time to leave, they wished each other a Merry Christmas and a Happy New Year. Afterwards, Rob and Helen had their dinner on the West Side, and then went back to Thirty-second Street for a night that was filled with tender loving and a nightlong embrace.

When morning came, Rob began his nearly three-week vacation. He couldn't really call it that because it was also the start of a whirlwind that would include his move to Hampden Lake. Kim spent every free hour with him that she could arrange. Then on Christmas Day, Regina put on another grand holiday feed, said good-bye to Rob, and got ready to welcome Mike to her family while he finished his senior year at Sheffield High. If all went as expected, he would graduate in June as a member of the class of 1972.

On the thirtieth, Rob drove Greg back to school. He'd had a good vacation and was able to say good-bye to his Sheffield friends. He didn't expect to see them again until he was released from the rehabilitation program that would continue into the foreseeable future. Rob had hoped to see Sarah, even though they hadn't made specific plans to meet. They'd talked and she told him she'd still be visiting her mother, sister, and new brother-in-law in Worcester until January 2.

Since Rob was close to what would be his new home starting next week, he decided to stop by the cottage to see if everything was all right. What he found was that Sarah had set the heat at a comfortable temperature, so the place was cozy. She'd also left a cute little card behind saying that she'd be thinking about him. "Sweet of her," Rob thought. "But then, that's Sarah!"

The trip back to Sheffield went smoothly. As he drove, Rob was continuing to fight reality and still refused to accept the fact that he'd be leaving Juniper Heights behind. He had loved the city and his home. The last two years had been fraught with problems, especially with the boys, but his personal life, and the hours he'd spent with Kim had, in contrast, been glorious. But it was another chapter that was closing, and he wasn't at all certain that what was on the pages to follow would ever be quite as fulfilling as the last twenty-seven months had been. Sarah would now be the centerpiece of his life, but putting thoughts of Kim behind him would take time, just as it had with Marianne. At that, and for as long as he would live, she'd always occupy a special place in his mind not very far below the conscious level. But he'd not forget her—neither the many wonderful hours they'd spent together, nor the several trials they'd shouldered.

New Year's Eve was a bittersweet affair. Gina, the perfect hostess, had as guests a small group of people who were both friendly and compatible. Rob and Kim truly enjoyed being a part of the festivities, yet they couldn't ignore the fact that in less than a week their relationship would be little more than the glorious memories that were the end product of all they'd shared. They tried hard not to let the days ahead spoil their evening and took pleasure from simply being in the company of others. When the clock struck midnight, they welcomed in the New Year in the same manner that others did. They shared a warm kiss and held each other tightly.

When the party yielded to the early hours of January 1, they all wished each other good health and happiness in the new year. But Rob and Kim saw little joy in the days immediately ahead. They made the drive back to Juniper Heights without saying much, each lost in their own thoughts about themselves and what the year would bring to their lives. Once at home, they gave themselves to each other passionately on this final Saturday they would love within these walls. As morning light turned shadows into familiar shapes, they both felt distress and it pervaded the hours they spent together during this initial weekend of 1972—their last together as companions and lovers. They made the best of it, recalled the good times and hoped that somehow there would be more. On Sunday evening, Kim went home to her sons, Chris and Ian. But before she left she made arrangements to stay with Rob during his last two nights in the place they had laughed, and loved, and shared difficult moments during the past twenty-seven months. Memoirs were just about all they had left.

On Wednesday morning, January 5, the movers arrived early and began loading the truck. Mike, now living at Regina's, came over from school before classes began to say good-bye. Kim took an early lunch and was at number 710 well before noon to see Rob off and to wish him well.

"If ever I fit into your plans again, I'm here and my love for you is here," Kim said. Rob had rarely seen such a grim face. It tore at his heart.

"I don't see how it can work out. It'll be hard for both of us, but it's best that we make the break and get on with our lives. I don't like any part of the idea, but you're here and I can't be. Time we dealt with the truth of what is. Part of it is that you're still married."

"What I wouldn't give to rearrange the circumstances. I'll never forget you Rob, and I'll always remember the love we've had."

"Let me go with you to your car. Best we say good-bye there."

"I'm parked outside. Before I forget it, here's the card to the garage. Thanks for letting me use the space next to yours. Don't suppose my car and your Mustang will have broken hearts quite like ours."

"Come down to the garage with me. I've got to pull outside, too. After I turn the cards in, I won't be able to get out. Let me drop you off where you're parked."

"Sort of a good-bye to your 'horse' before you head Down East." At Kim's car, they held each other, and shared one last kiss. "Thanks for some wonderful, wonderful memories," she said.

"No. It's for me to say thanks to you for more than all the great memories we have. You were tremendous support when I needed it. I'll not forget what you've meant to the boys and me."

When the time came for Kim to leave, there were no tears. They'd already shed them days before. There were only cruel aches as she waved, blew a kiss, then drove away and out of his life forever. Or so it would seem. Rob watched her car until it was out of sight, and then he went back to his vacant apartment. He stood at his big living room window one last time and looked out across Sheffield and Long Island Sound. Overcome with sadness, and not in total control of his emotions, he lost it.

After drying his eyes, and getting himself presentable, Rob went to the office to turn in all of the keys and his garage access card. A hopeless romantic, he kept the one Kim had used and put it in his pocket. He would save it for the rest of his life, together with a handful of other personal items that would forever be reminders of those who had been important to him. Among them was the amber water glass with Marianne's smudged fingerprints and a trace of her lipstick on it—the same one he'd taken from her Georgetown apartment just weeks before she died.

Chapter Twelve

On his way to what would become their new home in Hampden Lake, Rob waved as he passed the van that was carrying nearly all of his worldly possessions to the cottage on Colonial Trail. Having left Kim behind, his heart was leaden. Sarah's presence would give him a lift, but it would be weeks before Rob was able to reconcile what he had hoped for with the reality of what had to be. It was the third painful good-bye he'd been confronted with since December twenty-five months earlier. Still, it hadn't gotten any easier. He had yet to learn how to deal with those last moments with someone who'd mattered as much as Lu, and Marianne, and Kim. His eyes got blurry. Not a good idea at Interstate speeds. He stopped at a rest area adjacent I-86 to collect his thoughts and to begin the process of putting all the events of recent weeks behind him. Not easy. But life, he acknowledged, would go on—difficult as it might be at times.

Rob got to the cottage before Sarah did, and both were there ahead of the van. The driver and his two helpers had stopped for coffee, so it was mid-afternoon before they were ready to move the contents of his nest on Juniper Heights into new surroundings. The moving crew was efficient, so it took less than two hours to get all the furniture, and barrels, and cartons inside. After Rob signed the delivery release, Sarah surveyed the chaos and observed, "No point in letting all of this just sit here. Let's unpack. For sure there's enough stuff to make a roaring fire. Before we get to the boxes, though, I'll help you put the bed together. The essential things come first." Rob wanted to smile, but that it had played an important role in Kim's good-bye was impossible to ignore. To show that he was grateful, Rob gave Sarah a hug and thanked her for volunteering. An extra pair of hands would help.

With the two of them working, they made a big dent in getting unpacked and putting everything in its place before they went to bed. Sarah came back on Thursday afternoon and went right back to helping Rob settle in. By Friday evening, they were ready to treat themselves to dinner out, a little extra wine, and a satisfying late evening once they'd gotten to bed. Still very much in his thoughts, he made love to Kim. It would take time before she'd let go of his mind and the memories would fade. But he had to come to grips with the fact that she would find his replacement one day soon, and the thought of that made him irrationally jealous. To have moved to the cottage was his decision, so he made a concerted effort to deflect those kinds of thoughts.

By the morning of the tenth, Rob had fully conditioned himself to begin the long weekly commutes into New York. As he got into his Mustang, Sarah begged, "Be careful. Please?"

"I'll do it. Just because you asked. See you late on Thursday evening. Remember, the carpet guys are coming out on Friday morning."

"I know. I'll come by after school. Can't wait to see how it turns out."

Sarah leaned in, gave Rob an affectionate kiss, and then he was on his way. The drive went smoothly, but when he parked in Sheffield, it was all he could do to stick with his plan of getting on the 9:15 train. The thought of Kim was burning a hole in his mind, and he had an almost irresistible desire to stop and see her at the Prentiss Agency. But he didn't need to be reminded that he'd been through all the reasons why their long distance romance couldn't work, so he disciplined himself to get aboard the train and go on to Grand Central. In the weeks immediately ahead, when on Monday mornings and Friday afternoons he would pass within a half-mile of where Kim was at work, he continued to resist the temptation to see her. It was a test of strength—and one he would pass. As spring approached, he was certain that by then she had someone new in her life. Though he was far more jealous than he had any right to be, it somehow made his trips through Sheffield easier.

Living with Helen on East Thirty-second Street, which began on the second Monday in January, helped Rob blur the wonderful memories he had of his relationship with Kim. In the months following his move to Massachusetts, Rob generally stayed with Helen from Monday evening until Friday morning. The exception to the pattern was that first week when Rob left on Thursday afternoon so that he could be at home when the carpet installers came. After they'd finished, his little cottage at Hampden Lake now felt like home. Sarah approved of all he'd done to make it so. And as they'd talked about earlier, she eventually became a regular tenant on weekends. The pattern, then, was set. He left early on Monday morning for Sheffield, went into Manhattan, walked to Thirty-fifth Street, worked long hours at NAGE, spent his nights with Helen, and then returned to Hampden Lake on Friday to weekend with Sarah.

When Rob got home on February 18, Sarah announced that she had all of the following week off, the so-called Washington's birthday break. She planned to spend time with her mother, but proposed that she come into New York and have lunch with Rob, just as she had in early November. They set their plans, and she made the trip down—but drank too much at lunch. It was a case of trying to keep up with the boys. She lost and spent the afternoon sleeping on the sofa in Rob's little office. Newcombe was mostly responsible for her condition because he kept egging her on. It was a day when Sarah learned a great deal about her limitations. The NAGE crowd, except for Rob, had a good laugh over an inebriated Sarah Stuart. She did get upright in time to make the trip home, but there was no loving that night. She was badly hung over.

The following weekend, Rob left for New York on Sunday afternoon to keep a date with Justine. His simple explanation, for Sarah's benefit, was that they had an 8:00 a.m. interview with a senior level candidate, which in fact they did, and he wasn't interested in getting up well before daylight to make the long trip into Manhattan. Rob and Justine were glad to see each other again. They had a good visit, an enjoyable dinner out, and their usual fiery evening and morning in bed.

Over an early breakfast, Justine said, "I've missed all of what it is you can do for me. But I suppose I should plan on this coming to an end soon."

"Probably so. I've met someone up at the lake that has your kind of beauty within—and I don't mean physically. You recall my telling you that it wasn't exactly intentional, but when you came out for Thanksgiving dinner back in sixty-nine, you taught me what to look for inside a person. I remembered the lesson, so it was fairly easy for me to spot it. Sarah isn't exactly stunning, but the kind of person she is has turned out to be much more important."

"If it leads to something permanent, I'm happy for you, Rob. You've meant a great deal to me, but if I've helped in some way that gives me a good feeling."

"You have, and I'm grateful to you."

The work week was beginning for both Rob and Justine, so they said their good-byes at the Fifty-first Street stop on the Lexington Avenue subway. With just a hint of melancholy showing, Justine started up toward street level and was quickly out of sight. Rob took the next train, got off at Thirty-fourth Street and then walked back a block.

On the third Saturday afternoon in March, Alan Wilcox stopped by the cottage to talk further with Rob about the details of starting to work for him. They quickly came to an agreement about compensation since they'd already discussed most of it last October. Then Wilcox took Rob on a tour of his subdivisions and gave him building lot plans so he could see what was available. The surveys and individual lots were marked with numbers, and he saw that many of the boundary pins had been spray painted a bright orange. "Nothing complicated about any of this," Rob thought.

"Next weekend," Alan said, "I'll want to give you a tutorial on my contracts and support paperwork. Once you have them down pat, you'll need to sit for the salesman's exam. Here's book the Commonwealth puts out, and you'll need to study it. If you have any questions, I'll help you with them. Next step will be the broker's license. If you're to run my businesses here, which is what I've always had in mind, you'll need it. "

"When does the season begin?"

"There are already some people looking around, but usually it's the middle of April. This year is a little different because Easter is on the second, and I think from the inquiries I'm getting already that we ought to be open starting on Saturday, the first. I'll work alongside you until we're both comfortable with how you're coming along. After that, I'll expect you to be my man in charge out here around the lake. By the way, here are some ads from last year. I'm in the *New York Times* nearly every Sunday until mid-October because the area you came from is a gold mine. I'll want you to take over writing the ads each week and then getting them placed."

"I've written a fair amount of ad copy, going back more than ten years, so I understand what it's all about. It'll be a matter of learning the style to attract customers rather than candidates for employment. I'm doing some of the latter now in New York. Anyway, your Sunday ads were how Regina and I found you back in sixty-seven. It's strange that I'll be on the other side of them from now on. Ought to be interesting learning a new trade and working with tangible assets."

"I was hoping that we'd get together someday, and it's happened." Alan held out his hand as said, "Welcome to the Wilcox family, Rob. You'll do well. I'm sure of it."

"Thanks, Alan. I'll see you for more orientation next week. Two o'clock at your office be OK with you?"

"Fine. See you then. Enjoy your weekend."

Keeping his date on the twenty-fifth, Rob spent most of the afternoon with Wilcox going over his land contracts, buy-sell agreements used by local brokers, escrow details, bank contacts, the names of lawyers Wilcox used, and countless other details that he would have to master before he would be able to manage affairs at the lake. It would take time, but Wilcox was pleased with Rob's early progress and said, "You're taking to this like a duck takes to water. Your corporate experience has helped. It shows. My guess is, I'll be able to turn everything over to you by the Fourth of July. That would suit me, because my Connecticut partner and I are in serious negotiations now to buy the office building in downtown Springfield that I mentioned when we met last fall. We have in mind that you'll manage it for us during the off-season out here. There'll be renovations to cost out and supervise and new tenants to bring in. We'll talk about that after you've pulled out of New York and are living here full time. You still have plenty to learn before you can hit the ground running when we open for business next Saturday. I've got to go, but let me see how you'd write an ad for next weekend's *Times*. When you're done, we'll call it in."

Rob remembered from a marketing class he'd taken years ago that a good rule to follow was to write copy for something that would generate the most inquiries, not necessarily the best item for sale. Looking at what was available, he picked an inexpensive lot and also a cottage being built on "spec" that was priced to make a prospective buyer sit up and take notice. When he'd finished, Wilcox said, "Perfect. You've gotten the message across very effectively at a minimum of words and cost. I don't have to teach you a thing about writing ad copy—that is, if you keep doing them like this."

"New product, but I'm not exactly a novice. Same principles apply."

"That's all your corporate experience coming through. I'm happy with what we've accomplished today, so why don't you go home to Sarah and then maybe take her out for dinner."

"Good idea, Alan. I'll do it. See you here at a little before nine next Saturday to get the season underway. My aim over the next six months is to make a fair amount of money. I'm not getting into real estate just to occupy my time. I have other ways I can do that. The search business has slowed down just a tad, but I still have bills to pay."

"I know about things like that, and I'll give you all the support you need. Enjoy the rest of your weekend, have a good week, and be careful on your way into New York and back."

Rob spent some time on Sunday, and then again at Helen's during the week, familiarizing himself with the details he had to absorb if he was to do a good job for Wilcox *and* to earn extra money from real estate sales. It wasn't especially complicated, but he'd need to understand all the laws that governed transactions and that would take a little time. And even though it was several years back, it helped that Rob had taken both agency and contract law courses at Iowa State. He was sure to benefit from them.

On the last Wednesday in March, Rob called both Mike and Greg to work out the details for all of them to spend their Easter weekend together. Mike said he'd come down to the station and meet Rob's train coming in at 4:22 on Friday. Greg would be a problem, Rob thought, but it turned out not to be the case. A classmate of his was from Hartford, he'd been offered a ride and could be dropped off on the way. "Tell his folks thanks. Since I'll be starting to work for Wilcox on Saturday, it'll be a big help not having to drive up to school after we get home. Mike and I won't be in until about six thirty or so, but Sarah will be there to let you in."

"Glad we can have the weekend together, even if you are going to work. Sure is easier being close now."

"I agree with that. Gotta run, Greg. See you on Friday evening."

"Bye, Dad."

Rob saw the week through, and, to his surprise, was handed a sizeable check for a senior-level placement. Equally important, he was on his way up to the woods and launching a new career in fresh, pine-scented air. By the time he and Mike got to the cottage, which he now jokingly called Chateau Grant, Sarah had everything in the way of snacks organized for three guys coming in from two directions. Her attention to detail won their hearts and the goodies took the edge off their hunger.

"You've done yourself proud, teacher lady," Rob said. "You must have known we'd be starved by now."

"This is just the beginning. I'm taking you to Romulo's for pizza after we've had our drinks. Yours is in the fridge. Since I did all the rest, you can pour my wine."

"Got yourself a deal, babe."

They had their drinks, and snacks, and then pizza. It was good to be four around the table once again. But the memories of that fourth person, Kate, Lu, Marianne, and Kim were very much on Rob's mind. The only decision he still regretted was that his relationship with Kim couldn't have survived. What a wonderful companion and wife she would have made. But she, too, was history now, so there was absolutely *no* point in looking back and continuing to inflict further pain on an already agitated psyche. Her private moments were in someone else's hands by this time. The thought of that certainty still hurt some.

Before dinner was finished, Sarah proposed a toast to Rob's success in the new career he was about to undertake. "To a bunch of sales and loads of good commissions," she said. The wine she'd had caused her voice to project just a little too much. Rob laughed but didn't forget to thank Sarah. The guys cheered quietly.

Following an evening of gentle loving, a good night's rest, and a hearty breakfast, Rob was ready for his initiation into the world of real estate. It didn't matter that what he'd be selling were small lots and cottages. The way he looked at it, being tutored by Alan Wilcox was the right way to begin his new career.

Rob got to the office well before nine. After spending a few minutes getting his desk organized, he turned his attention to the prospects who had just come through their door—and then to observing how to go about selling properties to people with discretionary funds. A page was turned to another chapter in Rob's life, and his new career got underway on the morning of April Fool's Day 1972. Should that mean anything? For some strange reason he thought about Kim and wondered.

This first weekend of sales activity was mostly orientation for Rob. He watched Alan at work and found that his was a polished style that had evolved over a good many seasons of selling properties around the lake. The Wilcox approach was, at minimum, to write a contract or at least ask for a deposit. Rob could see that his own approach would be different, and he very quickly arrived at a philosophy that would be at odds with Alan's. Wilcox was a salesman. Rob saw himself as a counselor of sorts. He'd first get inside a customer's head, determine what they wanted, and then work with them to meet whatever goals they had. He would later call it finding the "hot wire" and then making good use of whatever it was he'd learned. Be interesting to see how Rob's notion of selling stacked up with Alan's. His idea was to nail customers the first time they showed up. Rob's aim would be to gain a prospective buyer's confidence, and then act more like a friend and investment advisor rather than a hotshot sales guy. As the season progressed, Wilcox had to admit that he'd never seen anyone who'd worked for him previously get so many "comebackers", as he called them. The difference was that there was no pressure in the Grant method. As it turned out, it led to repeat customers and referrals from satisfied buyers. Wilcox had no quarrel with Rob's approach, because his technique made a good many sales, and that's what both of them wanted to see happen.

On the second Friday in June, Rob stopped overnight in Sheffield for Mike's graduation ceremonies—which would take place the following morning. Regina had invited Rob to stay at her place. It would be the last night they'd bed before he returned to Massachusetts, and she and her two sons, Kyle and Denny, moved back to Des Moines.

Following graduation, the two of them loaded the Mustang with all of Mike's gear. As they got ready to leave, Rob paid Regina the balance of what he owed her for boarding Mike, wished her well, and thanked her for everything she'd done for them since Thanksgiving 1968. Regina, sadness in her eyes, hugged Rob tightly and said a tearful good-bye. He was touched. As the years passed, he would remember June 10, 1972, not only because it was Mike's graduation day, but also because he'd never see Regina again after they drove away that morning.

On their way to Hampden Lake, Mike became the last of the Grants to detach himself from Sheffield. He'd now call the little house on Colonial Trail his home as well. And there was good news, too. He had a job waiting for him since Wilcox needed someone to clean up around the newly completed cottages, and to paint or stain them if the new owners wanted their retreats dressed up some. From that exposure, he discovered that there was a steady flow of referrals by the mostly summer residents, so it worked out that Mike was busy and made good money right from the first week he was home.

But if there was a downside to Rob's keeping busy, it was that he had no time off. He worked long hours in New York and then the full weekend for Wilcox. What began to develop over the summer, however, were both a high comfort level with real estate and less patience with Newcombe's martini-induced outbursts. He could see his weekly trips into Manhattan coming to an end fairly soon.

By the time the first weekend in July came around, Wilcox sat down with Rob to assess how he'd done so far. Alan said he was pleased with the way things had gone and also that he'd been right about his being able to turn all of his operations at the lake over to Rob by about mid-season.

"You're a quick study. I'm very satisfied with your progress and am putting you in charge starting today," Wilcox said. "You've gotten your salesman's license in record time, but I'll want you to sit for the broker's exam as soon as you think you're ready. That way, you can handle anything and everything that comes up out here. I'm getting busy with the Springfield office building, so I'm glad you've made it possible for me to stay on top of things there. It's a big investment."

"Broker's license? Not just yet, Alan. I still have a job to do in New York, you remember, so I'm working eight days a week—if you include the women in my life." They both chuckled.

"I know, but it'll be important. You'll be able to handle listings, properties that aren't mine, and you can earn a good part of those commissions. It's a way to make even more money."

"Magic words, boss. Since I'm starting to think about pulling out of New York, I'll be able to use the time I spend on the road to study the manual."

"When do you think you'll be up here permanently?"

"Inside sixty days is a good guess. Figure around Labor Day weekend. I've got to negotiate the recovery of the money I invested to capitalize the new company. Shouldn't be a problem. It'll just take a little time. But that won't have any influence on when I pull out of the firm. The guy who hired me has been on my case for some reason, and I've had about enough of his crap. Since I eventually brought in eight new clients, I expected better treatment. Problem is, his mid-day martinis have gotten to be toxic, so it's unpleasant for everyone around him. But I have a career now in Hampden Lake, thanks to you, so I'm ready to pack it in. Only thing is, I'm leaving Helen Flynn behind, the feisty little redhead you met, and that'll hurt some."

"I remember her. She didn't have any trouble saying what was on her mind. I thought she was cute and I guess she took exception to my having looked her over."

"Alan, let me tell you something that you may not want to hear. Every woman I ever brought up here, going back to Kate Skowron in November of sixty-eight, complained about your having made them feel like you'd undressed them. Helen was the first one to call you on it. It made all of the other ones feel very uncomfortable. I tell you this in case you're not aware of it, and I hope you'll take what I'm saying in the friendly spirit in which it's offered. It's possible that it may have cost you some sales."

"You know I like to look at a pretty woman, and the ones you brought with you were really easy on the eyes. Not many like them around here. But I didn't realize that I was carrying it to the extreme, so thanks for saying something about it. You could be right about the sales. There have been times when I lost them and I wasn't sure what went wrong. You could have the answer. It says to me that you're a friend, too."

"I am that. But I'm also an ex corporate level manager. Even though you're the boss, there are times when it's hard for me to stop behaving like one. What you did is something I'd have called to the attention of an employee."

"We're going to be a good team. But then I said that going back at least a couple of years ago."

When Rob got back to "Chateau Grant", he told Sarah that from today he was to be in charge of operations around the lake and that he'd be called Wilcox's general manager. She beamed.

"That's *wonderful* news, Rob. I'm so happy for you. But I'd have been shocked if Wilcox hadn't recognized what he got when he asked you to come to work for him. He has to be pleased with what you've been able to do so far."

"It's a beginning. The nice part about it is that I'm out in the fresh air, and it's such pretty country. What could be nicer? A plus is that you're here, too." That comment earned Rob an extra big hug. To show his appreciation, he hugged back.

As the summer wore on, and the weekly and weekend routines continued, Helen began to see the handwriting on the wall. Rob had talked enough about the working environment at NAGE, and his discontent, to know that it was just a matter of time before he left the company—and New York. They'd been lovers for nearly two years, and since Rob had never talked seriously about marriage, she guessed that their relationship was coming to an end. If he were to go, she would miss him. Terribly. But Helen, thirty-three now, felt it was probably time to acknowledge the truth of how matters stood, make the separation, and then get on with her life. She was attractive and had admirers, so settling on a good man at some point wouldn't be all that hard. The problem was that there'd never be another Rob Grant and he'd be impossible to replace, she guessed. But, if anything, she regretted that she didn't have all of what it took to land him. They had such pleasant memories, an abundance of them, and she would undoubtedly make love to him after he was gone, just as she'd done before they got involved.

During the last week of July, Helen forced the issue some and asked Rob, "What're your plans, my love? I know you aren't happy up on Thirty-fifth Street, so something has to give soon."

"You're ahead of me by a few days. I've asked for a meeting with Paul late on the thirty-first, next Monday afternoon. Like you, I think, he knows what's coming. The romance has run its course and it's time to pull the plug."

"Like ours, too, I guess."

"No, not at all like ours, sweetheart. You'll always be *very* special to me. But you're here, and my home and my work are up in Massachusetts now. I'm running all of Wilcox's operations, and although I'm not making the kind of money I could in New York, assuming someone wanted me, it's a decent living. Being out in the open and moving around has a lot of appeal. The other part of it is that I can easily afford living at the lake. The costs are a whole lot less than they are around the New York metro area."

"So, you're about done with Manhattan—and me?"

"I honestly wish I could say I'm not done with you, but once I've pulled out of NAGE, I can't sit around here all day while you're at the office, and then drive up to the lake and work every weekend. Deep down inside I love you very much, Helen, but geography is against us. My future is elsewhere, and, distasteful as it may be, I have to face up to the reality of what is."

Helen had a show of tears. "I need a hug." Rob accommodated her and added a gentle kiss to confirm that he meant what he said.

"To answer the other part of your question, I'll tell Paul on Monday that my last day will be August 31, and that will be my last night here."

It was an unsteady voice that said, "*Ohhh, Rob*!" He held her tightly for a few minutes.

"It's something I'd rather not have to deal with," Rob said, "and it's obvious that you don't want to either."

"No, but I'm a realist, and I understand. I'll be OK eventually because, like you and Marianne did more than three years ago, we have to accept the circumstances. You know that I'd hoped we could spend our lives together, and I still want that, but none of the dots connect anymore. I'm so terribly, terribly sorry that they don't. What makes it easier for me is that I have lots of family and friends here. But Mom and Dad are going to be awfully disappointed when I tell them what's about to happen."

"We'll talk more about this later, but if you'll have me during the week until the end of August, I'd like to stay here with you."

"One option I have is to ask you to move out now. But there isn't any way I could do that, so, until you're gone, I'd like us to spend whatever time together that we can."

"We both feel the same way, then. And I have to confess something. I'm going to be jealous of whoever it is that comes along after me."

"It'll take a while for me to get over you. By then the thought of that won't be as painful as it is now. But, I have a request."

"Which is?"

"Take me to bed."

"My pleasure." And it was. For both of them.

Following a busy weekend at the lake, Rob had his Monday meeting with Paul Lenard. It was then that Rob told him that he'd be leaving NAGE, his resignation to be effective at the end of the day on Thursday, August 31.

"I was pretty certain that it was the reason you wanted to meet. Newcombe has made life pretty unpleasant for you lately, so I'm not exactly in deep shock. It seems that during the last two years you've brought in more clients and may have gotten better at the search business than he is. If he'd stayed off the booze that might not have been the case."

"Doesn't matter. My oar is in the water up in Massachusetts now, and I'm running the whole show at Hampden Lake. This winter, there'll be an office building to look after, and then I'm told there are some other things in the works. Another part of it is that Sarah and I are getting to be close."

"Later this week, I'll have Diane prepare your letter of resignation. I know you'll want to take your capital out, and I'll have your check ready by the time you leave. One question. No, two. I'd like you to allow us to leave 'Grant' in the corporate name. Second, and as personal favor, I want you to remain on the Board. You help bring some stability to it."

"Appreciate the compliment, Paul. And to answer your questions, I don't have a problem with either of your requests."

"I'd have been surprised if you said you did."

"I'm staying with Helen during the week while I'm still in New York. I know she'd like to continue the IMMCorp association with NAGE, so I'll make sure you have her private number at the office, one you don't have now.

"She's been good to us—and you," Lenard said, smiling.

"I've earned some good fees because of Helen. Truth be known, it's going to be *very* hard to walk away from her. She's an awfully good woman, and I hope she eventually finds all the happiness she damn well deserves. Now, I'm going down to Thirty-second Street and repay some of my debt." Paul smiled knowingly.

Before Rob left for the day, he called Justine.

"Hi, gal. You'll never guess who this is."

"Don't you believe it, guy. Hard to mistake a voice that's attached to someone from Iowa." She laughed. "Good to hear from you again. Are you calling to tell me that I'm on your agenda again? Hope so."

"Good guess. But not immediately. I'm going to be leaving New York, permanently, on Labor Day weekend. My last night here is September 1, a Friday, and I was wondering if I might spend it with you."

"Oh, Rob. *Yes*! I'm not into tears, as you know, but you've almost got me there and my office isn't the place to have them. What an honor you do me. I'm deeply touched."

"Now, the other part of it is that I have two tickets for *Man of La Mancha*. The show's been on tour for a year, but the original cast came back in late June to do 140 performances. This time they're at the Vivian Beaumont. Richard Kiley is singing the lead again. Interested?"

"*Extremely*! I can hardly believe this. You're incredible, Rob Grant. How exciting. And that includes when we get back to East Eighty-third."

"Thought you'd squeeze that in somehow." Rob chuckled.

"You haven't worked me into your schedule very much in recent months, but this makes up for it. That you'd spend your last night in New York with me is *so* special. I know it could have been someone else."

"It could have, but like I told you some time ago, you taught me something about people. You recall my comments about your having helped me find inner beauty, and I've met a young lady who has it. I've also mentioned her name, Sarah, and what we have is budding. It'll take a while, but we'll see how we do. One thing about it, she's a whole lot younger than I am."

"I'd like to meet her if ever you come back into New York to visit."

"No plans, but you never know. I've got to run, dear heart. We'll talk again before we have our last night together and then build up another big fire." They were chuckling as they hung up.

The weeks to follow all ran together and were a blur. Rob worked extra hours and earned some good fees in the days before he left NAGE. Late as he was some nights, Rob and Helen still looked after each other frequently and both were able to smile broadly when morning came. He'd miss Helen and her pixie-like smile.

As had been his routine since early April, Rob spent each weekend at the lake working for Alan Wilcox. Then, after closing the office for the day, he'd share his evenings with Sarah. What he hadn't told her until they were nearing the last holiday of the summer season was that he'd be making Hampden Lake his home, permanently, starting on that Labor Day weekend. It was pure coincidence that his first day "at home" would be exactly one year to the day since they'd met. She was euphoric!

When the last week of August was upon them, the NAGE countdown began. On Monday, the twenty-eighth, Rob would make his final trip into New York. This time, he'd be driving all the way into the city. But before he left, Sarah gave him a concerned look and pleaded with him to be extra careful. "I don't want anything to happen to you," she said.

"It was the weekend before my fortieth that Marianne called me 'Mr. Worrywart' because I was concerned about her. Maybe you can be Miss Worrywart and we'd be a pair of 'em. You know the story. I had every reason to be, because within a matter of a few days she found out that her disease was fatal."

"I don't like the comparison, Rob. Not a all."

"There's some valium in the medicine cabinet. Take half a tablet with water. It'll help."

"If it's OK with you, I'll pass."

"In that case, let me give you a big hug and a promise that I'll drive defensively. I'm going to come back to you whole because you're *very* important to me. OK?"

"You just got my attention with that. Gave me a shiver."

Rob gave Sarah a firm, reassuring hug and a soft kiss. They made her feel much better.

"Be back on Saturday afternoon. It should be just about the same time you showed up with Wilcox last year."

"When I see you coming up the road, I'll start getting our drinks ready."

"You know me. I'm nearly always thirsty. Alan is covering for me, so we can have a little welcome home party. Be a pleasure. I haven't had a Saturday off since last March."

Sarah waved as Rob turned into Old Town Road. She was already counting the hours until he was back—and exclusively hers. During the eight months he'd been driving back and forth, Sarah never asked where he was staying. She had an idea but didn't want to confirm her suspicions. During those lonely weeks, she got to calling herself "the queen of denial". But now the split weeks were at an end, and the thought of that gave her reason to be in high spirits—and with tears of happiness.

When Rob got into Manhattan, he never dreamed it would be possible to find a parking spot on East Thirty-second Street not far from Helen's apartment. Moving his stuff out later in the week would be fairly easy. There wasn't much of anything at the NAGE office that was his, and since late spring he'd worn winter clothes when he went back to the lake and then left them there. What was still hanging in Helen's closet didn't amount to much.

Once parked, Rob walked up to East Thirty-fifth Street and began the process of wrapping up work on his current searches. Since he was pretty much on top of them, there really wasn't a whole lot for him to do. He'd get the last of his fee checks during the week, and since it was a rather good sum of money, it would certainly help. One item on his agenda was to call Justine and confirm that they still had a theatre date on Friday night.

"Justine. Hi. I just wanted to make sure you haven't forgotten about *Man of La Mancha* this weekend."

"Not a chance, lover. And I'm planning on taking you fully captive afterwards. That doesn't have to be explained."

Rob laughed. "You're right. No need to. But before we go up to West Sixty-fifth, we can have a bite to eat. It'll be early, so what do you think?"

"Better that way than an after-theatre supper. I wouldn't want it to stand in the way of having you at home with me."

"Sounds like you're in that 'hot pants' condition again. Ought to be an exhilarating evening."

"That's still a crude way to put it, Rob, but you've always been able to recognize the signs. I've got to run now. See you at about six, or a little before?"

"I'm at loose ends here this week, so it'll most likely be sometime around five thirty."

They hung up feeling the fire building. It didn't matter what he and Helen would do during the week to say good-bye because Justine would make it a memorable final night in New York.

At the end of the day, Rob went back to East Thirty-second Street and into the arms of a waiting Helen. She was glad to see him and it seemed to Rob that she was holding up well given that their relationship was coming to an end. Very different than with Kim. He asked Helen about it.

"We're going to make this a good week, sweetheart. Had Marianne lived," there were those words again, "I'd never have been given the chance to share all of what we've had for almost two years now. I'm counting my blessings because, considering your loss, I've been happier than I had any right to hope for. I'll probably always love you, but I'm not going to let the weeks and months after Friday morning destroy me. I'm a liberated woman, Rob Grant, and I'll see to it that I find happiness again.

It'll no doubt take time, but I'm still young and I *will* have a life after you're gone. Seeing the Marzanos will help me get through the bumpy spots."

"You deserve the best, Helen. But it sounds as if I'm going to have a harder time on Friday than you are. You've willingly given me your love, without any questions, so there have been times when I felt like I've used you. That wasn't my intent. Had I been able to live and work in the New York area, we'd have most likely gotten to the altar. You're an absolute sweetheart, Helen, and you'll be on my mind for a long while to come."

"C'mon, Rob. I'm an adult, and clearly understood what was going on. If you hadn't cared for me, we wouldn't have come this far. Don't think about it. You're the man I want in my life, but since I can't have you, the least you can do is take me to bed. We've each had our say, so let's get on with a week we'll always remember."

They then made every attempt to do just that, and succeeded, they agreed, as the week was coming to an end. They ate out, walked the neighborhood, had late afternoon drinks, saw *Everything You Ever Wanted to Know about Sex*, which didn't do a thing for either of them, and loved every night through Thursday. On Friday morning, they decided there was no need for an encore because they'd done it all the evening before. "There isn't any way we could improve on last night," Helen said, "so let's call it a perfect ending to our affair. For certain, I'll remember it. You *were* an animal."

"Just trying to leave enough of my growl behind so that Rob Grant will always be a pleasant memory."

"I won't need any reminders. Ever."

After Rob put what was left of his clothes in the Mustang, he came back in to say good-bye to Helen.

"I just had a look in the closet. Sure is empty now. It breaks my heart." And then the liberated woman cried.

"Helen. *Ohhh*, sweetheart. It really hurts to see you like this." Rob showed tears of his own.

"We've had a good three and a half years, my love. Especially the last two." She smiled weakly. "I'm sorry it's over. That's no mystery. And there's really no need to tell you that I'll never forget what we've had. But my life goes on without you. So, I wish you success in your new career, and I hope you find another woman someday that you can love and make as happy as you have me."

"Thank you for your good wishes, dear heart. You're such a love, and I'm sure that a good man will come along one day—someone who can give you all the happiness you have a right to. I'll say a little prayer if it'll help make it happen."

Rob Grant and Helen Flynn hugged tightly, and shared a warm and affectionate kiss. Then he was out on Thirty-second Street and gone from her life. Helen remained behind closed doors just long enough to dry her tears, and then she left for Wall Street and IMMCorp. The company where the two of them had met would never be the same. And the empty office that Rob had at one time occupied would be a constant reminder of what they'd shared going back to his first day at work: April 14, 1969.

There was very little left for Rob to do at NAGE. One of the few things that remained was to turn a half-dozen search files over to Paul.

"I'll be giving these to some of our senior people with the hope they can finish your searches successfully. If they do, I'll see to it that you get half of your fee share. Since you've done most of the work on them, that may not be fair but there has to be an incentive on this end to follow them through to completion."

"I understand, Paul. It isn't a problem. If the files just sat here, then nothing would get done and 100 percent of zero is still zero. A couple of the mid-level searches should fly, I think."

"We'll see that they get finished. Change of subject. You've seen Helen?"

"I put what was left of my clothes in the Mustang and then said good-bye to her earlier this morning. She was fine all through the week until she looked inside the empty closet. That undid her. It was tough on me, too. We go back to our having first met in February of sixty-nine and you know what a sweetheart she is. I'd have given anything not to do what I did. But the reality of it is, I can't have an arrangement here part of the week and another one in Massachusetts. Helen's tough, a survivor, will find a good man, and eventually have a loving and contented life. If anyone on earth deserves that, she damn well does. But I *hate* what I've done to her."

"You gave Diane her private number down at IMMCorp?"

"I did."

"Well, about all I have to do is give you checks for the fees you've just earned, plus the certified check that represents the return of your initial capital investment."

Lenard handed Rob an envelope with three checks in it, and he asked that Rob sign an acknowledgment that he gotten them. "Now, I've got to be on my way. I'm going to miss not working together, but we're going to stay in touch. There'll be a little bit of business to finish up, as we discussed. My broader meaning is that both Jessie and I want you and Sarah, I presume, to come over to our little lakeside retreat in Columbia County. It's near Albany, but it'll be an easy drive for you now. Just come straight across on the Mass Pike and, after you cross into New York, take

Route 22 north. The directions are on one of the sheets in the envelope with your checks."

"First. Yes, it'll most likely be Sarah. It'll be a year tomorrow since we met, and we've grown closer. It may be that I've found that someone I've spent almost four years trying to find. My steps along the way have been very deliberate, but my self-imposed mandate was that I needed time to sort out my feelings. It hasn't been good for my guys—or the 'candidates' either, I guess. But now that I'm at Hampden Lake, my inventory is down to one. Usually I've had a three ring circus and a juggling act going on all the way back to the fall of sixty-eight." Rob laughed. "My son, Mike, used to say that I was pretty busy. He was right."

"Well, we'd love to have you come see us. All of our phone numbers are on the sheet."

"Thanks, Paul. I really appreciate it."

"Rob. Best of luck to you. If you and Sarah decide to become a team instead of two singles together, we'll want to be among the first to know. I like the girl—even if she did pass out on your sofa earlier in the year." Both Paul and Rob laughed gently at the memory. "But there's no mistaking it. She's a delight and would be good for you. It's time for you to settle down and stop trying to look after all the needy young women in the neighborhood."

"I'll take your comments under consideration. All the best, Paul."

"And to you, Rob."

Chapter Thirteen

After Paul Lenard left the building, Rob made two calls. The first was to Stan Baird to say good-bye and to thank him for giving NAGE a chance to do business with IMMCorp.

"Rob. Good to hear from you. I understand you're into a new career up in Massachusetts. Not much chance you'll be able to sell us any real estate." Stan chuckled softly.

"I'd suppose you're right. The reason I called is simply to express my appreciation, and to say that it's been a pleasure working with you."

"And I can say the same to you. I deeply regret that it went the way it did with your job here. By the way, you're leaving a pretty sad little girl behind. Helen's confessed all your sins, and I'm sorry about that, too. You were a great team and would have had a good marriage, too, I believe."

"I agree with you, completely, but Helen probably explained that the geography is all wrong. This is my last day in Manhattan and, try as I did to find an answer, there isn't any way we could make it work."

"She's already told me all about it. You've had a very difficult three years and something like this doesn't help. The plus side is that you've shown me what kind of spine you have. I'm proud to have known you."

"Thanks, Stan. That means a lot to me. Time to go. I wish you well."

"You, too, Rob. Best of luck."

Rob's second call was to RD.

"Boss. It's a voice from your checkered past."

"It is that." RD laughed. "How're you, Rob?"

"OK, I guess. This is my last day in New York. I'm pulling out of the search business and going to make my home in Hampden Lake. The new career is in real estate. The head man has made me general manager of his recreational properties businesses and it's a full time job. During the off-season, there'll be an office building to manage and there's a chance I *may* get involved with condo conversions in Florida."

"I assume you won't be making New York money, but you sound like you're in a positive frame of mind."

"Other than saying good-bye to Helen this morning, I'm fine. I'll miss her, but you know about Sarah. She's turning out to be a real sweetheart. There are lots of other things to talk about but time is short. I don't suppose there's a chance in hell that you're free for lunch."

"I'm spending the long weekend on the Cape with Marcia and am just about ready to leave. I make the trip fairly often, so what I'd like to propose is that I make a side trip once in a while to see you and Sarah."

"We'd love it. You have my number up there, so call me. Maybe when the leaves turn, we can arrange something then. Welcome news, RD."

"It's time to pick up Marcia, so I've got to go. We'll stay in touch, just as we have since we left Sentry. I'll call you out of the blue one of these days. Count on it."

"Really look forward to hearing from you. Say hi to Marcia. It's time all of us met."

"Couldn't agree more. Take care of yourself, Rob."

"You, too, RD. God bless."

At the end of the morning, Doug Newcombe came into Rob's little office and said that he wanted to chat for a few minutes.

"I've been a little hard on you during these last few months, and I want to apologize. As much as anything, I feel guilty because my attitude toward you recently is probably responsible for this being your last day with NAGE."

"It was a contributing factor I suppose it's fair to say. But there's more to it than that. Sarah is part of it. Having had about enough of New York is another, and the long commute was the final nail in the coffin, you might say. You wouldn't have done it for eight months like I did."

"Not even *one* month. But I guess part of my problem is that your search techniques are so different from mine. Yet you've been good at and have turned out to be one of the best people I've ever had. In some ways, the student has overtaken the mentor. I suppose that's irritated me some. But alcohol has obviously gotten to the point where it's taking more out of me than I'm taking out of it. It's a little late now, at least in your case, but I'm trying hard not to drive others away because of it."

"If it came down to the fundamental reason why I'll be gone at the end of the day, it's because I've gotten into something new and it's just plain enjoyable. Being outside appeals to me, so the farm boy has resurfaced. It's pretty country, the big pines smell good, and at the end of the day, I'm a pretty happy guy. Sarah contributes a great deal to that."

"You've had your share of escapades, so maybe it's time you found yourself a permanent companion, or even tied the knot."

"Could be Sarah someday. I've been cautious, and you know how many beds you have to test before you get it right." Newcombe liked that and laughed. "But by sheerest coincidence, I'm spending the night with the same gal I did that morning I called you in August two years ago. It was to ask if I could come by to talk about going to work for you."

"I remember it well. I thought you called pretty early for somebody who lived in Connecticut. And there was a line you used that I thought was hilarious. What was it? Oh, yeah. You said something about getting your ashes hauled, but that the fire was out and you we're cleaning up the mess. I could relate to that and liked your line. Still do. Obviously." Newcombe laughed again.

"Justine is quite a woman. Lots of interests similar to yours, meaning theatre, concerts, art shows, and the like. She's also noisy in bed when she does her thing. I'll miss that, too."

"My lady and I are going down to the Jersey shore, so I'm on my way. I wish you good luck, Rob, and I hope that you won't become a stranger."

"No reason to."

"You've put a lot of yourself into your work, brought in new clients, and earned some serious money for the new company. I want you to know that I'm grateful for all you've contributed."

"Thanks, Doug. I'm glad that you and I have made peace. I feel good about that."

"Me, too. I wish you well. Bye, Rob."

There was no one around at mid-day, so Rob fixed himself a small meal and ate in the office. Alone. "Not the way it should be on my last day here," he thought.

During the afternoon, he worked on files that he'd leave behind. He wanted to make sure they were complete and up to date. As the afternoon wound down, Rob made one last call, this one to the Marzanos. They were sorry to learn that Rob would be leaving New York but said they understood. Carlo promised that he'd continue to look after the roses at Marianne's grave. Before they finished, Rob let them know that Helen would continue to visit, probably on the same once-a-month schedule that the two of them had kept up for over two years. Then at about five o'clock, he collected the few items that were his, said good-bye to Diane, who, surprisingly, showed him a sad face. Rob then walked out of the offices of Newcombe Associates, Grant, Engelhardt—never to return.

Rob made the short walk back to his Mustang that he parked on Thirty-second Street and threw everything in the trunk. He looked back at Helen's building one last time, felt badly for the heartache he was leaving behind, brought his now very dirty Mustang to life and drove off. He didn't have all that far to go. Turning north into Third Avenue, Rob drove straight up to Eighty-third Street. With people having left town for the long weekend, he gambled that he'd find a space somewhere close to Justine's building located on the corner of the two streets. Eighty-third ran westbound, so he turned left, heading toward Lexington, and, bingo, he came upon someone just pulling out. He eased into the space, said a small prayer of thanks, and locked the car for the night.

Back on East Thirty-second street, Helen got home just minutes after Rob had left. She saw that his Mustang was gone from the place he'd parked it and then said quietly, "Guess that makes it official. It's over." The tears on her cheeks confirmed how painful this moment was for her.

When Rob got to Justine's building, he pressed the buzzer for 11B and heard a voice say, "Yes?"

"Guess who?"

"No need to. Come right up."

When he got to Justine's floor, she was standing at the door and showing Rob a bright smile. She'd lost a little weight and looked delicious.

"Hi, lover. Look at you. It isn't like it was when you came back from Australia, but you have a good tan." With that she gave him a warm kiss and a matching hug.

"Great to see you again, gal. It's been too long. My fault, and I apologize."

"Don't know why. That you'd spend your last night in New York with me makes me think *I'm* special, and it's really good to see you one last time before you leave me behind."

"You've always been near the top of my list, but I recall you telling me that I wasn't a keeper because I'm twice divorced, nearing forty, and a gentile. Two things haven't changed. One has. I'm forty two and a half now. Good grief! Has it been almost three years since we started building those big fires after dark?"

"Thanksgiving of sixty-nine. Yes, it has, and I remember that visit out to Sheffield very clearly. What a treat it was."

"And I remember the night we met a couple of weeks earlier. I hope you're still as noisy when you do your thing as you were then. Last time, I thought you'd mellowed some. But I like it when you sound very much like a lioness."

"We'll find out later on if I'm in good voice. But we have to stop talking like this or we'll never eat or get to the theatre."

"Save the excitement for later. What are we doing about food? It's your neighborhood, so I'll leave that in your capable hands."

"We're going to eat here. I've already got something started, and it'll be a whole lot simpler than going out and then trying to be on time for curtain call."

"Fine with me."

Justine whipped up a light but adequate meal and after they'd eaten, they talked on for a few minutes. Then once they'd cleaned up, they went down to hail a cab. It would make their trip over to West Sixty-fifth Street much easier than trying to drive it. Since they were close by, Rob pointed out where he'd parked.

"That's not the same car you had before. It's a newer model. Another Mustang, is it?"

"Yep. Mike took the other one out one night and tore it up. I've had this one a little over a year. But the fact that you haven't seen it tells me how long it's been since you were in Sheffield. I've really neglected you, dear heart." A cab driver saw Rob's hand signal and pulled up. "Vivian Beaumont, please." On their way, they continued their chat.

"You've had loads of things go wrong since early seventy, so I understood the reasons why your calls were few and far between. And since I'm not wife material, I couldn't make any demands. But you know I like spending time with you, and at one point I reconsidered how I'd respond if you ever asked me again to think about something longer-term. We're a good fit and it would've worked out very nicely. I'm sure of it."

"Damn, Justine! Where were you when I was hurting? After I lost Marianne, I'd have run straight into your arms had I known they were there. The calls helped, but you didn't give me *any* encouragement."

"No, I thought the initiative should be yours. Guess I was wrong to think that way."

"I agree with that. Well, whatever, it's too late now. The cottage is built, it's home, I have a new career, and a part-time roommate it seems. Sarah. The same girl I mentioned before."

"Sounds promising, Rob. I really do want you to find yourself, and a good woman, and finally know what happiness is. I mean that. You've had enough of the other, so it's time. You're a good man, and in my own way I care about you more than you know."

"It's sweet of you to say those things, dear heart. I hope we can stay in touch and remain friends. You're important to me, and you remember at least two of the reasons why I say that."

"I do, and I appreciate it that you give me credit for teaching you something about looking for inner beauty."

At the theatre, they were there in plenty of time to get situated and go through the Playbill. Before curtain call, Justine asked Rob if he'd seen many shows.

"Very few. Snag has been finding the time. While I was trying to deal with all the recent hits we've taken, I worked in a couple, though. A show I saw last year that I really enjoyed was *Butterflies are Free.* Good cast with Keir Dullea, Eileen Heckart, and Blythe Danner, I think it was. Well done. The other one was *Lost in the* Stars, based on the book, *Cry the Beloved*

Country, if I remember correctly. It was an off-Broadway show, but it didn't last long. I saw both shows by myself."

"Why didn't you ask me if I was interested in going with you?"

"Mostly because they were weekday matinees, and I knew you couldn't get away. I'd get caught up with my search work and would sneak off under the pretense of doing something productive." Rob chuckled. "I'd get to the point where I'd need a break from all the phone calls and that was my diversion. Twice over a period of eighteen months, so it wasn't major corporate theft."

"We might have gone in the evening."

"Time to confess. I've been staying with a young lady down in the Murray Hill area. There was a chance *that* would've worked, but with her job here, and a good one, my move to Massachusetts killed it. We're both sorry about the way it turned out, so maybe we should change the subject."

Before Justine could respond to Rob's appeal, the house lights dimmed. "Looks like it's being changed for us. We'll talk more about it later. Probably in the morning," she whispered. "No time for it tonight." She showed Rob a mischievous smile.

The show was a smash! It's no wonder it had a six year run before its current revival. Joan Diener's performance as Aldonza was vibrant. Richard Kiley was perfect as Don Quixote, and he had the audience in the palm of his hands when he sang *The Impossible Dream*. You could have heard a pin drop. But Rob thought Irving Jacobson, the actor who played the part of Sancho, stole the show. Justine was thrilled that she'd been invited to share the evening with Rob. "This was at the Martin Beck Theatre until they went on the road early last year," she said. "I had a chance to go and turned it down. What a mistake that was. But then, I couldn't have spent this last evening in New York with you. What a pleasure. Thank you, Rob."

"You're welcome, love. Maybe this helps get even for all you've done for me starting with that fiery night in November three years ago, and then the great job you did with the turkey a couple of weeks later. Made our holiday."

"And you made mine. It was so peaceful at your place in Sheffield, that is until late in the evening." She smiled at the recollection of those nights. "If we can find a cab, let's get back to East Eighty-third and see if we can't stir up more of the same kind of excitement."

It took a while, but their turn for a taxi did eventually come up and they went back to Justine's apartment. After they got comfortable, she poured two nightcaps.

"I see you still have the Fijian tapa I brought back from my last trip to Australia. Looks great."

"It's a conversation piece. I'm still crazy about it. So unusual, and I'll leave right where it is. It'll remind me of you."

"There were a couple more of them. One was for Marianne. She asked me to have it framed and then keep it for her until she got back from Washington. I did it just about like yours, but she never saw it. And I have to tell you that it's still hard for me to look at the building across the street, the one she lived in. I'll probably want to glance at it one more time before I leave in the morning. What memories. But enough of what was. It's time you and I got reacquainted."

And that they did. Justine was ready and when they joined, Rob heard a low moan. It was her way of letting him know how she felt. "Mmmm, you feel good. Now, love me."

"You still talk too much. Let the practice begin."

Always quick to respond to Rob's special treatment, she suddenly turned rigid and came to a pulsating climax. It was accompanied by her familiar animal-like wail. Then she wrapped her legs around Rob and orchestrated their movements again. There was no escape. She was after another of the same—and found it.

"You're good at waiting. Let's practice some more."

"How many more of those do you have left?"

"At least one. Maybe more."

"Let's find 'em.

They loved on until Justine had fully satisfied her ravenous appetite.

"That first night, remember what I asked you to do when I was ready for you."

"Never forget. 'Decorate my interior'."

"Do it. *Now*!"

She came back for another trip to the epicenter of exhilaration. Rob joined her as she arrived. When she felt his release and heard him add that deep growl of his own, the animal in her was heard one more time.

"It's all yours now. Interior decorated."

"Is it ever! Fully."

Then they rested. It was their only option.

When they'd recovered, Justine said, "You took me back to a place tonight that I've only been to once or twice before. It's at times like this that I regret my decision not to pursue a longer-term relationship. You've always been a joy to be around. We like many of the same things and are sensational in bed. I've made a mistake in judgment, Rob." She trembled ever so slightly.

"Sensational? That's a pretty big word to use on a short guy like me. But you're pretty good yourself, dear heart."

"I'm going to miss you. It's a shame that we won't have any more concerts, or theatre, or art exhibitions together."

"Justine, you know it couldn't have worked out for us any more than it might've with the little gal down on East Thirty-second Street. I'm up in the woods now and mostly out of circulation. New York is history—as is the kind of career I expected to go on forever. I have plenty of regrets myself, but there *is* one thing that will always make me smile."

"And that is?"

"When I called you from Sydney. I could visualize your papa rocking back and forth on his feet as he wondered what it was costing."

She laughed, and then said, "I was just about into tears now. Very rare. Thank you for saving me from more of a display." The mood was brightened by the simple recollection of what had happened late in December nearly three years ago.

"Tomorrow morning," Rob said, "I'm going to put you in charge."

"I'll be ready. That'll take me close to where I was tonight. I'm glad you're here. It'll be a night I'll want to remember."

"Me too, sweetheart."

Exhausted, they embraced and slept snugly all night long. It felt good to both of them.

When morning came, they spent a little extra time with preliminaries before Justine took charge. As she settled down on Rob, she fairly purred. Their movements were gentle, and it didn't take her long to reach a place that excited her. When they returned to a slower pace, she said, "I'd like you to make your last donation to the cause in the conventional way. I want you on top."

"Are you ready for more decorating?"

In an unsteady voice, she said, "Yes. And give me all you've got."

That turned Rob on, and he became an animal. It wasn't long before he delivered. His climax reached, Justine felt it and she joined him. Their growls were a duet. Simply magnificent!

After Rob and Justine had showered and dressed, they sat at breakfast and reminisced about how they'd met, and all they'd done since then.

"Hate to see this come to an end, but you were right about us last night. Like you said, we couldn't have made it work with me here and you there. Same situation with your lady down in Murray Hill. But you're leaving some heartaches in your wake. You know that."

"And I'm taking my own supply of them with me. Neither of you is alone when it comes to that. Helen was a candidate, if you can call her that. But, I've had the better part of five years behaving like a hummingbird."

"Meaning?"

"Going from flower to flower, and . . . well, you understand."

Justine smiled. "Interesting way to put it."

"I suggested that to Helen a long time ago. She didn't agree with the concept."

"Not sure I do either. But tell me about your Helen—and the girl up at the lake."

Rob replayed the story about the two different kinds of relationships he'd had with Helen and how it could well have been a good marriage. "She's an absolute sweetheart."

"And the one in Massachusetts?"

"Young, but she seems to be taken with this old relic. Name's Sarah Stuart, by the way. Age difference is about the same as it was with Marianne. She wasn't concerned about it and neither is Sarah. Could be it's because my people live forever. But I have to be mindful of it. We'll see. My inventory is down to one and the pickings are pretty slim up there in the woods. Could be that's exactly what I need and I'll be forced to stop behaving like a horny hummingbird." They both laughed. "Sarah, like Helen, is a love; very sweet. It's the wrong thing to say, maybe, but she has the same even disposition and gentle ways that my mother has. They'll get along well, assuming we get that far."

"You've sure got more going for you than I do, and I'm living in Manhattan. But you've known right along that I'm something of a recluse and am still fussy about my friends. It's one of the reasons I hate to lose you. Ever since we met, you've accepted me for what and who I am. Not many like you around, even in a city this size."

"We'll stay in touch. I'd like that, even though it's unlikely I'll come back to New York anytime soon. Maybe never. But you've reached a place inside that matters. I'll not forget that—or you."

"Those are lovely words, Rob. All of them. Thank you."

"Now, sweetheart, it's time I started for home. You have my address and my phone number. If ever you want to talk, call me. Or write. It'll tell me that I've meant something to you."

"You have, right from that first night we met at Capricorn's."

"Let me get my stuff together, and I'll be on my way."

"I'm going down to your car with you. All right?"

"You bet. Guess I do mean something to you after all."

As they got on the elevator, she said, "Not the way to put it, Rob. Your ego is fishing for something."

Rob laughed. "My dear, perceptive friend—and lover without equal. We *could* have made a go of it."

Across Third Avenue, and standing next to Rob's Mustang, Justine said, "About your comment, I agree. But don't do that to me. Not now. We know what the realities are. You have someone at home who matters. I sincerely hope it'll be right for both of you and that it leads to years and years of happiness."

Rob reached out and hugged Justine with feelings that surprised even him. He felt her react just a bit emotionally.

"I know you're not into public displays of affection, but I would give you a good-bye kiss if you don't mind."

"I don't mind at all, Rob. Public be damned. Make it a good one. Something I'll remember."

And he did. Justine trembled for a moment and then returned his kiss. It sent a message that Rob would try to sort out on his way out of New York and up the Merritt Parkway.

He slid into his Mustang, brought the big engine to life, and then rolled down the window. "Take good care of yourself, Justine. You matter a great deal to me. Always have."

She leaned in and gave Rob another warm kiss. "Bye, Rob Grant. I'll be thinking about you."

Rob eased out of the parking space, one that someone already wanted, and then he and Justine Siegel waved a final good-bye. Within a few minutes, he would leave New York behind. From this hour forward, these final moments in Manhattan would mark the end of several chapters of his professional and personal history. Later, when he'd think back about them, they'd alternately be the delight and despair of his years here between the ages of thirty-seven and forty-two. The memories, all of them, were to be savored. Hard as this day was for Rob, it was also difficult for Justine as well—someone who was never into tears. When she got back to her apartment, she laid down on her disheveled bed and cried.

Maneuvering through surprisingly heavy late Saturday morning traffic, Rob worked his way over to the Bruckner Expressway. From there, he got onto the Hutchinson River Parkway—and then finally the familiar Merritt. Once he'd passed through the upper end of Sheffield, he was on familiar ground, and really on his way home! Within three hours, Rob was driving up the slope at the lower end of Colonial Trail. As he turned into the road behind the cottage, and into his drive, he hit the horn. Sarah recognized it instantly and flew out the back door to welcome her man home.

"You sure are a sight for sore eyes. I'm *so* glad you're back safe and sound. I worried about the 'last trip' because I remember Daddy telling me about pilots who went out on that one last mission during World War II. Sometimes they never came back."

"Ah, my sweet little worrywart. It's hardly the same, but I'm pleased to know that you like this aging pilot. "

Sarah laughed. "You're a long way from that, I'm happy to say. But I need a big hug and a kiss, and then I'll help you get your things into the house."

Rob delivered and it was obvious that Sarah Stuart was delighted to see this man who, for some time now, had meant so much to her. Once they'd unloaded the car and got everything inside, he unzipped his garment bag, the same one that had gone all over the world with him when he was with IMMCorp. From under his shirts, he took out a long, narrow box.

"Since you've had to put up with travel worries and weeks alone, I brought you something to take the edge off your anxieties."

"I don't have any now. You're home—for good and ever."

"Does that mean you aren't going to open the box."

"Of course I am, you silly goose."

Sarah carefully removed the ribbon and paper and then opened the slim box. Inside, she found a simple gold necklace. "Ohhh, Rob! It's just gorgeous. You know how much I love gold jewelry—and you. Thank you so much. You didn't have to do this, but I'm glad you did. I'll put it on before we go out to dinner."

"It's my way of saying that you're important to me. And it's partly a first anniversary gift. We met just about now exactly one year ago today. Remember? So wear the necklace this evening, and then you can try me on afterwards."

"That's naughty talk, kind of, but I'm overdue for that."

"We both are. Where's Mike?" Rob asked.

"He's staining the inside of a chalet that some New York people had built by their own contractors. It's interesting that they're Norwegian. They came over to find Mike. Nice people."

"I guess he's still busy, then."

"Sure is. And he's making good money. Between Wilcox, and all the referrals, he's done very well since he came up in June."

"Has he been around much?"

"Not really. He's found some guys his age and they've been running around together. About the only time he stops by now is to get a change of clothes. But I imagine that since you're home he'll spend more time with us."

"With *us*? Sounds like you've mostly moved into Chateau Grant."

"I'd like it to continue. Unless you don't want me around."

"Aw, my Punkin. I hurt you when I said that. I'm sorry. So to erase any doubts you have, let me confess that I *really* do like having you here. It'll be a way of finding out if something longer-term will work."

Sarah showed Rob a beguiling smile and then gave him a bear hug of her own. "You don't very often tell me how you feel about us, but that says a lot to me. It makes me feel all warm and tingly inside. And I like my new pet name, too. Punkin. Cute."

"An impulse. It just popped out. But about being tingly, we'll add to that later on." Rob showed her a playful smile.

"I can tell what's on *your* mind. I've been that way ever since you drove in. Love the idea!"

"Yeah! Change of direction. Whatever happened to those drinks you promised on Monday to have ready when I got home?"

"They're already made. Well, mostly. Tall cool ones for a warm Labor Day weekend."

When Sarah finished putting their coolers together, she thanked Rob again for the pretty necklace and then offered a toast to their having met a year ago on this same Saturday afternoon. "I hope we have many more, Rob. And you know by now that I mean that. You've brought so much happiness into my life, and I'd like what we have to continue."

"And you also know by now how deliberate I am. Maybe it'll give you hope if I tell you that you're beginning to grow on me. I always enjoy it when we're together, and it's why I said I like having you here. You're easy to be with, and you're good for me in lots of ways ."

"Nice words. I'm feeling even better inside."

"Well then, just wait until tonight."

"There you go again. You sound deprived, but for some reason I don't think that's the case. What I want to believe is that it's me."

"It is. There were a couple of difficult good-byes, but never mind your suspicions. Let 'em die. You're what counts. We'll make my homecoming and the start of another new chapter in my life a memorable one."

"Hope I can find Sarah on some of the pages."

"I think you'll find that you're already there—with probably lots more of 'em to follow."

As they were finishing their drinks, Alan Wilcox drove up. He had customers with him, but he came up for a couple of minutes to welcome Rob home and also to ask if he'd be in the office tomorrow.

"Thanks for the welcome home, Alan. Yep, I'll be in before nine. You can spend your Sunday in Forest Park with your wife and kiddoes. Appreciate it that you could stand in for me. And that'll be it, because New York and I are now history. You predicted that some time ago, and I'm here permanently from now on."

"Welcome news, Rob. When we get into October, McCallum and I will want to talk to you about the office building in Springfield. We're just about to close on it, so by the time you're done here at the lake, we're going to need you full time on State Street."

"You can keep me current as we go along. You'll be out here from time to time, so let me have it in small doses if you will."

"Sure. Now, you'll have to excuse me. I've got to get back to the people I've left waiting in the car."

"OK. Thanks for stopping by, Alan. See you out here again soon I suppose."

"Yeah. And it will be fairly soon."

Rob and Sarah went off to the Oxen Pub and celebrated both a homecoming and an anniversary. They nursed drinks and then had a leisurely dinner. Their pace was slowed to the point that Skip Rydell, the local guitarist and singer, came on for his last set of the evening. Sarah knew him, at least casually, because he was also a teacher in one of the local schools. Sarah went up to the corner where he was seated to say hello and to make a request. Rob thought she probably didn't do things like that very often, so he guessed that the wine helped bring it about.

When Rydell was into his set, he publicly acknowledged Sarah and her partner, Rob Grant, who had just moved up from New York and was now calling Hampden Lake his permanent home. He welcomed Rob to the community. Heads turned in Rob and Sarah's direction. He waved at the guitarist and mouthed a thank you.

"You've gotten bolder in the past year. Or does the white wine have confidence built into it?"

"A little of both. But I was coming here before I knew you. Skip is a teacher in our system, so I met him quite a while ago. Even without the wine, I wouldn't have been uncomfortable saying hello to him."

About the time she finished her explanation, Rydell sang the request Sarah had made: *Bridge Over Troubled Waters*. He couldn't be mistaken for Paul Simon, but he did a respectable job with it.

"Should I interpret that to mean I'm troubled waters, Miss Sarah?"

"No, not at all. It's intended to mean that I know you've had your share of problems and if you have any more of them that maybe I could be your bridge."

"A nice thought, dear heart. But maybe I could be yours, too, if the day comes that you need one." Sarah smiled warmly, then reached over and squeezed Rob's hands.

"We seem to be in a romantic mood, so maybe we ought to go home and take advantage of the high we're on. What do think?"

"I'm ready whenever you are. Maybe more than ready." Sarah laughed warmly.

As they headed for the door, both Rob and Sarah waved at Rydell. Over the PA, he said good-bye and called Sarah by name. It was still a full restaurant and there were diners who looked as if they were wondering who these two people were.

At home and snuggling together, it wasn't long before that led to other things. Sarah *was* ready and they joined, each feeling the pleasure that accompanied it. Having been without her man all week, she set the tempo and soon got to the place that made her squeak—which then developed into something more robust.

"Don't wait," she said. "I'll be happy with express service."

"Very smooth. Let's enjoy."

"Tell me when. I'll be there."

Rob didn't realize how ready *he* was, so they both reached an animated finale moments later. He growled. Sarah purred.

"Brought that all the way up from New York. It's imported."

Sarah pitched upward and found a little something extra.

"Guess you didn't leave it all behind. Mmmm."

Rob ignored her comment. "Think you're glad I'm home."

"Sarah hugged him tightly and confirmed it with a simple, "Yesss."

They then burrowed down together and slept snugly the entire night.

Sunday was the beginning of Rob's fulltime commitment to working for Wilcox Enterprises. He and Sarah had breakfast, and then Rob went off to the real estate office well before nine o'clock. She followed him there because they'd agreed it was time for her to move a few of her clothes into his bedroom closet at the cottage. Not all of them, because it was necessary for her to maintain a different legal address if for no other reason than to hide the truth from the school board—and Sarah's mother. Rob then went to work and Sarah attended to the business of partly moving into Colonial Trail. It wasn't exactly a new experience for Rob since little Helen had done the same thing at Juniper Heights until the end of last year. But somehow this was different. There still wasn't any of the uncertainty he'd had then about it being "too much, too soon." He felt comfortable with Sarah, just as he'd been with Helen, but having been divorced for about four years now he felt none of the pressure to make up his mind about Sarah, or the path their relationship would take. He and Sarah had known each for a year, and she sensed that he was beyond the point of being excessively cautious. She was going to let him decide in his own good time about what the future held for the two them. Pushing him wouldn't be the answer so, being young, she was prepared to wait him out. Her motivation was easily explained. She loved Rob Grant. But what came to Rob's mind was a comment that his friend and former boss, RD, had made at least a couple of years earlier. It was along the lines that there'd eventually be a tolerant woman, a good woman, standing in the wings. She'd let him finish sowing his wild oats, and then suddenly pounce on this roguish old lion. RD predicted that Rob wouldn't know exactly what had happened, but it would be fait accompli. It was beginning to have the feel of an accurate prediction. Although Rob wasn't quite ready for Sarah, he had the dreams going back nearly three years now, his old premonitions, working on her behalf. Self-fulfilling prediction? It was entirely possible, he imagined. At that, the thought didn't especially trouble him.

Chapter Fourteen

The final weeks of the selling season at Hampden Lake went smoothly, made so in part because Rob no longer made the long commute into New York. And then given the fact that Sarah lived in the Wilcox building, he frequently had her by his side. She had a gentle nature, was a perfectly enjoyable companion, and when weekends came he thoroughly enjoyed having her at the cottage. As their schedules allowed, now very often shaped by Sarah's classroom workload and her various school activities, they had dinner out and it was always a treat for both of them.

As trees and shrubs turned from summer's verdant green into the brilliant colors of autumn, there was a sudden flurry of activity at the Wilcox sales office. Some of the prospects had seen Rob's ads earlier in the year. Others were simply enjoying nature's colorful display, liked the area, and stopped by the office to see what was available. Still others thought it prudent to take advantage of late season prices. The end result was that October turned out to be a banner month. When Wilcox came out on the twenty-ninth to close the office for the season, he let Rob know how pleased he was with how the year had turned out.

He repeated his earlier remarks. "I knew I was right about you going back just about three years ago. You've turned this office into a real moneymaker, and to show you my appreciation here's a little something extra for all you've done." Wilcox handed Rob a generous bonus check, at least a fairly sizeable amount of money for rural, central Massachusetts.

"This is an unexpected surprise, Alan. What can I say other than thank you very much."

"You've earned it. The part of the business that you've really expanded is the construction end. You've taken building lot buyers and sold them on the idea up putting up custom built chalets, or A-frames, or our standard cottages—most of 'em winterized. There's real money in that as you found out. The fact that you know construction, and then figured out how to put together a proposal that's tempting, made all the difference. Nobody I've ever had work for me could do that. You've been here seven months, only two of 'em fulltime, and you've done very nicely for yourself. Turns out you've made that 'fair amount of money' you talked about back at the beginning of the season. Only contract we didn't do well on was the one for Larson, but neither of us could have known that those two lots he bought were loaded with boulders that we had to have hauled away from the building site."

"Total surprise, especially since the lots on either side of his didn't have anything like that in them. Larson was a giant pain. He didn't want to bear any of the extra cost, so I had to fight with him to pick up part of it. His lots were the only problem we ran into. We did OK everyplace else."

"We have to get onto what's next. You've worked just about every day since Easter, so I suggest that you take next week off and then be ready to come into State Street a week from Monday, the sixth. I know Sarah's birthday is coming up on Wednesday, so I imagine you'll want to celebrate it with her." Wilcox showed Rob a mischievous smile.

"You're right, Alan—on both counts. Only day I've had off since March 26 was part of the Saturday on Labor Day weekend. Be good to sleep late and to look after some of the personal stuff I've let slide. Include Sarah in that. Last year, her birthday was on Monday, so I wasn't here for it. I'm glad to be around for this one so we can do it up proper-like. We'll have dinner out, probably a little champagne, and maybe a little lovin' afterwards if the season is right." Alan chuckled softly.

"I thought that might be part of the plan. Sarah's a sweet young lady, and I'm glad the two of you met. If you ever exchange vows, I want to be invited."

"Entirely possible, boss. I need to be more certain about my future with Wilcox Enterprises and about Sarah and me. The latter shows promise, but it won't happen anytime soon."

"Well, you sure don't need to have any worries about the Wilcox end of it. I'll have you work for me as long as you'd like. It's a drive into Springfield, but I think you'll enjoy the challenge of overseeing the renovation of an older office building and helping find tenants for it."

"By the time we get to the Thanksgiving break, I'll have a pretty good idea if you're right. Sounds interesting, I have to admit."

Alan Wilcox settled his account with Rob for all the commissions due. With the last of the fees he'd earned at NAGE and the amount Wilcox had paid him, plus the bonus, he was having a good year. If he were still living in Sheffield, it would have been more like hand to mouth. But the Hampden Lake economics, including mortgage payments on the cottage, were totally different. Rob's income from his various real estate activities alone would allow him to live comfortably. So, coming to the end of 1972, he was certainly much better off than he'd been in some time. But money wasn't the entire picture. What was still gnawing at him were those he'd left behind. He often thought of Helen, and especially Kim, so until he could add more layers of insulation between the hours when he'd said good-bye, and some point in the future when the vivid memories would eventually fade, it was unlikely that he'd be making a commitment to Sarah. Still, Rob's instincts led him to believe that her day would eventually come.

When Rob got home, Sarah greeted him with an affectionate hug. And to his surprise, Mike was there.

"Hello, stranger. What brings you home?" Rob asked.

"Aww, the guys I was staying with wanted to start charging me rent. No deal. Anyway, I'll be going into Springfield, too, so I figured it was easier to stay at home."

"What's in Springfield that's gotten your attention? A hot chick?"

"No. Didn't Mr. Wilcox tell you? I'm going to be working in his building for a Polish guy named Stash. He's in charge of maintenance. Maybe I'll decide to stay there during the week rather than go back and forth. There's a tiny office that has a cot, a little refrigerator and a hot plate in it. They don't expect to rent it, so they said it'd be OK for me to stay there."

"Well, young man, all of this is news to me. Guess Alan decided that it was between the two of you and not a subject that he should take up with me. But in case he didn't tell you, I'm not starting in Springfield until the sixth. Alan knows that I haven't had but part of one day off since the end of March, so he told me to take the week."

Mike turned to Sarah and asked, "Are you staying here tonight?"

"Usually do on Sunday."

"Could I ride over to Bloomdale with you in the morning? There's a bus at about eight thirty that goes straight into Springfield. I wouldn't be too late. Then I could stay in the building until Friday and come back here for the weekend."

"Sure. I'll be leaving at about a quarter of eight."

"I can be ready—and then maybe have time for a coffee at the Woodside."

"Now that you guys have your plans all set, how about a drink?" Rob asked.

"Great idea. And after that, I'm going to whip something up for dinner."

Mike knew that Sarah and his dad would want to talk about things that didn't include him, so he moved to the sofa in the living room and turned on the TV.

"I have something to show you, dear heart," Rob said. He pulled out an envelope with his commissions' settlement and bonus checks in it.

"Wow! Look at the bonus he paid you. I don't think he's ever done that before. Does that mean you're going to stay here? Permanently?"

"Kinda looks that way, doesn't it?"

Rob was standing at the bar and Sarah came around for the sole purpose of giving him an affectionate hug.

"You've made my weekend, Rob Grant. I'm *so* pleased to hear that."

"Could be, given time, that it'll mean something permanent for us, too. No promises, but the future looks one hellava lot brighter than it did a year ago. You're part of the reason, you know."

"You've got me on the edge of some happy tears. That'll keep me going all winter."

"But before we get to that, we have a dinner date on Wednesday evening. A little birdie told me that you're having another birthday. First thing you know, you'll be caught up with me."

"I accept your dinner offer, and maybe you'd let me stay overnight so we could extend the celebration a little."

"I was prepared for that, and I'm still trying to decide if it would be the proper thing to do." Rob couldn't pull off the sham and laughed. Sarah joined him.

"Could we eat down at the Lodge? You said it was our place, so it's where I'd like to go."

"Done and done. Just come back here when you're done at school."

"See if I can find the way."

Rob and Sarah had their drinks and then dinner. Mike wasn't into calves liver and onions but decided that it wasn't too bad after all. The three of them talked until almost ten o'clock. Then Sarah declared that it was time to call it a day and get ready for bed. "You're invited, too," she said. Her playful smile wasn't lost on Rob.

"Guess I don't have much choice." Mike, now almost nineteen, didn't have any doubts at all about what would follow. And he was right.

After a passionate loving, and a night of sleeping snugly, the week began for both Sarah and Mike. When they'd left for Bloomdale, Rob went back to bed. He couldn't remember the last time he'd done that, but he was feeling the effect of having worked more than seven months with only part of one day off. He thoroughly enjoyed the idea of being able to get another forty winks. At least he expected it would be restful. But it was a very bad idea. He dreamed of his dead Marianne, and of Lu, and of Kim, and of Helen. He awakened with a start and a resolution. "I am *not* going to do that again until I'm ancient. Those memories have to be put to rest. I can't continue to carry that kind of baggage around with me for the next thirty or forty years."

Unknown to Rob at the time, and certainly never to Sarah, that catnap signaled what would be the start of a turning point in their relationship. His resolve would be carried forward and over time all those wonderful memories would be put in their true perspective. They would always have a place in his mind, and in his heart, but he would *not* allow them to have an influence on how he lived out his remaining years.

On his feet, and feeling liberated to some extent, Rob got ready to start putting some of his neglected personal affairs in order. Among them was to open a new account at Guaranty Bank and deposit his checks, both from NAGE and Alan Wilcox. It felt good to have a sizeable amount of money sitting there at his disposal. Next was to see about some health and hospitalization insurance, and then to get service for his neglected Mustang. It had been a good many miles without proper attention. The Ford dealer's service department could see that and charged him an arm and a leg to put everything right. Last, Rob would pick up the gift for Sarah that he'd ordered—one he'd give her when they had a glass of champagne. Before he went home, he stopped by the Iandoli Market to pick up a few things they needed. And then, because he had the time, he drove around the area just to get acquainted with a neighborhood he'd had little time to survey until now. The USGS "Southbridge" topographic map, their #62916, that he'd bought weeks earlier was a big help.

That evening, since he was alone, he built himself a very dry Beefeater Gibson over ice, and then put together a simple dinner. He watched Monday Night Football, until he got bored and then went to bed. At a little after midnight, his phone rang. Expecting the worst, he answered it.

"Rob? It's Sarah. We've had some clown burning rubber outside the house and someone just threw a big rock through the picture window downstairs. Gwen, Jeanie, and I are leaving and going to spend the night someplace else. Would it be all right if I came over? We're all scared."

"No need to ask. *Absolutely*! But don't move. I'm coming over to make sure your roommates get on their way without any problems. After they're gone, I'll follow you back here. I have a Beretta pistol that I'll bring with me."

"I'd rather that you didn't do that. It shouldn't be necessary."

"The gun is more noisy than life threatening. I promise not to shoot the bastards. It's just to get their attention in case we get hassled. I'll call the town police before I leave. Feel better?"

"I do now. My fearless knight. See you in a few minutes." Rob felt a small twinge. The word "knight" brought back memories of both Kate and Marianne. Different context, but a reminder nonetheless.

It didn't take Rob long to get across to the other side of the lake. This was a sleepy town, except for the idiot who'd had too much beer and was behaving like a jerk. When he pulled up behind the Wilcox building, the burn rubber guys backed off—especially when the floodlights on the building clearly showed that Rob had a weapon in his hand. Seconds later, a police car showed up. He very quickly put the gun out of sight, and the tension eased. Officer Boudreau saw that Jeanie and Gwen got on their way safely, and then he stood by until Rob and Sarah left for Colonial Trail. Afterwards, he went looking for the white Firebird that had left black marks all over the pavement in front of the Wilcox building. The car and its owner were known to the police. With the broken window, they should have enough now to bring the guy for questioning.

When Rob got Sarah home, it was evident that she was badly shaken. The matter finished, and now feeling safe and sheltered, Sarah had tears of relief on her cheeks. Therapy began with a firm hug. They hung on until the worst of her anxieties were over.

"Thank you, my sweet. I needed that. We were being terrorized by that clown, and we're all really upset about what happened. When it started, you were the only person I thought of. I'm so glad you got there as fast as you did. I don't know what would have happened if you hadn't. Calling the town police never occurred to us because we all thought they only worked during the day. Having somebody on at night must be new. Anyway, you're our hero and Gwen and Jeanie asked me to say thank you. You can add me to that, too. Especially me."

"You knew I'd show up. I didn't want anybody giving my very own Punkin a hard time."

"It's funny. Gwen knows about a ground floor apartment in Palmyra that's available, and it was just this past Friday that we talked about the two of us sharing it. After the rock came through the window, and before you showed up, we decided that we're going to take it. She'll call Alan in the morning and tell him that we're all moving out. The police will give him the damage report."

"That means you'll be farther away. No more five-minute drives to visit my Sarah."

"It'll only take twenty minutes or so. One thing about it, the road from Palmyra to Bloomdale is much better than the one from here. You'll find that out yourself this winter. Since it's a U.S. highway, the state takes good care of it. For me, the driving distance is just about the same. Seven miles."

"In case you hadn't noticed, it's gotten to be early morning. Best we turn in." And they did. Sarah had unwound, snuggled with Rob, and then slept as soon as her head hit the pillow.

Over breakfast, Rob told Sarah that he wanted her to stay with him until the apartment was ready. She was quick to agree. When she came back on Tuesday evening, she said that Gwen had called the owner of the building, someone she knew, and told him that she and a friend would take the apartment. The owner said that it had just been repainted and that they could move in tomorrow, the first—Sarah's birthday.

"Timing couldn't be better," Rob said. "Since I'm off, I'll help you move. But don't count on spending your first night there. We already agreed to extend your birthday celebration so that it ends in my bed. Right?"

"It'll be a day to remember. Never made love, or even slept with anybody on my birthday before. What a wonderful way to celebrate my twenty-fifth."

"We'll try to make it verrry memorable."

"Especially since I have the day off."

"IMMCorp used to let us take our birthdays off, but I wouldn't have ever guessed that a school district would have the same policy."

"They don't." Sarah smiled amiably. "Just imagine something like that. No. It's that schools in Union 16 allow teachers to take a moving day if they need it. You're on vacation, so, sure, I want to spend the day with you. We can sleep late, fool around maybe, and then move my stuff over to Palmyra. I don't have much, except clothes, so it won't take very long. You can see the place that I'll be calling my legal address."

"Well, babe, you'll have a day-long date tomorrow. I'll help get you situated. Then we'll have your birthday dinner tomorrow evening, and a sleepover."

"Sounds wonderful. All of it."

On Wednesday morning, they did sleep in but decided not to "fool around", as Sarah had called it. They both wanted to make sure there were plenty of fireworks to conclude festivities at day's end. Rob settled on wishing Sarah a happy birthday and then giving her a tender kiss to show that he was pleased to have her there. In turn, she gave him a loving hug to confirm that she was just as happy as he was that she could wake up in the cottage on Colonial Trail.

Over breakfast, Rob gave Sarah a birthday card. A hug came with it. It was apparent that she was already enjoying a very different kind of birthday. She was all smiles.

At mid-morning, they drove off to the Wilcox building, emptied out Sarah's closet and then loaded everything in her big Galaxie. "You're right. There really isn't all that much to move," Rob said.

"You have a few of my things at your place, but you'll have more of them before the end of the day if that's all right. I keep most of my summer stuff in Worcester at my mom's apartment. Believe it or not, I'm not a clothes horse like some people—even if it looks like I am."

"With more of your clothes in my closet, it sounds as if you'll be spending more time at Chateau Grant."

"Weekends like we've been doing, and maybe you'd let me stay over one night during the week. I like this Wednesday arrangement."

"You already know that I like having you here, so I can't object to your being up on the 'Trail' on Wednesday evenings. Remember, I'll be coming out from Springfield now, so you'd likely be home first."

"Not a problem. I can stir up your drink and have a little fire going before you pull around in back. By the way, I don't think I ever mentioned that bringing a driveway in from the road behind was a smart idea. Sure makes it easier than coming up all those steps in front. I'll *really* appreciate it today when we drop off my clothes."

Rob and Sarah had loaded her car in two heaps. The bigger one would go into the apartment in Palmyra, and the second lot, on the bottom, would come back to the cottage later in the day. Since Rob didn't have a clue about where they were going, he asked Sarah to take the lead. Good thing he did. Their apartment was in a decent residential neighborhood, one with winding streets, so he would never have found it without her first showing him the way.

Parked in front, finally, Rob could see that it was a neat little building with what looked like four units on each of three levels. Sarah had called the owner, a Mr. Dumont, and made arrangements to meet him there to get the keys. He was waiting for Rob and Sarah when they arrived. Turns out it wasn't necessary because Gwen was already in the apartment and busy putting her things put away. But Rob figured that Dumont probably wanted to see who the "other" tenant was. They introduced themselves and then the landlord took them on a quick tour of the building, showed Sarah her parking space in the back, and told her where she and Gwen could find retail outlets and services in town. He was a pleasant man with a full beard and a very friendly smile. Rob liked him immediately.

Unloading Sarah's car, Rob discovered a third pile of clothes, and he asked Sarah about it.

"Dirty stuff. The building doesn't have a laundry, so I'll be taking my clothes, and yours, to the laundromat in Fiskdell on weekends. When we moved out of Wilcox's building, we lost the washer and dryer."

"I have a key, so we could still use 'em."

"Not now. Since the building is empty, Alan will have a plumber in, probably today, to drain everything that has water in it. That includes the heating system, so the place is shut down until you open up again on April 14. That's the date I think he mentioned to Gwen."

"So you're going to be my laundry lady?"

"I was hoping that we could do it together. My thought was that if we go late enough in the afternoon on Saturday, or even Sunday, that maybe we could find a place to have a drink while everything's drying."

"Sold! My 'Country Punkin' is way ahead of me when it comes to getting things done. I'm impressed."

With everything inside the apartment, Sarah hung her clothes, put undies and the like in her dresser drawer and then made sure she had a duplicate set of her cosmetics in the bathroom. That done, she declared that she was ready to go back to the cottage and reminded Rob that when they were all finished, she'd stir up their drinks. The proclamation of the day was that she was going to have a Harvey Wallbanger to kick off tonight's festivities.

"You have to work tomorrow. Maybe you ought to take it easy. Remember, you have a lion to beard later this evening."

"I'll be fine. Just you wait and see. It's mostly orange juice anyway. The lion and his lioness will be verrry satisfied by the end of the evening."

Before they left, Sarah had her Harvey Wallbanger and Rob drank his usual Beefeater Gibson over ice. A good beginning, he thought.

Drinks finished, they went to the Lodge for dinner. For openers, Rob ordered a split of champagne and offered a toast to Sarah's having survived her first quarter century. "And many more years of good health and happiness," he said.

"The latter part of that will depend on you, I have a feeling."

"We're getting there. Patience, sweetheart." That was enough for Sarah, and she showed Rob that sweet smile that he liked so much.

When it was time to order, they both decided on baked stuffed lobster, a house specialty. Then as the food was put before them, they said "Yumm" in unison. The bartender, Bob, recommended a dry white wine, which they both enjoyed as they ate their fill and talked about Rob's future, Sarah's move, the holidays, Mike's birthday coming up soon—and Sarah's mother.

"She's known about you for quite a while. And since we've been seeing each other for almost fourteen months now, she's beginning to think we're serious about each other."

"Think I'll agree with her," Rob said.

Sarah grinned. "She wants to meet you, and I thought we could do that over the Christmas holidays if that's all right with you."

"Fine with me. Perfect, in fact, especially since Alan thinks we ought to start our holiday on Friday evening, the twenty-second, and then come back on Tuesday morning, January 2."

"That's identical to the school calendar. It *is* perfect."

"Then put this on *your* calendar. I want you to stay with us during your vacation. We'll get at least some idea about how well we do together over, what, ten days? It's a place to start."

Sarah reached across to let Rob know that he was invited to take her hands in his. He accepted the invitation and saw happy, misty eyes looking back at him.

"Those words are the best birthday present I could ever have. You've made me very happy tonight. How I feel about you is no secret, but I'll say it anyway. I love you very much, Rob Grant. Those ten days will be special. I'll see to it."

"In that case, I guess it's time to pull up the birthday box."

He went to the rack where their jackets were hung and took a long, narrow box from the inside pocket. Back at the table, he handed it to Sarah.

Not knowing what was inside, she took care opening it. When she saw that it was a small fern leaf that had been dipped in gold and suspended from its stem by a delicate gold chain, Sarah Stuart was thrilled. "Oh, *Rob*! It's absolutely stunning. What a unique gift. I have to put it right on." And she did. With her dark blue turtleneck sweater serving as the background, it was exquisite. To show her appreciation, Sarah got out of her chair and gave Rob a very affectionate kiss.

"Whew! That had something behind it. Maybe I should pay the bill."

"That's to say thank you for a wonderful birthday and an elegant present. You already know how much I like gold."

"Well, you're birthday isn't over yet. Or have you forgotten?"

"Not a chance! And I'll make my birthday memorable for you, too. I'm ready if you are. In fact I have been for a while." Sarah giggled.

Back at the cottage, they wasted no time in finding their way into Rob's bed. It wasn't a night for preliminaries—no need for them. Sarah went on the attack and took charge. Completely. It wasn't long before she'd reached a place that made her exclaim, "*Yessss*!" loudly. Gone was the little squeak. It was confirmation that she'd found paradise.

"You're right. It's already memorable."

"Now *you* talk too much. Roll over. I want you on top. Better way to take extra-large deliveries."

They made an attempt to prolong their loving. But their movements were silken, and arousing in the extreme, so their plan was destined to fail. It was Sarah who helped that along when she said, "Don't wait. I'm *waaay* up there, and I want it now. All of it!"

That was all Rob needed to hear. He increased the pace, brought Sarah to a vigorous climax and then joined her. She groaned noisily after he'd touched nearly every nerve in her body that had passion in it.

When they'd rested for a moment, Rob said, "Another birthday gift. I think you liked this one, too."

"*Ohhh*, yes. The feelings. Unbelievable. I understand now what it is that makes it so special. You're patient. And it's all the things you do to bring me along. Mmmm. So after you've gotten me *really* turned on, and then stay with me until I come, it's pure ecstasy. No. It's more than that. Closer to temporary insanity. Could I be a regular guest at your chateau? I really enjoy the late evening therapy."

"Since you kept your promise and made it a night for me to remember, too, I think we can work out arrangements for a permanent reservation under the name of Stuart."

"I'll try to arrive before six p.m. so you don't cancel it. Would a credit card number help?"

"Won't be necessary. You're a regular guest." They chuckled at their silliness.

"You've made me a very happy Punkin today. I don't mean just now, but all the help you gave me to get moved in, then a wonderfully romantic dinner, your gift. I don't know. I've never had a birthday that made me feel anywhere close to this happy. Loving me the way you do is part of it, but you've been so sweet. That goes back to what you did on Monday night. You've gotten to be *so* important to me, especially since I know more about how you think, the way you do things, and how thoughtful you can be. There's a lot about you that's taken a year to learn. I love all of it—and all of you."

"I'm not ready to say those words yet, Sarah. You know my story, so you understand why. But the things you just said should tell you how much I care about you. Maybe they say 'I love you' in a different way."

"What you do isn't lost on me. You're a lovable Punkin, too, you know."

"Good Lord. I wonder what senior management at IMMCorp would say if they knew that I was a bona fide Punkin. For sure, Wall Street would never be the same if the word got out." They had a good laugh and then shared a loving hug.

"One day, Rob Grant, I think maybe you'll have me as your partner. Could be that what I want to believe is influencing what the real truth is, maybe, but let me think that way. I'll be like Dorothy in the *Wizard of Oz*. She believed—and it worked."

"You aren't too far off the mark. Like I've said before, just be patient with me for a while. Remember, you have all of my dreams, and the foreshadowing, working for you."

"Gives me lots of confidence, because you told me how often they've been accurate before. I like the odds."

"We'll see, sweetheart."

"If it isn't too late, would you love me again? If you can't, that's all right, too."

"Ahhh, it's possible, I think, and I want to. Says something else about my feelings for you."

Love again they did, and it was every bit as fulfilling a gift as the one earlier. When they were fully satisfied, they rested. Then Sarah tensed and had a few tears that wouldn't be denied.

"Hey, now. Those aren't supposed to a part of a happy birthday celebration."

"I know. It's just that I've never felt this way about anyone. I'm not sure what it is you've done, but you've brought something into my life that I've never known before. I feel a kind of contentment that's completely new to me. The tears are happy ones, and it's a way of saying to myself how glad I am we had that chance meeting a year ago on September 4. I'm going to declare it a national holiday, even if the government won't." They laughed at the idea.

"You'll like this. One day when I had nothing else to do, I figured out that the fourth will be on Labor Day in 1978. So you'll get your wish. But we'll be all right. You just have to be confident that I'll come around. My feeling is that we'll be an item in the Sunday paper someday. One of the things I have to be certain about is that I can do all of what Alan expects of me. At this stage, he thinks I can walk on water."

"He's never had anybody like you before, so I know you'll do just fine. And about me, don't worry. I'll be here. You're inside me now—in more ways than one." Sarah smiled warmly.

"You're being more understanding about this than I have any right to expect."

"We both know that if I press you I'll never see my dream come true."

"I'm not sure that's true. Maybe it's time I had an external push. It might be that I'd finally see that the right thing to do is to take that next step. But in the meantime, don't worry about me, dear heart."

"We've done enough on the subject of us, I think. Could I interest you in a world-class snuggle? I have to be back in school tomorrow, you remember."

"Yep. A snuggle? Sounds delightful. I'm all yours—in lots of ways." With that, they got close and stayed that way throughout the night.

Sarah returned to her classroom, and then late on Friday afternoon she showed up with Mike in tow. Rob gave Sarah a hug and then asked his son, "Hi, guy. How was your first week on State Street?"

"I like it there. Different things to do and it's great being inside this time of year. Stash is a little flaky, but he's easy to work with. I got paid, too, so I'd like to go over to the guys' place if I can get a ride."

"No problem. I'll drop you off. Be good to find out where you spend some of your time."

"Thanks, Dad."

"Sarah, did you tell Mike about your little adventure earlier in the week?"

"He knows, and I also told him about your helping me move."

"I know the guy who owns the white Firebird. Yeah, he'd peel rubber, but throwing rocks doesn't sound like him. It had to be somebody else in the car who did that."

"The cops know who he is, too. One thing about it, he flushed the building. All three of the gals have moved out."

Rob took Mike across to the other side of the lake and dropped him off in front of a building that was more shack than cottage. It also sounded as if the party had begun. The loud music seemed to confirm it.

"Enjoy yourself, but don't spend all your paycheck on whatever it is that goes on in there."

"I won't. They're good friends. We usually talk a lot and take it easy. I'll probably stay over until Sunday afternoon."

"OK. We'd like you to have dinner with us, spend the night, and then you can ride in with me on Monday morning. It'll be my first day as the building manager—and your boss."

"Glad I won't have to take the bus in. Great! See you in time for the second NFL game. Bye, Dad."

Rob and Sarah went out to dinner after he got back from dropping Mike off. They did some shopping, *all* the laundry on Saturday, and then spent a quiet Sunday together. None of what they did over the weekend could in any way be considered exciting—that is, not until after dark. They took full advantage of their nights together and awakened each morning with sleepy eyes and affectionate smiles.

"You've known right along how much I've liked spending my weekends with you," Sarah remarked. "I thought that maybe after a year they'd lose their edge, or wouldn't mean as much. If anything, I enjoy them more, need them even more than I did a year ago. It tells me that my feelings for you are still growing. I really hope we can make things work out. If not, you'll have a badly broken heart on your hands."

"Mine, too, I'm beginning to think. What I worry about sometimes is our age difference. I have to consider that our being married maybe isn't the right thing for you."

"I'd rather that you didn't keep seeing it as an issue. I'm not going to. You've been good for me, and I want nothing more than to be your partner. I won't crowd you, though. You know that, too."

"Sarah, you're a love, and the way I feel about you translates into just about the same thing, I think. Stick with me, Punkin."

"I'm not going anyplace. I care too much."

As Sunday afternoon began to wind down, they poured drinks and Sarah started to get dinner organized. Mike came home, and the three of them visited some, watched part of the football game, and then ate. The lady of the house knew how to cook, but Rob had found that out long before November 5. Afterwards, Sarah had some school work to finish up. When she was done with her students' workbooks, it was time for bed.

Mike said he wanted to watch the end of a movie and would stay up a little longer.

"Remember, we have to be out of here at a little after eight. I'm not sure what the driving time is into downtown Springfield."

"That'll be plenty of time, but I'll be up so I can have breakfast with you. Night, Dad. Night, Sarah."

Chapter Fifteen

The start to their week wasn't nearly as frantic as it had been in Sheffield when Rob had to catch the Penn Central into New York. Even so, they were now a working threesome and it *was* a Monday morning. Sarah and Rob teamed up and got breakfast ready quickly. Their goal was to have a few extra minutes to enjoy a leisurely coffee before they had to be on their way. They easily accomplished what they intended, and the aura of "family" was pervasive. Neither said a word about it. They simply smiled affectionately at each other to acknowledge what was at work. Both Rob and Sarah had sensed it and before they left for the day they agreed that it felt awfully good.

"Maybe you should come back here tonight," Rob said. "I like the feel of this. The other part of it is that it's nice having you here—not to mention that eating alone doesn't have much appeal."

The sweet, captivating smile that Sarah showed Rob closely rivaled Marianne's. Even at nearly thirty months on, Rob felt a pang when he retrieved the mental image of it.

"We only talked about Wednesdays, but I'll come back tonight—and every night if you'd like me to. That would make me one very happy girl. You know that, too."

"Yeah, why don't you, and we can talk about it."

"Love to, Rob. See you at about six?"

"I imagine so."

"I'll have your drink ready."

"Be sure to make one for yourself."

"You don't have to worry about that. But, I've got to be going."

"See you tonight. And as we used to say in New York, 'Have a good day.'"

Sarah Stuart waved as she left for Bloomdale Elementary. Once there, she spent the entire day in her classroom with a song in her heart and smiles that came easily.

Rob got his things together and then he and Mike made their first thirty-plus mile trip together into Springfield.

As they were passing close to Sarah's school in Bloomdale, Mike commented, "You've had a lot of women during the last four years, and they were all pretty neat. There wasn't any of 'em I didn't like. They were all different, and nice, too, so when it was over with one of 'em it had to be hard. When Marianne died, that was rough on all of us. But I really like Sarah, and I'm glad you're seeing each other. I think she was lonely before she met you. You have been, I know, so maybe something good will finally happen. She's real sweet. We don't need a mom anymore, but it sure would be nice to have somebody like her around."

"Looking back, four of the women I was close to would have been fine, I think. But out of those who were left after we lost Marianne, the one I really miss is Helen. Surprised?"

"Yeah. I am."

"Like Marianne, she and Sarah have a special something going for them. They're both even-tempered, considerate, lovable, and just plain easy to be with. I see a lot of the other two in Sarah, so there isn't much doubt it's why I'm taken with her. Still, I need a little more time to sort it out. Part of it is the age difference."

"That was part of the problem before."

"What was?"

"The time you took. You lost Kate that way, but I understand the reasons. Like, if you'd married Lu that would've been a big mistake because of the way she turned goofy."

"And she's still that way. I heard that other than her customers, she's like a clam that's shut itself inside its shell. Her mother died, and she's become a recluse almost."

"What's a recluse?"

"A hermit, someone who prefers to be alone."

"I still think what happened, and the reason why she walked away from us, was weird."

"Yep. Me, too."

They both fell silent for a few minutes. When it was clear that his dad was finished talking about the past, Mike reached over and turned on the radio.

As they continued west on the Mass Pike, Mike listened to music while Rob thought about the enjoyable weekend he and Sarah had just shared. How could it have been otherwise? Composed, she always seemed to be at peace, so whenever they were together Rob felt a special kind of contentment. Simply put, he was pleased when she could spend time with him at the cottage on Colonial Trail. As had been the case with Justine, Sarah's beauty within transcended her physical appearance, but Rob had finally learned that it was the heart, and the mind, and the soul of a companion that were more important. He was fortunate that three Thanksgivings ago Justine had inadvertently shown him the difference. He decided at the time that it would be an essential trait he'd look for in the woman he'd ask to share his life. The more time they spent together, the more Sarah reminded Rob of his mother—a gentle Christian woman who saw that the home he grew up in was filled with love. Sarah brought that same kind warmth to Rob's cottage when she came through his door. Other women in his life had as well, but they were all history now.

Arriving at the building on State Street, Rob parked in the lot behind it. Since he wasn't aware that there was a back door into the office, Mike took pleasure in knowing something that his dad didn't.

Alan was busy in his private office and never looked up. Rob was greeted by a dark-haired nymphet with sparkling blue eyes and an alluring smile. He liked what he saw. It showed.

"Good morning. I know who you are. You're Mr. Grant. I'm Deana Forster, Mr. Wilcox's receptionist and secretary."

"Good morning, Deana. Happy to meet you." Mike knew his dad all too well, and he could read what was going on in his mind. He grimaced.

"Mr. Wilcox should be free in a few minutes. Could I get you a coffee?" She used her playful smile to charm Rob Grant. Mike had seen enough, said he had to get to work, and took off.

"Thanks, no. Any idea where I'll be sitting?"

"That desk right over there." She pointed out which one it was. "It's right where I can keep an eye on you." She smiled warmly.

Rob had only been in the office for a couple of minutes, but he was already beginning to feel just a little uncomfortable. Deana was petite and a cutie, but as he studied her more closely, he decided that she wasn't much older than Mike. Her leer told Rob's practiced eye that she was on the make and apparently willing to accommodate someone old enough to be her father. To take the edge off her ardor, Rob asked, "Who are you voting for tomorrow, Nixon or McGovern?"

"I won't be able to vote until the seventy-six election, but probably McGovern if I could."

Rob was right. "Do *not* touch. Ever!" his inner voice said.

While he was waiting to see Wilcox, Rob went out to the car to get a small box with personal items he wanted in and on his desk. They'd certainly been around—some of them from his Los Angeles days, then in Chicago, back to L.A., at two companies in New York, NAGE, his office at Hampden Lake, and now downtown Springfield, Mass. He wondered where else they would have been by, say, the early 1990s.

Wilcox finished whatever it was he was working on and came out of his private office to greet his new building manager. It was his typical, "Hi, Rob. How you doin'?"

"Fine. Not a bad drive, at least until we have a foot of snow on the ground. The week off did me good. And it also helped to have had some company. " It was his turn to smile. Alan understood his meaning—as did Miss Forster.

"Come on in. Deana, hold the calls. Rob and I need to talk for a while about our plans for the building."

And "a while" it was, because they spent the balance of the morning together.

Just before lunch, Alan Wilcox concluded their first meeting by summarizing all of what had to be done to this older eight-story office building to make it a viable investment. Foremost among them was to get tenants. Because it hadn't been well maintained, businesses had moved out and cash flow was thin. But Alan saw potential, and he was the kind of man who almost always turned his vision into reality. If his plan was to succeed, Rob Grant would be the human resource that would make it happen. It would be a challenge, and a huge undertaking. It'd also draw heavily on Rob's years of experience and raw intelligence if there was any chance at all that it would turn out the way Alan Wilcox expected it to.

After they got back from lunch, Alan took Rob on a tour of all eight floors, the roof, and the basement level. He was nearly overwhelmed by what had to be done. The building had been let go and it was obvious that the previous owners had taken everything out of it and put nothing back in. He was depressed by what he saw, but Alan's demeanor was at all times positive and Rob was soon infected with his contagious enthusiasm.

Late in the afternoon, Wilcox went off to meet with his bankers. It was interesting that he took Rob's resumé with him. He'd now become a marketable asset. So with everyone busy elsewhere, Rob went straight to the business of setting up a master work plan, or a kind of flow chart of what had to be done—and how to sequence, and accomplish, each of the tasks. Apart from attracting tenants, he'd need a complete list of contractors and suppliers who would be the key to putting the building back into shape and giving it far more appeal than it had at the moment. When he paused, he looked up and saw Deana smiling at him.

"Do you always smile at people hard at work?" She came out from behind her desk, walked slowly over to Rob's and sat down.

"No, I was just wondering what you'd be like in bed."

"Not again!" he thought. His recollection of how Marianne had approached him in his office nearly four years ago came flooding back. She'd had no experience making love. Rob was certain that Miss Forster did. Plenty of it.

"Isn't it a little early in our love affair to be thinking about such things?" Rob asked.

"Love doesn't have anything to do with it. I just like getting laid. A lot." She smiled provocatively.

"Deana, I'm more than twice your age, and even if I weren't, I don't bed co-workers—at any age. Added to that, I have a lady of my own who looks after me very satisfactorily."

"I thought that's what you meant when you said you had company last week. But there's something animal about you. It turns me on."

"You need a good man to look after of you, someone who isn't closing in on forty-three. No, Deana. You're doing good things for my ego, but I'm not a candidate to put out your fire."

"I do have a man, but he's under contract and working up in the Alaskan oil fields. Lotsa bucks. He'll come back pretty well off, but in the meantime I have needs. Big ones. And I prefer mature men because they know what they're doing, aren't in a hurry, and I always get where I want to go. You understand these things."

"This has been a pretty frank first-day discussion between a man and his daughter. I'm not a prude, but let this be the last time we talk about your biological needs."

"OK, but I hope you aren't mad at me because I tried to put the make on you."

"Not especially, just as long as your fantasies don't interfere with whatever it is I ask you to do here in the office. If they do, then I'll most likely be grumpy about it."

Deana laughed sweetly, and said, "They won't, but you might want to remember that I'd do what you ask outside the office, too."

"I hear you. Now, where do I find Mike?"

"This late in the afternoon, he's probably in the maintenance office. I can get him on the intercom."

"Ask him to come up, would you?"

Rob was about to finish with a general outline of his renovations and management plan when Mike sauntered in.

"What's up, Dad?"

"I just wanted to know where you're going to be sleeping."

"No reason for me to make the trip back and forth, so I'll stay in town during the week and go out with you on Friday nights. The guys at the cottage said I could stay there on weekends, rent free, if I wanted to. We have a good time, so I'll probably do that and then come home late on Sunday afternoon—just like yesterday."

"If you're staying in that little room up on six, you could probably have some company." Deana was off running an errand and Rob aimed a thumb at her empty chair.

"Yeah. I know. She's oversexed and would probably screw a male snake if she could get somebody to hold it. I'm guessing she's already been after you. I saw how she licked her lips this morning. Thing is, I don't want to get tangled up with anybody in the same place I work."

"Good for you. If things went bad, it could get messy. I just told the little lady the same thing about twenty minutes ago."

"The way you looked at her when we came in, I thought maybe you'd want to check her oil. I figure she's always about a quart low."

"A temptation at first glance. Then I realized she's roughly the same age as the sister you don't have."

"Well, she'll be legal on December 14," Mike said.

"Doesn't change a thing. It would worry me to bed a minor. And besides, there's Sarah. She matters."

"Best reason I can think of to play it straight."

"Well, if you're staying in, I might as well be on my way. Not much else I can do today. See you in the morning."

"Night, Dad."

On his way home, Rob thought about the woman-child, Deana. He'd turned her on, she said, and if the truth be known, she did the same to him. But this was one instance when he'd have to draw the line.

As Rob came into the end of his driveway, Sarah heard him and looked out the back door. He could see that she had a glass in her hand. They both chuckled.

"Hi, Punkin. Good to be home—and so warmly welcomed." With the glass still in her hand, he gave her a gentle half hug.

"I like this. Makes me feel like this is my home now, too."

"Let's sit and talk about it."

They went to the eating bar and chatted for a couple of minutes before Rob said, "I like it, too. But this was a special kind of day with me going into a real office again, tie and all, so I wanted you here. Felt good to see a smiling face at the door when I drove in. I could get used to this rather easily, but if we start living together, then the day we say 'I do' wouldn't be much different than any other day. It'd be a case of rolling over one morning and saying, 'Well, why don't we go off someplace and get married'. It's the convention that would be missing. I'd like us to be a little hungry for each other if ever we get to a wedding ceremony. I don't know, maybe I'm all hung up on the idea of two people coming from different directions to form their union. Sleeping together right up to a few hours before an exchange of vows lacks a certain something."

"You know me. I nearly always agree with you, and as I think about how my mom would look at it, there isn't any way I can disagree. She doesn't know how close we've become and would almost certainly disapprove if she did. So, what do you propose?"

"Much as I don't like spending evenings alone, maybe we should go back to what we decided about having you here over the weekend, and then possibly Wednesday night, too. We can see how well we do with that, keeping in mind that there could be that occasional night when we break the rules. For example, one of us might have special needs."

"You've taught me about those, but I can live with a four here, three there schedule. Who knows? At that, we might get tired of each other."

"With three free nights, that would leave me free to service some hot chick who's in need."

Sarah showed Rob a pained expression.

"*Ohh, Rob*. I hope not. You were busy in New York, I'm sure. And I don't really have any control over you here, so that smarts."

"Aww, Punkin, I didn't think you'd take me seriously. I'm sorry. Really. You're the only woman in my life. Forgive me?"

"Well, maybe. If you'll take me to your bed, it'll fix the hurt, I think."

"You don't have to ask me twice. No dinner, so we'll have our dessert first."

"And third." They both chuckled at her having used Rob's words.

They gave themselves time for gentle foreplay. When they'd coupled, Rob had a fleeting thought of Deana. It turned him on and he was ablaze with passion. That brought Sarah to a fever pitch, and it wasn't long before they each enjoyed a spirited climax. Sarah led the way; Rob followed moments later and added his customary growl.

After they'd rested, Sarah inhaled deeply and asked, "Where'd you find that volcano? *Whew*! If being in the city does that for you, maybe I should be here on Monday nights, too." She laughed softly. "Your body told me you're sorry. You're forgiven."

"Shhh. There's more to come. Rob kissed her affectionately and then went back for seconds. He resumed his smooth, even movements and since Sarah was still afire, it didn't take but a minute or so for her to get close to that special place that always left her fulfilled. She reached the brink, exclaimed "*Now*!" and then came to a pulsating, world-class orgasm. She felt Rob respond immediately, joined him again with more contractions and uttered a long, hoarse moan. Suddenly, the exhilaration associated with physical love gave way to a whimper and a tear. Just as abruptly, she smiled.

"You'll have to decide which it is you want to show me, dear heart. Tears or smiles."

"The tears came from thinking about you maybe making love with somebody else. Call it being selfish because I like the idea of looking after all your needs, and I want to believe that it's the way it'll always be. The smile? Then I thought about the way you just made love to me. Mmmm. I couldn't help it because I'm overflowing with a feeling of contentment."

"That's better. I've asked you not to worry, so if you'll keep that in mind, we'll be fine. You're such a sweetheart. What you give of yourself to make our relationship work, and the kind of person you are, touch me in places that haven't gotten much attention, at least not recently. What I'm trying to say, I guess, is that the way my feelings for you have begun to grow is much like a bud that's starting to open." Rob smiled at Sarah warmly to let her know that his words were sincere. She responded with an affectionate look that would have melted a heart of stone.

"I'm going to believe absolutely everything you've just said and have faith that one day I'll be part of the Grant family. Until that day comes, I'll be glad to look after your heart, and your mind, and your body—and your deliveries. Especially them." Sarah attached a cute giggle to her words. "And it all begins with us finishing the drinks we left on the bar, and then having me get dinner ready."

"Since it looks like there won't be any more deliveries today, I'll join you." Sarah, totally fulfilled, reached over and hugged Rob tightly.

At breakfast on Tuesday morning, Sarah said she'd plan on keeping her Wednesday evening date. Rob happily agreed. "I'll have drinks ready and a little fire going. No. Probably two."

"I should be out at about the same time. Around six. But now I should get going. Be a good idea to stop at town hall and vote before I go in. Just leave the dishes. There'll be time enough to do them tonight."

"No, love. I don't have to leave just yet, at least today, so I'll do them. That way, you can come home and relax."

"Like I said last night, you're a sweetheart. And you are. See you tomorrow tonight, Punkin."

Rob voted without any delay and was in the office on State Street pretty much on time. Deana had settled down and was off her "bed Rob Grant" mission. She was pleasant and helpful, so the atmosphere was greatly improved. Rob considered that she may have found someone else last night to unwind her mainspring.

When Wilcox came in later that morning, he spent some time talking with Rob about how he thought they should go about soliciting new tenants. Rob had his own ideas on the subject. He and Alan didn't agree.

"Sounds as if you'd have me out knocking on doors," Rob said. "I'd have to be two people because managing the building and getting leased space ready is just about a full time job the way I see it. Just getting a team of good suppliers and contractors together is going to take some time."

"You spent too many years with corporate responsibilities not to have some ideas of your own. Let's have 'em."

"During our meeting yesterday, I got a pretty good idea of what you and McCallum have to get per square foot to make the bottom line show a reasonable return on borrowed and invested capital. The first thing I'd do is negotiate a rate holder contract with the *Union* and the *Republican.* We'd have small-ish ads run every day so they'd be at the lowest rates available. People who're seriously looking for space will read them. Count on it. Then, knowing something about lease numbers, ours and others, is essential. For the last three months or so, I've been tracking what the owners of other high-rise buildings are asking. I'm convinced that we can offer newly renovated space at lower rates. That assumes I'm able to find the right suppliers and that I also monitor their charges so they don't go wobbling out of control. Contractors? I want outfits that perform! Those that do quality work and get on and off the job quickly are the ones I'm after. It'll take some time to find them."

"Sounds like something I should see in detail," Alan said. "Work up your suggestions and figures and then show me how it all looks on paper."

"Now, on another subject. We have a handful of tenants that have been here for years. I'd offer them an incentive. Specifically, give them a month's free rent if they deliver a prospect that signs a lease. What triggered the thought is the old lawyer, Buckley, up on five. His office is a gloomy place, and I have to assume he's not all that well off. At the same time, I'll bet he knows a ton of people around town."

"Don't let appearances fool you, Rob. He does better for himself than you might think. But I like the idea. Most of the tenants' rents are low, so we can afford to do what you suggest. I should have thought of something like that myself."

"Next, I propose that we pick out some space on a higher floor and then turn it into a sexy model office. I have some ideas on that already. But in the ad we'll run, assuming we do, I'll invite readers to come in and see the model. Tract homes developers do it all the time. Anyway, prospects would get an idea, firsthand, what we could do for them. In case they don't have much imagination, we could show them options, simple artist's renderings, of offices that run from plain vanilla to plush."

"Good ideas. All of them."

"There are maybe some other enticements we could offer. You know more about the exact numbers than I do, but we might consider a ninety-day run up to the full rent, depending on the length of the lease, or skipping the first month's rent, and free or reduced parking fees in our lot. Then we should be writing press releases for the local papers and stations. I propose to give them just enough information so they'll get curious and want to dig into the details about the new ownership and renovations that are underway. Ten-second radio spots at commute time, both morning and evenings, might be something else to look at."

"You've figured out all kinds of ways to spend money we don't really have yet. But you're doing a good job of brainstorming, so I have to give you credit for that."

"One other suggestion that I didn't get to. Instead of having me run around town knocking on doors, I'd put together a colorful flyer about us, and our rents, and have your oldest boy, or all three of your youngsters, stuff mailboxes in buildings in the central business district. They'd be much cheaper to hire than a very highly paid executive like me." Rob couldn't help but laugh. Wilcox wasn't quite sure how he should take his comment and declined to touch it.

"Another good idea. Since it looks like you won't be knocking on doors, as you call it, you'll have all kinds of free time, so I'll put you in charge of implanting your various ideas."

"There goes my cushy thirty-five hour week. Does a pay raise come with it?"

"You just said you're highly paid." It was Alan's turn to laugh. Rob joined him. "Seriously, you've had sound ideas going back to last spring. If the ones you have about the building work out by the time you open at the lake again in mid-April, there'll be something in it for you. It'll be an incentive, let's call it."

"I hear you. Now, are you buying lunch?"

"After all the work you've done already, it looks like I don't have a choice." Wilcox's pained expression was all an act.

On the afternoon of Election Day 1972, Rob Grant took the first steps toward developing and executing some of the programs he'd outlined for Wilcox. His aim was to get as many of them in place as was humanly possible before the start of the long Thanksgiving weekend. He'd also quickly discovered that it meant longer hours. Sarah began to wonder if he'd found another love interest until he showed her his projects list and the progress he'd made on each of them.

"I know what kind of commitment you make to whatever it is you're doing, so I shouldn't have raised the kind of question I just did. I owe you an apology."

"Not necessary. At the outset, what took the most time was working up all the numbers before we went public with them. And then I had to figure out how to write a press release. I'm not a PR guy, but I vaguely remembered how it was done at the three companies I worked for. It meant fiddling around with the words until I was satisfied that an editor would at least look at what I was submitting. They're done, and I've sent them in as 'run at will' releases, as opposed to 'immediately', but the papers jumped on them right away—as did some of the radio stations. One of the TV outlets said they'd send a crew around at some point. Not urgent. It'll spread the coverage out. Important thing is, we've gotten exposure and it's already paying off. Wilcox is pleased as punch. For my part, I will *not* confess that I'm surprised at how well it's worked."

"I told you that you'd be able to do whatever it was he wanted done. You're able to draw on all your corporate experience. It's possible you've forgotten some of the things you know how to do because it's second nature. I'm *sooo* proud of you."

"Aww, go on. I'm blushing." Sarah smiled.

"I should come in after school some day and see where you work. Take me on a tour of the building?"

"Sure. Just say when."

"Probably after Thanksgiving. And on that subject, I'd talked about having you meet my mom at Christmastime. But, she's invited you in for Thanksgiving dinner. Time you met, she thinks."

"I agree. Great! We're closing down for the weekend after lunch on the twenty-second. Mike's birthday, you may recall, is on the twentieth, but he plans on staying in the city to celebrate. Seems there's a young lady who wants to help him do that. I have a good idea what that means. Anyway, he said we could do something for his birthday over the long weekend. Fine with me. Greg's comes up on the sixth, a Wednesday, but I'll call him on Thanksgiving Day. If your mother doesn't object, I'll do it from her place. I can get time and charges and pay her for the call."

"Won't matter, I'm sure. I'll be staying with you the night before Thanksgiving, and we can all go in together. Mike's coming out with you on that Wednesday?"

"Yep. He'll go back in with me the following Monday, but I don't imagine we'll see much of him. It's amazing how many friends he found here over the summer months."

"I have to say it. You're a good planner."

"A holdover from my corporate days—especially IMMCorp when I was doing a lot of international travel."

"Well, since we're organized now for weeks in advance, could I interest you in joining me in your bed? I'm suddenly in bad need of a big delivery."

"I guess that's our new word for mating."

"There's probably a sexier way of saying it. But, yes."

And mate they did. It had been several days, so they enjoyed every minute of their union, and both of them fell asleep smiling.

In the run-up to the Thanksgiving break, there was a fairly steady flow of inquiries about office space. The traffic wasn't especially heavy, but those who came in or called seemed to be serious prospects. It was nearly a case of too much, too soon because the hours Rob spent qualifying them, and then matching what they needed versus the space they had available, ate away at some of the time he wanted to develop new marketing strategies. It meant that his longer hours would continue for the time being. Three nights a week it wasn't important, but he refused to let his work load cut into his Wednesday nights with Sarah. So he saw to it that it didn't.

Mike then decided that he did want come out to the cottage the weekend just prior to his birthday on Monday. Before they left to start their week in Springfield, Rob wished him a happy birthday and gave him some new work clothes. Since he didn't have anything that was specifically suited to that purpose, he was pleased. Sarah gave him a gift certificate for work shoes, and in return he gave her a big hug to show his appreciation.

"I don't have any decent clothes like this because some of my good jeans and shoes are beginning to look pretty bad. Thank you. I can really use these things—and I'll look sharp, too."

Two days later, the eve of Thanksgiving, Alan stopped by Rob's desk and suggested that he take the afternoon like everyone else. "You've put in a lot of extra hours to get your projects off the ground, and we're already seeing the results. I want you to know how satisfied I am with what you've been able to accomplish in a very short time. You need to take the break and spend some time with Sarah."

"I'll do that. Tomorrow's the day I finally meet her mother, and her sister and brother-in-law. It'll be over a big turkey and trimmings, I'm told. Sarah and I have been seeing each other since the first week of September last year, and I still haven't met any of her family. Her mother thinks it's time. So do I, because we seem to be getting serious about something longer term."

"I like hearing that, Rob. She's a wonderful girl."

"That she is. A very special young lady, I'm discovering. I've been divorced for over four years now, and maybe it's time I settled down. You know about all the other women. I think you met every one of them I brought up to the lake. Except Marianne. I thought for a time that you had a built-in Rob sensor because whenever I showed up *you'd* show up. It was uncanny." Alan Wilcox laughed robustly.

"I'll give you this, you bedded some real beauties. I was envious, and you've already told me that it showed. Sarah isn't quite in their league, but the kind of sweet person she is makes up for it."

"My label for it is inner beauty. Interesting that it was a Jewish gal, another one you never met, who taught me about it. She had it. Gentle.

Very much at peace with the world and herself. By coincidence, it'll be three years tomorrow that she came out to Sheffield and had dinner with us. Like Sarah, Justine wasn't a knockout, but she had that special something inside that made her one the most beautiful people I've ever known. Sarah's much the same way. A lesson learned."

"Well, enjoy yourself. I know you'll come back next Monday and hit the ground running."

"Thanks, Alan. I'm pleased you're satisfied with our results so far. Have a great Thanksgiving."

"We're getting an awful lot of talent and experience for what we're paying you, so I have a lot to be thankful for this year. You have a good Thanksgiving, too."

Rob collected Mike, and then as Deana headed for the door, they both wished her a good holiday. Before they left, Rob gathered up some of his paperwork, stuffed his attaché case, and then he and Mike were on their way, too. The Mass Pike was busy, but not overly so. Rob didn't have much to say because he got lost in his thoughts, mostly about plans for the building, so before he knew it they were home. Mike plopped on the sofa, turned on the TV, and immediately got wrapped up in an old Three Stooges movie. Rob changed into something casual and warm, got a little fire going, and stuck a bottle of white wine in the fridge for Sarah. It wasn't long before she pulled into the drive in back and they began their long holiday weekend with a hug and an affectionate kiss.

"Mmmm, that felt good. I'm really looking forward to our weekend together. It's just enough days to make me feel like we're a family. Christmas will be even better."

"I understand what you're saying, so it's time to confess that I like the feeling, too."

Thursday morning dawned frosty and bright. A good omen for all that was on their agenda later in the day. Before Rob and Sarah stirred, his fingertips traced patterns on her bare skin. She got goose bumps and shivered. "What would you think about making a quick delivery before we get up?" she asked.

"I think it's a splendid idea. Would you like to be in charge of things at the loading dock?"

"*Yesss*!

They joined and extracted immense pleasure from their smooth, even movements until Rob said hoarsely, "No fair. I'm losing control."

"Mmmm! Let go. I want it."

With that, he came to an explosive release and growled quietly to confirm that the delivery had been made. She quickly joined him with a vigorous climax of her own, and, as a finishing touch, added a soft squeal. Their union was brief, but perfectly delightful.

"Purrrr," she said. "This was one of the few times I knew when your delivery arrived. No mistaking it."

"Don't start thinking about more of them, or we'll never get to your mother's."

Still joined, Rob's words made her squirm just a little. "We've got the whole four days ahead of us. I can wait for another one later in the weekend. Like tonight." They couldn't help but smile at the thought.

"Sure you can wait that long?"

"We'll manage. Have to."

By the time Mike got out of bed, Rob and Sarah had showered, were dressed, and had breakfast about ready.

"Hello, sleepyhead. You must have been tired. It's already the day after Thanksgiving."

"*What*!"

Rob broke up. "It is kinda late."

"I stayed up and watched *Ivanhoe*. Good movie but it wasn't over until after midnight."

"Too late for breakfast. You'll just have to go hungry."

"Why are you on my case this morning?"

"I don't know. Feeling extra good, I guess. The stuff I'm doing in the building is working, Alan is happy, and I've got my arm around a sweet young lady who loves me. How could I ask for more than that? You're just a good target for my monkey business." Sarah was getting a kick out of Rob's playfulness.

"OK, just as long as you don't go crazy with it."

"I won't. Let's eat."

Early in the afternoon, Rob brought his Mustang to life and they drove to Sylvan Knoll in Worcester. He couldn't help but remember that it was the city where Lu Cappelletti's Uncle Gino had lived and then died of cancer the morning following New Year's Day nearly three years ago. He wondered where in the city he'd lived—and also how Lu was doing with all the ladies specialty shops she had by now. With Exit 10 off the Mass Pike coming up, his thoughts about the past came to an end.

Then onto I-290, Rob asked "How many times did we make this trip last year, dear heart? I'm surprised the Mustang didn't steer itself right into Swanson Road from Exit 9. Let's see if it remembers to pull into the Auburn Mall all by itself. It should." The idea of that made them chuckle.

After they were past the Mall, Sarah gave Rob directions as they drove. It was then up Pakachoag Street until they pulled up in front of the apartment building where Sarah's mother lived.

"Mom's ferocious, so I'll lead the way." She laughed cutely.

Sarah's mother had been watching for them out her living room window and came to the door to welcome them. "Mom. I'd you like to meet someone very special to me. This is Rob Grant. Rob. My mother."

"Mrs. Stuart. I'm glad we're finally more than just names." They showed each other friendly smiles.

"Happy to meet you, Rob. I'm Margaret, but everybody calls me Peg."

"Peg it is, then. And this is my son, Mike."

"Hello, Mike."

"Pleased to meet you Mrs. Stuart."

"Come in. Let's sit for a few minutes and get acquainted before I have to get back to the kitchen. Could I get you a glass of wine?"

"Love one."

"Red or white? I don't have to ask Sarah. Hers is Boone's Farm." She chuckled.

"Ohh, *Mom*!"

"Red if you have it."

"I do. Mike? A Coke or a Pepsi?"

"Coke, please."

When Peg Stuart came back with their drinks, she proposed a toast to welcome her guests and they all took a sip.

"I like your apartment, Peg."

"It's only one bedroom, but I'm alone so it suits me perfectly."

"Something else I like. No, two things. First. Your daughter." Sarah blushed slightly. "Second, the aroma coming from your kitchen."

"Thank you. Twice. But Sarah hasn't told me all that much about you, Rob, so now that you're here I hope we can get better acquainted."

"Don't get me started. I talk a lot sometimes and it could be I'd bore you to tears."

The four of them chatted for about twenty minutes and then Peg Stuart said she needed to get back to the kitchen.

"Sarah, could you help me out for a little while? Be nice to have some company for a change."

"Sure, Mom. Be right there."

Sarah turned on the TV and invited Rob and Mike to relax while she helped her mother. Before she left, she said that her sister, Valerie, and her husband, Erik, would be coming along soon.

"I assumed they'd be sitting at the other two places at the table."

"We'll be six. Just the right size. Now, you two just relax while I go help Mom and visit with her until Sis gets here. Since I'm at the cottage most weekends, we haven't seen each other for quite a while."

"Don't worry about us. We'll be fine."

When Sarah got to the kitchen, her mother wasted no time getting into the subject of Rob Grant.

"He seems nice, Sarah. And good looking, too. How old did you say he is?"

"Be forty-three in late April."

"Looks a lot younger than that. And you said he works in real estate for the Wilcox organization?"

"Started Easter weekend. It's been a year or so since I mentioned it, but you may remember I told you that he was in corporate management in New York right up until the time he moved to the lake—and a little after that. He was driving down on Mondays and then back on Fridays afternoons. He did so well this past summer with Wilcox that he paid him a big bonus. I don't think that he's *ever* done that before. But I know Rob's been a success at just about everything he's ever tackled. He's Alan's general manager now."

"Would you peel the potatoes for me, honey?"

"Sure."

"You also said he's been married twice and that you thought there were women in New York that he was seeing. Sounds to me like he's kind of a playboy and maybe not a very good risk. Sure you aren't setting yourself up to get hurt? I don't want to see that happen."

"I believe we have a relationship that will survive and grow, and it's something I really want. It's worth the risk, if that's what you think it is, because I'm in love with him. Very much. He's a good man, and you'd have had to overhear the talks we've had. He needs time, and I'm going to see that he has it. Part of it is, he's been hurt and he wants to be sure about us first."

"I don't know, Sarah."

"Mom, he's raised the same questions—that is, about our age difference, and he's worried that our being married might not be the best thing for me. He's concerned about my welfare, and as much as anything he's giving me time to decide if *I'm* making the right decision. I think that's an honorable thing for him to do. He's thoughtful, and kind, and considerate, and I love him dearly for the person he is. But another reason he's being deliberate is that his fiancée died of leukemia in the summer of seventy and the wound was very deep. Mike told me how hard he took it. I can help him put those memories to rest. I've done some of it already because little by little I can see a difference. Just from the way he says things, he'll have me one day. I'm sure of it. But you couldn't know that unless you'd heard some of the things he's said to me. If I'm right, and I think I am, you'll have a very happy daughter."

"Looks like you're done with the potatoes. Here. Let me have them. Well, I hope you're right, dear. He has a lot of assets it seems, and it's obvious that he's lifted your spirits. I've been worried about you at times. That other guy sure wasn't the answer. Your color is good now and you look happy—that is, as if life finally has meaning. I'll say a prayer for you. Every mother wants good marriages for her children. In the end it's your decision, and I'll not interfere. Have you talked about family?"

"I'll leave that up to Val and Erik. I have children all day long. It may be the wrong thing to say, but being a mother isn't high on my list of things I want to do."

"How does Rob feel about that?"

"He's had his and really isn't interested in starting over, even if he could."

"What do you mean by that?"

"He was put out of business surgically a long time ago and we like things just the way they are. It's one of the reasons I want to see if what we have will work out. I'll do my part. No, probably more than my part because I've found the man I want in my life. All of it."

"I've only spent a few minutes with Rob, but my first impression is positive. I like him. You have my support, honey."

"Thanks, Mom. One day, you'll love him as much as I do, in a different way of course."

"Maybe you should get back to your man. I can finish up here now."

"What's happened to Val and Erik?"

"They were going to stop by his folk's house first. You know how the Hansson's like to talk." She smiled at the thought. "They should be here before too much longer."

Sarah went back to the living room and joined the Grant 'boys' and an NFL game. Mike was watching it. Rob was reading the paper. When it was apparent that she'd be joining them, he put it down and commented, "You had quite a chat with your mother. Did you ask her what she thought about the election?"

"Don't have to. My grandmother, her mother, is very active in the Republican Party and worked for Nixon's reelection."

"With all but eighteen electoral votes and over 60 percent of the popular vote, they have to be happy as clams at high tide."

"They are. I have to tell you that my mom's four number license plate was a thank you for helping John Volpe get elected governor in 1960. Not often Massachusetts has a Republican governor. He lost in '62, and then they worked for him again when he was reelected in '64 and '66. That last election was the first of the four-year terms."

"I'm in good company then. You and I have never talked politics very much, but I can remember Dad backing Willkie and McNary back in 1940, and Dewey four years later, so I grew up in a Republican household."

"Mom will be glad you're a political friend and not a foe."

"That may not always be the case because I tend to look at the candidates and their views on various subjects rather than to follow the party line. An example is the Roe vs. Wade debate. I tend to be pretty much pro-choice, so I was more aligned with McGovern than Nixon on that issue."

"I don't think any of us will get into a fight over that."

"It's interesting that when I was at Sentry Oil, I was drafted by the CEO to 'volunteer' time to help the Republican finance committee. The guy heading it was Maurice Stans and we were housed in the Drake Hotel up on Park Ave. We sat at phones and worked lists of people from all over the country. The idea, obviously, was to raise funds to support the Nixon-Agnew election campaign. The one call I remember most vividly was to Alf Landon, the candidate who ran against Roosevelt in 1936. He was dead set against what we were doing and told me, 'No, dammit, I didn't beg for money when I ran for president, and I'm not giving that Nixon feller any either.' Then he hung up on me."

"You have to tell my mother that story. She'll love it."

Sarah was just about finished with her comment when two young people came through the door. "Hi, you two," she said, then jumped up and gave each of them a big hug.

"We got cornered by my folks," the tall young man said. "Hard to break away." The pretty girl with rusty hair and blue eyes agreed.

"Rob, I'd like you to meet my brother-in-law, Erik Hansson, and my sister, Valerie. Erik, Val, this is the light of my life, Rob Grant."

Rob and Erik shook hands, and to Rob's surprise Val gave him a hug.

"Looks like I'm not a complete stranger," Rob observed. Both Erik and Val confirmed it.

"We've heard quite a bit about you," Val said. "After all these months, I'm glad that we could finally meet."

"Then you probably know what kind of schedule I've had this year, and the reasons for it."

"Sarah told us you were driving back and forth to New York and then working at Hampden Lake on weekends."

"That's it. From late March until October 30, I had only one day off."

"Wow. You must have been beat by then."

"I was, but Sarah was welcome therapy." His comment wasn't lost on Erik.

As they talked before dinner, Rob discovered that both Erik and Val were younger than Sarah. He'd just gotten a degree in June and Val had been at UMass until they were married a year ago last summer. Neither had permanent jobs yet, but they were looking. Both were interested in Rob and his career, and it was obvious from the questions they asked that Sarah had shared some of his story with them. Since New York was history now, it gave him a chance to reminisce. Moreover, he was happy to share part of his story with them. From Val's attentive expression, Rob could see that she was taken with Sarah's new love and the many things he'd done in recent years.

When dinner was ready to be served, the girls helped, Peg Stuart gave thanks, and they then dug in. Previous Thanksgivings crossed Rob's mind, especially those with Regina and the one with Justine. But this one was special because it could well signal the start of a long string of holiday meals with the Peg Stuart and Hansson families. It gave him an especially good feeling.

As was often the case, they all ate too much. Those around the table enjoyed Rob's oyster dressing that he was called on at the last minute to put together.

"Rob, your dressing was different—and delicious. I can say that if for no other reason than it's all gone. Where did you learn how to make it?"

"My mother. She's good in the kitchen, and although there aren't many oysters in Iowa, she found the recipe somewhere."

"She taught you well. It was scrumptious, and I want the recipe before you go back to the lake."

"Me, too," Val said. "It was *great*!"

By the time dessert was finished, something no one needed, and the dishes were washed, they'd all gotten to know each other fairly well. Rob felt comfortable with the family and enjoyed spending time with them. He would fit, he decided. Not unlike the way he felt sitting at Kim's table. But that was a thought that he shouldn't have let cross his mind. She was gone from his life, but those memories were still very warm and pleasant and always would be.

At dusk, Sarah suggested that they get their things together and start for home.

"By 'home' I suppose you mean Rob's place?" Val asked.

"No, I'll stop by for a little while before I go on to Palmyra. It's fun to make up a little fire and then have a nightcap at the end of a pleasant day like this one."

They said their good-byes to Rob and Sarah, and also wished Mike a belated happy birthday. After they'd left for Hampden Lake, Peg Stuart observed, "It looks to me like I'll eventually have another new son-in-law.

Sarah certainly is in love with him and it shows. It's the best I've seen her look in a long, long time. It's obvious to me that he's good for her."

"I like him," Val said. "I don't care about the difference in their ages, or his personal history, because he seems like a really nice guy. Sis thinks so, and that's what matters, doesn't it? Just watching the two of them, I think they're good for each other—and they're so cute together. He thinks the world of her. It shows."

"I'm not going to worry about it, Val. I had my doubts earlier in the day, but they'll be just fine, I think."

"One thing about it," Erik said, "he's had loads of good experience and will always be able to take care of her. To have made it in the New York corporate world says a lot about him, I think. You didn't hear some of his stories about global responsibilities and all the international travel he did. I'm really impressed. I'd have him as a brother-in-law. Bet he could teach me something."

After they'd gotten back to Colonial Trail, Sarah asked, "Weren't you going to call Greg from Mom's place?"

"We were having such a good time I decided that instead of calling we ought to run up and see him for a little while on Saturday afternoon. That assumes you want to go along."

"Oh, I'd love to. Be good to see him."

"Done, then. We'll have lunch here and plan to be up there by around two o'clock. It doesn't take long to make the trip now."

Rob and Sarah spent a quiet day together on Friday. Mike found a ride and left to stay with his friends. He promised he'd be back in time, like always, to see the second NFL game late on Sunday afternoon.

"Well, sweetheart. It looks like we're empty nesters again. I'm all out of anything to deliver, and it's too soon to go looking for any. Until I find another consignment, why don't we do the laundry and get the shopping done?"

"Good idea. Then we can spend the rest of the weekend trying to find something for you to deliver." She giggled sweetly.

"Are you fertile by any chance? You're all wound up."

"No, I'm past that and closer to the end of my cycle, I think."

"Well whatever it is, if you have a fire going, I'll do my best to keep up. But let's get our chores out of the way, and then maybe we could go have dinner someplace in Sturbridge."

"Could we do the Oxen Pub?" Sarah asked. "We haven't been there since Labor Day weekend."

"Just what I had in mind. By now, Skip probably wonders what's happened to us."

When they arrived at the Pub, Skip was just setting up and they stopped to talk with him for a minute.

"Hi, Sarah. Rob. Where have you been keeping yourself? I can get paranoid pretty easy, so I thought maybe you got tired of my music."

Rob laughed. "No, young man, we've just been awfully busy. You know Wilcox—at least by name. Over the winter months, I'm managing a building in Springfield that he and a partner just bought. Lots of work to be done on and to it, so my days have gotten longer. Sarah can tell you all about that."

"Is Rob telling me the truth, Sarah, or is he just trying to make me feel good?"

"It's the truth, but I do get him for the whole weekend."

"I've got to get to work. Good seeing you again. About the time you get your meals, I'll play something just for the two of you."

"Appreciate it, Skip."

Sarah and Rob made a romantic evening of it. Skip Rydell kept his promise, introduced the two of them, and then the song he had chosen.

"Here's something for Sarah and Rob, good friends of ours. They met a little over a year ago so here's a song from last year. It's very appropriate, I think. The title of the song, made popular by Andy Williams, is *Love Story,* or *Where Do I Begin*. For Sarah and Rob."

Rob pointed at Skip and mouthed 'Thank you'. Diners looked in their direction and there was a ripple of applause. Sarah looked at her man with the unmistakable look of all the love she felt for him.

When Skip had finished, Sarah blew a kiss in his direction. Then she turned to Rob and said, "I'm close to tears, you know. What he did has touched a warm place inside, the one where I keep all the love I have for you. I always like our evenings out, but this one's special because we *do* have a love story. I'll tell Skip that on the way out."

"You can speak for me, too, sweetheart. Adding to what you just said, there are words I remember from a ballad someone wrote years and years ago that have a lot of meaning to me at this moment. They were, 'I've got you under my skin', and it's time for me to acknowledge that you've taken up residency there—and in my heart."

Sarah reached across the table and took Rob's hands. She smiled warmly, then looked into his eyes to show him how much his words meant to her. She didn't say a thing. There was no need.

Chapter Sixteen

When Rob and Sarah got back to the cottage, they were eager to take their feelings for each other to another level. This was a night when the physical aspect of their union was less important than sharing what was in their hearts. For all the nights they'd spent together over the past fifteen months, this was a fresh and meaningful expression of their emotions. It was especially important to Rob because he was finally at the threshold of shedding the unpleasant and sometimes painful memories of those he'd been very close to during the past five years. Foremost among them was Marianne Marzano. After they'd loved, Sarah whispered a simple. "I love you, Rob," and then she held him close all night long.

As Rob was drifting off to sleep, the question that had crossed his mind so often with Lu was there again. "How could I possibly turn my back on this?" In his heart, he felt the time was coming when he wouldn't. But he was still cautious, and, as had been the case in the past, the day that he would make the commitment was still probably months off. But the difference this time was that he had none of the questions, or doubts of the kind that had deferred his earlier decisions about marriage. With Kate and Lu, the delays proved to be the right thing to do. In Sarah's, case there was little of that. She was stable and patient, and he had the feeling that she'd wait him out until he was hers. The thought of that left him with a feeling of total contentment when sleep finally laid his thoughts to rest.

Up at a reasonable hour, Rob and Sarah had just finished breakfast when Derek Erwin called.

"Hi, guys. It's been a while since we saw you last. Any interest in some Chinese tonight? There's a new place up in Ware that we thought you might like to try."

"With a new job, at least over the winter, I've been in hibernation you might say. But, you're right. It's been close to a couple of months. We're going up to see Greg this afternoon. It's up north of Worcester in the Princeton area. Why don't we stop by your place on the way back?"

"Sure. I'll stir up a martini for you."

"You got me hooked. It'll be late afternoon, I imagine."

"Perfect. See you when you get here. Not before." Derek chuckled.

After they'd had lunch, Rob got a map out and tried to figure out if there was a more direct way to get up to Duchene by going cross country and using less traveled state roads. It wound up looking like the last trip. So, wiggling their way north, they got on Route 62 and within an hour they were on the school grounds. When Greg was brought into reception, his jaw dropped and he said, "Oh, *wow*!" He hugged both his dad and Sarah affectionately.

"How're you, young man?"

"I don't believe this. Super! What a neat surprise."

"Well, we haven't been up for a while, and since we have the long weekend, we thought you might like to know that we're still alive."

The three of them talked about all manner of things and visited until fairly late in the afternoon, in fact later than Rob had expected to stay. But Greg was so glad to see his dad and Sarah that he couldn't stop talking. And he had questions, too. Among them, he wanted to know if Rob had heard anything about Kim, or Helen, or Justine. Sarah might have objected, but she was confident that she was the woman in Rob's life now and didn't even raise an eyebrow.

"Justine is still Justine. A wonderful gal and she remains a good friend. Helen? I haven't heard anything about her, but I had reason to talk with Will Cable, and he said Kim's 'gone bad'. That was the way he put it. She tried a reconciliation with Vince. It didn't work, and then she moved out of the house on Perrin Drive. The odd part is that she left the boys behind. Hard to believe that—considering how close they were. Chris and Ian were her life. What happened, I guess, is that she got used to loving and being loved regularly, missed it, and then among other things she took to drinking pretty heavily. That led to her sleeping around, which included her immediate boss, and then after she moved on to someone new, he saw to it that she lost her job. She's a mess from the way Cable described it. Kim was a strong, compassionate woman. You know that, so you wouldn't have expected to hear the kind of story he had to tell. Will said she's finally divorced now. I knew how much she cared about me, but my sense of it is that her feelings ran *much* deeper than I thought. So, when I walked out of her life, something must have snapped. I have to admit that I feel awful about it. Makes me think I'm at least partly responsible for what's happened to her. She gave me so much support when you got into trouble and then again when Marianne died. But she and I couldn't have gone anywhere since she was still married when I moved out of Juniper Heights. Such a good woman, and I just hate to think about what's happened to her. It's terribly, terribly sad."

"I don't want to hear stories like that. She was always nice to us. Maybe when I'm outta here, I can go see her. There's a chance I'll be released at the end of the spring term. It'll be over three years by then."

"That's *wonderful* news, Greg. But before then, you'll get to come home for Christmas, right?"

"Yeah, from Saturday the twenty-third, and I can stay through to the thirty-first, a Sunday. Like before, I can get a ride down since one of the kids lives in West Hartford. Different family than the one last spring and they'll be driving down I-86. His dad's already told him they'll drop me off at Goody's truck stop, the one on the west side of Exit 106."

"You going to hitchhike up to the cottage then?" Rob chuckled.

"If I ask real nice, maybe you'll pick me up."

"Sure. It's only about five minutes down to the exit. We can do that."

"Sounds like they're getting ready to feed us. This has been a real surprise and it's great that you could come too, Sarah."

"Wouldn't have missed it for anything." She gave him a hug.

"Tell my ugly brother that I'll see him in four weeks. And you have to make some of that great chili soup for me. I miss it."

"You got it. Now we should probably be on our way."

"Thanks for coming up. It's been really super."

"See you on the twenty-third. Drop me a note and give me some idea when I need to be down at Goody's."

"I will. Bye, Dad. Bye, Sarah."

Hugs and good-byes finished, Rob pulled onto Route 62 to start their drive to Bloomdale and the Erwin's house.

As they drove, Sarah asked, "Why is it you were talking with Cable, and how'd the subject of Kim come up?"

"I got a letter from him early last week asking me to call. He wanted to talk about my share of the cost to board and educate Greg. When he found out that I'm not making New York money anymore, he didn't ask for much this time around. My share has always been keyed to what I'm earning. We'd finished with that and since he knew that Kim and I had been close for more than two years, he thought I'd be interested in her story. He and Kim, and Lu, were all in high school together in the early to mid-fifties, so call it a personal thing. It really bothered me to hear what he had to say. I would *never* have imagined that she'd turn out the way she has. I'm still really upset by it."

"Have you thought about calling her—or seeing her again?"

"Will said she's slept in an awful lot of beds since I left, not the least of them the salesman who sold her a car recently. I guess she busted up her other one. I'm positive that she wouldn't have turned out this way had I stayed in Sheffield. But the fact remains she *has* gone bad. To answer your question, I couldn't be interested in a woman with the kind of life she's let herself slide into. It wouldn't ever work now. Her boys, Chris and Ian, must really be disappointed to see their mother go to hell. Same with you if you slept around. It's a double standard, I suppose, but it's the way I see things, right, wrong, or otherwise."

"Which, in part, explains why you've been so cautious. It's also the reason why I'm willing to be patient. You've told me about the two divorces, and I think you had good cause to file. I don't blame you, my sweet. I know who and what you are and as long as there's hope, I'll stand beside you. It helps, too, to know what's happened before me, but I think you've just about finished sowing your wild oats. I've never had any, so you needn't worry about me. Ever. All I ask is that if we ever marry, please don't cheat on me. I wouldn't be angry, just very deeply hurt that at that moment you'd think *she* was more important than us."

"Ahhh, Sarah. You're too sweet to hurt. It would do a lot of damage to me and my psyche. It's called conscience."

They drove for several miles in silence. All the while, Sarah held Rob's right hand until they pulled into the drive at the Erwin's house.

"We made pretty good time, dear heart."

"Sure did. It was the frank discussion about some personal subjects that made the trip back seem shorter than the trip up. One thing that came out of it is I'm discovering that the more I know what's inside your head, the more I love you. Much more, and I'll come apart at the seams."

"Don't do that. I like you just the way you are—and I'm not at all good at stitching."

At the door, Derek said, "We thought maybe you'd forgotten about our date."

"No, not at all. We had a really long visit with Greg. He didn't know we were coming up so he took advantage of our being there. It was clear that he badly needed to be with family for a while."

"I understand. Let me have your things, and then I'll make you a drink. Both of you. Sarah, you still drinking Boone's Farm?" He laughed.

"Ohh, no! Not you, too? Mom just did that to me at Thanksgiving."

"We can do better than that."

Out of their coats, Julia said hello to Sarah, then Rob. For some reason she didn't look at all cheerful.

They had their drinks, chatted for a bit and then left for Wang's. Rob said he'd drive, too, so they could cut across country afterwards. Derek agreed. "Be a lot shorter than doing two sides of the triangle."

The restaurant was right on Route 9, so it was easy to find. The interior was of an oriental motif, of course, and very stylishly done. Once seated and drinks served, the chatter began. What Rob quickly found out was that when you put educators together, that's all they talk about. Drinks led into dinner and Rob had said hardly a word from the time they walked in. But that gave him time to listen with one ear and also think about various plans for the building. Wilcox was right. He would be able to hit the ground running on Monday morning. But all through the meal, he smiled and nodded when he deemed it appropriate so those at the table thought him pleasant company. At the same time, Julia still wasn't especially cheery, and he wondered what her problem was? A "lady thing", maybe?

When they finished dinner and were cracking open their fortune cookies, Derek asked two questions. "What did you think about your meal, and how does your fortune look?"

"Dinner. You probably didn't notice, but I had Egg Foo Young and it was nothing short of terrific. My fortune? It says you're paying for it and I *have* to believe what I read." Rob laughed. Derek grimaced. "No, it's more personal and 'spot on' as the British sometimes say. '*The greatest peril could be your caution*'." Sarah turned and looked squarely into Rob's eyes. Her wicked grin was absolutely priceless.

After the foursome had split the bill down the middle, they said their goodnights in the parking lot and then Rob followed the Erwins until they reached their turnoff to Hampden Lake.

As Rob was driving, he asked Sarah, "You liked my fortune?"

"I thought it was an amazing coincidence, especially after what we talked about on our way down from seeing Greg."

"Maybe I should put it under the glass on my dresser. That way it can be a reminder that I haven't proposed yet."

"Good idea. I'll help you do it."

"Change of subject. What was bothering Julia? She wasn't herself, unless I don't really have any idea what she's like most of the time."

"No, I think you're right. Because she's in the office most of the day, I don't see her that much. But I agree. It isn't their kids. My guess is their marriage isn't what it might be. There have been rumors that Derek is seeing a younger teacher on the sly. Don't know who or where she is, and no one has ever seen him with anybody else, but the rumors persist."

"Well it isn't likely he'll tell me about it, and if he did I'd be obliged to keep my mouth shut. But if he hasn't said anything to anyone or been caught, I don't understand why there are rumors. So why don't we forget about the whole thing, slip into bed and make mad, passionate love when we get home."

"*Yeah*! I like that idea. No caution when it comes to that subject."

And when they got to Colonial Trail, that's exactly what they did.

Sunday morning was a time when Rob and Sarah liked to make love, at least once, and then continue their day in a leisurely fashion. It was that one morning during the week when they had the time to snuggle and to share some of the passion they felt for each other. This last Sunday of November was no exception.

Then before they had breakfast, Rob went to the Hampden Market and bought the *Globe*, a good paper with lots to it that would keep both of them occupied for hours. At one o'clock, they turned on the Patriots-Colts game but by the time they got into the second quarter, it was obvious the Pats were going to continue their losing ways. And that's the way it turned out: 31 to 0, Colts. In Derek's words, when he called later, "They stunk out the joint." Then as Mike promised, he was home in time to watch the second game, Kansas City at Oakland. As a fanatical Raiders fan, he'd make every effort to be in front of a TV, somewhere, for the 4 p.m. kickoff. He made it. Just barely.

By the time the game was over and Oakland had made Mike happy with a 26-3 win, Sarah had dinner ready. They ate, and exchanged news about what they'd done since Friday. Rob made sure Mike knew they'd seen Greg and passed along his message about seeing his "ugly brother" on the twenty-third.

"Wish you'd told me you were going up to see him," Mike said.

"Guess you didn't hear us talking about it on Thursday evening. You'll see him at Christmas, though. He'll be here for eight days."

"And about the 'ugly brother' business, we'll see about that."

"Easy on the physical stuff. This place isn't big enough for that."

"Just kidding. It'll be good to see him."

No one had much interest in Sunday evening TV programming so they all busied themselves with other things. Mike took a look at the Boston paper, Sarah finished up a little bit of school work, and Rob decided what needed to be tackled first in the building tomorrow. The long weekend had run its course and it was back to work in the morning.

Everyone went down at a reasonable hour, so on Monday morning they were all up bright-eyed and bushy-tailed by seven o'clock. Sarah was up first, showered, and then had breakfast going by the time Rob and Mike were ready to sit.

"I've decided we did pretty well as a family over the past several days," Sarah suggested.

Rob was quick to agree and added, "It's been a very tranquil and comfortable long weekend." Mike nodded that he concurred. Want to try it again over Christmas—like I suggested a while back?"

Sarah responded immediately with an emphatic "*Yes*!" A bright smile accompanied her answer.

"We'll work out the details later. Wilcox will have a little Christmas get together on the twenty-second, the Friday that's the start of our ten-day shutdown. The party includes all his people, wherever they're located, and McCallum's, too. They've taken a small room at the country club. We're not talking about a lot of people, so I guess we'll all fit."

"The school's doing the same thing at the Banjo Pub. I'll be over after it's done. It won't be late because most everyone has family they'll have to get home to. Amy Porter and I are about the only ones who're single. By the way, she and I are talking about rooming together. I'll tell you about that, and the reasons why, if we decide to do it."

"I've got to scoot, Punkin. It's been a wonderful weekend."

"Can't wait until Christmas. We'll go back to Mom's again, OK?"

"Sure is."

They hugged, shared a gentle kiss and then Rob and Mike left to start their week in Springfield.

Sarah waved as they pulled up over the hill in back. And then, alone in the cottage, an empty feeling swept over her. "*Sarah*! He's not going to New York, and we'll be together on Wednesday. Stop it!" Even so, she still felt an ache of loneliness in her chest. It had been a marvelous four days and she hated to see the time they'd shared come to an end.

The week began and Rob went right to work getting additional marketing and PR programs launched. The first thing he did was put together a simple leaflet, had it printed, and then hired the Wilcox kids to stuff it in every office mailbox in the city. It was a simple device, but it worked. The inquiries increased and new leases were written. Having gotten a small model office ready quickly helped sell prospects on the idea of taking space in the McCallum-Wilcox Building. And some of the tenants were useful, too. Old attorney Buckley brought in two tenants and got two months rent free. He loved it! Then at the end of that first week of December, there were serious inquiries from two major prospects. An acupuncture center expressed interest in leasing the entire third floor and the four branches of the U.S. Military wanted all of the remaining free space on the ground floor to set up recruiting centers. Wilcox himself took charge of those negotiations. Rob's part would be to oversee the renovations if they went to firm leases. They soon did and Alan Wilcox was jubilant. A plus was the press coverage of their success story, and both the owners and Rob Grant were getting an excellent reputation around this metro area of some 400,000 residents.

In the midst of all this activity, Sarah made a late afternoon trip into Springfield just before the Christmas break to see the building and all the renovations that were going on. She met Deana, of course. There was no love lost between the two of them from the moment they met, but Deana got the message that the likelihood of getting Rob Grant into bed was indeed slim. His Sarah wasn't stunning, but she *was* attractive, pretty well built, and had enough sex appeal in her own right to keep her man from straying too far. Rob was glad they'd met. It might keep Deana out of his hair. Busy as he was, he had neither the time nor very much interest in dealing with her fantasies.

After the tour was over, Sarah said she was impressed by what she'd seen. She also pointed out that they were right across from the brand new Civic Center, home of the AHL hockey team, the Kings.

"Maybe some Friday evening I could come in for dinner and then go with you to see a game. If the local players move up from here, it's generally to Los Angeles in the NHL."

"You know more about sports than most gals."

"Daddy and I used to watch the Giants every Sunday. He taught me football. I love sports."

"OK, you're on, but with everything else I have on my plate here, it'll be sometime into the new year before I can spring loose."

"No rush. Be a fun evening and something to look forward to."

December wound down, and the McCallum-Wilcox organization could look back on the last two months with satisfaction. The expenses for improvements were substantial, but they had new, long-term tenants that would dramatically improve how their financial statements looked.

The late afternoon and early evening of the twenty-second had been set aside to celebrate the start of the holiday break. The room at the country club was the right size for the small-ish McCallum-Wilcox group and there were plenty of hors d'oeuvres and drinks. It was a congenial bunch and a pleasant way to start the holidays.

At about eight o'clock, Deana came to Rob, said she was ready to go and asked him if he'd mind dropping her off on his way out to the lake.

"You came with Alan. He's not taking you home?"

"He's the host and told me he has to stay until everyone's left. If you're not ready yet, I can wait."

"No, I've had enough drinks and hors d'oeuvres." Rob knew what to expect but consented to be Deana's chauffeur.

Rob wished Wilcox and the handful of other people he knew at the party a Merry Christmas and a Happy New Year. Then, as they were on their way, Deana expressed her continuing interest in bedding Rob Grant.

"I had a chance to visit with your Sarah for a few minutes," Deana said. "She seems nice, but I thought you might like a little variety."

Rob pulled over and parked at the side of U.S. 20.

"I thought we were done with that subject weeks ago."

"You were, but I wasn't. I still want some of you. The idea of getting into your pants turns me on."

"I don't believe you. One thing for sure is that you aren't shy. But we've already been thorough this. I'm old enough to be your father. Plus, I have a good woman I care about and someone who cares about me."

"You're not being at all cooperative. The age thing doesn't bother me because older men have had time to get it right. Much easier for me to do my thing, to really go *all* the way. I told you that before."

Rob was about to reply to that when a patrol car, blue light flashing, pulled up behind them.

"State Police. Is everything all right here?"

"No problems. She and I work together and just came from a holiday party over at the country club. We were having a little conference, you might call it, before I drop the young lady off at her house in Hampden."

"You look familiar for some reason."

"The owners of the building at 153 State and I were on WHYN-TV earlier in the week."

"Could be that's it. But let me suggest that you move along. Russell Road isn't a good place to park. It's way too busy."

"We'll be on our way, Officer."

"Appreciate your cooperation. Merry Christmas to both of you."

"Thanks. You, too."

As they drove on, Rob said, "Polite guy."

"Sure did chill what I had in mind."

"Let it go, Deana."

The two of them didn't have much more to say until they were about to turn into Chapin Road in Hampden. When Deana showed Rob where she lived, he pulled up in front and waited until she got her things together. Before she got out of the car she asked, "Could I at least have a kiss? I'd like to have something from tonight that's worth remembering."

"In the sprit of the season, sure."

Deana leaned over and made it wet and passionate.

"*Whew*! Lots of fire behind that."

"If you only knew. I could give you a loving you'd never forget."

"I'll take your word for it. Have a great Christmas."

"Rather have one of your presents."

Rob ignored her comment. "Behave yourself on New Year's Eve."

"No fun in that. See you on January 2. Bye, Rob."

"G'night, Deana."

As Rob drove home, he reflected on Deana's suggestion that she was a world-class lover. Given her youth and her obvious passion, she might well be. If so, he'd probably risk having cardiac arrest. It would most likely be extremely athletic.

When he pulled up in back of the cottage, he saw that Sarah was already home, and the smoke coming from the chimney told him that she'd taken the time to add a romantic touch to the start of their holiday weekend. Sarah met him at the door and gave him a loving hug. "Vacation time!" she exclaimed.

"That it is, and I'm all yours for the duration."

"Promise?"

"Yep. And if I hadn't had too many nibbles, I'd take you out for a bite. But, it's gotten late, so you'll have to settle for a good lovin' and some serious nuzzling afterwards."

"I like the items on *your* menu much better."

"Let's have a sip of something first and then go find a couple of lofty peaks to climb."

"There's a little Baileys left. I'll have that. What would you like?"

"A nip of Drambuie. Not much, though. I'm about ready to start the climb." Rob had no difficulty at all recognizing that Deana's hot pants and fiery kiss had turned him on again. She was 'legal' now, but that didn't change anything. She was very young. Too young. Looking back, it wasn't often that he felt the need to discipline himself, but this was one instance when he had to say no—in spite of the fact that the thought of bedding her was very appealing.

When they finished their liqueurs, Sarah took Rob by the hand and led him to what would be *their* bed for the next eleven nights. "We're going to get an even better idea how it would be if we were married. You can think whatever you like, but I'm going to pretend."

"Recollections of Lu," Rob thought. "Difference is, this has a good chance to turn out that way. First time the odds have been this good."

With both of them turned on, this was a night of searing passion and the finale was spectacular. Sarah's squeal was world-class and Rob's animal growl was at its very best. Finished with their deliveries, they slept like two cuddling logs.

The gray light of the early December morning was brightened by Sarah's radiant smile and her softly spoken words. "Morning, my sweet. You sure fixed me up last night. It helped that you were verry animated."

"Once in a while I feel your little contractions when you get where you want to go. Drives me wild and straight to making *my* delivery. We're pretty good, I've decided."

"Pretty good? Much, much better than that, mister."

"'Mister'. Marianne's word again," Rob remembered. For the first time, the memory of her, and that expression, didn't hurt as much. Maybe Sarah *would* be the beneficiary of the opal ring that Marianne had taken from her finger and, unknown to Rob, bequeathed it just before she died "to the wife of Rob Grant". All the images surrounding the stone were vivid. He saw the shop in Sydney where he'd bought it three years ago yesterday, the jeweler in Sheffield where Marianne had picked out the setting, and the afternoon of January 4, 1970 when he'd slipped it on her ring finger when he saw her off at Penn Station. It also brought back the image of her papa, Carlo Marzano, and he wondered how he and Anna were doing. He decided that he'd call them over the holidays just to say hello. Wonderful people who would have been his in-laws, "had she lived". Carlo's words were still there.

"Where are you?" Sarah asked. "You seem lost in thought."

"I am. I was thinking about what was going on three years ago. I'd left Fiji, Nadi, and was on my way back to Kennedy. The day before, a Monday, I'd bought an opal, brought it back for Marianne, and then she'd picked out a simple ring to have it set in. Just before she died, she took it off and put it in a little envelope with a note she'd written to the woman I would marry. She wanted her to have it. That's what I was thinking about."

"That's so touching, Rob. But if someday I become that woman, I couldn't accept it or wear it. That was something special between the two of you, and I couldn't be a part of that memory. It wouldn't be right."

"I bought it, she wore it, but it would be yours to decide what should happen to it. That assumes I propose and you accept."

"Let me put you on notice. If you propose, I'll accept. Instantly."

"I thought as much."

"Do you have a picture of Marianne? I've never seen what she looked like."

"All those pictures are in a shoe box up in the closet. I'll dig one out after breakfast."

"It's a shame I didn't know you when you were traveling all over. It would have been exciting to meet you when you came in from wherever you'd been around the world."

"That's when the age thing rears its ugly head. But you told me not to bring it up again, so I won't."

"Thank you."

"Now, I'm hungry. What's on the menu?"

"Scrambled and sausage. By the way, I meant to ask about Mike last night but ran into a *verrry* interesting detour." Sarah grinned broadly.

"He was at the party and some of the other people coaxed him into going off to a club that had live music. He'll come out to Bloomdale on a bus and will have made arrangements with one of his pals here to pick him up. He and Greg may show up at about the same time."

"Oh, that's right! He's coming home today, too."

"Good thing we got the tree up last weekend. There wouldn't be any time for it today."

"It's so pretty. You did a good job."

"One of my many talents." Rob smiled.

"I know some of the other ones better." Sarah giggled.

"Since Greg won't be down until this afternoon, why don't we do the shopping and get the laundry behind us after we finish breakfast?"

"I'd already planned on doing that."

They ate and then Rob kept his promise to get out a photo of Marianne, the same one he'd showed Kim ages ago. It was among those he'd taken in late December 1969, well before she'd started losing weight and the leukemia had begun taking its toll. She looked tan and healthy.

"She was gorgeous, Rob. What an incredible smile. And she had such beautiful eyes, too. Seeing her picture explains a lot of things. It *is* worth a thousand words."

"What we had and all we'd have shared, have been very hard to put aside, or forget. That won't happen. But you'd have had to know her to fully understand. Like you, she had a special something inside and because of it everyone loved her. Her expression and that charming smile were projections of her inner self—or her soul, maybe."

"I know how you felt about Marianne, so it would be wrong for me to imitate how and what she was to you. But from the way you've described her, I think we're alike in some ways."

"You are. Very much so. Where I see the greatest similarity is that you're even-tempered and have a gentle nature like she did."

"But she couldn't have loved you any more than I do."

"Hard to measure. On the other hand, I can't disagree with you."

"I'm not her, Rob, but I hope you'll keep an open mind and let me show you that I can make you happy, too."

"You already have, but we're saying essentially the same thing—that is, both agreeing to give ourselves a little more time to find out if what we have now is right for us over the long haul."

"I've said it before. You'll have it. I'm not going anywhere, unless you throw me away. And what I'm going to do is wait you out until you see that I'm the best thing that could happen to you."

"Throw you away? No. You mean too much to me now. It's not very likely that I'd give any thought to doing something like that. Not to worry. What I *am* concerned about is getting the laundry and shopping done before we run out of time."

Sarah chuckled sweetly. "*That's* a change of pace if I ever heard one. Not at all romantic, but you're right. We need to get going."

After they got their chores out of the way, they went down to meet Greg at Goody's truck stop adjacent Exit 106. It wasn't long before a big black Cadillac pulled up and a smiling face was waving from the back seat. When the driver pulled to a stop, Greg exploded out the door and gave Rob and Sarah a bear hug. He wasn't too excited.

The driver, his woman companion, and a boy about Greg's age, got out of the car to say hello.

"Dad, Sarah, I'd like to meet Mr. and Mrs. Kohler, and my good friend, Casey. They live in West Hartford."

They said hello, shook hands all around and then Mr. Kohler said, "It's more like the west side of West Hartford. We live on the other side of a street called Mountain Road."

"Not having lived outside the New York metro area very long, I don't know much about the Hartford area except to drive through it."

"Greg said you lived up on Juniper Heights in Sheffield. I grew up not far from there. Really nice area."

"We had a two bedroom apartment at number 71. But after I was made redundant, as an Australian lady called it, we couldn't afford the Heights any longer. I had a chance to get into real estate up here and during the winter months I manage an office building in Springfield. Come April, I'll be back out here again and in charge of sales and construction around the lake. Big change from corporate life in Manhattan."

"I'm with Travelers Insurance, so I can relate to what you're saying. But if you're involved with summer properties, we ought to come back up and see you. We've been looking around for a cottage. This would be close enough so that I could leave the family here and commute. Do you have a card? Could be I'll call you when you open in the spring."

"That'll be mid-April, the fourteenth I think it is. Here's my card."

"Ahh, the general manager of Leisurely Times, Ltd., a unit of Wilcox Enterprises. Well, you're the right man to know. Can't miss all of his signs. He seems to be a major player locally. And here's my card."

They chatted for a few more minutes and then Wendell Kohler said it was time for them to be on their way.

"Glad to have met you. If it works out that you come up for the summer, the boys could spend time together here, too. But about the ride down, what do I owe you?"

"Not a thing. Glad to do it. Anytime."

"Much obliged."

They all said their good-byes and the big Cadillac eased into the on ramp and headed down I-86 toward Hartford.

"Mrs. Kohler is very nice," Sarah remarked. "We had a few minutes to talk. I gather they're pretty well off. A classmate at UMass lived in their part of West Hartford and there are mostly very big homes out there."

"Well, Kohler's card says he's an executive vice president, so I guess you're right. Ready to go?"

"Yeah!" Greg said.

By the time they got back to the cottage, Mike was home.

"Geez. Go way for a half-hour and look what the cat drags in."

Greg and Mike hugged each other, bobbed like two dancing bears, and finished off their greeting with another fancy teenage handshake. It was obvious they were glad to see each other.

"I don't know if I like your comment about the cat," Mike said, finally. "That sounds like Iowa farm boy talk." Sarah was watching their exchange and smiled.

"It was, and there's nothing unpleasant about it. It's an expression your Gram uses all the time. Call it a friendly negative."

"In that case, I forgive you."

The two boys went off to their room and carried on a non-stop conversation, accompanied by their kind of music, for at least a couple of hours. The only break they took was when Greg came out of their room to ask, "Could we have chili soup tonight? It's been a long time."

"I thought you might ask for something like that, and we bought all the makings earlier this afternoon. See how smart your old man is?"

"Yeah. I've finally figured that out. Not the old man part, but it's amazing how much smarter you've gotten in the last three years." They all had a good laugh. Their holiday break was off to a good start.

Sarah had told her mother that she was coming to Hampden Lake to open presents with Rob and his sons. Of course, there was no mention that she'd also be spending the night with them. So after they'd exchanged gifts, they got everything together and just after mid-morning headed for Peg Stuart's apartment. The roads were a little tricky until they got to Sturbridge, but the Mass Pike had been well cared for and was fine.

After Greg was introduced, and they'd opened their gifts, Peg served eggnog with more than just a little punch to it. By early afternoon, both Rob and Erik were feeling no pain.

"Guess I better slow down," Rob said. "I've got twenty-five or so miles to do later in the day. If the snow keeps up, it might be a good idea to minimize the risk to the valuable assets I have riding with me. The Pike should be OK, but some of the city streets, and the country roads near us, could be a driving test I don't need on Christmas Day."

Taking his own advice, Rob sipped a single glass of wine before, during, and after dinner. By the end of the afternoon, he was fine. Val wasn't a drinker, so she was all right, but Sarah took St. Thomas's advice and drank to the point of hilarity. Feeling good, she also quit.

All in all, it was an enjoyable afternoon. They had a great meal, and a very pleasant visit. The boys also enjoyed themselves. They didn't have to say so. It was obvious. And Rob sensed that he'd been accepted as part of the Stuart and Hansson families. All of the warm feelings he felt at Thanksgiving time continued to grow.

As dusk merged with darkness, Rob suggested that it might be a good idea if they got on their way before the roads got any worse. Sarah was quick to agree. Peg Stuart didn't ask if Sarah would be able to get home to Palmyra yet this evening. She'd probably have gotten an answer she wasn't ready to hear just yet.

After they'd all hugged and said their good-byes, Rob discovered that he needed to be careful on the local streets. They were messy and there were a couple of drivers who'd already discovered that cars do spin on snow. Unlike Rob, they may have kept on drinking eggnog, or whatever.

On the Pike, Rob said, "I thought your mother was going to ask how you were going to get home, or if you were even going to attempt it."

"She wouldn't have wanted to get into the subject."

"So, I shouldn't have said that you're sleeping with me tonight?"

"No, Rob, you shouldn't have volunteered that I'm sleeping with you tonight—or any other night."

"I get the picture, but it reminds me that you said something about maybe rooming with Amy Porter. You were going tell me about it but the subject hasn't come up again."

"There wasn't anything to talk about until the end of last week. We've taught together for three years and are good friends. She wants to move out of her parent's house and has said I'm about the only person she'd share a place with. Nice of her to say that. When she first asked me about it, I wasn't interested in moving again so soon, but two things have happened. First is, Gwen is spending most nights with her guy, Scott. The other thing is that we have some kind of odor in the apartment now and the owner, Dumont, hasn't been able to figure out what's causing it. He said that he'd cancel our lease and let us move into another building he owns, one that's near the center of town. We could walk to the big market, too. It's a much better location."

"Hang on a second. With all the blue lights flashing down there, it looks like we've got an auto entanglement up ahead."

"Oooh, Rob. It's a mess. Please take it easy."

"I don't have much choice. I thought the Pike would be OK. On the other hand, you can't blame that on road conditions. The crews are taking good care of it. That's just too much Christmas cheer at work I suspect."

"This is exactly the kind of thing I worried about all the time you were driving back and forth to Sheffield. If we'd been a few minutes earlier, we might have been involved."

"I'm sober. At least a couple of those drivers aren't. I'll bet on it."

"There's somebody on a stretcher," Greg said. "Look at the blood."

"Don't ask me to do that, Greg," Sarah said. "I'll pass out. Really."

"Dad's a good driver," Mike pointed out. "But you need to take it slow, too," he added.

As they were waved on, Rob said, "You don't need to worry. It's one of the reasons I nursed a single glass of wine all afternoon. I'm fine."

They got home without incident by driving carefully, especially on the back roads. The few people out were doing the same.

"I think we need to build a little fire and get ourselves warm and cozy." Sarah and the boys liked the sound of that.

"And just for being a good driver, I'll make you a drink—unless you want to go out again."

"With the snow coming down the way it is now, not a chance. We're in for the night. Mix away and I'll drink it."

Sarah gave Rob an affectionate hug and said, "I'll join you."

When morning came, they discovered that they'd had a pretty good snow. But Rob was up during the night to visit the bathroom—and also to keep the fire alive. He pulled the "back log" out of the ashes at the rear of the fireplace and it burst into flames immediately. He then put heavy pieces of split wood on top of it and quickly had the start of another good fire. When Sarah got up not long after first light, she was surprised to see that there was a good, slow burning fire going.

"How did you do that?" she asked. "You must have been up off and on all night long."

"Nope, it's a matter of burning seasoned wood, oak preferably, and then doing what I call the fore log, back log principle. They keep the fire contained in the middle, the one in back doesn't burn much until you roll it out of the ashes. It ignites when it gets oxygen and you're in business. Later in the day, I'll show you how it works. It's something I learned from an old guy when I was growing up. Just call me the fireman. I can build one up or, in your case, put one out." Rob chuckled.

"Well now, it's early yet and the boys are still sound asleep. Does that suggest anything to you?"

"Yep. Two things. First, build up a roaring fire, *then* extinguish it."

"You won't need to build it up. It's already going," Sarah confessed.

"You horny thing you. In that case, I have everything required to put it out."

Snowed in, sort of, it was a romantic early morning and it enhanced all the pleasure they found. The peaks were towering and the finale they shared was spectacular.

"You certainly are a good fireman. The blaze is under control and I just decided that this is exactly what at least part of my Christmas vacation should be like. Our first, and I hope we have lots, lots more."

"If they could all be like this, I second your motion."

After everyone was up, Sarah made breakfast and then Mike and Greg shoveled off the stairs and pathways. The town got Colonial Trail plowed, salted, and sanded, and Rob called Ben Neely to plow out the back drive. By early afternoon, they could access the world again and Mike and Greg went looking for someone to take them across the lake on a snowmobile. They found a couple of guys who were more than willing to show off their new Arctic Cats.

Rob and Sarah decided to sit near the fire, put on some gentle music and just enjoy each other's company. They were now into their fourth day of living together and they were really looking forward to spending the rest of their vacation discovering how life might be if they made this a longer term arrangement. Rob wasn't at all bothered by the thought and felt that their relationship was becoming a firm bond. What they were sharing was comfortable and he was feeling very contented. But he'd been this far before—and then seen it go wrong. He'd still needed more time to make reasonably certain that it would endure. Sarah had assured him, repeatedly, that he could have it.

On Wednesday, Mike and Greg were invited to spend some time with Mike's friends across the lake. Rob agreed, but he took Mike aside and asked him to keep an eye on his brother. Rob then sat with Greg and cautioned him that if he got into funny stuff, and was caught, that it would destroy everything he'd worked toward.

"I'm not going to risk it, Dad. There isn't anything worth that. At the end of March, it'll be three years since Connecticut put me away. I've learned my lesson."

"I'll count on you to say no because I'm sure there's junk in that place. You fall and it'll be another three years. Count on it."

"This is a neat little place. I want to come home, be with you and Sarah, and finish high school here."

"There has to be a time when I can start trusting you. It's today. And remember, we have to run you back up to school early Sunday afternoon. You can sleep late, and then we'll have a late breakfast before we go."

"Thanks, Dad. I'll be OK. And I'll be ready for that good breakfast."

Chapter Seventeen

The boys got organized to leave for the rundown cottage across the lake and promised they'd be back no later than Saturday afternoon. There's a hockey game on and I'd like to watch it, Mike said. "Toronto's at St. Louis. You know I like the Leafs."

"OK. See you on Saturday. We can go out to eat before the game if you'd like."

"If you don't mind, I'd rather eat at home," Greg said

"Fine. But no more chili soup. Please?" They all laughed because they'd had plenty of it during the past week. "Sarah and I will come up with something."

With the guys gone, Rob asked Sarah what she'd like to do.

"Let's go have a burger or something and then maybe we could go to a movie. *The Getaway* came out about two weeks ago. I'd like to see it."

"I would, too. We have a date. But it means going into Eastfield Mall. That be all right?"

"Sure. Then we could eat at the Flaming Pit."

The evening turned out to be one of contrasts. They had a good dinner, loved the movie with Steve McQueen and Ali McGraw—and a small part at the end beautifully played by Slim Pickens. The unpleasant part of the evening was that when they came out of Cine 2, Springfield was encased in a coat of ice.

"Ohhh my," Rob said. "It looks like we're in for some fun."

As he said that, Sarah was looking to the west and saw flashing orange lights atop a narrow echelon of salt trucks moving east on Boston Road, U.S. 20. "Yea! Here comes the infantry," she said.

"Good news, babe. Mustangs do *not* do well in this kind of weather," Rob noted. "There's no one on the move yet, but with the thick layer of stuff they're putting down I'm going to try following the trucks by five to ten minutes. The ice coating looks pretty thin, so the salt should do a number on it quick-like. And the sand will help, too. The way the state has jumped on this, I don't expect serious problems if we take 20 all the way to the lake cutoff—and then go slow."

"Ordinarily I'd object, but I think you're right. Rob. Look. There are already some people who've pulled out onto 20 and they don't seem to be having any problems."

"I just had a thought."

"Another bright idea? What?"

"You were planning on moving into the new apartment on Friday. Why don't we stay at your old place tonight? You can call Dumont in the morning, ask him if you can have the keys, and I'll help move you in a day early."

"Good thought, Rob. But you won't like the odor."

"We should be able to handle almost anything for one night."

"Amy may have already moved in. She's done all the work to put this together. I'll find out when we get to the stinky place."

When they got onto Route 20, it was slow going, but they got to Palmyra without too many problems. It helped that people weren't venturing out. It was also a relief not to have to drive the dozen or so miles home to Colonial Trail.

As they got near Sarah's door, they heard her phone ringing. Before she found her keys and could get the door open, it had stopped. Then it rang again.

"Sarah? Mom. Where-have-you-been? I've tried to reach you since late this afternoon. With this ice storm, I was worried."

"Rob came by and picked me up. We went into Springfield, had dinner, saw a movie, and then had a slow time getting back. Did you just call a few minutes ago?"

"No, it's been a half-hour or so. Why"

"Just wondered. The phone was ringing when I came in."

"Is Rob there?"

"No. He's gone on home. I tried to talk him out of it, but he can be pretty stubborn at times." Sarah winked at Rob.

"Well, you sound like you're OK, so I'll let you get to bed."

"I'm fine. If you tried to get me over the last couple of days, I'm moving and have been over at the new place. I'll be sharing it with another teacher. We don't have a phone yet, so I'll be out of touch for a few days. Rob's coming back tomorrow to help me finish moving."

"Make sure you give me your new number when you have it."

"I will. Thanks for calling, Mom. Night."

"You cover your tracks very nicely." That was all Rob got out before the phone rang again. A husky male voice on the other end said hello and identified himself.

"Hello, Matt. Surprised to hear from you. It's been quite a while."

A fairly long monologue was followed by a question that he obviously put to Sarah.

"No. I'm afraid not. I'm involved with someone now and not seeing anyone but him. Nice of you to think of me, though."

Another mumbled comment and a short question.

"Not possible. It's like I said. I'm committed and out of circulation. But I've really got to go, Matt. Thanks again. Bye."

"An old boyfriend sniffing around, I gather."

"No. We only went out a couple of times, and it's been ages since he's called. Yeah, it was last summer just before you and I met. He must have run out of names. Sounded like he was in a bar and that maybe he'd been there too long. Wonder how he got my number? Gwen and I haven't been here but about two months. Operator probably. Anyway, nothing went on, and he was history well over a year ago. I decided after we went out the second time that I didn't want to see him again. Nothing to worry about."

"I'm not, but I liked it when you let him know you're my girl. The sound of that made me feel good all over."

"And I loved saying it, mister."

"Now that we're in and snug, maybe we should take all those good feelings and christen your bed. Again."

"I'm completely yours for the taking. You can stand the odor?"

"It's noticeable, but not overwhelming. Reminds me of something that you'd smell at a petrochemical facility. I'm guessing it's related. It's best that you're moving. I would be too, but for a different reason."

Rob and Sarah loved with deep feeling, but she didn't sleep well afterwards. Rob's comment about *his* reason for wanting to move bothered her. She finally understood what he meant and was pleased that he'd be around to help her get her things over to the new place tomorrow.

The day began early. Dumont brought the key by, and Rob turned out to be a regular workhorse when it came to getting Sarah relocated into the Pleasant Street apartment. It was up on the second floor, brighter, and a much nicer arrangement. Rob felt better about Sarah being here. That it was centrally located made it even more attractive.

"I like your new digs, Punkin. You can walk to everything. Could be I'll stop on my way out from Springfield and maybe spend the night with you, especially if the weather's crummy."

"That ought to be interesting because Amy and I will share the same bedroom."

"Well, now. I've never slept in a shared bedroom before. Could lead to a very stimulating evening!"

"Am I going to have trouble with you? Don't turn out to be the rascal you probably were in New York. This is too close to home."

"Aww, Sarah. Don't be too hard on him," Amy Porter said as she came through the door. "Might be fun."

"Sounds like I'm going to have trouble with both of you."

"No, babe. I'll be a good boy. It was just the idea of it that gave me a buzz." Rob chuckled at what was going on.

"In that case, I'll introduce the two of you, although it really isn't necessary. Amy's already seen your picture."

"So you're the Amy I've heard so much about. Glad we finally met."

"Sarah, I have to say he's even better looking than his photo."

"Looks like you're going to be a thorn in my side, too. You're putting a less than subtle move on my guy."

Amy laughed. "All this has been at your expense, Sarah, and it isn't fair. No, our friendship is too important for me to do something like that. I apologize. It's the wrong way to get our boarding arrangement off the ground. But I have to confess that I am envious."

"Don't stop now, ladies. This has been a first and kinda fun."

"Maybe you can convince Amy that it's a first, but I've been around you for sixteen months, and I think I know better."

"Time to call a ceasefire, dear heart. I don't want you to have hurt feelings, not for anything, or for there to be friction between the two of you. A truce?"

"Yes. Please."

"Now I feel bad. Let me give you a hug and make it right."

"That's better."

It did, but Rob felt a tiny shudder. She'd been bruised, and it helped him discover that Sarah Stuart had a fragile side. An innocent and playful exchange had gone a little bit awry and it told Rob two things. She'd confirmed just how much she loved him, and it also said that in her young life she'd taken an emotional hit of some kind. Put to the test for the first time, her fear of losing him had surfaced. He vowed not to play with her feelings again. Ever. She was sweet and didn't deserve conduct that would cause her pain.

Rob finished bringing up the last of Sarah's personal effects and then they went about the business of getting them all put away. In the meantime, damaged feelings were repaired and they were able to laugh at simple little things before they got ready to leave for Hampden Lake.

Just before they left, Amy asked, "Should I assume you won't be spending much time here?"

"Hardly ever on weekends. No, probably never. And more often than not I'll be at the lake on Wednesday evening. We need that." Amy showed both of them an understanding smile.

"Good to have your schedule. I'll know when I can have friends in. Now that I've left home, maybe I can finally lose my virginity."

That got Rob's attention and it was obvious to both girls that it had.

"Surprised, Rob?" Amy asked.

"Yeah. For two reasons. The first one you can figure out. Your age. The second was your having been so blunt about it." Rob chuckled.

"Well, I'll not share stories, so you'll never know when it happens."

"Don't you believe that. You can't hide it. The male animal knows."

As Rob and Sarah drove back to the cottage, they were mesmerized by the spectacle of a landscape that looked as if it had been fashioned from glass. The temperatures had remained just below freezing so the coating of ice remained. The roads were nearly dry, but as far as the eye could see the countryside was a glittering panorama. The sun was out and it made the scene come to life.

"How many times have there been beautiful shots like this that I've missed because I didn't have a camera. Never fails. But we couldn't have known about this last night. It's dazzling, and a good opportunity missed, at least in this part of the county."

"And the beauty of it all is a huge contrast to my mood earlier. I owe you an apology for acting like a high school freshman. I got my period this morning, and I'll blame it on that."

"Don't worry your pretty little head about it. It said to me that you care enough to worry about our relationship falling apart."

"But if that happened, I should be able to deal with it as an adult, not the way I behaved. Amy must wonder about me."

"I understand, but your reaction was positive reinforcement. I don't have any reservations about where you and your feelings stand."

"You're being kind."

"I'm being honest, Sarah. What came out of our exchange was more important than you might imagine. Look at it positively, sweetheart."

"What I don't want you to do is treat me like I'm a fragile butterfly." Sharon Kerner flashed across Rob's memory. That was what he'd called her. Had it really been four years ago?

"You aren't, and I won't. But I will be mindful of your feelings, especially at this time of the month. What we did was a little bit over the top."

"Not all that much. But you *are* good looking, you're smooth, and because of those things you've not had a shortage of women in your life since your divorce. You're a magnet. You attract them. I know, because I'm one of them. I'll bide my time, as I've said before, because I think we're something special. Well, at least I know you are."

"And we are. But there you go again. You're good for my ego. Just for that I'll give you a juicy kiss when we get home."

And that's exactly what he did.

"Too bad we can't take that a couple of steps further."

"I know. But we'll survive until next Wednesday."

Early on Saturday afternoon the guys came sauntering in. Both of them were grubby and hungry.

"First thing you're going to do is shower and then get into some clean clothes. I'd be pleased if you'd look like the sons of Rob Grant and not the guy who runs the town dump."

"You're in a good mood," Mike said.

"Mood has nothing to do with it. Since we came up here, you seem to be less interested in your appearance. Take pride in your heritage. Gram would be as disappointed in the two of you—as am I. Your friends in Sheffield would be, too. Take a good look in the mirror."

"Yeah, guess you're right."

"After you're cleaned up, we'll get the laundry done, and that includes yours. While it's doing, we'll go for a burger."

"I like that idea," Greg said.

And that's how the afternoon played out. Toward evening, Sarah put together a fine dinner, Greg's last until Easter, and then they all watched the Toronto at St. Louis NHL game, which the Leafs won, 5-4.

On Sunday morning, Sarah was up early and turned out a man-sized breakfast. The aroma of bacon frying and coffee brewing got the boys up and dressed without much delay. The guys were nearly always hungry.

As they ate, Rob asked Greg if he'd be given time at Easter to come home.

"We have a week starting on Good Friday. I can probably get a ride with the Kohlers again."

"That would help because I'll be opening the office out here the weekend before. If you're due back the Sunday following, I'll ask Wilcox to come out and cover the office for maybe two or three hours. Let me see, what's the date? It's, uhhh, the twenty-ninth. You'll be here for my birthday! I'll be thirty-nine again." They all chuckled at his starting to lie about his age already. The truth was, he'd be forty-three.

"This year, I'll buy you a present," Greg said. "Finally."

"Don't worry about it. My present will be to have you home again."

As they'd finished their leisurely breakfast, Rob asked Greg to get his things together. While they were waiting for him to finish packing, the phone rang.

"*RD Borger*! What a wonderful surprise! Good to hear your voice, boss. How are you? Where are you?"

Rob's former boss at Sentry Oil said he was in the Boston area and would be driving back to New York tomorrow, New Year's Day, and wondered if it would be OK if he stopped by for a little while.

"Absolutely! We'd love to see you. We'll be here all day, so you don't have to set a time. Terrific! What a way to start the new year."

RD said it would be early afternoon and Rob suggested that he have lunch with them.

"You can finally meet Sarah, the love of my life."

They finalized their arrangements and Rob gave RD directions out to exit 106 on I-86. They agreed that they'd meet there at around 1:00 p.m.

When they'd hung up, Rob was elated. "What a treat!"

"I like what you said about me being the love of your life," Sarah commented. "Feels like I've been moved up another notch."

"That was spontaneous, so I guess you're right." He hugged her to confirm it.

As they got on their way to Duchene Academy, Greg said he was really sorry that he wouldn't get to see RD.

"Next time, guy," Rob said. "You'll be home when he stops by this summer. He generally vacations for a week or two with his parents. They have a house on Long Pond. You might remember that Regina and I spent a long weekend there once. Nice place. Right on the water."

"Say hello for me. I always thought he was a cool guy."

"I'll tell him what you said. Princeton and then Columbia Law. That's probably the first time he's ever been called 'cool'."

"Aw, you know what I mean."

When they got to Duchene, the place was alive with cars, and kids, and parents. Given the congestion, Rob pulled to the side of the access road just long enough for them to say their good-byes.

"I had a great time, Dad. Thanks for everything. I should be able to see you at Easter and then come home in June. I'll have that date by the end of April." Greg did his fancy handshake with Mike and then gave Sarah a big hug. She loved it. His last hug was reserved for Rob.

"Let me know about your ride arrangements at Easter. But you can write anytime, you know."

"Yeah, I know. Thanks again, Dad."

"Behave yourself, young man."

"I will. I'm close to coming home now so I'm not gonna blow it."

"Good. See you in April."

With that, Rob got the car turned around and they headed home. As Greg had said, it was a good visit.

By the time they got back to Hampden Lake, Mike asked to be dropped off at his friend's place.

"OK, but take it easy on the beer. The word's out that you like it more than you should at your age—or any age for that matter.

"Greg's a fink. That twerp!"

"Nope. But what you're telling me is that he knows, too. No, when you're in the kind of high exposure business I'm in, people get to know you. And when it's in a community this small, you can't get away with much. People talk. But I should tell you that it was Will Cable who first brought your taste for beer to my attention, so it isn't a new subject. In a way, you have an addiction of your own, one similar to Greg's. I suggest you ease up. If it causes problems, the state won't put you away in some school. The local cops will want to see you in jail—or at least fined. Not a good way to come out of your teen years."

"Why are you on my case?"

"I'm not. And if what I've just said isn't going to sink in, especially after you busted up my other Mustang, then you *do* have a problem. Just don't bring it home."

"Guess I'm an outcast, then."

"Mike, *stop it*! If I haven't shown you over the past five years how much a dad can love a son, two sons, then I'm not sure where *I* went wrong. I want what's best for you, but you have to meet me part way."

"Yeah. OK, you found out about me, and I'm being a turd."

"That's a little strong, but I think you need to understand that alcoholism can be every bit as deadly as drugs. You two guys seem to have the same kind of problem, and I don't know where it's come from. No one back to my grandparents did. Your mother doesn't drink at all, and neither did her parents. I care about you, Mike. I don't want to see you in trouble or injured. If I can help, let me try. OK?"

"I hear you. Greg said he needed what he's going through, and I guess I need to know that I'm important to you."

"There's never been a time when you haven't been. Remember that."

"OK. We'll party tonight but maybe I should cool it."

"You don't know how pleased I am to hear that. See you tomorrow?"

"Yeah. The Bruins are at Vancouver. I want see to the game."

"You'll eat with us, then?" Sarah asked. "I'd like it if you did. It'll feel like we're family."

"I'll be home in time for dinner."

After they dropped Mike off, Sarah was quiet until they were almost back to the cottage.

"Hardly a week goes by . . ." Sarah said quietly.

"'Hardly a week', what?"

"It's rare when I *don't* discover something new about you. That bit with Mike was so well done. Val could get out of hand at times and the way you handled him reminded me so much of the way Daddy would've dealt with her. He was good at it. So are you."

"I always feel afterwards that it lacks something. Still it got his attention, and he's coming home for dinner, so I guess it was OK. But, the day may come when you might discover something about me that you don't like."

"After all this time, I doubt it. You've got an unbroken string, and you should take pride in yourself—and what you just did."

"If you're still learning about me, then you understand why I'm cautious about making a commitment. I'm a two-time loser, and I want the next marriage to be right. For a lifetime."

"I said not long ago that I didn't blame you for the marriages having gone bad. You've shown me there's so much good in you."

"Suppose I can live up to that kind of billing?"

"I'll bet on it. Now, love, what are we doing on this New Year's Eve? I'll agree to whatever you suggest."

Rob thought back over the last four. Three were with the different women in his life—Marianne, Justine, one at home alone, and then Kim. He had a feeling that from this one on, he'd celebrate it with the same woman: Sarah.

"I suggest we make a little fire, have a drink, and then go to the Lodge for dinner. Afterwards, we'll build up the fire, not you in your monthly condition, and bring in the year privately and quietly. I'm not big on some kind of bash and too much booze. For years, I've called New Year's Eve amateur's night."

"Your plan suits me perfectly. I love it."

And that was exactly the way Rob Grant and Sarah Stuart brought in their first New Year together. They would have preferred to love 1973 in, but they both had reason to think there would be other years to do that.

Just before one o'clock on New Year's Day, Rob and Sarah drove down to Exit 106 and waited for RD. Since it was hard to know how long it would take him to drive out from wherever he was in the Boston area, or exactly when he'd left, their timing wasn't all that bad. The wait amounted to a little over ten minutes. But it wasn't a problem since they could always find something to talk about. What occupied Sarah's mind was the week and a half she'd spent at the cottage—and how their life together might be if it were a permanent arrangement.

"Except when my self-confidence deserted me for an hour or so last Thursday, I think we have at least some idea how smoothly it would work," she suggested.

"Given your gentle nature, I can't imagine that you'd ever be hard to live with. You don't have highs and lows. I do and can be downright rowdy at times."

"I know that, but you've noticed that I back off until you're done blowing off steam. It's the only way to avoid a fight. Like you said, I don't have extremes so I can't imagine that we'd ever get into a row. My rule is, two people should never be angry at the same time."

"I'll try to remember that. The only time it's permitted is if our anger is directed at something or someone else," Rob suggested.

They talked on for a few minutes until a familiar face showed up driving an unfamiliar car. Rob jumped out, as did RD.

"Hello, stranger. Damn, its good to see my favorite ex-boss again, How're you?"

"Good. And I don't have ask how you are. You look terrific. Country living agrees with you."

"Not as much pressure, and I have a gentle young woman helping stabilize my life. A lot like Marianne in that respect. Come on. I want you to meet her."

As they walked to Rob's Mustang, Sarah got out and showed RD a charming smile.

"You're RD. Rob has told me *so* many stories about you, and I'm glad we've finally met."

"Sarah. It's my pleasure. I'm delighted to meet the woman who's looking after one of my favorite people."

"Follow me, boss. It's only about five minutes to the cottage."

Once they were inside, RD said, "Ahh, a fire. I may just move in. No wonder you look so good. Beautiful country, a charming little house, and a sweet woman. This is the stuff of peaceful dreams. I envy you, Rob."

"All of this doesn't have the energy of Manhattan, but it sure is easier on my innards. Very little stress associated with living here—other than what's self imposed. I'm a tough boss to work for."

"I know exactly what you're saying. When we were at Sentry, you set goals and *always* met them." To Sarah he said, "Rob was one of my superstars. Day in and day out, he delivered."

"He's doing the same thing here. For the first time ever, the guy he works for paid his general manager, meaning Rob, a bonus. During the winter season he's managing an office building in Springfield and in two months has done a great job of finding new tenants. On top of that, he's managing all the renovation projects. I'm terribly proud of him."

"His boss is a fortunate man. I'm guessing he wouldn't find Rob's kind of self-discipline and experience locally. Who is it you work for?"

"Alan Wilcox. He has his fingers in lots of pies."

"You could hardly miss the fact that he's a big operator in this area. His signs are everywhere. Looks like you made a good connection."

"Truth be known, I met him not long after I went to work at Sentry. He's been after me ever since then to move up here and run some of his businesses. I don't make New York money, but living here is much less expensive. My mortgage payment on this place isn't much more than what I paid for a monthly commuter ticket in from Sheffield. That's my favorite line, by the way. But enough about me. Too much, in fact. What are you up to these days?"

"I'm still at *The Week's News, TWN.* Problem is, we have a new man running the show and it's become unbearably political. After three years, I'm looking again. Believe it or not, in the retail business. Difference is, it's the parent of some very well known names in New York and elsewhere around the U.S."

"Lunch is served, gentlemen."

"Gentlemen?" Rob asked. "Not if you'd known the two of us in New York about four years ago." Both Rob and RD snickered. Sarah didn't.

They had their lunch and a good visit. As RD was about to leave, he had a few minutes to talk with Rob privately.

"Your Sarah is an absolute sweetheart. In lots of ways, she reminds me of Marianne. Not her appearance, but her gentle nature. Any plans to turn your roommate into a bride? If you have, I want to be here for it."

"Since she spends three nights a week at her place in Palmyra, a town west of here, she isn't exactly a roomy. But I understand your question. Could be. You know how guarded I've been. And it's served me well with Kate and her impatience, Lu having gone around the bend, and Marianne, well, you know that story. Kim and I could have made it work, I think, but she's gone bad. A painful shock. And Helen? You met her at Marianne's funeral. I'd have married her and it would have been near perfect. But she couldn't leave New York and given my situation—that is, with Mike still in school, and me having pulled out of NAGE, there were lots of hurdles. I still miss her."

"Been an uneven road for you at times. We'll stay in touch. I expect to be back next summer, and I'll stop by. Bet it's beautiful around here in July and August."

"It is that. And October, too. You have my number, so call and let us know when you'll be nearby. We'd love to see you whenever you can make it." Sarah, who'd just come back into the living room, agreed.

"I'll do it. Now, I won't have any trouble finding my way out. See you soon, Rob. And, Sarah, I'm really glad we've met. Look after this guy."

"I'll be happy to. You think he's special. So do I."

Later on, Rob, Sarah and Mike had a pleasant dinner together, and as the first day of 1973 was coming to an end they all went down for the night at a reasonable hour. Their vacations were over. It was back to work, and the real world again, starting tomorrow morning.

Chapter Eighteen

The new year began where the old one left off. There was a modest level of inquiries and little by little the building was being leased out. All the ideas Rob had set out early in November had been implemented and the local press was following the McCallum-Wilcox success story. That they saw an opportunity, paid very little per square foot for the aging building, renovated it, and ultimately turned it into a moneymaker was a story business editors were delighted to follow.

The last full week in February was a school vacation for Sarah that always coincided with Washington's birthday. Since Rob could show that he was current with all his projects, he asked Wilcox if he could take the week. He explained that he wanted to take Sarah out to eastern Iowa to meet his mother. Alan smiled and gladly approved his request.

When Sarah came over on the second Wednesday of the month, which was also Valentine's Day, Rob took his very own valentine out to dinner. As they were having a drink, he sprung his surprise.

"Have any plans for your vacation?"

"Spending the whole week with you—assuming you'll have me."

"You bet I will. Happily so. But what would you think about driving out to Iowa to see mother?"

"Ohhh, *Rob*! I'd love to. Are you serious?"

"I am. I asked Alan for the week, told him why I wanted it, and he said yes with a big grin. Looks to him like I'm trotting you by Mother to get her OK. I don't need that, but I think it's time the two of you met."

"I'm *so* excited! But you're not giving me much time to get ready."

"Casual clothes. Jeans. Take you fifteen minutes to pack. You won't even need a dress. We'll drive a bit west of Cleveland on Saturday, and the rest of the way on Sunday. Altogether, it's around 1,100 miles."

"I'll pack tomorrow night and come over after school on Friday. We can eat here. Make it simpler."

"And leave your car in back. I'll put a couple of lights on timers so that it'll look like somebody's here."

"What fun it'll be."

"By the time we finally get off I-90 south of Chicago sometime on Sunday, your backside may think differently about that."

Early on Saturday morning, Sarah made breakfast, packed some munchies in a bag, and shortly afterwards they were on their way. By the time they'd gotten west of Cleveland to the second of the two Sandusky exits, they decided it was enough for one day and pulled off the Turnpike. Then early the following morning, they resumed their drive west and by mid-afternoon, Rob came off I-80 and onto Highway 130 at Davenport. Heading northwest, they drove through farm country until they got to Cedar County and a side road to the farm.

"There it is, sweetheart. The house my dad's father built back in the late 1880s. As you can see, it's still standing and looks pretty good."

"It's beautiful, Rob. And there's your mother coming out to meet us. It is a long ride, but it's worth it. I'm *so* glad we're doing this."

With both of them out of the car, Rob said, "Mother, I'd like you to meet a very special young lady. This is my Sarah."

"Sarah. I'm delighted that Robin has made it possible for us to meet. He's told me a good deal about you, so now I'm glad I can put a face with all his stories."

"Mrs. Grant. This is such an important day to me, and I share your feelings. Our trip, and being able to spend some time with you, is a dream come true."

"Well, Sarah, we should be on a first name basis. I'm Margaret, and Robin tells me that it's your mother's name, too."

"She goes by Peg. It's been that for as long as I can remember."

"I was Peg in high school and a couple of my friends from those years still call me that. Most everyone else I know well calls me Margie. But we shouldn't be standing around in February weather. Let's get inside."

When they walked into the living room, Sarah commented, "This is lovely. It's so comfortable."

"When you live in the same house for almost a half century, you have time to figure out where you want to put things." Margaret Grant chuckled softly.

"It's perfect. Think I'll move in."

"Then you could be the daughter I never had. Rob was supposed to be a girl and the name we'd picked out was Elizabeth Anne. He wouldn't have told you that, I imagine."

"No. And I like him just the way he is." It was Sarah's turn to chuckle.

"How long can you stay, Robin? You didn't say when you called."

"Until Thursday morning. We're going to make it a more leisurely drive back—meaning three days."

"That'll give Sarah and me time to get in several games of Scrabble, then. I know you don't care all that much for it, but maybe Sarah does."

"Oh, yes! I'd love to play. But I'm pretty rusty."

"It's always a friendly game. I like making good words more than getting a big score. And around here, if we get three of the same letter, we can put one back and draw again without any penalty."

"I like your rules. Should be fun," Sarah quickly decided.

At the end of the day, Rob's mother said, "I don't suppose this is the way it is in Massachusetts, but I'm old fashioned and you'll have separate bedrooms."

"Same as at my cottage." Rob smiled. Margaret Grant looked over the top of her glasses and gave him a very skeptical motherly look.

"I know something about Grant passion, so I'll let that comment lie."

Monday was the holiday, even though it was three days short of the twenty-second. They spent most of the day just visiting—part of which involved Sarah and Rob's mother getting better acquainted. Working together in the kitchen accelerated that process. There was local news and it was amazing how many people his mother's age were gone. She'd turned seventy-five just two weeks earlier, so it was to be expected, he thought. After supper, as the evening meal was called in Iowa farm country, the ladies got into their Scrabble game and played each other about even. "You're good," Margaret Grant said of Sarah. "Given a little more practice and time, you'd be hard to beat. Younger minds are more agile, I have a feeling."

"Thank you, but you're the best I've played. Good training." They both smiled.

The following morning, while Sarah was taking a bath, Rob's mother poured coffee and sat with her son at the dining room table.

"She's a *very* sweet girl, Robin. Even tempered, gentle. I hope the two of you can make a go of it. She's a lot younger, but there isn't much doubt how she feels about you. And in this case, I don't think the age gap amounts to a hill of beans. But Sarah is unquestionably different from the other two. I've never criticized you for the marriages that didn't last, but if you two take vows, I have a hunch they'll finally mean something. It shows in the way you treat her. There's a degree of respect that was never there before. The best noun I can come up with is deference. And that leads me to believe I know more about your feelings than you do. On the other hand, I understand why you're being careful."

"And so do I," Sarah agreed as she came through the door.

"Morning, dear heart. Guess you took a speedy bath so you could come down and listen in." Rob gave her a quick but loving kiss.

"Morning, Mum. *Oops*! Guess my subconscious just let the cat out of the bag."

"Not really. It's all right, dear. But if you call me 'Mother G.' it's sort of half way in between until Rob makes up his mind."

"I like your compromise. 'Mother G.' it is then."

"Glad we could come to terms so easily. But I have an idea that's the way you are about most things. Me, too."

"You're right. Ordinarily that's the case, especially when it comes to this guy." Sarah aimed a thumb at Rob.

"Same with Rob's dad, Sam. I see a lot of me in you. I worshipped the ground he walked on."

"I don't want to give away too many of my secrets, but let's just say I can relate to that. Anyway, coming back to the beginning, it's been a long time since I've been in a tub, so I wasn't sure what to do first." She grinned. "But it didn't take long to get scrubbed."

After they'd had a good breakfast, Rob took Sarah for a walk around the farm. She had some watertight boots from L. L. Bean and was really better prepared for their tour than he was.

As they got started, he pointed out the barn where his dad had been working the morning he died. "He began to feel bad and thought it was something he'd eaten. But then he starting having severe pain in his shoulders and arms and within an hour he was gone. I know what mother went through. Thirty-two months ago I had a taste of the same thing. She was your age. But you know the story—and I've already spent too much time talking about it. Sorry."

"No need to be. I understand. But if you're still at it five years from now, assuming you keep me around, I'll remind you that it's enough."

The balance of the morning was spent looking at fields, seeing what crops had been harvested and where the wheat had been sown. As they walked, Sarah asked about Rob's dad.

"Born in 1894, had rheumatic fever as a young man and that was part of what shortened his life. At that, he was seventy-three. My uncle, a surgeon, was amazed that he lived as long as he did."

"He died when?"

"At the end of October sixty-seven." Then Rob abruptly changed the subject. "As Iowa farmland goes, I don't know that I'd call this the best of it. Maybe it is, and I've forgotten what Dad said about it. I've been gone almost twenty-five years and things like that have gotten away from me. Sign of old age, I guess."

"I don't see it that way at all, love. If the cemetery is close, could I go pay my respects to your dad? "

"It's nearby—just a little bit further up the road from where we turned off Route 130. We'll do that after lunch and then go on and make a quick pass through Tipton. It's where Regina grew up and also where I ran into her in late sixty-two."

Sarah was thrilled that could see some of the places that were a part of Rob's early life. "You know that seeing all of this will make it impossible for me to let go of you now. This is just about the final part of our bond."

"I don't have any problem with that." Rob smiled at her.

After they'd been to the cemetery, and then drove on to Tipton, the pass through was, as he'd said earlier, quick. He showed her the high school he'd gone to and the restaurant, Ambers, where he'd met Regina. They drove up and down Cedar Street, then got on Route 130 east and went back to the farm.

"Wasn't that exciting? It's roughly the same seven mile bus route I had to take into school every day. Bennett High was closer, but we were led to believe that Tipton High was a better school. Guess the teachers did their job because just look at how important I've become—at least to you."

"You are. But I suppose somebody might one day say the same thing about Hampden Lake versus Bloomdale. That aside, I've enjoyed every minute of your tour. The terrain is so different. Not much farming in our area. Too many rocks and it isn't mostly flat like this. And without many trees, it'd be hard to find a place to hide so you could make love."

"There isn't enough traffic to worry about late in the evening. Back in the late forties, you could have spread a blanket out in the middle of Route 130 and done your thing. Leisurely."

Sarah laughed heartily at the thought. "I'll bet you didn't test the odds. Now, be honest."

"You're right. I didn't"

Back from their outing, Rob was ready for a dry Gibson on the rocks, but "Mother G." didn't drink so it was a dry house. Sarah agreed that a glass of crisp white wine would hit the spot. Doing without, they had an early dinner and then the 'girls' got involved in another serious game of Scrabble. They were thoroughly enjoying each other's company.

After "goodnights" all around, they went upstairs to bed. On their way, Rob said he'd tell Sarah the story about his bed. She hadn't seen his room yet and was taken with the four-poster that he was sleeping in.

"First thing you have to understand is this. When I finish telling you about it, and I'll be brief, we're going to make love in it. Quietly."

"I'm ready for a large delivery. By now, I imagine it will be."

"Don't go turning me on or you'll never hear the story."

"OK. I'll behave myself—at least for a few minutes."

"The bed is solid cherry and was brought here by covered wagon from eastern Pennsylvania. It was originally a rope bed, and it's where the expression 'sleep tight' comes from. You had to keep them pulled snug. I suppose if you made love energetically, like we do, they'd break and we'd be on the floor."

"That'd hurt. The mattress must be three feet off the floor."

"It is. This was Mother and Dad's bed, and he fixed it with slats so they wouldn't break any bones."

"And it looks smaller than a standard double bed."

"The mattress has always had to be custom made because it *is* a little narrower than mine, for example. Mother said they slept like spoons, which is where I picked up that expression. But I saved the best for last. I was conceived in this bed. Does that turn you on?"

"It does, but not to do the same thing. Even if you weren't fixed, I'm about a week beyond being ripe so it wouldn't work anyway."

"Out of your jeans and undies. I'm going to fill you right up."

Their union was brief, *and* quiet, but they quickly discovered they were both fired up. Even with gentle movements, it didn't take long to find exactly what they were looking for. They shared a perfectly timed finale that met their needs.

"Delivery completed," Rob said. "That'll have to do until Thursday night."

"I was right about you. Some delivery. Good thing there's a bath close by. I don't have to explain that, do I?"

"Nope."

When Sarah came back, she said, "I wish I could spend the night with you. This old bed does something to my libido."

"Let's chance it." They did and didn't get caught. It was wonderful.

Their last day at the farm was spent quietly. Sarah finally told Rob's mother about their trip west and how different Iowa was from New England—really about the only part of the U.S. she knew. During the early evening hours, there was more Scrabble. Rob's mother loved having an opponent who was a challenge.

On the morning of the twenty-second, Washington's actual birthday, Margie Grant made sure her guests were well fed before seeing them on their way. When it was time for good-byes, Rob was deeply touched by his mother's words.

"Sarah, you're the daughter I always wanted and didn't have. I've never said anything like that before. But I'd have been pleased, and proud of you, if you had been my own. Maybe someday you will be anyhow."

Rob could see that her words got to Sarah. They hugged tightly. It was fair to say that the two women, born nearly fifty years apart, had become close during their visit. Not at all surprising, because their personalities were so much alike and Rob understood clearly why he was fond of Sarah.

Then it was Rob and his mother's turn to share a hug. "It's been short, but I've enjoyed being here. Always have. But let me go back for a moment to the help you gave me when I ran out of money and had some big medical bills facing me. You can't know how much it helped us out, so I want to thank you again from the bottom of my heart for what you did."

"Life's road isn't always smooth, Robin, so I was glad to help. I accept your thanks. You've gotten part of your inheritance early—at a time when you needed it, so now let's call it a closed matter. If you want to say thanks in another way, ask your Sarah to be the last of your Mrs. Grants. You were right when you introduced her to me as someone special because I think she's all of that. So, I'd be delighted if one day she could be a member of our family."

Sarah, misty eyed, said, "Thank you, Mother G. Those are lovely words. I like what you've suggested and will pray that it turns out that way. I'd be proud to add 'Grant' to my name—and I would honor it. I also want you to know that I *will* write, just like I promised last night."

"It'll be a treat to hear from you. Robin doesn't always have time. Now, drive carefully, and please call me when you get home."

"We will. Probably be on Sunday. Take care of yourself, Mother."

"You, too. Both of you."

As they drove down the lane, they all waved. And then when they turned into Route 130, Rob looked toward Sarah and saw that she had tears on her cheeks.

"Aww, sweetheart."

"These have been five days I'll never, ever forget. I hate to see them come to an end. Your mother is a rare woman. I just love her. To use one of your expressions. She's *so* special. And if she gets to be my mother-in-law someday, I'll love her as if I *am* the daughter she never had."

"We'll come back if you'd like to."

"Oh, Rob, yes! Please?"

They pulled onto I-80 and drove for a while without either of them saying much. Then Sarah asked how they were going home.

"By car. All the way." Rob chuckled.

"I know *that*. Which way, silly."

"We'll stay on 80 until we get to I-94 southeast of Chicago, and then stay overnight in Benton Harbor on the eastern shore of Lake Michigan. Tomorrow, we'll drive across Michigan to Detroit and cross into Canada at Windsor. Our day ends on the Ontario side of Niagara Falls, and we'll spend the night there. Then on Saturday, we get on I-90 in Buffalo and take it all the way to Exit 8 in Palmyra. Long day."

"My Rob, the planner guy. You sure have everything worked out. I suppose we have reservations, too?"

"Wouldn't be without 'em. I try not to leave much to chance."

"I like the way you do things. Making travel arrangements, among many others."

Their trip went as planned, and on Friday evening Sarah loved having a view of the Falls. Then on Saturday, their day across New York and nearly half of Massachusetts began at a reasonable hour. To Rob's surprise, Sarah didn't complain, but he knew that her bottom side was probably getting tired. When they'd gone past Utica, Rob pulled into the Indian Castle Plaza to get fuel. "Ready for a bite, dear heart?"

"I'm not very hungry, but I could go for a sandwich and a visit to the ladies room."

"Ditto. We're a little over halfway home so this ought to be the last of our stops since we left Iowa."

"Thinking about that, and your mom all alone, makes me a little sad. She's such a sweetie."

"So are you, dear heart."

When they got to a table and had ordered, Sarah stared out the window for a moment.

"Thinking about our week together?"

"I was. It's been simply wonderful. It was a surprise you pulled on me and it's left me with such fond memories. You've taken me places I've never seen, I got to meet your mother, and saw where you grew up. I couldn't have asked for more. I'll be talking about it right into our summer break."

After their food was brought, Sarah chuckled about something that crossed her mind.

"What's funny?"

"I was just thinking about the last Scrabble game your mother and I played on Wednesday evening. She was getting such crummy letters, often three of a kind. You could tell she was getting exasperated. Finally she said, 'Oh, I think I'll just quit!' She didn't mean it, but just the way she said it was so cute. What a love she is."

"I've known that for a long time. You're so much like her, and there's no doubt in my mind that it's one of the reasons I'm so taken with you. I'm feisty at times, but you, like mother, are a good stabilizer."

"And those are sweet words, too. You Grants have a way with them, I've discovered. Maybe you *should* write a book. Some of the things you've done and the experiences you've had, good and bad, would make a good story, I think."

"I'm not as certain about that as you seem to be, but it's something to think about when I'm retired, maybe. Now, my horse has been fed, as have we, so it's time to head for Colonial Trail."

"I'm ready. Tonight I'm going to pour myself a glass of wine, and I'll stir up a *very* dry Gibson for you if you'd like."

"I'd like. And while you're doing that, I'll get a little fire going."

"We've eaten pretty well for the last three days, so I'll make a light meal, let's call it supper, and we'll have ourselves a romantic evening at home sipping and munching on whatever it is I can find."

"We're already beginning to think alike. Scares me just a little. On the other hand, maybe I should start believing that I'm becoming a completely domesticated lion."

"Think tamed. You swept me off my feet a long time ago, so maybe you should take your mother's advice and make an honest woman out of me. I won't lean on you, though. I know that's the wrong approach, so I have to make you think it's your idea."

"That sounds just a tad calculating. If you mean it, that's one way you and mother are entirely different."

"I'm just kidding, Rob. But part of it's true. Making me an addition to the Grant family has to be your decision. Sarah Grant. I like the sound of it, and you know I'd honor the name—like I promised on Thursday."

"And I have to confess that I rather like the sound of it, too." Sarah smiled at him warmly.

When they got into the Berkshire Hills of western Massachusetts, Mother Nature arranged for them to drive through a snow shower. It slowed them down quite a bit, but once they were down in the Connecticut River Valley Rob was able to let his horse run and they got to the cottage just before 5:00 p.m.

"It was a wonderful trip, my love, but it's good to be back. Thank you for everything."

"You don't have to thank me. No reason to. I wanted you to make this trip. It was important to me, too. Now, I'm covered up with trail dust and verrry thirsty, so let's go pour something into glasses."

They had their drinks, and a fire, and dinner, *and* a night of fervent loving. Sarah confessed afterwards that the memory of having made love in Rob's bed at the farm turned her on.

"I wondered what was behind all the passion. I have a photo of the bed. Maybe I should have an enlargement made and hang it on the wall."

"No need. You know all the steps needed to get me worked up. With you, it doesn't take much. Just being next to you usually does that."

Sunday was the quiet, restful day they needed to get ready for their return to work. Sarah had been amply loved and might have purred if she were a kitten. In a way she was behaving like one. She was at peace with herself and the world about her. It was contagious and Rob became infected with a severe case of tranquility. It was a very agreeable feeling.

Then before the day was out, Rob called his mother to let her know that they'd gotten home safe and sound. Sarah also had a chance to talk with "Mother G." and it brought her week's vacation to a perfect conclusion.

When the work week began, they had their breakfast and got ready to leave.

"This past week has been one I'll always remember," Sarah said. "My bonding with you has grown even more, if that's possible, so I'm already looking forward to coming back on Wednesday."

"Who said you're invited."

"Please don't say things like that, Rob. After the week we've just had, that hurt a little. No, more than a little."

"I just wanted to see if you still love me." Rob smiled at the pained expression that was facing him.

"Oh, *you*!" Sarah smiled back and then kissed him tenderly.

"I guess there isn't much doubt," Rob said.

"None at all."

"In that case, we can continue all this on Wednesday evening."

"I'll be here, have fires going, and be ready—*if* my body will let me."

"Hope so. Sounds delightful. But I've got to scoot, dear heart."

"So do I shortly."

They hugged, and as Rob drove up over the little hill in back, they waved. Sarah didn't move from her station on the back stoop until he was gone from view. There was no reason for it, but Sarah felt just a touch of emptiness. Why? Simple. She loved Rob Grant with all her heart, but she didn't need to remind herself of that.

The workweek began with Deana showing Rob a naughty smile and asking, "How was your week, lover?"

"Absolutely delightful." Then to tease her a bit, he added, "And I made *several* contributions to Sarah's well being."

"I'd like a serving of it myself."

"Deana, there must be fifty good-looking studs in this town who can look after you. I'm not a candidate. You know that, so let it go."

"But the aged product, like good wine, is the best."

Rob saw that he wasn't about to make a dent in her ardor, so he turned and walked back to his desk.

When Wilcox came in, they compared notes and Alan was pleased to report there were a couple small leases signed in Rob's absence.

"Good news, boss."

"We're getting close to being leased up. McCallum's amazed. He can't believe what you've done in four months."

"Timing is everything. In sex and in business. We hit the market right. Leases were running out, and we had the right product, at the right lease rates, at precisely the right time. I'm no miracle worker, but we put some tools to work that helped bring it all together."

"You're being modest. But say it whatever way you like. We've got people talking to themselves about what we've done. I'm *very* pleased." Alan Wilcox laughed raucously. For him to have done so didn't surprise Rob one bit.

"OK, but I've got to get back to work."

"You haven't offered to tell me about your week. How'd it go?"

"Margaret Grant and Sarah Stuart fell in love with each other. Sarah, my mother believes, is the daughter I was supposed to be, so she's adopted her. What it means is, I have to start thinking seriously about our relationship and where it's going."

"I remember all the beauties you brought up to the lake, but I have to agree with your mother. Maybe it's time you settled down. Be hard to do better than Sarah."

"Looks like I'm outnumbered."

"It's for you to decide, but I hope it works out for the two of you."

"Thanks, Alan. It's still a case of needing a little more time."

As Rob was making his rounds of the building to check on the various renovation projects that were still underway, he ran across Mike.

"Mike! How're you?"

"Hi, Dad. I'm fine. With all the stuff you've got going on, Stash and I have been real busy."

"Helps keep you out of trouble."

"Not exactly."

"I thought you might spend some time out at the cottage, like maybe this past weekend."

"No, I met a gal here in town. She isn't much older than me, but she's got her own place. We hit it off right from the start. I remember when I asked you about Justine and how you could know about her so fast. Now I understand. Nothing serious. We just have fun together."

"If she's got her own place, I suppose so."

"You've done the same thing since sixty-eight, so what's different?"

"I was thirty-eight. You're nineteen. That's what's different. Just don't come to me someday and tell me I'm going to be a grandfather. I'm too young for that, and you're still a minor."

"Won't happen. Promise."

"Thanks."

"How was your trip? How's Gram?"

"Great. She's adopted Sarah. Says she's the daughter she never had, or that I was supposed to be. I'd have been Elizabeth Anne."

Mike cackled. "Never thought about anything like that before."

"Sarah loved seeing where I grew up. And we had a good trip both ways. Weather wasn't too bad, and I enjoyed having Sarah with me. It's beginning to feel like she belongs by my side—both night *and* day."

"I don't have to tell you she's nuts about you, and I'd like it if she could be my stepmom. There's something about her. She's real sweet."

"I know, Mike. I know."

When late February fused with early March, Rob could see that his projects in the building were coming to an end. The timing was perfect because the start of the season at the lake was drawing near. Whatever leasing there was to do was minimal since there wasn't much space left to rent. As spring approached, Rob took satisfaction in how well he'd done after having gotten totally immersed in a new career. He also welcomed the rather sizeable bonus the two owners paid him for a job well done. Never mind that they were pleased. It was just as important to Rob that his inner man was satisfied. That was what *really* mattered.

Then at the beginning of April, Wilcox told Rob that he was going out of town but that he'd probably be back before it was time to open the office at the lake. If not, Rob knew what had to be done. Alan wasn't talking about what it was he was up to and Rob didn't ask. Knowing that his boss saw himself as something of a Casanova, and was even bedding the lady lawyer who looked after most of his legal affairs, he assumed that it was a tryst of some sort—maybe with someone Rob knew. His guess was well off the mark, but he wouldn't know that until late in the summer.

As it happened, Alan *didn't* make it back by April 14. It was neither necessary nor important. Rob called the plumber in to see that the office utilities were up and running. He then wrote and placed the first ads in the *New York Times*, and then got everything organized so that he was ready to do business on opening day. Sarah helped with the office setup because she liked having her man back at the lake all week. At the same time, she was delighted to work along side him for a couple of hours. And for Rob, it felt good to be 'home' and in the casual environment of Hampden Lake. It occurred to him that maybe he was still a country boy at heart.

Rob opened on schedule and had some buyer traffic during their first weekend. Sarah breezed in and out of the office since she'd grown used to having him all to herself from Friday evening to Monday morning during the off-season. But now she'd have to share him with his job until October 21, or maybe a week later. That would depend on the weather and late season inquiries. When her vacation started, she was counting on their spending lots of time together. It might be that Rob would even agree to let her move into the cottage when summer came. She'd want to talk about it sometime soon.

On April 21, Greg came home for the Easter break. He was able to get a ride with the Koehler family again, and Sarah said she'd meet them at the foot of the Exit 106 off ramp. She wasn't gone long and brought Greg by the office to say hello before she took him over to the cottage. Mike had come out for the weekend, so they'd have plenty of time to visit before he had to go back into Springfield on Monday morning. When Rob got home, Mike told him he'd asked Wilcox for the week off and that he'd agreed to it. A stipulation was that Mike had to work out arrangements for Greg and Alan to meet. The reason behind it was that he was interested in talking with Greg about the possibility of his working for him—at least part-time.

"Guess we'll need to talk about this some," Rob said to Greg. "You *will* be coming home this summer, right?"

"It's definite now. I don't know why they haven't told you yet."

"Maybe they will after the break. About Wilcox, if he wants you to work around the lake, that's fine. If he has the office building in mind, I won't agree to that. He hasn't said a word to me about what his plans are, so there are some unanswered questions. But, you haven't seen your mother since the summer of sixty-nine, so I thought you might like to spend part of your vacation in California."

"Sounds like it'd be great fun," Sarah remarked.

"I've thought about it, but I'm not as excited about doing that as I was four years ago. The letters Mom wrote, and the way she dumped on Dad turned me off. She didn't have a clue about how hard 1970 was for him. Me getting into trouble, Marianne dying, and then him losing his job. It was the pits. Let me think about it. I may decide to stay here and work around the lake if that's what Mr. Wilcox wants me to do. Be a good chance to earn some money. But thanks for offering, Dad."

The Grant 'boys' had a good week together and then on Saturday, April 28, the four of them celebrated Rob's forth-third birthday. "This is the happiest one I've had in quite a while. It's good to have the guys here, and with my Sarah sharing it, too, it's turning out to be a very special day."

Sarah showed Rob an affectionate smile. "That you wanted me to be a part of it makes me feel good, you know. Maybe we can do it again next year, and the year after, and the year after that, and…."

"I like that idea," Greg said. Mike agreed. It was Rob's turn to smile.

Greg had told the Kohlers that his dad would be working, so they agreed to pick him up early on Sunday afternoon for the return trip. It wasn't out of their way. At the time they'd arranged, Rob had customers. Both he and Sarah thought that might happen so she took Greg down to the restaurant that was at the foot of the eastbound off ramp for Exit 106. As they waited, Sarah had a coffee. Greg thought it best not to add anything to all the orange juice he'd had before they left the cottage.

From the chair that Sarah had taken, she easily recognized the Kohler's big Cadillac as they drove up. She and Greg went out to greet them. After hellos and before Greg got in the car, he said, "Not long now. We're finished on June 21, the first day of summer. I'm probably going to work for Mr. Wilcox out here at the lake and skip California. I can probably do that some other time."

"We'll come get you in June. I saw on the calendar that it's a Thursday, so your dad will be able to have someone cover for him by then. He'll be hiring at least one other person to work for him."

"Great. Be good to come home. Finally."

"Be good to have you home, Greg. See you soon."

As the Kohlers drove off, they all waved. Sarah stood fixed until the Cadillac was up the road toward Sturbridge and gone from view. She already missed Greg. But he was coming home, and that made her smile.

With early season activity customarily light, Rob decided that since he now had a broker's license he'd start taking listings in his free time. They would be properties owned by individuals who had decided that it was time to sell. Owners paid good commissions, but Rob had to keep in mind that his chief responsibility was to sell Alan's lots, with or without a building. But to take listings, he'd need one or two brokers to work alongside him in the office. The first person he brought in was, like Sarah, an educator. Her name was Cassie Naylor. The plus was that she'd worked part-time in real estate before, so the training she needed was minimal. It wasn't long before she was in the swing of things and Rob went off to solicit listings as time allowed.

When the weather turned warmer, traffic increased and it brought an end to Rob's listing efforts—except when sellers came to the office and asked him to put their property on the market. Now into his second season, Rob was beginning to find out that Alan Wilcox's reputation wasn't what it might be. But the word had gotten around that Rob Grant was running things, that he was honest, and that he also treated customers with respect. When that got back to Rob, it made him feel good. Sam and Margaret Grant's upbringing was paying dividends. Customers were coming back to do repeat business and also to list their properties when they were ready to sell. They had other choices in the real estate community, so the increase in their brokerage business was evident. Alan Wilcox took note of it.

The reputation that Rob was building was confirmed by a local summer tenant, Sonia Smolenski. She and her husband lived in western

Connecticut, but for years they'd spent four to five months at their little waterfront cottage. Sonia dropped by the Wilcox office one afternoon mainly because, Rob thought, she had nothing else to do. A short, round woman who liked her Scotch, she got onto the subject of Wilcox. "You know, in all the years we've been coming up here, you're the first guy Al's had that treats people decent. He tries to squeeze every nickel he can out of a customer. It's almost like he don't care about tomorrow. You're different. It's like when you do business you want to make a friend at the same time—somebody who'll come back maybe."

"Smart business, but I'm serious about what I do. I've always tried to make a customer feel like they're the one person I really wanted to see that day. In most cases, it's true."

"Well, since we came up for the season, I've talked to a lot of summer regulars around the lake and we all feel the same way. We hope you stick around."

"You may know that I'm a Midwestern farm kid who was raised on the Christian principal of do unto others, etc. But I'm also a fugitive from corporate New York and you can be gutted down there for trying to shaft somebody. Thing is, I haven't needed the fear of that to teach me what's right. And I learned a long time ago that I wouldn't be worth a damn in a cutthroat business."

"Just stay with it, Robbie. You've made a lot of friends around the lake, people you don't know. And we've seen you around with that nice teacher lady. Any plans that include her?"

"Could be, Sonia. Might very well happen."

The period between the Memorial Day and Labor Day holidays was a busy time, both in the real estate office *and* personally, as it turned out. On the Memorial Day weekend, Sarah had gone to her mother's for a couple of days just for a visit. After he'd gotten home on that Sunday evening, Sarah's roommate, Amy Porter, stopped by. She knew Sarah had gone to Worcester but pretended that she didn't.

Rob offered her a drink, and when the booze hit her, Amy began to open up. "It's time you found out that I'm in love with you, too. Ever since that first day we met, the one when you helped Sarah move in, and now every time I've seen you since then, I've wanted to change places with her. I guess that's a way of saying that my feelings for you grew little by little and now they're nearly out of hand. Something else. I'm *still* a virgin and I want you to be the one to change that for me."

Rob gulped. "Sweet of you to say these things. Good for my ego, but as long as Sarah and I are as close as we are, I don't see how we can do something like that to a mutual friend."

"I predicted that you'd say something like that, but I want you to know that the love and the desire to have you bed me, are there for the taking. Like I said, it's just about gotten out of hand. I even have dreams about me having your baby."

"Sounds like your emotions *are* running rampant, but I have to say that you've kept it pretty well hidden."

"I have to because I can't let Sarah know how I feel."

"Let me put it this way. If she and I ever go separate directions, I'd most likely be accommodating."

"Sure you don't want to show me what you'd feel like—and then do your thing? Not even once?"

"Amy, you're a sweetheart, but I can't do that to Sarah. She wouldn't know, but my conscience would and it'd hurt me to do what you want done. She's very trusting, but she's also fragile. It wouldn't be fair—in spite of the fact that taking you to bed is awfully tempting."

"I understand. So, in that case, I'll save myself for you. Maybe the time will come, and you will, too." She giggled.

"You're being a naughty girl."

"It's all right. I'll make believe and then look after myself when I get home."

As Amy was leaving, she gave Rob a genuinely affectionate hug and a very steamy kiss.

"That's to show you what's inside."

"I know very well what's in there. But I have to confess that your kiss was delightful."

"It'll help you remember me, then."

"No reminders needed."

"See you, Rob."

"Maybe so."

Amy Porter was on Rob's mind at various times during the Memorial Day holiday. Given her internal fire, he had no doubt that she'd figure out very quickly how to become highly animated. A year ago, he'd have gladly satisfied her request, but by now Sarah was much too far inside him to do what she'd proposed yesterday. Besides she was local, and a friend of Sarah's, so it could lead to serious repercussions at some point.

When Sarah came home, the thought of Amy was on his mind but Sarah was the one who benefited from the internal blaze he had going on.

"Maybe I should go away more often," she said. "That was sizzling and a spectacular welcome home. *Whew*!"

Then, in mid-June, RD Borger stopped by the cottage unannounced. Sarah was there and told him Rob was working but that he would be home before much longer.

"I can't stay. Spent my birthday, yesterday, with my folks out on the Cape. Good day all around. Got in a little boating and some swimming even if the water is still pretty cold."

When Rob got home soon afterwards, he was delighted to see RD. "How're you, boss? Good to see you again."

"Fine. Changed jobs, something I was considering when I saw you at the beginning of the year. Bigger title, lots more money, and expanded responsibilities. Far better than my last exposure to retailing."

They had a drink, Sarah put out some munchies and they exchanged news until RD said he wanted to get back to Manhattan and see Marcia. He added that their relationship was in full bloom now and that he would most likely propose before long.

"Not sure we could come down, but let us know if you do tie the knot again. After all the chasing around we've done, be good to see you settle down. Not that you were anywhere close to the rascal I was."

"Your turn next. When?"

"It's under assessment. You know how deliberate I've been. There's always been something important about knowing someone two years or so. Sarah and I are getting close to that. Patience, RD."

"I hear you. Now, I've really got to get going. See you again soon, or at *your* ceremony." They all chuckled. "I want to be a part of it."

On June 21, Rob and Sarah drove to Duchene to bring Greg home. Permanently. He had lots of good-byes to look after and while he was about that, Rob went to the office to pick up Greg's release papers and grade reports. Something that was in his folder was a comment by the soccer coach. It said that Greg was one of the best forwards he'd ever coached. Rob was completely surprised. Greg had never said a word about being involved in Duchene's soccer program. Something to talk about on the way home. Sarah was the consummate female sports fan and she'd go to games if he was to continue playing.

And that was the main topic of conversation as they made their way back to Hampden Lake. "Yeah, I want to see if I can get on the team when I start at Truman High."

"You never mentioned that you were into soccer."

"It's not a big deal in the U.S., but I love it. I didn't think it would matter to you."

"You're wrong about that. And your grades are pretty good, too."

"We had to work at Duchene. They have some really good teachers."

"Well, it's good to have you back. I don't have to tell you that you'll have to behave because you'll be eighteen in December. If you screw up after that you'll be in deep doo-doo."

"You won't have to worry about that. But one of the things I have to do is get in touch with Mr. Wilcox to see if he still wants me to work around the lake."

"You have a letter from him. Came at the beginning of the week. Maybe that's what you're looking for."

And it was. Alan said he'd be out at the lake office on Sunday and that Greg should come over so they could talk further about a summer job.

When he shared his news, he added, "This is great! I'll get to do the same things Mike did. I've got lots of old clothes now that I can paint in."

"We'll have to get you some new ones before long. School will be back in session before you know it. Sarah has the calendar. I'll get you over to Truman one of these days so you can pre-register. I've got your grade reports and everything else they'll need."

Chapter Nineteen

The weekend before July 4 was hectic. One of the customers who stopped by the office was an attractive, dark haired, thirty-plus gal from New York—something Rob discovered later. She introduced herself as Holly Kimball. She was interested in buying a building lot or two and had plans to put up a cottage at some stage. Since Cassie was out, Rob left their part-time secretary to cover the office.

Holly said she'd drive. Since this was the first time Rob had seen the new Audi Fox, he readily agreed. They spent maybe close to an hour looking at various lots and eventually wound up at the far south end of Colonial Trail.

"I live down there." Rob pointed past the cottage that he and Regina had almost bought before they divorced—and the same one where he'd made love with Kate just before Memorial Day 1969.

"Neat place. And you'd be my neighbor. I like that idea. But aside from your proximity, these are the best lots you've shown me."

"Shall we go back and draw up the agreement?"

"Not just yet, that is if you have the time. This is a very romantic setting, and I'd just like to sit here with you for a few minutes."

Rob shrugged and said, "You're driving. Sure. Be delighted. I don't see many attractive lady buyers—especially ones with sexy new Audis."

"And you're the first nifty real estate tomcat I've come across in the past four months. Most of them are overweight, ugly or overage. You come from a different lair."

"Yeah, I'm shorter than most of 'em." Rob chuckled. "But maybe it's because I spent a lot of time in Manhattan at Forty-eighth and Fifth and later on at an address on lower Wall Street."

"That has to be it. What did you do?"

Rob told her and then he asked Holly what she did.

"I'm part of the in-house legal staff at CMZ International. They pay me well."

"I suppose so. What law school."

"Columbia."

"That's where my former boss at Sentry Oil went to school."

"What's his name?"

"RD Borger."

"*That's* a coincidence. He's remembered around the law school because when he was still a very young attorney he was chosen to work directly for Rockefeller—right after he became governor in fifty-nine. Quite an honor. Yeah. You really are different. Never expected to find someone like you up here in the trees."

"Life's full of surprises, huh?"

"For sure. Now, let's go back so I can sign an agreement. Otherwise, I'll put a move on you that your wife wouldn't approve of."

"I don't have one—and haven't for almost five years."

"Sorry it's still daylight."

"Easy, Holly. You're a customer. There are rules, you know."

"I'm the one in pursuit. None of 'em are relevant in this instance."

When they got back to the office, Holly Kimball signed an agreement to buy on or before the first day of August, 1973.

"I don't need financing. When I come back on the twenty-ninth I'll bring you a bank draft for the full amount, less the five hundred I'm going to give you now."

"Good. You're my kind of a customer."

"And I like your kind of salesman." She showed Rob a devilish grin. "There's something animal about you. What is it? Sure you aren't part lion or related?"

That brought back memories of Kate, and he laughed warmly. "There have been others who've suggested the same thing."

"Good to know that you have your own stable. I thought you might. Someone like you couldn't live in New York, single, and not be in demand. It's a shame you don't live in the neighborhood any longer."

"I was a commuter. Sheffield. Had a great place overlooking the city and the Sound."

"Very nice. I'll say it again—in a different way. Too bad I didn't know you before you got away."

"That was at the beginning of January last year. But it seems that my herd is down to one these days."

"You don't sound very sure of your numbers."

"A former New York stud never really learns how to count."

"I'm looking forward to coming back at the end of the month."

"Me, too. Means a commission." Rob smiled.

"You can do better than that. I know where your head is. Mine, too."

"See you, Holly. Been fun."

"You might say that. Bye, Rob. I'll be thinking about you."

And obviously she did just that because late in the afternoon of Friday the thirteenth, Holly Kimball called Rob to say hello.

"Just wanted to make sure you hadn't left Wilcox's employ."

"Nope. I have a career in the woods. Grows on you because you get to meet beguiling lawyer ladies on the make."

"How would you know something like that?" Holly giggled brightly.

"I'd have to be at death's door not to. Remember, I'm part lion."

"I'll bet you growl, too."

"Only during the finale. But how would you know *that*?"

"Sixth sense. I've got to run, guy. You've made my day. See you late in the afternoon on the twenty-eighth—maybe in hot pants."

"That's a day earlier than what I have on my calendar. But is that in 'em or with 'em?"

"Maybe both. I decided not to wait until the twenty-ninth."

"I'll make the change so I don't leave early."

As it happened, Sarah had told Rob only a few days earlier that her mother had vacation time during the week that bridged the last two days of July and the beginning of August. Peg Stuart had asked Sarah if she'd be her driver on a trip into Canada that she wanted to make. What it meant was that Sarah would be going into Worcester on the afternoon of the twenty-seventh, and then staying overnight so they could get an early start on the Saturday morning following. Rob was sorry it was working out that way. Having Sarah around would insure that he wouldn't get into trouble. Following the conversation he'd just had, he had to ask himself what the hell he was doing. But he knew full well what he was up to. Holly was New York and he was back into the kind of exchange of come-ons he'd been a part of countless times since sixty-eight. He couldn't ignore the fact that it was fun, and something he'd missed after all these months. He'd been totally monogamous since detaching himself from New York, but maybe it wasn't possible for an animal to change its stripes. If so, it would be wrong to marry his Sarah. All of this began to bother him. Difference between Holly, and Deana and Amy, was that the latter two were local and, among other things, they had none of the mystique, or any of the words that came with playing around Manhattan style. Now he would be tested. Holly Kimball was attractive, seductive, in need, and a 1970s liberated New York woman. But Rob was off the mark some—as he would find out on the last weekend in July.

On the afternoon of the twenty-eighth, Holly showed up wearing a jumpsuit with legs that were cuffed just above the knee. Not hot pants at all. But nothing could hide the fact that she had great legs. As she walked in, Rob was just finishing up with customers who wanted a year-round 'A' frame built. Holly smiled, said nothing, and sat quietly until Rob had concluded his business with them. Since it was well after six o'clock, and there were no other customers waiting, he hung a "Closed" sign in the window, shut the door, and drew the drapes.

"Well, Miss Holly. Here we are again. Welcome back."

"Good to see you again, Rob. It's been a long month. If we couldn't have had that sort of naughty phone call two weeks ago it would have been even longer. Any chance we could we go over to your place?"

"Sure. I'll buy you a drink. Then we're going out to dinner. We'll get to our other business tomorrow."

"Sounds like a good proposal. Your one and only isn't around?"

"No. Believe it or not, she and her mother are on a trip into Canada. They left early this morning. If the timing had been different, I'd have taken your check and sent you on your way. But I have to confess that I'm glad we can have a little time together, counselor."

"Me, too. You still belong in New York. The corporate animal in you sticks out all over. You're a fish out of water doing what you're doing."

When they got to the cottage, Rob invited Holly to sit at the bar and then asked her what she'd like to drink.

"Something gentle. White wine would be fine." As he poured, she said, "It's a small place but very tastefully done. Really comfy, and masculine, but there's evidence of a female companion."

"I'm not trying to hide a thing from you, or to show you anything other than what my life is at the moment. I've gone beyond images and role playing. I've had some very rough sledding going back about three years ago. That included my fiancée dying of leukemia. And then I nearly lost my son, the one who's here with me now, from an OD. What I did lose was a *very* good corporate job on Wall Street. And then my sons helped me get kicked out of the great place we had in Sheffield. I finally got to the point where I said to hell with it, moved up here and changed careers."

"Wow. You should have lots of scars, but if you do they don't show. I have one, too. A big one, but we can talk about that over dinner. Could we go? The wine was first-rate—and gone."

"Sure, but I have to find a place where I'm not known. Whatever happens tonight isn't worth losing Sarah."

"I'm very familiar with those kinds of feelings. But just so you'll understand, I'm not here to break up a relationship. My aim is to find a little bit of peace and maybe add some spice to our evening together."

Since it was still fairly early, Rob drove off to a place in Southbridge that he knew about but had never been to before. When they arrived, he thought the reviews could be right. It *was* a decent restaurant.

Drinks ordered, they settled down and looked forward to enjoying each other's company.

"You were going to tell me about your scar. A big one, you said."

"I've been married. Not long, though. Loved the guy dearly, but one morning, when he was on his way to meet a client, a truck jumped the center divider and rammed his Mercedes head on. He never knew what hit him. Killed instantly. I'm guessing you went through a long process of watching your fiancée die, but a fatal accident doesn't hurt any less. We've both been there. Now let's wind forward to four weeks ago. You have an awful lot going for you. What struck me, immediately, was that you reminded me so much of my Gary. He was a little taller. You joked about your height, but when I first saw you, there was a tender place that you unknowingly reached inside and touched. It's why I asked you to sit on those lots for a little while. It was a romantic setting and for those few minutes I was trying to recapture something permanently lost."

"I'm so sorry, Holly. I couldn't have known any of this, of course. But we *have* shared something extremely painful. I'm pretty much over my loss. You have a ways to go."

Rob and Holly ordered dinner, and another drink, and then went back to the subject that had been interrupted.

"I know. I know. But I haven't been with a man since Gary died. No interest. And I had to come all the way up here to meet you, someone who's actually rekindled my need to make love. Our first exchanges were fun, and I loved the give and take. Sort of like old times, but I was serious about my wanting to put a move on you. Still am. I need to feel what it's like to be with a man again. Tonight, that means you—if you'll agree to it. But you know that if we start playing around that we have to go all the way. I'll want it all, start to finish. And I'll gladly share *my* special moment with you. I need to go there. Badly. Maybe more than once." Holly paused. "I'm sorry, Rob. I've never said these kinds of things to anyone before so I'm a little bit embarrassed that I'm being so forward."

"Don't be. I understand where you are. After Marianne died, I was like you. But then I called a woman who'd been part of my support team, someone who also cared about me. I told her that I woke up that morning having discovered that I was still very much alive. She understood exactly what I meant and said she'd be up right after work. Didn't take long to reach the same place you want to go. It was deliverance. The finale was spectacular."

Dinner came and they let the subjects of heartbreaks and the healing processes rest for a moment.

"In a way, I'm glad to discover that we've both had to deal with old hurts. Mine is more recent. It was just a few months ago," Holly said, "but I hope you'll be willing to help me start putting mine to rest."

"Let's have dinner. Then we'll see about afterwards."

Rob and Holly enjoyed their meal and the idle chatter about all manner of things. She wanted to hear more about his New York jobs, the traveling he'd done, the places he'd lived, and his two sons. He talked at length about each. Rob liked to talk. Holly was a good listener.

"You've already had an interesting career. That you worked through Benewitz at CMZ when you were doing search work is another surprise. If you were in the New York area again, I'd want to see you regularly, or maybe even have you move in with me. The better we get to know each other, the more taken I am with you. In the end it might not work out for us, but I'd surely want to give it a try."

"Not much point in talking about things that won't happen. I left three very sweet gals behind when I unplugged from New York. There's a perky little redhead down on East Thirty-second Street that I'd have probably married had I stayed in or near the city. We worked together at IMMCorp on Wall Street. She'd met Marianne and then came to her funeral. Now, I'd offer you an after dinner drink but I sense that you'd like to get back to the cottage."

"You're perceptive, too. Maybe I'll move up here just so I could chase after you."

As they started back to the lake, Rob finally responded to Holly's comment. "Wouldn't *that* bring things to a head?"

"If it turned out to be me, I'd take the Massachusetts bar exam, we could have a couple of little ones, and I'd see that you were a very happy husband."

"No babies, thanks."

"Why not?"

"Two reasons. One is I'm forty-three and I've had my two little ones, now both grown. The other is, I've been put out of the baby business."

"Guess it wouldn't work for us after all unless I changed my mind. No, I'd probably want the babies before long, but it doesn't change how I feel about you. You're a neat guy. Being realistic, then, what I can say about our relationship is that tonight maybe you'll help me take another step forward in the recovery process, and whatever it is we share will have to be brief. I said earlier that I didn't come into your life to break up a romance, and then for a moment I forgot what I'd said. Reason is that over the past month I discovered it wouldn't take much more for me to fall in love with you. Babies or no babies. I'm already part way there, so I'll have to ease up. But not until after you've taken me to your bed. What I feel for you will help me get where I want to go as you put it. And I *will* get there. I know that for certain."

"Don't recall having invited you to share my bed. If I did, I should have told you that you can have my bed and I'll sleep on the sofa." Rob laughed.

"I think I know better than that. But don't say things like that, Rob. I need you. Really. I don't want to say desperately, but it's close. And it won't take me long to find satisfaction."

"You're beginning to turn me on, girl."

"That's the idea."

"OK. Here we are back at Chateau Grant."

"I like your layout and what you've done with it inside. When I build, I'll want a cottage like yours."

"Nightcap, babe?"

"You're my nightcap." Holly Kimball held Rob tightly and kissed him with intense passion. It turned him on. She felt him and trembled.

"That had feeling in it. Lots of it," Rob said.

"And it stirred you up. Now, make love to me."

In his bedroom, Holly unbuttoned his shirt and loosened his belt. Then Rob slowly ran the zipper on her jumpsuit down its full length. She watched and was captivated. Out of the rest of their clothes, Rob saw that she was *very* well built and what he saw finished turning him on. She responded with "Oooh, imposing!"

Rob was fully ready. Obviously. Holly wasn't. "I must be nervous. Much as I want you, I didn't expect anything like this."

"Don't worry about it. There are those who know me well who would say that I'm patient. What I'll do is 'take you through the steps', as I like to call it. We'll start at the beginning and before you know it, you'll be ready."

The process began with passionate kissing, and touching, and gentle massaging, and then fingertips tracing patterns across erogenous areas. All of them. Holly soon stiffened and said "Mmmm. You've just about got me to that place we talked about. I'm relaxed now and you've found out that I'm ready for you. You're good. Now I want you. Be gentle. It's been months."

"I'll be careful." And with that promise, Rob slowly, gently made their union complete.

"Ohhhh. You feel *sooo* good. You don't know."

"Oh, yes I do. Shhh. Just enjoy."

And she did. It wasn't long before Holly tensed and whispered, "Oh, Rob! There. *Ohh . . . Yesss*! Beautiful."

"Let's have another one of those." Rob shifted upwards and resumed his even movements. Holly wrapped her legs around him and helped set the pace.

Within minutes, Holly stiffened and whispered, "I'm there again." Then, "*Now*! Ohhhh. I want another one. Can you wait?"

"Say when."

"Soon."

They loved on until Holly told Rob she wanted him. "Next one, I want you with me."

Rob increased the tempo and it brought Holly to a vigorous climax. He felt contractions and whispered, "You've arrived."

"*Yes*! Now I want you. *Come*!"

Rob responded immediately. She felt his release and cried out with joy. His deep growl simply reconfirmed that he'd done what she asked.

Afterwards, they rested for a minute or so.

Then Rob said, "You wanted it all. You got it all. And that's how babies get made."

"Thought you were fixed. I'm close to being fertile and that would take some explaining. At that, it's an interesting idea."

"Just a manner of speaking. But you were taking a risk because you didn't know anything about my condition until this evening."

"No, but your being fixed didn't have any effect on either your performance or your deposit. I'm amply supplied. Whew! I guess so."

"So, you might say I'm a competent interior decorator?"

Holly laughed softly. "That's a cute way to put it. Yes. Very. But what's hard to believe is how you were able to wait until I was ready for you to unload."

"Nearly always been able to do that. Well, sometimes it doesn't work. But having good control made me popular with the ladies in New York and Sheffield. Thing is, if my partner isn't getting all the delights she can out of a loving, then it really isn't all that enjoyable for me. Prolonging the session is a way to make sure we both have a good time."

"Amazing. You're right, though. I don't know when I've felt so good after making love. You're not just 'competent', you're terrific. Maybe I'll reconsider my position about having babies and chase you after all. You'd sure keep me happy. In a way, I'm sorry that what we've just done won't bear fruit. And I was right. You *do* growl when you supply the goods, and there *is* something animal about you. Really turns me on."

"If we wait a bit, I may be able to come back for an encore. Any interest in having another nightcap?"

"You serious?"

"Could be. Worth a try?"

"You're incredible. Yes. Definitely. Got anything left?"

"I don't know. We'll find out."

Later on, they had their repeat performance and then settled down for the night. Before they slept, Holly said, "I feel very thoroughly loved. If you could still propagate, my little egg would have lots of choices by now. Seriously, this has been more than I ever dreamed it would be. Will you marry me?" They both laughed at her proposal.

"You're visit isn't over. There's still tomorrow morning."

"I don't believe you. If you're up to it, I'll gladly let you decorate my interior again." Holly leaned over and gave Rob a very passionate kiss. "Now I'm going to purr like a contented kitty." They then got all tangled up with each other and slept like a pair of affectionate logs.

Rob awakened early and studied the attractive face across from him. Holly was still asleep but she wore just the trace of a smile. It was easy to guess why. Then he thought back to all the mornings during the past five years he'd done this very same thing. He went through all the names and faces and decided that Holly Kimball was every bit as appealing as the others. In a way, he was sorry they hadn't met during his IMMCorp or NAGE days. They hadn't known each other long, but there was something about her that made him feel as if they'd been long-time friends and lovers. She was a woman of character and someone who, given time, he could almost certainly love. Yet her needs were the same as Marianne's: she wanted babies. But he was comfortable with Holly, and she with him. He saw it as a good start of a relationship that would most likely end later this morning. The thought of that was just a touch painful. What surprised him, though, was that he didn't feel all that much guilt about having bedded a woman other than Sarah. Rob thought he'd be remorseful, but the emotion wasn't there—at least yet. At the same time, what he'd done was essentially physical and it didn't alter how he felt about his Sarah. Recognizing that truth, it was a defining moment for Rob as well. He was beginning to understand, finally, what was most important to him. True, he and Sarah weren't engaged, and in a sense were still dating. But the reality was that Holly would be gone from his life, so this little eighteen hour fling wasn't at all important in the overall scheme of things. Still, it *was* important to Holly, Rob convinced himself, because it helped put her life back on track. The plus, if there was one, was that she was *very* good in bed. Rob closed his eyes for a few minutes. When he reopened them, he saw Holly studying him.

"Good morning, lover," she said.

"Morning, babe."

"I've been looking at you and came to the conclusion that I could be very happy waking up and seeing your handsome face every morning. I'm making the mistake of caring about you because by midday our mini romance will be over. And years from now when I look back on these few hours together, I'll thank you for liberating me from a weight I've had on my shoulders. I know. It's been self imposed. But when I wasn't ready for you last night, you might have turned your back on me and gone to sleep. But like you advertised, you were patient and then took me places I haven't been before. And I want you to do me again. Will you?"

"I promised that to you last night. And since we'll be going in different directions before the morning is out, we'll make it special."

"I envy your Sarah. Is that her picture on your dresser?"

"It is. Taken during her Easter vacation."

"Looks like she's a lot younger, but the expression on her face tells me she's crazy about you."

"She'd agree with that, but the age difference is my main concern."

"Guess it doesn't bother her. What about babies?"

"No real interest. She's a teacher and has kids all day long. Her favorite line is that she can give 'em back to their owners at 3:00 p.m."

Holly liked that and laughed. "You two will do just fine. I'd like to be in the competition. But you know my priorities, so with you I'll just pretend. When I marry again, there isn't much doubt that the feel of you will be on my mind. I'll surely make love to you from time to time."

"As I will you. But the memories of us will fade—and that's as it should be."

"Oh, Rob." Holly tensed a little and showed him misty eyes. "Start from the beginning and then love me one last time. I want all of you."

The caressing, and the fingertips, and the touching made her squirm. She was soon ready. Very. Rob suggested that she take charge and explained what he meant. As Holly settled on him gently, she inhaled deeply and whispered, "Won't take me long this way. It's new. Exciting. *Ooooh*!"

They loved on until she reached high peaks. When they paused, Rob said, "I guess you like this."

"Can't believe I never tried it. Erotic. Call it a deep satisfaction." She smiled broadly. "But I want you on top."

They turned over and loved on until she said she was ready for him. "Make it special." Rob stepped up the pace and as he neared his crest Holly said, "I'm almost there. Make a baby in me." Within seconds they both came to a noisy, pulsating climax. Then they wilted.

Minutes later, Holly added, "You said last night that it would be special. And it was. You've aroused a woman inside me that I didn't know lived there. Never had an orgasm like that before. Mmmm. This is a morning never to be forgotten. And it won't be. Ever. Could be you've ruined me for anyone else."

"No. Not so. I'm sure there are other guys out there who're reasonably good at loving."

"You call yourself just reasonably good? You're that and a whole lot more. Whew! Like I said before, I envy your Sarah. If you could put me in a family way, I'd fight for you."

"Holly, we're still talking about things that won't happen. I've grown to like you over the past month, and your fantasy has tons of allure, but the geography, and careers, and personal needs are on familiar but different paths. You know, it's interesting that you're like my late Marianne. We have some time, so let me indulge my need and tell you about her.

Rob told Holly how he and Marianne had worked together, found that they were in love but ended their romance because of babies. He went on to tell her about their chance meeting in Sydney, how they learned that their love was still alive and then how Marianne decided later on that Rob was more important than family. It was after they'd made plans to marry that she discovered she had leukemia and died soon afterwards. When Rob finished, Holly had tears welling up.

"That's such a painful story, Rob. But you've managed to survive. Says something about what you're made of."

"You've been through the same kind of trauma, and *you've* made it."

"And you've helped. The night together is part of it. But for lots of other reasons, I'm glad I stumbled across Hampden Lake—and you. You'll always be an inspiration."

"Sweet of you to say something like that. And to show you how you've come to mean something to me, I want to love you again."

"You can't mean that."

"Oh, but I do."

"Now, *that's* special! And I'm verrry ready for you."

Rob was slow to recover so their loving was extended to include several different positions, all of them highly satisfying. Holly reached crests that made her gasp with pleasure before Rob was finally able to deliver what she begged for again.

When they'd gone the limit, Holly said, "Ohh, I'm tender. But I'm not complaining. It'll be a reminder of everything we've done since yesterday. You certainly have left a lot of you with me," she said chuckling. "I can understand now why Marianne changed her mind."

"Next thing you'll imagine is that we'll run into each other in Springfield, and you'll have changed *your* mind, too."

"I wouldn't have to go there to do that. Woman's prerogative." They both smiled.

"Hate to break up a good party, but I've got to get ready to show up at the office."

"Hold me for a minute, Rob. I need it, because I've rediscovered my emotions—and how to love. That you and Gary are so much alike has to be a big part of it. Maybe I'm trying to fool myself. Make you him when you aren't. You have your own life and I've marched in and disrupted it in a way. I should apologize."

No, Holly, don't do that. These hours have been important to me, too. This is the first time I've cheated on Sarah, so I have to ask myself what I'd have done if we were married. Maybe the same thing and that wouldn't do. Either you're married, and monogamous, or your not. I wouldn't stand for her cheating on me, so it's a serious question that's been raised."

"Then I really should apologize. I've focused only on my needs and ignored yours."

"Please don't. I wouldn't substitute this time we've had together for any alternative that I could think of. Remember, I was the one who wanted to love you one more time. It's because I looked inside myself and found you there. If it weren't for the little ones you want, you and I could make a marriage succeed. I'm certain of it, even though we've only known each other for a month or so."

"I have exactly the same feeling. And it's a lot more than what we've done in bed. That's world-class, but in a matter of hours, we've discovered that we have a compatibility that lots of couples could only hope for. I'd like to stay on and confirm it, but you have work to do, and I have to get back to New York and sit in on a high powered meeting at eight o'clock tomorrow morning."

"We have some rich memories, dear heart."

"Ohhh, yes. Do we ever."

"Shower with me?"

"Yes! Love to."

They showered, and Rob put a good breakfast together before they each drove to the Wilcox office. When they arrived, separately of course, they were all business.

"Good morning, Miss Kimball."

"No, Mr. Grant, it's Mrs. Kimball. My maiden name was Warren."

"Sorry."

"No need to be." The smile they exchanged was precious.

"Now, you have a check for me, I believe."

"I do. It's for the balance I owe you. Here you are."

Rob got busy making out a receipt and then getting all of Holly's details so that Deana could prepare the deed and mail it to her at her New York address.

"I'd really like to come back, but if I did that I'd probably want to stay here. It's such pretty country." Holly smiled at Rob warmly and he knew what she really meant.

"Well Mr. Grant, it's time for me to be on my way."

"Do you mind if I take another look at your new Audi? Neat car."

"Not at all."

Rob walked with Holly to her car. She'd parked out of view of the office—and most everything else.

"You've leaving behind a lot for me to think about, Holly Warren."

She smiled. "No one has called me that for quite a while. Felt good to hear you say it. And like I said earlier, you've left a lot with me, too. I don't have to explain that. But before we say good-bye, would you hold me again? Having you do that gives me comfort. A very special kind."

As they held each other, Rob felt Holly tremble. As he leaned back, he could see tears on her cheeks.

"Oh, babe. I don't want to see you hurt like this."

"Can't help it. It's the end of some days and hours that have been as happy as the ones following Gary's death were sad. You've left a big imprint, Rob Grant, and I'll remember you. Always. And in all ways."

"Bye, dear heart."

"Bye, lover."

They kissed tenderly and then Holly was on her way home. What she left behind was a hollow Rob Grant—and his bedroom at the cottage filled with a new set of memories.

"Not likely that I'll ever forget what's happened here this weekend."

But Holly Kimball's visit accomplished two things. She'd laid to rest even more of Rob's memories of Marianne Marzano. And she had also introduced him to something new, an emotion he thought earlier that he'd easily escaped: a feeling of extreme guilt. Both would figure into how the months to follow would unfold.

Chapter Twenty

Late on Sunday afternoon, Greg came home and shared what he'd been up to during the week. It was mostly bits and pieces about cottages he was working on and other projects Wilcox had given him. They sounded identical to what he'd heard Mike tell him when he was working on properties around the lake. And just as Mike had built up a client base of summer people, Greg was doing the same and making pretty good money for a teenager.

"This'll all come to an end on September 5," Rob said. "Sarah told me that teachers go in the day after Labor Day, the fourth, and students start classes the day after. I have to make sure the school administration knows about you."

"Maybe Sarah could help get me registered. She's kinda like a mom now, and it'd be neat if she could do that."

"Sure, and I'll bet she'll be tickled to do it. I know the soccer part will interest her. She's a lady jock, you know."

Greg laughed. "Yeah, I know. Justine was sorta like that but Sarah's really into sports. She said her dad taught her all about football."

"Yep, that's my gal."

"Are you going to marry Sarah? She'd be a good wife and mom, I think. It's always real nice when she's here. Lots of things have gone wrong with your women, so I hope this time it'll be OK. You've sure had a lot of 'em in your bed, but I never thought it would take five years." Greg showed Rob a funny little grin.

"I think it's possible that Sarah and I could have a good marriage. As much as anything it's the age difference. I thought the time would come when she'd see that, but it hasn't happened. If anything, her feelings are even stronger now."

"I know. She's really likes you—at least that's the way she acts. That's me, the expert, talking."

"You're right. But I had something happen yesterday that makes me think I should wait a little longer. It has to do with me, not her."

"Those messy sheets on your bedroom floor have anything to do with it? Somebody was here. Looks like you're up to your old tricks."

"Yep, they have everything to do with it. And, yes, someone was here. A New York gal, and I still speak the same language. Thing is, if I'm still going to play around, that's no good for Sarah. But let's get off the subject.

I've got to sort this one out on my own, so I'll want you to keep still about it. But, what I have to do now is go over to Fiskdell and get the laundry done. If you want to come along, we'll go get a burger or something while everything is in the dryer."

"Sure. With us working crazy hours, we don't get to eat out all that much anymore."

"We will when school starts. Sarah's usually here on weekends and then on Wednesday nights most of the time."

"I know you wanted to change the subject, but maybe I know who was here. Reason I say that is that just before the Fourth I was in the office and there was a customer you got real chummy with. You rode with her in her car, a foreign one."

"*Damn*! I've been caught. That's her."

"She was really pretty. Was she good?"

"*Greg*! Sons don't ask their fathers questions like that."

"In Sheffield, we didn't have to. Mike and I could hear who was and who wasn't. Justine was super noisy. No way we couldn't hear her."

"Ohhh, boy. The things you learn after the fact. OK, we're changing the subject. Permanently. But to answer your question first: sensational! Her husband was killed in a head-on collision and she wanted me to help her get over it. End of discussion."

"Thought so. The expression on your face said she was."

"And I'll give you the same lecture I gave Mike about protection."

"Don't have to. Mike told me all about it. I won't give you any more problems."

"That's good news. Thanks for letting me know."

Late on Wednesday afternoon, Rob got two long distance calls. The first came from Sarah who was up in Canada's Atlantic Provinces.

"Hi, sweet. The first two things I have to tell you are that I miss you like crazy and that I also love you to pieces."

"Say, those are two bits of good news. I figured that by now you'd have run off with some handsome fisherman."

"Not a chance. The other news is we got caught in a tropical storm that had tourists running to get out of its way. It wasn't quite a hurricane, but it had a name anyway. It was called Alfa. We were in Nova Scotia when we got the first warnings and we we're able to catch the last ferry across the Bay of Fundy to Saint John in New Brunswick. The sea was rough, so we were both nervous during the crossing. We're in St. Stephen now, just over from Calais, Maine. Tomorrow morning we'll get on U.S. 1 and come down the coastal route. We're going to take our time and stop along the way. I know Mom wants to see Acadia National Park. Other than the storm, and missing you, it's been a good trip so far."

"It's good to hear from you, but this call has to be costing you a small fortune."

"Mom's paying for it. She said that since I'm driving, she'd let me make one call to you. We won't be gone all that much longer. Should be home sometime on Saturday afternoon."

"Say hi to your mother, and a here's big squeeze for you."

"And a big kiss for you. Mwah! Bye, love. See you in a few days."

The second call, to Rob's surprise, was from Holly.

"Is this Mr. Grant?"

"You know it is, and I recognize the voice."

"Aw, c'mon, Rob, let me have a little fun."

"What's the occasion, Holly?"

"You. I can't stop thinking about you and our Saturday night and Sunday morning together. You won't let go of my head."

"I'd be less than honest if I said I'd forgotten all about you by now. But do you think this is a good thing for you to do? That is, to call me. I got the impression that Sunday was it."

"You'd rather not hear from me then?"

"No. I'm glad you called."

"I had to hear that smooth voice of yours at least one more time. And it means I can thank you, again, for all you've done. Only drawback is that when I go home you're not there to take me to all those exciting places you helped me find. Mmmm."

"You're turning me on, gal. Not good."

"For me either."

"But it's good to hear your voice, too. Sweet to listen to."

"It wouldn't be right for me to see you if I came back up to the lake. Same reason as before. I can't ask you to compromise your relationship with Sarah, but will you at least let me call you once in a while?"

"Sure. But when you get ready to build you'll have to deal with me."

"Lovely. Then you can take me to bed again and love me all night long." Holly burst out with a hearty laugh. "No, Rob, I respect you too much to pull that kind of trick."

"I like the sound of your proposal. For a shaky start, you got it all together and were magnificent."

"Glad to know I was adequate."

"Adequate? I guess so."

"What I wanted to tell you is that the Monday session had more to do with me than the high-powered legal meeting I was told it would be. Looks like it'll be a while before I'll build because I'm probably going to be promoted and transferred to CMZ domestic. They're talking about Ohio, Cincinnati, specifically. Not my first choice because I'm a New Yorker and it would also take me further away from you."

"But…."

"I know. That shouldn't be a consideration, but you've become very important to me and I'd like us to remain friends if nothing else."

"You'll always be that, dear heart," Rob said.

"Dear heart? I like hearing you say that. You used those same words on Sunday, but today I especially like the sound of them."

"You're important, too. But you need to find a good man and have those babies you want. Still, I'd like to be your friend."

"You will be, but like your Marianne, I'm beginning to think twice about the little ones. I've just turned thirty-five and could run out of time. The other thing is, I might find a man I care about who's in the same dismantled condition you are, and it would be dumb to kill a good relationship for that reason alone. You taught me that. What it also says is that if I thought you'd have me, I'd undoubtedly have you."

"Ahhh, Holly. That's an awful lot of something you just put on my shoulders. And it *does* compromise my situation. You've given me some difficult things to think about."

"No, I haven't. There's no pressure. I just want you to know how I feel. But if it happened that someday you started thinking your romance with Sarah wasn't working out and you decided that you'd have me, I'd simply tell CMZ corporate that I'd want to be in the Northeast."

"It sounds like you're proposing again. When I get home, I'm going to stir up a double Gibson on the rocks, make it very, very dry, and reflect on all this. The drink will make me ever so much more incisive."

Holly chuckled. "Sarah isn't back yet?"

"No. Saturday afternoon. By the way, my son, Greg, saw my sheets and accused me of being up to my old tricks of spreading my love around again. Then, believe it or not, he remembered a very pretty lady with a foreign car, as he identified you, that I'd gotten 'chummy with' just before the Fourth. He's almost eighteen and he asked me if you were good. I told him that sons didn't ask fathers questions like that. In the end I felt the need to confess that you were sensational. He said he already knew that because of the way I smiled."

"That's a hoot, Rob." Holly laughed brightly. "Does your boy have a big mop of dark hair?"

"He does that."

"I remember him. He won't have any problem finding girls."

"He's already found them, I think. I had by his age."

"No surprise there. But, I should probably let you go."

"Yeah, there are some things I have to do here before I leave, but I *am* glad to hear from you. Call me again one of these days. Will you?"

"I promise. Our little chat has helped. I feel better now. But if I call, and you can't talk, just tell me. I'll understand."

"I'll do it. Look after yourself, gal."

"I will. You too, lover. Bye."

Sarah was back in Hampden Lake by late afternoon on Saturday. She got to the Wilcox office just as Rob was saying good-bye to a customer. As soon as they were alone she gave him a bear hug and a big kiss to go with it.

"Oh, sweetheart. I'm glad your back. Guess you are, too. But what's with the pained expression?"

"I had a terrible dream on Thursday night. You'd quit your job with Alan, sold the cottage, and moved back to New York. My pillow was all wet, and because I was crying I woke Mom up."

"Come here, Punkin. Let me hold you. Everything's all right. I'm here, I'm at work, and I *haven't* sold the cottage." He kissed her tenderly.

"That helps a lot. I feel better now. But the dream was so real."

"Just wait until tonight. You'll find out that everything is perfectly OK—or as we used to say on the farm, 'hunky dory'. Ahhh, there's a smile. That's much better."

"I'm so glad to be back and to find out the dream was all wrong."

Rob was feeling shame, but he made a determined effort not to let Sarah know what was going on inside. And it was a moment when he had to recognize, once again, what was in his heart. An outsider, a stranger, had tested his resolve and he quickly rationalized that perhaps his one night stand with Holly Kimball had a positive side to it. During the minutes that followed, his guilt eased some. Then he convinced himself that a few hours with Sarah would give him the time he needed to repair his mental damage and also to reconfirm that she was the most important person in his life. It was wonderful to have her back and in his arms again.

Sarah stayed at the office, almost as if to ensure that Rob didn't get away. When his day ended, she followed him back to the cottage. A note from Greg said there wasn't much for him to do there so he was spending the night with Mike's friends again. A postscript said they shouldn't worry about him because he'd be all right.

"Looks like we're empty nesters, Miss Sarah. Since we have the place to ourselves does that suggest anything to you?"

She was half undressed before he finished the question.

"I need an extra large delivery to make up for what I've missed over the last nine days. Time to get caught up."

In bed, they joined immediately and Sarah's legs held him in place. It wasn't but minutes later that she reached the epicenter of pleasure and she wailed loudly from the pleasure of it.

"That's a new sound."

"I'm in bad need. There are others."

"They loved and loved some more until Rob said, "You're testing my limits."

"Don't wait. I want it!"

The pace quickened, and Rob did what Sarah asked. Having arrived, there was no mistaking the energy behind his robust finale. She joined him with a vigorous climax that was accompanied by a baying sound. It nearly drowned out Rob's deep growl.

They were utterly spent and rested quietly for several minutes.

"I presume you're glad to be home." They both laughed softly.

"My body's been hungry all week and it couldn't wait to be fed. It has been. *Very* generously. Whew!"

"I'm guessing there'll be an encore."

"Several if I have my way. What's odd is that when you were driving in and out of New York, I never got this turned on. And I'm not even fertile. What it says, I think, is that my love for you continues to grow, but it's in a different way somehow. I'm at a place where I really need you in my life. You're so important to me. It's almost like what your mother said about worshiping the ground your dad walked on. It maybe shouldn't be that way, but I can't help what I feel. I love you *so* much."

"It's time for me to start thinking seriously about what I'm going to do with you. No. Not just you. Us. We've had our first real taste of separation now after having been together for several months. I'm beginning to understand what you mean to me. It's a feeling of affection that's maturing. Think of it as the bud that's opening. I used the same analogy once before. Remember? But today it has more meaning than it did then."

"I love hearing you say words like that. They give me goose bumps."

"My feelings aren't in full flower yet, but I seem to be getting there. That you're patient with me helps. Pressure wouldn't. You know that—a dozen times over."

"I'm patient because I want you in my life. All of it. And I think I can see that the flower you talk about *is* beginning to open."

"Let's have an encore and then go have dinner."

"I like your plan. Let me take charge."

They had a delightful repeat performance and then an enjoyable dinner at the Oxen Pub. Skip Rydell was glad to see them again and said he'd have a song for them later in the evening. He kept his promise.

"It's good to see Sarah and Rob again," Skip said, "and I'd like to dedicate a song to them. It's Stevie Wonder's number one hit from this past May. You remember it. It's called *You Are the Sunshine of My Life*. I think the words apply to the two of them very nicely."

As Skip sang, Rob and Sarah glanced at each other and smiled warmly. To anyone watching, there wasn't much doubt that they cared about each other. When Skip was finished, and the ripple of applause had died away, he asked, "Set a date yet?"

"We don't own a calendar," Rob said. "As soon as we find one, we'll let you know, Skip." Rob laughed. "Want to play at the ceremony?"

"Just tell me when."

"That's novel," Sarah commented. "I like the idea. It also says that maybe you're beginning to think about adding Grant to Sarah Stuart's name. Possible?"

"Could be, sweetheart. Now, how 'bout another encore?"

"I'm all for that. Whenever you're ready to go, I am."

Once they were home, they loved again and were happy to share their night side by side after more than a week's break. For Rob, it came down to the reality that he'd really missed his Sarah.

As it had been a year earlier, mid to late summer was an extremely busy time. Rob put in long days, but with Sarah now back from Canada she put her foot down and got him to agree that he'd take at least one mid-week afternoon off. So, on the second Wednesday in August, a new routine was initiated. Sarah made up a picnic lunch and then introduced Rob to Connecticut's Bigelow Hollow, a nearby state park. Heavily forested, and at the edge of a big pond, it was tranquil almost to a fault. And it did help Rob unwind. A bottle of chilled wine played a part in accomplishing that. Although there were a fair number of heavy wooden tables in the picnic area, they nearly always had the place to themselves. Rob decided that, longer term, Sarah would probably be good at looking after both his physical and mental health. With their seventeen-year age difference, it would be her way of doing all she could to see that he lived well into the next century.

And throughout August, they were busy in other ways. Greg asked Sarah to drive him to Truman High so he could register. She was most willing to help out. Toward the end of the month she took him to the Truman administrative office, and the matter was done.

Then, as Rob's schedule would allow, they were active socially. Sarah's roommate, Amy, came by—as did the Erwins. They'd become good friends and were enjoyable company. Then on the last day of the month, a Friday, and the beginning of the Labor Day weekend, RD dropped in on them. It was another surprise visit—this one also late in the afternoon. As usual, Rob hadn't gotten home yet so Sarah was happy to play hostess until he was.

When Rob walked out onto the deck, he said, "What a pleasure, RD. It's awfully good to see you again. We always had news to exchange when we had drinks during our Friday afternoon summit meetings in New York. This is different, but not really. Bring us up to date."

RD talked at length about his new company, a conglomerate in the retailing business, and his role as Vice President-Personnel at the corporate level. Big job—and big money from the way it sounded. And not to be overlooked was his romance with Marcia. "In some ways, I'm as deliberate as you've been. Like me, she's divorced so we're taking the time we think is necessary to decide if marriage will work. The way things are progressing, it looks as if we'll probably tie the knot late next spring. That assumes there are no changes in the meantime. But what about you two? You've known each other, what, a couple of years now?"

"Good guess, RD. It'll be two years tomorrow. Sarah came over with the guy I work for now. You know the story. She and a couple of other teachers were living upstairs in the real estate office. Sarah was at loose ends that afternoon and Alan asked her if she wanted to tag along and see how our do-it-yourself projects were coming along."

"I have to assume that you're glad she did. I remember during our Sentry days, and after, that you were sure it would take a couple of years to find out if a relationship felt right. It may be a question I shouldn't ask in front of both of you, but have you made any plans yet?"

"You're right. It isn't. But the answer is that Sarah has plans, so she's ahead of me on that score. I'll let you know if there's a change. We have a very solid footing, and I'd be less than honest if I didn't confess that what we have shows great promise." Sarah smiled at Rob's words because she knew there *were* signs that he was coming to terms with himself about how he saw their future.

"It's interesting," RD said, "how much Sarah reminds me of Marianne. I don't mean that from an appearance standpoint, but Sarah is gentle and seems to have an even disposition just like Marianne did."

"Shall I leave you two alone so you can compare notes?" Sarah asked.

"No, love. We'll not be going much further with this. But, yes, you're right, RD. I should confess that I have thought about it some, and I can confirm that Sarah, like Marianne, doesn't have extremes. Given the fact that I do, she keeps me stabilized. And she does a good job of it. Justine was that way, too. She taught me how to look inside a person for answers, and it's one of the reasons why I have the feeling that Sarah and I could make a marriage work. But what's also interesting, at least to me, is that they, like Sarah, were composed, in much the same way my mother is."

Sarah reached over and squeezed one of Rob's hands, smiled, and said, "It takes a visit by a good friend to find out what's going on inside your head. Thank you, RD." She got up and kissed him on the forehead.

"Sure glad I came by. That was the icing on the cake. But with that, I have to be on my way. I'm going on to my sister's place in North Carver, and then I'll drive out to Long Pond on the Cape early tomorrow morning. Sunrise is a few minutes after six, and I plan to be on the road before then so I can get to the Sagamore Bridge ahead of the mob. It's always a good idea to attach a prayer to the plan. The traffic jams can be awful at times."

"Sorry you can't stay longer, RD. Maybe you can stick around for a while the next time you're up. You know we're always glad to see you."

"I'll keep you posted. And if you decide to ask Sarah to be part of the Grant family, you know I'll want to come to the wedding."

"You'll be among the first to know. But let me walk down front with you. Looks like you've got a new Pontiac. I'd like to take a look at it."

"Sure. I bought it a couple of months ago. Never owned a red car before and I'm not at all certain that I like being that conspicuous."

When they were at street level, Rob told RD the real reason he wanted to come down with him had to do with a woman he'd had a fling with at the end of July. He went into some detail about Holly Kimball, how he felt about her, and the conflicts he'd had since.

"You were never much into cars, so I thought you had something else on your mind. I still read you fairly well."

"That you do. Well, my feelings have been that if I'm still inclined to be on the prowl, then it would be wrong to marry Sarah. But in the five weeks since then, I've sorted out who and what's important long-term. Geography plays a part in it because if I were still in the New York area, Holly and I would very likely be an item in the Sunday paper someday. Not immediately, but there was much more to us than the fact that she's phenomenal in bed. Where I am with all of this, RD, is that I have to recognize that I'm forty-three now and that it's also time to stop playing the field. Sarah would be good for me, I'm firmly convinced of that, and I'm starting to weigh the pros and cons of asking her to be a permanent part of my life. My age and the two divorces don't seem to bother her, so I think it might work. No. It *would* work, but the success of our marriage would be up to me."

"When Marianne died, I told you at the time that you'd have been a perfect match—or words to that effect. You've been fortunate, Rob. I can say the same thing about Sarah. Stop being a playboy and marry her. She'll be solid as a rock for the rest of your days. I'm absolutely sure of it."

"Going back to the time when we first worked together, now well over six years ago, I always valued your opinions. I still do. What you've just said will carry a lot of weight as I come to a decision about us. I still have doubts about me because I've liked variety. You know that. I'd nearly forgotten about it, but Holly brought it all back to life again. There are two local gals who want a piece of Rob Grant. I can't let that happen because in the end Sarah would find out, she'd be deeply hurt, and I could *not* do that to her. Yeah, I know. Turning my back on Sarah would too, but bedding her roommate would be totally indefensible."

"You'll be all right, Rob. When you set the date, let me know. It's as I said before, I want to be a part of the festivities."

"You're more certain of my decision than I am, so we'll see."

"It's because I understand what your heart is saying. Pay attention to it. Now, I've really got to go."

"Thanks again for stopping by. You know you're always welcome."

"Take care, Rob."

"So long, RD."

After Rob went up the long flight of steps and then onto the deck, Sarah greeted him with, "You didn't spend much time looking at RD's car. I guess you had something else on your mind."

"There you go being perceptive again. But, yeah, it was mostly about you, and me, and us. The same subject and questions that we both know. RD is planning on being part of a wedding one of these days."

"See? He's on my side. Good for him. Now all we have to do is convince you of the same thing."

"I'm getting closer, sweetheart."

On Sunday of the Labor Day weekend, Holly Kimball called Rob at the office. He'd just come back in from a showing and was still with his customers.

"Hi, gal. I'm busy. Could you call me back in about a half-hour?"

"Sure. We need to talk. That'll make it close to six o'clock."

"Fine."

When Holly called back, Rob was free. "What's up, babe?"

"First is, I've been offered a new job, a promotion, and I've accepted it. But it isn't Cincinnati, it's Houston. Not sure how a New York girl will do in Texas, but I'll find out soon enough. I had hoped to see you again before I leave, that is if it'd been possible, but my transfer is effective immediately—in fact yesterday, the first. I'm really sorry, Rob, because what I have to say to you now is something I wanted to do face to face. And I'd hoped that somehow you might have been able send me off properly loved. But before I go on, I ought to ask how you are. And Sarah, too."

"I'm OK. And Sarah is, well, Sarah. She's just fine. And my old boss was here late on Friday afternoon. You remember his name. RD Borger. Told him about you and all the soul searching it led to. I said that if I were still in the New York area that we'd have most likely gotten to be an item in the Sunday paper. That's an expression I've used fairly often."

"I'm sure of it, too. But what I wanted to tell you is, the reason I haven't called sooner is that I've been doing a lot of soul searching of my own. I finally came to the conclusion that I *was* trying to make you a Gary reincarnate. You can't be that and it was wrong of me to think that way, even though I now clearly understand the reasons for wanting to. At the same time, I'm grateful that we met and that you helped me begin the process of getting my life back in order. I'll never forget the way you loved me, so the memories of my Gary aren't nearly as painful now. What it comes down to is that the way I feel about you is wholly independent of him and there is clarity, finally. I'm *very* fond of you, but it's because you're Rob Grant, and the person you are, and not a Gary-like image. I had the two of you mixed up. And talking about that, it's a good thing I'm not writing a brief because I'm not making much sense, I think."

"No, Holly. I understand. I'm not important to you because I'm like him. I matter simply because I'm me and nothing more than that. I'm really touched. It's likely that I'll always remember you. But, much as I care about my Sarah, you've reached a place inside that, for a time, will make me wonder about the road not taken. In recent years, I seem to have cared about two women with nearly equal fervor, so I've regularly had to face that same question—that is, which road is the right one? But nearly everyone has crossroads in their path."

"You're not making this easy for me, Rob. I think we agree that if the timing and the geography had been different, we could have had a wonderful life together."

"I'm just sorry that I couldn't have been around during the time you needed moral support. I could have helped."

"No question about it. My mourning period wouldn't have lasted nearly as long as it did. But, Rob Grant, I've got to go. Just so you'll know, I'm going to hang onto my land. It'll give me a reason to come back. Life's path isn't ever very clear, so who knows which direction yours will follow. Your affair with Sarah may not work—or last. If so, and I'm still unattached, we may yet have our day. You're a hard act to follow. Whatever happens, I'm eventually going to build on my lots. It'll give me a way to escape Texas humidity for a while during the summer."

"I expect to be here. If you come back, I'll want you to find me."

"I'll do that, Rob. Now, take care of yourself, lover."

"You too, Holly. Good luck, and bye-bye."

Rob put the receiver back on its cradle and sat motionless. What had just happened, stung. Badly. He stared out the window for perhaps a quarter of an hour. Another painful good-bye because Holly Warren Kimball really mattered. But his sixth sense told him that he'd never hear from her again. And he was right.

When Rob got home at the end of the day, Mike was there. He, Greg, and Sarah were sitting on the deck, each of them sipping something cool.

"Hello, stranger," Rob said to Mike. When he looked down at Colonial Trail, there was a yellow sports car sitting there. "Yours, young man?"

"Yeah. The son of one of our tenants was killed in Vietnam and they just wanted to get rid of it. Bought it really cheap."

"Sure small. What is it?"

"A Triumph. It's their model 250. Runs like a scared cat and it's lotsa fun to drive."

"So what are you doing these days? We don't see you very often."

"Still in the building and living with the same gal. She's off with her family, so I'm going over across the lake to show the guys my car and then spend the night. Greg's invited, too."

The four of them visited for about another half-hour and then the guys took off for the shack on Harmony Lane. When Rob and Sarah we're alone, he asked, "What's on the menu tonight, Punkin?"

"I have potatoes ready to bake, and if you'll get the grill fired up there are a couple of beautiful sirloin strips sitting in the fridge. I bought them down at the little market and they're ready to barbeque. How does that suit you?"

"Perfect! And just for that, you get a bear hug and a fiery kiss." Then Rob delivered. Later on, they had their steaks, done to perfection of course, cleaned up afterwards, and chatted on until it was time for bed. It had been a day with a kaleidoscope of emotions, but Rob badly needed his Sarah and he loved her passionately. When they'd given every bit of themselves to each other, Rob found peace. Sarah purred.

Labor Day was upon them, and it was likely that the Wilcox office would be busy through about mid-afternoon. After that, Rob was sure that customers from outside the area would be starting back to New York or wherever else it was they'd come from. And it worked out that way. Then late in the afternoon, and much to Rob's surprise, Alan Wilcox showed up. His face wore a serious look.

"Hi, Alan. Didn't expect to see you out here on the holiday. What's up, boss?"

"I have something I need to talk over with you."

"You make it sound like I'm in serious trouble."

Alan chuckled almost inaudibly, and the stern look vanished. "No, no. Not at all. It's more like I'm the one in trouble because I didn't take you into my confidence earlier in the year. You remember when I disappeared just before you opened up out here last spring?"

"Yep, I do. You thought you'd be back in time to help get things underway."

"Well, I was in Florida. Last fall, I told you about my interest in properties down there. A broker I've known for quite a while in a place called Cocoa Beach had an apartment building available that was classified by the lender, a bank, as 'other real estate owned'. That means they took it back through foreclosure. To make a long story short, it had some of the paperwork done to convert it to condos. The property looked pretty good, the price was a steal, the bank offered to carry a new mortgage, so I bought it. I'm in the condo conversion business now. Problem is, I didn't ask if you'd be willing to manage it for me. I took it for granted that you would."

"Sounds like I don't too have many options."

"You've taken on every assignment I've given you—and you've done them all well. I'd really need you to see this through for me."

"Why doesn't the Florida broker handle the sales? Why me? I'm a long way from the property."

"First thing is, there's construction work to be done, renovations mostly, then lots of painting, a security fence to put up, landscaping, and so on. You're very good at overseeing things like that. Then there's a pool I've contracted to have put in. Somebody has to be on site to make sure everything's done and done right. The broker, a woman by the way, doesn't have the experience you do. She's tops in her field, and that's one of the reasons she doesn't have the time to look after just this one project, even if she knew what she was doing."

"*Damn*! You've just given me a lot to think about. I'd have to figure out what to do with Greg, and I'd be leaving my Sarah behind. Interferes with my love life in a big way."

"I don't have an answer to your question about Greg, but the real estate gal has a good looking daughter, divorced now, who could maybe look after you while you're there."

"I don't understand, Alan. It's been your feeling right along that Sarah and I are a pretty good match and that maybe we'd go on and tie the knot. If I leave her behind, she might just find my replacement while I'm away. I have to assume that I'd probably be down there until all the refurbishing is done and the season opens out here again."

"That's about the way I see it, too."

"I don't know. You've stuck my feet to the fire, at least as far as Sarah's concerned."

"Why don't you talk it over with her and then let me know. I'd really like you to be in charge of the project. I'll make it worth your while and look after all of your expenses. What I'd want you to do is fly down to Melbourne at the end of October, get familiar with what's going on, come home for Thanksgiving, and then drive back sometime after that."

"Been a while since I've been handed a surprise like this. Last one came from Kate. You remember her—the good looking dark-haired gal you met back in May of sixty-nine. It was at the cottage just down the road from mine."

"Sure do. Nearly caught you in the saddle, I think."

"No comment."

"Think it over, Rob, and let's talk later in the week."

"OK. Looks as if things have slowed down today so I'm going to ask Cassie to close up. It's time to go sit with my Sarah and see how she reacts to what you've just asked me to do. I don't want to lose her."

"I understand. Call me. Or if you'd like, I'll come out and talk to both of you about it."

"I'll let you know."

As Rob drove back to Colonial Trail, Sarah's tearful dream about his leaving Wilcox, selling his house, and moving back to New York crossed his mind. Except that now it would be Houston, not New York. For a fleeting moment he considered the idea and then rejected it. Totally!

When he got home, Sarah was on the deck reading. She greeted the love of her life with a hello and warm smile.

Rob gave her a kiss and then said, "We need to pour a couple of drinks and then have a you and me summit meeting."

"Why? What's wrong, love? You look like there's trouble."

"Let's get the drinks first, then we'll talk."

When they got back to the deck, drinks in hand, Rob told Sarah about the bombshell Wilcox had just dropped on him. He also expressed his genuine concern that it might spell the end of their relationship and that he *really* didn't want to see that happen.

"That says quite a lot about what your feelings are for me."

"I guess it does at that. Well, sweet, they're very real, I'm finding out."

"You've made my day, Rob. But let me take that worried look off your face. First, you need to remember that you left me behind every week for eight months when you were going back and forth to New York. You also know that I was always here when you came home. This would be longer, but you don't have to worry about me. I'm your girl, and you're the man I want in my life. I'll still be here even if I have to wait until your fiftieth birthday." Rob smiled. "Then, about Greg, I'll move at least some of my things over from Palmyra and stay here with him—just like a wife and a mother whose man is off on an assignment somewhere. I don't think you understand how deeply committed I am to you, Rob. There's a lighter side to this, too. It's that when my February vacation starts, I could come to Florida. A good time *not* to be in New England. Any questions, my love?"

"Not a one. You're being a whole lot better about this than I thought you'd be. But then, that's my Sarah Grant."

They stared at each other expressionless for a couple of seconds. Then Rob said, "*Ooops*!"

Sarah chuckled first—and then was in hysterics. Rob wore a silly grin. When she'd stopped laughing, and had wiped the tears off her cheeks, she remarked, "It sounds to me like your subconscious knows more about your plans than you're willing to admit. Even to yourself."

"That was some slip. Well, maybe it's an accurate one."

"Love it! But if I'm to be abandoned for a few months, maybe you can tell me what the schedule looks like, assuming you have some notion of what it'll be."

"I have a rough idea of what Alan has in mind, but he understands that the specific details are up to me. All of this is a surprise, and he knows that I could still turn him down. He's come to me with hat in hand, so my negotiating position is a fairly strong one."

"You won't close the office here until late October, will you?"

"Probably not unless the weather turns bad, really bad. I've had a long look at the calendar and plan to lock up on the twenty-eighth. It's the last Sunday. I'll need a few days to get organized. Then I plan to fly down on the following Sunday, November 4. I *have* to be here for your birthday."

"I was hoping you'd want to do that. Wonderful!"

"After that, I'd come back up for a few days over Thanksgiving and then probably go back the Sunday after. Christmas? I'm not sure yet. All of this still isn't wrapped very tight. So if you really don't object, I'll tell Alan that I'll do it. Among other things, it means extra money. But that's much less important than making sure that what we have survives."

"*Ohhh*, Rob. That makes me feel *so* good. My objections are small ones. Call them personal. I'll miss you, and my regular loving, but we can make up for it when you're home. Being here will let me feel like I really am Sarah Grant. You won't object, will you, if I pretend?"

"I knew you'd want to do that, but how could I say no? Maybe it'll eventually be more than just pretending. I don't know. It's beginning to feel right, Punkin."

"That sounds promising. Could we go out tonight? You remember that I'm back to school in the morning. The kids come in on Wednesday and a new year begins all over again. I'm ready—mostly because it's been a wonderful summer."

"Sure. It'll be a good way to end your vacation. And since I'll be taking on the Florida assignment, I'd like you to spend most of your evenings here."

"I'll have to put in an appearance at the apartment once in a while. Maybe Tuesdays and Thursdays."

"Not very much different from last year. Fine. That'll give me time to have a little variety."

"Oh, *you*! I hope you're not serious."

"I'm not. Just wanted to see if you were paying attention."

Rob and Sarah had their dinner out and had just gotten home when Mike dropped Greg off. They all visited for a few minutes, and Rob told both boys about the Florida job.

"What are you going to do with me?" Greg asked.

"For the first time in years, you're going to have an adult female person looking after you. Every day. Sarah's too young to be your mom, but she'll be here and be like one while I'm away. Tell you more about my schedule tomorrow evening."

"*Super*!" Greg said. "But you won't be here. Maybe someday we can all be together."

"It'll work out one of these days," Mike suggested. "But it's time I got started back."

"Don't say anything to Alan about Florida. He doesn't know yet that I've decided to go ahead and take it on."

"I won't. When will you tell him?"

"Early in the week, probably. Keep him in suspense for a little while since what he sprung on me was a complete surprise."

September 4 was the day Sarah and Rob had met two years earlier. In 1971, it was a Saturday. This year, it was the start of the academic year for the lovable young woman Rob knew would one day be pleased to sign her name Sarah Grant.

And then on the following morning, the year also began for Greg. He had to be fed early because his bus would pick him on the main road below Colonial Trail at half past seven. Sarah, who had stayed over, got his breakfast together. Rob gave him lunch money.

When he was on his way out the door, Rob said, "Glad you're home, Greg. Do good work at Truman."

"I will, Dad. It's great to be a part of the family again."

Sarah and Rob ate, and then she got ready to leave, earlier than usual, so she could finish up work in her classroom.

"When I'm done, bulletin boards will have been put up, class lists gone over, again, materials counted and put out, etc., etc. I'm not very good with the boards, too little imagination, but they have to be done. I'll see you tonight, love."

"Like I said to Greg: do good, Miss S."

"I will. You too, Mr. Real Estate Man. Love you."

"Ditto, Punkin. Bye."

Rob straightened up a little, gathered up some paperwork that he *didn't* get to late yesterday and then left for the Wilcox office. When he arrived to open up, there was already a customer waiting. This was the beginning of the roughly eight week stretch, Alan had told him, when people came in hoping to find a post Labor Day bargain of some kind. There wouldn't be any among Wilcox's holdings because they were listed at a set price. But once in a while individual sellers, due to the time of year, or their personal circumstances, would accept a lower offer.

The prospect, and openly friendly man who'd waited patiently for the office to open, introduced himself as Dom Amorelli, a retired New York fireman. He said he was interested in buying a cottage. After walking through the qualifying steps, Rob showed him three and Amorelli made a full price offer on the second of those he'd seen. Within an hour, Rob had a signed buy-sell agreement and a four figure deposit in hand. A good way to start the off-season.

When the customer was on his way to visit Old Sturbridge Village, Rob called Wilcox and told him he'd take on the Florida project. Alan was elated. He then listened to the travel schedule Rob laid out for him and raised no objections to it. He was especially pleased that Rob had already set the date to open in the spring of 1974. It would be Saturday, April 13, the day before Easter.

"Perfect, Rob! Easter weekend nearly always gives us a good start to the season."

The weather held up during the weeks leading into the end of October and it turned out to be another banner year—in spite of the fact that gas was now in shorter supply and the price per gallon was on its way up. When the twenty-eighth came, Rob shut down all of the utilities and made sure the plumber had a key so he could drain both the water and heating systems. Power off, blinds drawn and a "Closed Until April 13" sign in the window, Rob went home to his Sarah and a very dry Gibson on the rocks.

"Last year, I was glad when we got to the end of the season. Not so this year. Different from when you were going into New York. You're the spark that keeps me going, you know. But I have family and friends and colleagues here, so I'll be OK. Mostly."

"In case you hadn't noticed, I haven't left yet. But if this OPEC thing and the gas shortage gets any worse, I'm wondering if I'll be able to make it down there. It's over a thousand miles. I called AAA and they said there aren't any problems along I-95. Maybe it'll all get sorted out before I start driving south after Thanksgiving."

The Thursday following, November 1, was Sarah's birthday and they began the celebration with a fiery early morning loving. "Not often that I'm completely satisfied before daylight," she said. "You put a little extra into that, my love. I'll be smiling all day long."

"That's what I was after. A vigorous finale and a big smile."

"Maybe we can end the day the way it's begun."

"Plan on it, but we'll have dinner out first, and I'll have a little gift for you at breakfast, and then another one at dinner."

"You've already given me one just now. Mmmm."

"Well then, there'll be four altogether."

At breakfast, Greg gave Sarah a cute birthday card. Rob added another to the collection and then handed her a long narrow box. "This isn't the big event, but it'll do until we get there tonight."

Sarah grinned. She was showing Rob that she was interpreting his comment two ways. He understood. When she opened the box, little fires danced in her eyes. Inside was a small topaz pendant suspended on a gold chain.

"My birthstone! What a sweetheart you are. It's lovely, Rob. Thank you very much. Put it on for me, will you? I *have* to show everyone at school. I've never had anything with my stone in it. This is really special." She leaned over and gave him a tender kiss.

"You're welcome, Punkin. You're special too, you know. I'm just glad to do nice things for you because you bring a lot of happiness into my life. Been a long time since I've felt this way about someone. Maybe part of what I'm feeling is that I know I'm really going to miss you. But this is the wrong end of the day to get this romantic. There'll be time enough for that later this evening."

Sarah's expression showed Rob just a touch of sadness. Then she recovered and said, "This is also not the day to talk about your leaving."

"I agree."

Rob spent much of the day getting his personal affairs in order so that he'd be ready to leave at about mid-day on Sunday. He also picked up his tickets. Instead of fighting Boston traffic and the Callahan Tunnel, he'd opted to leave from Bradley Field north of Hartford. An easier drive and a smaller airport. But no matter which one he used, he couldn't fly directly into Melbourne. The travel agent had booked him through Atlanta. With a good connection, he'd be on the ground in Florida at a little after 5:00 p.m. Not bad at all.

Sarah was usually home from school before Greg. But the staff at Bloomdale Elementary had organized a little party for her so the two of them arrived at about the same time. As they were hanging up their coats, Greg said, "I know you asked me to go to dinner with you, Dad, but I think it should be just the two of you. You'll be leaving on Sunday and maybe you have things to talk about."

It was Sarah who replied. "We'd love to have you go with us, Greg."

"I know, but maybe next year." Sarah looked at Rob. He showed her an affectionate smile.

"In that case, I'll put something together for you."

Rob and Sarah had a drink and, before they left, she made sure that Greg had been fed.

"You're a good cook. I'm going to like having you here while Dad's gone."

"Thank you."

"Just don't steal my girl away from me while I'm in Florida," Rob pleaded.

Greg cackled at his dad's silly comment.

As they were getting ready to leave for dinner, Rob said, "Tomorrow's a work day for Sarah, so we won't be late. We're just going down to the Lodge. It was where we went two years ago when we were new to each other. It's kinda like our place."

Sarah's glow told Rob exactly how she felt about that.

Thursday nights weren't usually busy so they had a leisurely and very peaceful meal. As they were having their liqueurs, Rob pulled another small box out of his pocket.

"What now?" Sarah asked.

"The other gift I told you about."

"You mean the third of four?"

Rob laughed softly. "You might say that."

"The box is too big for a ring—unless you're trying to fool me into thinking it isn't."

"You'll just have to wait and see."

Sarah opened the box and saw that it wasn't a ring, but she was absolutely delighted with what she did find inside: a gold Omega watch. "You've gotten to me again, Rob. You're incredible. It's beautiful! How can I ever thank you?"

"Just keep on being the sweetheart you are."

"That's easy. But if this is part of a plan to convince me that you'd be good to keep around permanently, you did that a long time ago."

"Then you're not terribly disappointed that it isn't a ring?"

"No, my love. The watch is elegant. I love it. But about the ring. Will you let me believe there'll be one someday soon?"

"Yes, Sarah. I'll let you think there'll be one someday soon."

"That's good enough for me. Now, could we go home so I can collect the last of my four gifts? I want more of you after Greg's gone to bed."

"It's your birthday. Your servant, dear heart."

"Listen to you. I like your attitude and am interested in an ample delivery, if you please."

And they did all of what was necessary to deal with the passion Sarah felt. At the end of their spirited lovemaking, they both said, "Mmmm."

On Saturday, Rob and Sarah shopped, did laundry, and then spent the balance of the day quietly. Rob started packing his big bag because he'd be taking plenty of lighter clothes to Florida that would be left there when he came back at Thanksgiving. Wilcox stopped by to give him a progress report on where the conversion stood and was pleased to tell him that he could start selling individual units. "You don't need a Florida license because my corporation owns them and you're an officer in it. About your salary, I'll have Deana put a check in the mail every week. And if you'll tell me when you're coming back for the holiday, we'll have our travel agent send tickets down to you."

"That isn't necessary, Alan. I already have my return ticket and then on the twenty-fifth, the Sunday after Thanksgiving, I'm on my way back in the Mustang."

"Ahh, that's right. I've completely lost track of what's going on. It's because I know you're on top of things and I don't have to spend much time with the details. You're good at looking after them. I'll need to find out what mileage rates are these days and will see that you're reimbursed. You'll be stopping overnight someplace. Just send me the receipts."

"Mileage from here is right at 1,075. That's Triple A's figure."

"There's an outside chance that I may have to come down before Thanksgiving. Both the bank and the lawyers have asked for a meeting sometime soon. If I do, I'll let you know and will probably have our attorney here come with me."

Rob knew that Wilcox was sleeping with her on occasion, so he was certain that he and Monica would try to make the trip.

When Alan was done with all the odds and ends, he wished Rob a good trip and then went on his way back to Springfield.

“Now,” Sarah said, “I’ve got you to myself for the next twenty hours or so, and we’re going to hold hands, kiss a lot, and just spend time with each other until I take you to Bradley tomorrow.”

“Sold! I’ll have some of each—starting with a kiss.”

“Didn’t tell you. I called Mom from school on my birthday. She complained that I’m never at home at the apartment anymore and hinted that she assumed I was spending a lot of time here. I didn’t admit a thing. But be prepared. You’re invited for Thanksgiving. I haven’t seen Val and Erik in ages, so I’m looking forward to that. I hope you’ll come, too. You will, won’t you?”

“You bet! Your mom’s a first-rate cook and great fun to be around. Wouldn’t miss it for anything! Say hi and let her know that I’m looking forward to a good visit and a world-class feast.”

“I’ll see her next weekend and will tell her what you said. I know she’ll be pleased.”

Chapter Twenty-One

On Sunday morning, Rob and Sarah made love with an intensity that was an unmistakable expression of how important they were to each other. It also confirmed that they'd miss their nights and mornings together.

After they'd had breakfast, Greg took his dad aside and wished him a good trip. But he had more on his mind. "I really like Sarah, and I'm glad she's going to stay here with me. You said she really isn't a mom, but I've grown up not having one so that's what it'll feel like. I gave you lots of problems. You didn't need 'em because of Lu, and Marianne, and then you had to leave Kim back in Sheffield. When Marianne died, it was real hard. For me, too. Sarah's neat, so I hope it'll be OK for you and her."

"Thanks, Greg. You've touched a special place inside, and I'm glad to know how you feel. As I fly, I'll think about what you've just said. She's younger, and I've needed time to think about that. I know where she stands, but I still have to decide if she's the wife Marianne thought I'd find someday. The weeks ahead, when we aren't together, should give me an even better idea what's inside my heart. The dreams I had about being patient, and waiting for the woman with inner beauty, may have seemed odd, but now I'm starting to think they really were telling me something."

"Be good if they came true. See you at Thanksgiving. Bye, Dad."

He hugged his younger son and said, "Behave yourself, Greg."

Rob slipped in behind the wheel of his Mustang, brought the cold engine to life, and then headed for I-86. Sarah sat quietly for the first few minutes. As much as anything, she was reflecting on what the coming weeks and months would mean, or possibly do, to their now closer relationship. Their separation would be their longest since they'd known each other. Guessing how socially active Rob had been in New York gave her at least some justification to worry that things could change.

When they got to Bradley, Rob checked in and was told that boarding would begin at eleven forty.

"We have time for a coffee. Interested?"

"Love one—and you too, mister."

There again was that expression Marianne liked to use. "Well, I'm a big spender, so I'll treat. But before I forget it, here are the keys to my 'horse'. The house and office keys are on the other ring."

"I never even thought about them. Good thing *you* did."

"Now, you won't forget that I come back two weeks from tomorrow?"

"I sure won't! You don't need to tell me that. It's all written down in my head. Arrival time is at a quarter after five, right?"

"Yep. I'm coming in from Atlanta. It's the reverse of today's flights. I also leave Melbourne just before noon on the nineteenth. Mike's birthday is the following day. Maybe you can talk to him and see what he'd like to do. Same thing with Thanksgiving. He mumbled something about eating with his girlfriend's parents. Don't know if that's still on or if he wants to go with us to your mother's."

"I'll get it all sorted out before you're back."

They talked about Christmas, and Rob's trip back to Florida. He reminded Sarah that he planned to start driving on the twenty-fifth, the Sunday after Thanksgiving. It was then close to boarding time so they walked to the gate and started the process of saying their good-byes.

"I'll miss you, my love. I just hope you don't run off with some cute blonde down there. That terrible dream I had back in early August still bothers me some."

"Not to worry, sweetheart. There's a lot to do to get settled in. I'll call you as soon as I can after I get there. Then it'll probably be time to go find something to eat, assuming there's a restaurant I can walk to."

"You're not renting a car?"

"No, the broker lady Alan works with is picking me up at the airport, giving me the keys to the unit I'm staying in and then dropping me off."

"Should I be worried about her putting a move on my very own ex New York corporate guy?"

"Hardly. Alan says she's close to retirement age. I'll be just fine, Punkin. You're worrying too much. Please don't."

"All right. I'll try not to."

"Time for me to get aboard, sweetheart." Rob held Sarah tightly and then kissed her in a way that said she really needn't worry. It made her feel much, much better.

"I'll write every day. You'll want to know how the Bruins are doing, I know. Expect to get some game reports." Sarah laughed.

Rob joined her, and said, "I'll start checking the mailbox along about Wednesday. Now, gotta go."

They hugged again before Rob headed for the gate. As he was about to disappear from view, he turned, smiled, and waved. Sarah blew a kiss.

On the flight into Atlanta, Rob suffered that empty feeling again, the one that always accompanied having said good-bye to someone important. It gave him just enough of an ache to let him know how much Sarah meant to him now.

Then on the ground in Melbourne, he didn't have any trouble spotting Alan's broker-partner, Ginny Helmond. She had a rather nice looking someone with her.

"You're Rob Grant. The description Alan gave me was perfect, right down to your handsome face."

"Ginny. Happy to meet you. Alan did a good job for both of us. He gave me one of your business cards with your picture on it. Smart idea. But I guess we'll get to know each other better from the way he described your business relationship."

"We will. Can't be helped, so we have to be nice to each other." She smiled genially. Rob returned it. "Now, I'd like you to meet my daughter, Dawn Hylton. I turned my ankle, not real bad, but she has to be my driver for a few more days."

"Dawn. Happy to meet you."

"Hi, Rob. Mr. Wilcox told Mom quite a bit about you, so I'm pleased that I can attach a face to the glowing reputation you have. In a way, I'm glad Mom's on the disabled list. It'll give us a chance to get acquainted."

"So my modest reputation precedes me by a few days."

"It's more than modest if Mom has the stories right."

"You're sweet, Dawn. Thanks. Now, I'm going to blush."

"While you're doing that, I'll give you the plan for the evening. We're dropping Mom off at home, and then I'm taking you on to the condos. Since you're new to Cocoa Beach, Helmond Realty will spring for dinner and I'm your hostess—unless you have other plans."

"None at all. It isn't often that a member of the welcoming committee includes an attractive young lady with bright blue eyes."

"Ahhh, Mr. Wilcox said you were in New York before you went to work for him. I can believe it. It shows." Dawn's smile radiated warmth.

"OK, I'll ease off, then." All the while, Ginny's expression showed how amused she was at what was going on.

Dawn took her mother up to their waterfront home on Capri Road. It was a lovely setting, Rob thought, and it was obvious that the real estate business had served Ginny Helmond very well over the years.

After Dawn helped her mother out of the car and into the house, they doubled back to the condos on Woodland Avenue.

"Decent looking," Rob said. "Maybe I'll move in."

"I'd like that." Dawn left it there, but her meaning was clear.

"Since I don't have a car, is there shopping nearby?"

"After I show you around the condo, and before we go to dinner, I'll take you on a quickie tour."

"I'm sort of familiar with the area because when I was with Trident Aviation, I came here from California a couple of times. It was when there were launches at Kennedy, and I usually stayed at the Ramada. In fact, there's a little bar not too far from here, as I recall, where the bartender showed me how to make an 'in and outer Gibson' on the rocks. It was super dry!"

Dawn laughed. "Yeah. It was an astronaut's hangout and well known. You have a good memory. It's over at First Street North just off A1A."

While Dawn was showing Rob around his quarters, she explained that this was the model. "Mom wanted me to ask you to keep it orderly because this is the one, at least initially, you'll be showing to prospective buyers."

"It's a neat unit. Sure, I'll make sure it's tidy."

"And you aren't without food and beverage. The refrigerator is stuffed—as is the liquor cabinet. I was the one who saw to that."

"Well, then, as a way of saying thanks, could I buy you a drink?"

"Sure. Make mine tequila and orange juice. No grenadine, thanks. You have the other two ingredients—and a ton of ice cubes."

"A tequila sunrise, almost."

They had their drinks, the quickie tour Dawn had promised, and then went to dinner at a place called the Surf & Turf. "What great ambiance," Rob thought. "Dimly lighted. Romantic." He had to wonder if this wasn't something that had been carefully orchestrated.

After they were seated, and drinks had been ordered, Dawn said she wanted to know all about Rob.

"We really don't have all that much time." He couldn't help but grin.

"In that case, we'll have to go out again soon. It's no fun being here alone, not knowing anybody, so if you'd like company, just call me."

"That's very kind of you, but it wouldn't be fair to your family. Still, if we could work it out, it would be fun, I imagine."

"My family, as you called it, is just me and my two daughters. I've been divorced for a while, live with my folks, and work with Mom in the real estate business. It's just possible that I'll see you fairly often, at least for professional reasons. But I'd like it if we could do dinner once in a while. Maybe next week sometime?"

"I have no idea what my schedule looks like, but it's likely I'll know more about that tomorrow."

"One thing that's on your agenda is to get the pool people to finish the job they've left undone. Oh, and another one is the painter. He's very laid back. Look for a gold Ford Torino. That'll tell you that he's at least on the premises. If you can get him off his butt, and have him finish something, it'll tell me that you're as good as Mr. Wilcox says you are."

"Why don't we get off business and eat. My engine says it needs fuel. We can get into this other stuff later in the week."

Dawn smiled pleasantly and said, "You're absolutely right. I like your style. We'll get along just fine."

They had a very good dinner and then Dawn dropped Rob off on Woodland Avenue.

"Thanks for everything. I've really enjoyed the evening. You're a bona fide sweetheart."

"You shouldn't use words like that, but I understand what you're saying. I may be back with Mom later in the week. If not, or even so, could we plan on dinner again soon?"

"Once I get things sorted out. Sure. You're good company."

"Nice of you to say so. OK, I'm on my way. Night, Rob."

"Night, gal."

As soon as Rob was in the door, he picked up the phone and dialed 413 245-9076. A soft voice said, "Hello."

"It's a Florida real estate Punkin."

Sarah laughed. "That's not *your* name, but I'll be glad to share it. How're you, my love? I've been worried. I thought you'd call before this."

"The real estate gal picked me up, drove me up to the condo so I could drop off all my stuff and then took me on a tour of the area. After that, she treated me to dinner, and I just walked in the door. I'm exhausted."

"Poor love. But I'm glad to know you're there and all right. It's kind of lonely around here so it'll be good to have you back, even for just a few days. I was going to watch the Bruins, but they're on the West Coast. Gave me time to work the crossword."

"How did you and Greg get along?"

"Fine. He went off for a little while to see a couple of his friends from school, but he was back in time for dinner. Says he likes my cooking and gave me a big hug afterwards. I may not be a mom, exactly, so maybe I'm an older sister. Whichever, he really likes it that I'm here."

"I get the message, dear heart."

"Thought you should know that I called Mom so I could tell her how she'd be able to reach me now. She doesn't seem to have any problem at all with my staying with Greg."

"Good. I wouldn't want there to be any friction between the two of you. That's because you're both sweethearts."

Rob and Sarah talked on for a few minutes and then said their goodnights. Sarah promised to call over the weekend just to see how Rob was getting along.

Monday was a day given over to putting the various contractors on notice that the hotshot from up north was on site now. Rob made it clear, in a diplomatic way, that he expected to see the contractors' employees on the premises every day until their work was completed. He also had them understand that he was the guy with the checkbook and that if projects were slow to get finished, then progress payments would also be slow in coming. The typical response he heard, truthful or not, was that without anyone on the premises to give them guidance, or to answer their questions, they should expect that progress would be slow. Then Rob spotted the gold Torino and as the driver was getting out of the car, he introduced himself.

"Rob Grant. Good morning."

"Hi. I'm Tom Wyatt, painter. You don't have any tan, so I'm guessing you're the guy from Massachusetts."

"The very same. I've had a look at what's been done so far and I was wondering if we might be able to step up the cadence just a little."

"No problem, but we need somebody to tell us what colors go where. Answers have been hard to come by. The real estate gal is here a lot but she doesn't have any of 'em."

"I do. Show me your exterior paint samples. You'll have an answer inside five minutes."

"*Damn*! That's what I like. Now we can knock off this job and go on to some of our other ones that we haven't even started yet."

"You have a New England accent."

"Yea-uh. Grew up in East Boston, " Tom said.

"Well, we ought to get along just fine. How'd the Bruins make out last night in California?"

"They won, 4-1. You a fan."

"Yep," Rob admitted. "With guys like Esposito, Orr, Hodge, Bucyk, Cashman, and young O'Reilly, who wouldn't be?"

"Might go all the way this year. Good team. OK, these are the samples of the exterior paint I use."

Rob went through them and picked out the stucco paint, one called "Soft Narcissus". Within no more than two minutes, he decided on "Swiss Chocolate" for doors, jambs, window frames and related.

"Geez, you're a regular white tornado. I'm gonna like workin' with you. I already know how much paint it'll take, so I'll get one of my guys to go get what we need. Next thing you have to tell me is how you want me to finish off all the units that are left."

"Basically a neutral color, like a very faint beige. The doors and windows? An off white, or a soft ivory."

"I have interior samples, too. Let me get 'em."

Rob leafed through the pages and then said, "That and that."

"Guess that's it. If you'd been down here a month ago, we'd have been long gone by now."

"I have other businesses to look after. But if you've got questions, I'm in that unit on the end."

"The model?"

"That's it."

Right after lunch, the pool crew showed up and went right to work after Rob answered the various questions they had. Suddenly the condo complex known as "Woodland Gardens" was a beehive of activity.

At the end of the afternoon, Rob called Wilcox and gave him a progress report. He was pleased with what Rob had to tell him, and then added, "I should've sent you down there before now."

Rob laughed and said, "I've already heard that comment today."

Late in the week, Dawn stopped by to say hello. "*Wow*! I can see a difference already. I'm impressed. No wonder Mr. Wilcox is so high on you."

"All in a day's work, dear lady. Buy you a drink? The sun's over the yardarm by now, I think."

"Sure can. I'll have tequila again. That Cuervo's good stuff."

It was very clear that Dawn Hylton liked Rob. Her body language and the formfitting clothes she was wearing told him that. It was his turn to ask a question. "Any interest in dinner, say, sometime early in the week?"

"Love to. Pick an evening. I'm usually free because Dad will look after my girls if Mom's out with a customer."

"Let's shoot for Tuesday. Come by at six or so, and we can have a drink first. You'll have to do the driving for me, too. But I won't have to lean on you after I'm back late in the month. By then, I'll have my 'horse' with me, assuming I can find the gas I'll need to make the trip down. From what I read in the *Sentinel*, shortages have gotten pretty bad in places."

"Your 'horse'?"

"My Mustang. It's about two years old now, but I'm in love with it."

"Neat car. Now, I've got to go, Rob. Have a good weekend."

"You too, Dawn. See you on Tuesday."

Sarah's letters were coming in almost daily now. On Monday, he got a replay of the Bruin's mid-week loss at New York and then their win over Montreal at Boston Garden the following night. A bona fide sports fan, she was having fun giving Rob the highlights—and telling him how much she loved him. He missed Sarah and her gentle ways.

On Tuesday, Dawn showed up at a little after six and was dressed in a way that got Rob's attention. He was certain it was intentional. They had their drink and then went off to a place called Blackbeard's. The pace was slowed since Dawn was insisting that Rob tell her about himself. When he'd finished, he repeated his earlier comment that it would take a while.

"It did, but it's fascinating. All the really interesting things you've managed to squeeze into forty-three years is amazing. You've already had a full life. But I have to ask you a question."

"Such as?"

"Any interest in moving to a warm and friendly place like Cocoa Beach? You can probably guess why I'm asking."

"Yeah, I most likely can. But it's too soon to decide. I haven't seen much of the area and wouldn't have been able to even if I had my horse down here. Been too busy getting the contractors up and running, opening a bank account, finding a laundry, doing some shopping and so on. But I'm most of the way settled in. Anyway, I don't have an answer for you."

When they went back to Rob's unit, Dawn invited herself in and asked if she might have an after dinner drink.

"I'll join you, I think," Rob said.

The two of them talked on until their drinks were gone. Suddenly, Dawn got up from her chair, and to Rob's surprise, took him by the hand and led him to his bedroom.

"Nothing shy about you," Rob said. "I guess I know what you have in mind."

"I hope you don't object. I've been divorced for nearly two years and haven't made love for quite a while. My body's in bad need of a refill. I've wanted you since the day you got here. I don't know. There's something animal-like about you. "

Rob laughed. "*Incredible*! You're not exactly the first person to have suggested that. But we haven't kissed, or even hugged. A little different."

"Then let the preliminaries begin." With that, she undressed and helped Rob do the same. He could certify that Dawn was trim and well built. She came forward and kissed him with passion. It was obvious that he was now fully ready to do what she wanted. Then she commented, "Ohh, that'll do very nicely. In fact maybe a little too much so."

"Meaning?"

"I'm built junior size. My little girls were painful deliveries."

"In that case, I'll make sure we take whatever time you need to get ready—and then I'll be gentle with you."

"You'll have to be."

Under the covers, Dawn kissed Rob again feverishly. Then with his hands and fingertips, he touched all the places, and each of the nerves, that had passion in them. "You'll be fine," he said.

"You know what you're doing. I can take you now. I'll be OK if you go easy."

"Promise."

Slowly they joined. "Oooh, I'd almost forgotten how good this feels. You're right. I'm fine."

"You talk too much."

Rob was gentle nevertheless and confined his movements to those that were rhythmic and silken. He sensed that Dawn had reached a place where her sensuous needs were met. But she seemed to remain there. After they'd made love for a while, Rob decided that this was a woman who'd perhaps never known an animated climax. Still, the murmurs and the gurgling sounds she made left no doubt in his mind that she was finding complete satisfaction. Then Dawn whispered, "I'm where I want to be. I need your refill now. All of it."

"You still talk too much."

"Give it to me."

With that, he increased the tempo and then quickly came to a pulsating release. "A refill, as requested," he said moments later.

"Ohhhh, *yes*. I know. Unbelievable!"

"That tells me you're satisfied."

"Very. It was wonderful. You're wonderful. But why do I have the feeling that maybe you could be even better, that you were holding back a just a little?"

"You're right, I guess. Might be because it's our first time together, and that I was worried about hurting you." But Rob knew full well what it was. He was suffering from a bad case of being ashamed of himself.

"You felt so good, and on a scale of ten I'd rate you a solid twelve. Not much doubt the refill was a good one." Dawn laughed softly at the ongoing use of her metaphor.

After they'd rested, Dawn said that she ought to get ready to go home. Personal matters attended to, and dressed, Rob walked with her to her car.

"Thank you, Rob. That was *so* good and for the first time in a long while I'm feeling very contented. That you were patient with me made it all possible. And I think I'm bigger than a junior size now. Mmm." They shared a gentle laugh. She kissed him softly, they hugged for a moment, and then Dawn Hylton left for Capri Road.

Rob Grant spent a restless night while trying to deal with his guilt feelings. He dreamed that Sarah had done as he had done and made love to someone else—in *his* bed! He knew that something like that was highly unlikely, but his conscience had sent him a clear signal. He'd be cruelly hurt, and if that was his reaction then Sarah meant far more to him than he'd been willing to admit. It was time to take stock and decide if he wanted to continue being a playboy or if it was time to ask Sarah if she'd accept his proposal to marry. He was beginning to lean *very* heavily in her direction. But he also gave himself a stern lecture. "Should you ask her to marry, then the business of bedding other women will come to an end. If you don't believe in being monogamous, then don't enter into the contract and later on break the promises you'd make in the Lord's house."

The balance of the week went by quickly. The renovations were coming along very nicely, and when Dawn dropped by on Saturday she commented on it again. "You've gotten more out the contractors in two weeks than we did in two months. Helps to have a pro look after things."

"It's simply a matter of staying on top of them. It gets results."

With that, Dawn's expression turned naughty. "Just like with me on Tuesday night."

"Easy, girl."

"Not to worry. I could use another refill, but Mother Nature has had other ideas. You understand."

"I do." And Rob was pleased that he wouldn't have to test his resolve. He wanted to go home needing his Sarah.

"You'll want a ride down to Melbourne on Monday. I'll pick you up at about ten o'clock. That be OK?"

"No farther than it is from here, that'll be fine. Give us plenty of time."

"I've got to work at the office tomorrow, but would you like to go get a bite after I'm done at around six?"

"Sure. What do you have in mind?"

"There's a Mexican place I'd like to show you. Good food."

"I'd like that. You're on."

"See you then, Bye, Rob."

"Bye, gal."

On Monday morning. Rob packed a small bag and was ready when Dawn showed up at 10:00 a.m. As they drove, she talked about their Tuesday night together. "You were unbelievably good. I could get used to you, and that, but I'm guessing you have another someone in your life up in New England. Was that her picture on the dresser?"

"Yep. That's my Sarah."

"Cute, but she looks awfully young."

"She's twenty-six. That's been part of my dilemma—for over two years now."

"Well, I have to say you're a very young looking forty-three. If I'd had to guess your age I'd have been off by nearly ten years. My age."

"Thank you."

"Too bad. For all the younger people there are around here, they either drift in and out of the area, or they're Air Force, or NASA. Not a good supply of people my age, or your age for that matter. Your Sarah's a very lucky girl."

"Under other circumstances, we might have something going for us. Thing is, I'm not sure if Florida is for me. Your real estate license laws are tough, so I'd have to find some other line of work while I was getting a broker's license. My corporate experience might be useful, I suppose."

"What little I've been around you, I've decided that you're a keeper. What you've done at Woodland is remarkable. Mom's amazed. I think she'd like to have you in the family so you could take over the business when she retires in two or three years."

"I should imagine there's another broker, and son-in-law prospect, out there somewhere."

"Possible, but I'm really taken with you, Rob."

"There's another piece of the picture that I haven't mentioned yet. No need to until now. I'm past the point where I want to father little ones. My younger guy is a senior in high school, so my parenting days are over. And at forty-three that's as it should be."

"You wouldn't want any with me, then?"

"Given how hard your deliveries have been, I can't imagine you'd want to go through that again. But the point is, I *couldn't* have any with you—or anyone else. I'm out of business." Rob then told his story about Marianne, how her hope to have children delayed their planned marriage, and then how she'd died. Dawn said she was sorry to hear a story like that and then went on to comment on Rob's condition.

"You didn't have to explain. But that's a shame, and I mean it. I'd almost let you father one even if we didn't have a long-term affair."

"With all the women I've known, I can't ever recall having had an 'I'd almost' offer like that. Says your feelings run deeper than 'I'm really taken with you', like you just said. With our having only known each other for a couple of weeks, aren't you deciding on something like that pretty fast?"

"Not really. But there's no risk. I'm not a candidate to have another baby, that is with you—or to be a wife, the way it sounds. So I'll change the subject and just remember what you did for me on Tuesday night. But I was right about you, and I now know why I felt you weren't all that fired up. I'll bet when you are that you're somethin' else. A real ferocious lion."

"And *that's* a label that goes back to November of sixty-eight."

"You've had an active single life, it sounds like, and it helps explain why you're terrific in bed."

"Thank you. Again."

They chatted until they got to Melbourne airport.

"OK, here we are. I'll come in and see you off."

"That's sweet of you."

After Rob had checked in, he and Dawn had a coke before he boarded.

"Any chance I could get you to look after me once in a while after you're back—and when's that, by the way?"

"Two questions. Last first. I'll be in sometime early next week. The second question. I don't know. I had a serious bout with my conscience after Tuesday night. I'm not saying no, because the male animal does get hungry from time to time."

"It's probably best to ask you after you're back. Several days after." They were both smiling as Rob's flight was called.

Near the gate, Dawn gave Rob a firm hug. It was followed by an amorous kiss.

"I really do like you, Rob. You already know that. Now, have a great Thanksgiving."

"You too, Dawn."

"Drive safely, and I'll see you sometime next week. When there's a neat Mustang with Massachusetts plates parked in the lot, I'll knock on your door."

"See ya, babe."

"Bye, you sexy thing you."

Chapter Twenty-Two

At Bradley Field, Sarah was waiting for her man with a face that was aglow with happiness. She grabbed Rob, gave him a bear hug and an affectionate kiss.

"Wow! That tells me that you're glad to see your very own antique."

"The last two days, I couldn't sit still. And I drove so fast getting here that I got a ticket. Well, not really. But the State Trooper did give me a warning. At that, I still got here in plenty of time."

"You're OK otherwise?"

"Now that you're back. *Yessss*!"

When Rob picked up his bag, he suggested that Sarah drive. "You don't mind?"

"I love your Mustang. Be delighted. And we're going back through Springfield. It's a little farther but much faster, I think. The I-291 cutoff into Chicopee helps. I made really good time, even with my being stopped."

"So, what's the plan, kiddo?"

Sarah laughed. "Kiddo? Didn't you use that same word out at your mother's place?"

"I don't remember. It's one of my Aunt Mary's favorites."

"Fun word. I like it, too. An alternative to Punkin. To answer your question, Mike's coming out for dinner tomorrow, and then going back into Springfield after that. He's also having Thanksgiving dinner with his girlfriend's parents. Must be serious."

"He's too young for it to be that serious. Uncle Sam won't even let him vote yet. He'll only be twenty tomorrow. But he's old enough to decide what he wants to do."

"Greg's all excited about going back to Mum's on Thursday. I have to work the next two days, so you can be a man of leisure while I'm slaving away in a hot classroom. Between now and tomorrow morning, I have to somehow scrub off all your tan. I can't have you walking around looking that scrumptious. Somebody might want to run off with you."

"Wouldn't work. We're a package deal. Can't have me without you." Sarah squeezed Rob's hand. "But what I have to do in the morning is get over to the Ford dealer and get my horse serviced." Rob laughed at what he'd just said. Sarah did, too.

"Easy, Rob. You're first in line for that kind of care."

"Thought I might be. Anytime privacy permits."

"Let me say it again. Easy, Rob."

When they got home, Greg greeted his dad with a smile, a hello, and a hug. Sarah got busy making Rob's favorite drink and then pouring a glass of wine for herself. Then as was his custom when he'd traveled all over the world, Rob gave Greg a sweatshirt. This one came from the Kennedy Space Center. He was tickled.

Drinks poured Sarah said, "Cheers, my love." Rob offered the same toast and they clinked glasses.

The three of them exchanged news over drinks and dinner, and since both Sarah and Greg had to be up much earlier than Rob would want to be, they all went to bed at a reasonable hour.

But sleep in Rob's bedroom was delayed for nearly a half-hour as Sarah needed hugs and then "a delivery", as she frequently called it. After the finale, she admitted to feeling much better than she had at any time since Rob had left. Needs met, they slept entangled.

Rob got up early and had breakfast with the teacher and the student. He then went off to get his Mustang thoroughly checked over and serviced for the long drive that would now begin on *Monday* morning. He'd decided days earlier that Sarah would like to have him around for the extra night, and arriving at the condo on Tuesday afternoon rather than late on Monday wasn't important. At the same time, the day later departure meant that Sarah would be back in school, and Rob felt that it would make it easier on her if she was busy all day.

On Tuesday afternoon, Mike showed up just before dark and gave Rob a big hug.

"Good to see you, Dad. And look at that tan! Need anybody to help out down there? Be better than working in the building. It'd have to be."

"I don't do any hiring. Everything is done by contractors. Even the janitorial services."

"Well, it wouldn't work anyway. I won't be around."

"What's that supposed to mean? Going back to California?"

"Nope. You remember that the military has recruiting offices in our building?"

"Yeah. I had a part in that."

"The news is that I've enlisted in the Navy and will be leaving for boot camp at the beginning of January."

"Wow! That *is* news. When do you go?"

"On the seventh."

"When I'm up for the holidays, we'll have to throw a little party for you. I'll be flying back on the third, so it'll have to be before that."

"Some of my friends here said they're going to have one, too. I'll tell 'em we can do it after you go."

"So, you're following in your dad's footsteps. I'm proud of you, Mike. If you like the Navy, you might want to make a career of it. You could go to a service school, retire at forty, and come out with a trade."

"I've already signed up for a school where I'll get training to be a machinist. There's a guy in Springfield I met who works for Smith and Wesson. That's what he does, and he makes real good money."

"Better than being in the building, I guess."

"Yeah, you might say that."

"You're here to celebrate being twenty. You remember what I used to bring back when I traveled all the time?"

"Sure do. A 'T' shirt."

"Not this time of year. But I haven't missed a beat. Here."

"A Space Center sweatshirt. Wow! Neat. Thanks, Dad. My other ones are starting to wear out—especially the one from Australia."

The four of them visited for a while and then went to the Lodge for dinner. As they ate, Sarah asked Mike about his Thanksgiving plans.

"Tell your mom thanks, but I'm going to eat with my girlfriend's parents. They're good people, and they live close. This way I don't have to make the forty mile drive there and back."

"Your choice. It's nice to be invited to two places."

"Maybe if I have leave, I could come back next year. Depends on where I'll be, I suppose. Going into the Navy will let me get out of the thing I'm doing now. It's time for a change."

"Glad to know that at your age you're not ready to hear wedding bells either. It's a little early for that."

"I may still see the same girl, but there are lots of other ones out there. Those bells are a long way off. I'm a lot like you."

Over dinner, Mike said he'd like to know when Rob would be back and what his schedule was.

"First, I'm not leaving for Florida now until Monday."

Sarah turned, smiled broadly and said, "That's news. *Wonderful*!"

"Thought you wouldn't object, but I was sure that I'd mentioned it earlier. Guess not. Anyway, I'll fly up on the twenty-first and then go back on January 3, like I just told Mike. After that, I don't expect to start home until April 4, a Thursday. That'll put me back here at the beginning of the weekend and then give me a week to get settled in before I open the office on the thirteenth."

"My dad, the planner," Greg said.

"Got to do it—if only because the sweetheart sitting next to me here doesn't like to be left in the dark. She's not a mushroom." They laughed.

"I don't either," Greg added.

When they'd finished, Mike thanked the three of them for their cards and gifts and started back for Springfield. Like Sarah, he had be at work in the morning and didn't want to be too late.

"See you in December, Dad."

"Drive carefully, young man."

Thanksgiving at Peg Stuart's was another big hit, and there was now no mystery associated with where Sarah had learned how to turn out tasty meals. Then considering that it'd been months since Rob had been to Worcester, it was good to see Peg again and to visit with her for a while. Everyone welcomed Greg back and said they were glad he was home now. It made him feel good that he was a part of the family gathering. There wasn't but about a five year age difference between Greg, and Val and Erik, so they got along well. Then everyone wanted to hear about Rob's most recent assignment, and he regaled them with stories about Cocoa Beach and the nearby Kennedy Space Center. They had a great meal, and a full afternoon of chatter, so they all had a wonderful holiday.

Before they started home, Peg gave Sarah a healthy portion of the turkey, and added that she was sure they could figure out how to share it. Her expression suggested that she had the feeling they were living together. Then Rob made a special point of saying good-bye to Erik and Val and said he hoped to see them at Christmastime.

After they were home, Greg got into TV and Sarah poured drinks. As they sipped, she said, Mom asked me where I thought our relationship was going. I think she thinks we're living together, but I ignored her hints and also said that I'm satisfied with how things are with us. I didn't get into how lonely I am when you aren't around, but that wasn't really what she wanted to know."

"You handled it well. You know how much you matter to me now, but you're still giving me the breathing room I need. And you're confident that your patience will pay off. I think you're absolutely right."

Sarah came around from behind the serving bar and gave Rob a hug and a loving kiss.

"You know I'm always pleased to hear words like that. You're special to me, but you've known that for a long time. You also know that my heart is so full of love for you that it could still come apart at the seams."

"Maybe I can help you keep it intact. When our young man goes to bed, let's see what we can do to show each other how much love we have to share." And they did exactly what Rob proposed.

The three days before Rob would leave on Monday morning were spent quietly. They did manage to slip in a movie, Disney's *Robin Hood*, and then had dinner out on Saturday evening. Greg visited with high school friends much of Friday and Saturday, but on Sunday he wanted to be at home with his dad and Sarah. On Sunday evening, when it came time to load the car with Rob's clothes and personal effects, Greg volunteered to help.

Before first light on November 26, Rob and Sarah loved passionately and then faced up to the fact that it was a Monday. It also meant that Rob would be on his way south within the hour.

"It's been wonderful having you home, love. And you were right. I'll be much better off in my classroom and being occupied all day. But you know that I'm going to worry about you until you get there."

"I'll be especially careful. Just for you."

Sarah smiled thinly. "Please do. Where are you stopping tonight?"

"A place called South of the Border on the two Carolinas' state lines. Sounds like quite a complex. I'm doing about two-thirds of the trip today, roughly 650 miles, and then a little over 400 tomorrow. My new hidden radar detector is in place because the official speed limit, as of yesterday, is 55 MPH. I'll probably find myself doing more than that—or falling asleep."

"*Don't-you-dare*!"

"Just kidding. I understand the Virginia cops are really tough. If they find a detector, they're authorized to confiscate it."

"Just be careful, Rob."

"I will, Punkin."

"Anything new on gas supplies?"

"Triple A insists that I won't have any problems along I-95. They should know. Time to go, babe."

"Call me when you get there. Please?"

"I promise."

"I have to say it again. I'm going to miss you, but expect a letter by about Wednesday or Thursday."

"You don't have a corner on the missing, and I'll drop everything when your letter shows up."

"More than one letter, my sweet. One every day."

"Great! But let me leave you with a thought or two. I'll only be gone three weekends before I come back, and then I'll be home for almost two weeks. The long stretch is after that."

"I already have every bit of it memorized, love."

Greg hugged his dad and wished him a good trip. And then Sarah went with Rob to the car. They hugged and shared an affectionate kiss. Door closed, Rob brought his Mustang's big Cleveland engine to life. One more kiss and he was on his way. Just before he turned the corner and disappeared from view, Sarah waved and blew a kiss. He waved back.

As Rob pulled onto I-86, he thought about Sarah. She'd held up well. No tears, and in fact she'd even shown him a smile as he left. A strong woman he was beginning to understand, and he was certain the smile was intended to send him off in a positive frame of mind. And she'd very nicely accomplished that.

Settling down to the day ahead, Rob went over the route before him in his mind's eye. In Hartford it would be I-95 to Port Chester, NY, then across the Tappan Zee Bridge, I-87 to the Garden State Parkway and the New Jersey Turnpike. He'd be on it all the way down state to the high Delaware Memorial Bridge and then back on I-95. From that point on it was easy—except for the traffic around Philadelphia, Baltimore, and Washington. Some of it would be the reverse trip he'd made with Marianne's little red Falcon on Memorial day weekend 1970, and the first time he'd have been on that part of I-95 since then. No escaping it. His memories of her would always be there. But after Richmond, it really would be easy, all the way to the Carolina lines and South of the Border.

At the end of the afternoon, Rob pulled into the "Border" complex and quickly found his motel. After he'd registered, there was time to poke around inside some of the shops. Tourist stuff mostly, but he bought a couple of souvenirs, including a cute ceramic mouse for Sarah.

After a tasty dinner and a good night's rest, Rob had breakfast and was on his way again by mid morning. Driving south, it seemed as if he was reversing the seasons from winter to fall to summer. Kind of fun to watch it happen and to see green again.

Then at just a little after 4:00 p.m., Rob pulled into a street side parking space at Woodland Gardens. What struck him immediately was how much progress they'd made in the past eight days—even with Thanksgiving stuck in the middle. The first person he saw was Tom Wyatt. From the ladder he was on, he waved and asked, "How was your trip down, Rob?"

"Slow. Slept most of the way." Tom laughed so hard that he nearly lost his balance on the ladder.

"Easy. Don't say things like that. I don't want to die laughing."

"I didn't think it was *that* funny. I've got to unload the car. When you're finished, let's have a beer."

"Great! I'm ready for one. Been hot. By the way, Dawn Hylton's been here nearly every day. You got somethin' going on with her?"

"Nope. She does. I don't."

"She looks like she's hot to trot."

"Maybe I should check her oil. Could be she's a quart low." Tom had another healthy laugh.

Rob opened the trunk and starting moving his clothes and personal effects into unit 1A. By the time he was finished, Wyatt was done for the day and showed up for his beer.

"Let's go outside and sit in the shade. There's a nice breeze now."

"OK by me."

"You've made a lot of progress in the past week. The place is really beginning to shape up. And I can't believe what the pool outfit has done since a week ago yesterday. I guess they want their money sooner rather than later."

"Same with me. We have all the inside work done. I'll have to show you after I've had my beer." Tom pronounced it Boston style: "bee-ah".

"You're due a progress payment. After I've had a look, let's go into the office."

They chatted for a while, finished their beers, and then Rob inspected the units that had been painted. "Lookin' good, Tom."

"You picked a good color. Anything will go with it. And we had some extra off-white, called oyster, so we did the ceilings with that and saved you some money on the soft beige that we used on the walls."

"Appreciate it. OK, let me write you a check. How much more to go? Looks like you're about done."

"We still have a little more to do in the back, but we'll be off the premises by Saturday."

"I'll do a final inspection with you then, and if everything's all right I'll cut your check for the balance due. I'll need your invoice, though."

"I can do that. Terrific!"

After Tom left, Rob went to the phone and called Sarah.

"Hi, babe. How're you doing?"

"*Oh*, Rob. It's so good to hear your voice. You know I worry a lot. Everything all right?"

"Fine. No close calls on the road. No gas problems. Only thing is that you're there, and I'm here."

"I don't need any reminders. Three weeks from Friday. But I'll be writing, and I'll call you on Sunday nights to talk for a few minutes."

"I'd like that. But about yesterday and today, there's not much to tell you. Good trip down and the people here have really gotten on the stick. The plumbers are done. Same with the electricians, and the painters will be gone by the weekend. What's left is to get the pool completed, and then put a fence around it. When that's done, I can bring in the landscape people to do the finishing touches. It's beginning to look really good."

"Love to see it."

"Maybe I can take some pictures and bring them with me when I come back on the twenty-first."

"Not the same as being there with you."

"I know, Punkin."

"I love you, Rob Grant."

"And I love you, too, Sarah Stuart."

"Do you know that's the first time you've ever said those words to me? Oh, *Rob*! I've got tears."

"Truth is, I miss you. So now that I've told you what's in my heart, the next 'I love you' should be much easier."

"I hope so. You've broken the ice. Took over two years for me to hear you say that."

"I won't make you wait anywhere near that long again. Promise. Listen, babe, someone just walked in. Call me on Sunday?"

"At about the same time. I know you can't say anything, so I'll be the one to say it. Love you, Rob. Bye."

"Ditto, babe. Bye."

The "someone" who'd just walked in was none other than Dawn Hylton.

"Hi, Rob. How was your trip north—and south?"

"Fine. Had a nice Thanksgiving, and a remarkably good drive down. No problems with gas, to my surprise."

"Like your car. Sexy. Like you. And that's some license plate. YG?"

"It's a 'vanity plate'. My initials weren't available, so I went for something at the end of the alphabet. That worked—as you can see. My 'horse' is over two years old now. But it's in good shape. I'm lots older."

"I know. But you're in good shape, too. Thought about you a lot while you were gone."

"Have to be honest and say that you were on my mind, too."

"So?"

"Not much I can add to that. I thought about you, and that Tuesday night before I left."

"I had big ideas that maybe you'd be ready to take me to your service station for another fill-up."

"Haven't been away from home long enough for me to start thinking about something like that. How's your mom doing?"

"You're changing the subject. But she's OK finally. The sprain was worse than she thought at first. So, now that I know you're back, why don't I come over on Saturday afternoon? We could have a drink and then go to dinner, maybe."

"Sounds like a good idea. You buying?" Rob smiled. So did Dawn.

"No, but the company will. Meaning ours."

"It's a deal."

Rob was kept busy during the balance of the week with a variety of details involving the property and also with a handful of prospects who were interested in possibly buying a unit. The time went by quickly and then late on Saturday afternoon, as promised, Dawn was at Rob's door. It was clear that she'd made the effort to look as desirable as possible, and she'd succeeded.

"Hi, girl. I thought maybe you'd forgotten about this evening."

"Not a chance. If you're pouring, I'll have some of that good tequila again. Maybe with a little OJ?"

"I can deliver." An impish look was her reaction to his words.

They each had a drink and talked about a myriad of subjects but, as always, it came back to a discussion about the two of them.

"I thought we'd covered the subject of us pretty thoroughly when we were on our way down to Melbourne airport on the nineteenth."

"We probably did, but I discovered while you were gone that I missed you. It's a way of saying that I have such good feelings about you." Rob started to respond. "I know, I know. There's Sarah, and *she* matters."

"She does that."

"Then it's wrong of me to interfere. But with you I don't have any scruples or want to know anything about the rules of fair play."

"Why don't we go to dinner? I can't think very clearly on an empty stomach."

And that's what they did. As they ate, their topics continued to be many and varied and they mostly stayed away from anything having to do with their relationship. Dawn got interested in how Rob had met Sarah, and more particularly how he wound up in Hampden Lake after having worked in New York. Her questions weren't raised just to fill time. She really was interested.

When they'd finished with dinner, and were on their way back to Woodland, Rob asked Dawn if she'd like a Cointreau or something.

"If you don't mind, yes."

After he'd poured, Dawn sat close to him on the sofa.

"Let me see if I have this right," Rob said. "If I remember your condition when I left two weeks ago, then that means…."

"You're right. I'm on fire." With that, Dawn leaned over and kissed Rob with the kind of passion that her condition dictated.

"How do I get out of this," Rob wondered.

Dawn pursued, and then as she did in mid-November, she got up, took Rob by the hand and led him back to his bedroom. His conscience bothered him again, but he let himself be taken. "I'm a weakling," he thought. The problem was that he was now also in need.

There were very few preliminaries this night because Dawn was ready and took the initiative. And as she'd said on that Tuesday night, she wasn't exactly "junior size" any longer. Then Rob suggested that she take charge and explained what he meant. When they joined, she gasped. Then, "Unnhh! The sensations. *Ooooh.*"

Rob felt much the same way.

They began their movements, and then Dawn's passion and all she was feeling, spun out of control. Within minutes, she groaned huskily and said, "I just went somewhere new. I think I just came. First time."

"I think so, too. Felt like it. Electrifying, isn't it?

"Better than that. I want you to mount me now."

"Don't count on me lasting very long."

"Now you're talking too much."

Rob was right. He *had* lost control. Dawn let him know that she was ready for her refill and that he shouldn't wait. He responded moments later with a surge that she couldn't miss. A deep growl accompanied it.

Afterwards, she said, "That's the kind of loving I thought was possible the first time. You *are* better than a twelve on a scale of ten. And in case you were too busy to notice, I came again. It's incredible, and the refill is nearly an overfill, I think."

Rob was fully satisfied, but he said nothing. His conscience was chewing up his insides and his inner voice told him, "This is it!"

"Was it good for you, too? That new feeling you helped me find was something I can't describe—other than it felt like complete insanity for a few moments."

"It was good. We both got something out of this one."

When Dawn came out of the bathroom, she said, "I was right about the overfill." Rob ignored her comment. Totally.

Both dressed now, Rob went with Dawn to her car. "Are you all right?" he asked.

"Very! I've *never* felt this good afterwards. Not ever. It was that exciting thing you helped me find." She hugged Rob, kissed him warmly, said goodnight, and then left for home on Capri Road.

Chapter Twenty-Three

Before Rob went to bed, he stood before his bedroom mirror and had a serious talk with himself. He now clearly understood what was in his heart and came to a decision about the way he wanted to see his future unfold. As it had been with Holly, he had to accept the fact that it was time to make his commitment and stop sowing wild oats all over the eastern United States. Following tonight's encounter, his conscience was troubling him. Badly. If Sarah knew what had happened, she'd be terribly, terribly hurt, and he didn't want to do that to her. She was far too lovable to injure.

When Rob awakened from a restless night, he rationalized that the good that had come from bedding Dawn Hylton was that he'd confirmed, without much doubt, that Sarah Stuart was the most important force in his life—to the exclusion of anyone else. But, if they were to exchange vows, he must pledge to be hers alone. And he would do that.

The week ahead consisted of three parts. The first was that Rob continued to oversee the work that still needed to be done at Woodland Gardens. The second was that he called Greg on Thursday to wish him a happy eighteenth. He thanked Rob for his birthday card and the money in it. The third was to give serious thought to what path his personal life should follow from these days forward.

It wasn't until Friday afternoon that Rob began to think critically about the various women he knew and what they meant to him. Suddenly, all of the pieces coalesced and the road ahead became crystal clear. The decision he reached at just after five o'clock on the afternoon of December 7 would result in a fundamental and unalterable turning point in his life.

The catalyst was that Rob had just gotten a letter from Sarah. In it she had answered his question about what she wanted for Christmas.

Among other suggestions, she wrote, "You could always give me a diamond." Rob sat perfectly motionless for several minutes before he picked up the phone and called Bloomdale Elementary School.

Julia Erwin, administrative assistant, and friend, answered the phone.

"Hi, Julia. It's Rob."

"*Rob*?"

"Is Sarah there?"

"*Oh*! She just left. Let me see if I can catch her." Rob heard her office door open and then the echo of her footfall as she ran up the tiled corridor.

A couple of minutes later, she came back on the phone. "I just caught her. She'll be right here."

Then Sarah's voice. "Rob? Is anything wrong?"

"No, dear heart. Everything's perfectly all right. Very much so. You said in the letter I just got that I could give you a diamond for Christmas. Would you settle for a plain gold band instead?"

"Are . . . are you saying what I think you're saying?"

"I am."

In an unsteady voice, he heard her reply, "*Ohh*, *Rob*! You know the answer is yes—and yes again in case you didn't hear me the first time."

"Would you agree to being married down here?"

"We couldn't do that. I've got to have Mom and Gram and Val and Erik at the ceremony. And you'd want Mike and Greg there. Derek and Julia will want to come and probably lots of others I can't think of."

"You're right. OK. Let's set a date, then. I'd like it to be while I'm home two weeks from today."

"There'll be an awful lot to do. You're coming up on the twenty-first, so the twenty-ninth is about the only Saturday open to us."

"The twenty-ninth it is then. I can get blood work done here, but I'm not sure if the Commonwealth will accept Florida results. If not, I'll have to go over to Harrington Hospital the following day to do it. Could you find out for me? The license is another thing. What else?"

"A ton of things. Looks like I'm going to be awfully busy before you get home. But I don't mind one bit. You've made me *so* happy, Rob. Deliriously happy." He heard a mumbled question in the background and Sarah's reply, "Rob's proposed, and you heard my answer."

"We'll have to talk. Maybe every day. Use my phone, of course."

"I'll make up a list of whatever it is I can think of that needs to be done. You should probably do the same."

"Sure. At this stage, I have more time than you do."

"I'm going to be Mrs. Rob Grant. I love the sound of that. And I love you, Rob."

"And I love you, too, Sarah. With all my heart."

"Your words make me feel all tingly inside. Can't wait to tell Mom, and Val, and Erik, too. I'm *sooo* excited."

"I'll let you go so you can start making phone calls—and whatever else you want to do. You can tell Greg. Be interested in his reaction."

"I'll let you know. And I'll call you on Sunday, just like last week. Give you a progress report then. Now, let's see if I can get any sleep tonight. Bye, my love."

"Bye, sweetheart."

When Sarah was off the phone, Julia had all kinds of questions. No surprise there. Then as she left the building, Sarah *floated* all the way to her car.

On Saturday afternoon, Dawn stopped by. She was probably looking for another refill. Rob didn't give her a chance to suggest it.

"Hi, Dawn. How are you?"

"Fine. Still feeling good about the other night. You're a real artist when it comes to making love."

"Thanks. But I have some news that I need to share with you."

"You're going home?"

"Eventually, yes. But Sarah and I are to be married at the end of the month. The twenty-ninth to be exact."

"When did all this happen?"

"About twenty-four hours ago. I finally had to acknowledge what's been inside my heart for quite a while now. And it's time to stop sowing wild oats, something I've been doing for almost six years since my last separation."

"Like I said before, it's easy to understand, then, how you got to be so good in bed. Does that mean there'll be no more refills?"

"That's what it means. From this day forward, the refills belong to her. But from what you said the other night, I thought you were oversupplied."

"I was, but my consumption rate has gotten to be fairly high. Ah well, sorry to hear your news. You introduced me to a new kind of feeling, and I assumed there were still others that, given time, you could help me find. I envy your Sarah. But I hope we can still be friends."

"Of course we can. Our wedding doesn't change anything other than I'm Sarah's guy now—solely. Before I fly back on the twenty-first, we can still have a drink here or dinner out. But that'll be the end of it."

"I'd like to do that, but with you across the table, it'll be hard for me to go in a different direction afterwards. On the other hand, I have to respect your feelings and the commitment you've made. Most guys, at least around here, would cheat."

"I've pledged to be her man, and I'll honor it."

"You're a rare animal, Rob. And you *are* part animal. I'm sure of it."

Over the next two weeks, Rob stayed on top of the work still to be done at Woodland, and showed the few prospective buyers he had the various units that were now finished and available. It was obvious that the gas shortage had reduced the number of those driving in from the northern states. Those people, called "snowbirds", were few and far between.

During her frequent calls, Sarah discussed wedding plans with Rob and they exchanged lists of names of people to invite. She also told him she'd had invitations printed and that she'd had a meeting with Reverend Gordon, the pastor at the Congregational Church in Bloomdale. Flowers were ordered, and, yes, Skip Rydell would be thrilled to provide the music during their ceremony. She'd also taken a small meeting room at the Village Inn where family and invited guests would have dinner after they exchanged vows. Sarah also told Rob that she'd worked out arrangements with the owners of the Lodge to have their wedding party there that same evening, December 29.

When they talked on the sixteenth, Rob said, "I'm *very* impressed. All of this has been on your back and what you've gotten done since the seventh absolutely amazes me. And a little piece of news that may brighten your day is that I'm coming up a day earlier—meaning this coming Thursday, and I'll be on the same flight I was at Thanksgiving."

"Wonderful news, Rob! I'm going to be so glad to see you. I know you have to go back around the fifth or sixth, but I'll be able to handle it now. You'll be mine and I'll have that trip down during our February vacation. And my surprise is that I've asked for, and been granted, two weeks leave. We'll be together there for three whole weeks."

"*Ahhh*, sweetheart. That's great! When you go back, it won't be all that long before I'll be home. Remember, it's the first weekend in April. This is working out so well. And it's all because of my lovable Punkin!"

"Well, if you want to get something done, ask a busy person. But I'm on a high and not even tired at the end of the day. It's all because of you and all the love I feel. And I have to tell you. Wilcox is happy for us and is taking credit for playing a big part in it because he brought me over to the cottage on Labor Day weekend two years ago. I guess he has a right to feel that way. And, Mum? She's beside herself."

"Did you call RD and ask him if he'd be my best man."

"He's overjoyed. And since Daddy's gone, I've asked Erik to walk me down the aisle. Val will be my maid of honor."

"Anything else up your sleeve?"

"I've seen a wide gold band at the jeweler's shop in Palmyra that I really like. I asked him to hold it until Saturday. But since you'll be here on Thursday evening, we can apply for the license and get the ring all at the same time. Your Florida blood test will be all right here."

"Sounds like about all I have to do is show up and say 'I do'."

"I'll be one *verrry* happy girl when I hear you say those words. And I'm just about in tears. Ones of joy, of course."

"If there's anything else, we can work it in because I have the extra day. I guess we don't have to see the reverend until next week."

"Next Thursday or Friday. I'll set a time."

"OK. See you late on Thursday afternoon."

"I'm ready. Oh, by the way. After Christmas Day, I'll be staying with Amy. We're not going to roll out of our bed on the twenty-ninth and then go from there to the church. I think we should come from different directions and different beds. We talked about that before. Remember?"

"Funny. I was going to say the same thing to you. But we've always agreed on that subject."

"See you in four days. Love you, Rob Grant."

"Love *you*, Sarah Stuart. Love you, Sarah Grant. Bye, sweetheart."

Sarah was giggling sweetly as they hung up.

Before Rob left for the airport on Thursday morning, he made progress payments to the two contractors who had yet to finish. The pool was nearly done; the fence and the landscaping jobs weren't. He told both of them what was going on and that he'd be back no later than the evening of January 6.

Then as he was about to leave, Dawn called to wish him well. "We didn't get to dinner, but maybe we can do that, just as friends, when you're back in January. Mom has your schedule."

"Thanks, Dawn. That you would call is special. You're a love in your own right. I'll be glad to share a table with you after I'm back. And I'll want you to meet my Sarah. She has three weeks off and will be down late on February 15."

"I look forward to meeting the young woman who owns your heart. Have a good trip home, Rob. My love goes with you."

Not entirely surprised at her words, all Rob could manage was, "Thank you, Dawn. Bye-bye."

Chapter Twenty-Four

On the ground at Bradley once again, it was a brightly smiling Sarah who greeted her man. They hugged tightly and then kissed with warmth.

"That feels awfully good, Miss Stuart," Rob said.

"I'll use your expression: 'ditto'. But I won't be a Stuart much longer."

"Nine days, the way I figure it. No traffic tickets this time?"

"No. And I still made it with time to spare. News, good news, is that I asked for tomorrow off, and administration granted it. They don't usually do that just before a vacation, but when I reminded them of what was about to happen, they agreed that it was an exception, said OK, and my hard-nosed principal even added her congratulations."

"A good beginning to a string of festive occasions. Now, since I've just driven two different aircraft all the way up from Florida, would you do the honors?"

Sarah chuckled. "Love to."

"I suppose that by now you have a master schedule to lay on me."

"You guessed it." As they drove across the Mass Pike, Sarah filled Rob in on all the pieces. "Mike is coming out on Christmas Eve and will have Christmas with us—which includes going into Mum's after we've opened our gifts. He'll stay over until the day after. Before that, you already know about tomorrow. On Saturday, I'm going to introduce you to Reverend Gordon. We'll walk through the steps with him a week from tonight. Everyone involved in the ceremony will be there, except RD. He's traveling. Skip will make some suggestions about what he might play. I have some ideas, too. After the ceremony and the party, we don't have time to go far, so we're spending the night at the best motel in Sturbridge. I've talked with Alan and he's going to give you time off when I have my Easter break, so we can honeymoon then. I've looked into the south of Spain. What do think?"

"I'm out of breath, but I like your honeymoon plans. Let's do it!"

"Before we get home I have something to tell you that I wanted to save until you got back. When I told Greg that we were going to be married, he hugged me and bawled. He said he was glad that something was going to work out for 'my dad' as he put it. He went on and told me about Kate, and Lu, and especially the tragic story, the details, about Marianne. That got to me, too. He feels good about us, but he's really sorry about all the grief he's given you. His attempted suicide was something I didn't know about, and he told me how the Lu person was a part of it. We've known each other for over two years but some of this was new to me. What I was able to get out of him is that your life has been far from easy. You've been tested, Rob Grant, and I think you could be called a survivor. It's a wonder you didn't lose your mind."

"He probably didn't tell you all of the stories, meaning the problems I've had with Mike. He's been very expensive and it was Mother who bailed me out at a time I was broke and had no major medical insurance. I brought that up, and we talked about it briefly, just before we left the farm on Washington 's Birthday."

"I remember, but let's leave all those things for another time. We have enough to do at the moment, and I'd like these next few days to be a happy time for both of us."

"Then it'll be nothing but pure, unadulterated bliss from this moment forward. But thanks for sharing your story about Greg. Someday I'll tell you the rest of it, and what he said when Marianne died."

"OK. Here we are, love."

Rob was barely out of the car when Greg came tearing out of the house and gave Rob a bear hug.

"Glad you're home, Dad. And I'm real happy about you and Sarah. Something's finally going right—and I've got a mom, kind of."

"Thanks, Greg. It feels good to think about what Sarah and I have. Life for me, at forty-three, has begun again. Would you come to dinner with us someplace?"

"I didn't know what time you'd be back, so I had a bowl of soup and fixed myself a sandwich. While you're home, you know I'll want you to make chili soup." Sarah wore a broad smile to show that she agreed.

Friday played out as planned. Rob and Sarah went to the clerk's office in Palmyra, applied for a wedding license, and then visited Main Street Jewelers to look at the ring Sarah had picked out. The owner, a Mr. Byrnes, greeted them cordially.

"Hello, Miss Stuart. And you have to be the groom up from Florida. Your good tan tells me that."

"Rob Grant, sir. I understand I'm buying a ring today."

"The one you're fiancée liked is in this tray. Here. See if you can pick out which one it is."

"That's a novel approach. Hmmm, let me see. Sure, this one."

"You two are on the same frequency. That's the one. Amazing!"

"Sarah and I like the same things, and she gave me a clue that it was gold, simple, and a wide band. I love it. Sold. And I'll want our initials and 12.29.73 engraved on the inside." Having asked that it be done reminded

Rob of the words he'd had etched on the ID bracelet he'd given Marianne at the end of March 1969.

"It's the busy season, but you don't have much time so we'll have it ready for you by Monday."

"I really appreciate it." Rob paid for the ring, hugged Sarah and then they went back to Colonial Trail.

"I'm on cloud nine, you know. My patience had paid off—like you said it would."

"Looks like almost everything's in place, other than picking up the license and the ring on Monday. But we have one little painful item, at least for me, that has to be dealt with. Not sure how well I can't handle it today because it's something I've dreaded since June of seventy. It's the ring I gave Marianne, a subject I introduced to you exactly a year ago. I brought the stone back from Australia at the end of sixty-nine, had it set in the ring she wanted and then gave it to her just as we were into the new year. Before she died, her papa, as she called him, told me she'd written a note to the wife of Rob Grant, put it and the ring in a little envelope. I wasn't to open it and I haven't. Since you'll now be the wife she was sure I'd meet one day, the message and the ring are yours. When the envelope is in your hands, I will have kept my promise to both Marianne and her dad. I remember the ring. Clearly. But I won't read what she wrote simply because she left me with so many wonderful memories and I'll always cherish them. Her note to you, if I read it, will only reopen an old wound. A look back, and resurrection, isn't what the day calls for. You're my life, and my future, and I don't want any distractions."

"Those are sweet words, Rob. I remember the story. But these are very happy days for me, my love, and it could be that I'd hurt some, too. I'm probably being selfish, but I don't want to take the edge off all the good feelings I have inside. When you asked me to share your life, you meant all of it. I happily accept that. What happened then was a sad time for you, so I agree. No distractions—at least for the time being."

"Thanks, sweetheart. We see things the same way, then."

"My feeling is, there should be just one ring between now and a week from tomorrow. Yes, I'll read what she wrote, and honor her memory, but I'd like it to be after I'm a member of the family. Thing is, I'm not sure about the ring. It was special of her to offer it to the wife she couldn't know, but it was something between the two of you. I don't know. If I have a niece someday, maybe she'd like to have it."

"Or I might give it to Mother," Rob suggested.

"That's an even better idea. But we don't have to decide today. There are other things we have to do. One of them is to get all our banking arrangements sorted out. I think it's best if we have joint accounts."

"I agree. Shouldn't take long. I'm with Guaranty Bank in Sturbridge now. We can make all the changes on the thirty-first. And thinking of that, we should get some tax money back from Uncle Sam. Might pay for our trip to Spain."

"Ahhh, you like my idea."

"I do, and I've already talked it over with the travel agent down on Route 131 in Sturbridge. It'll most likely be a tour. Prices are better. I've always had my international trips paid for, so it'll be a new experience."

With all the running around Rob and Sarah had to do, Saturday went by quickly. It was a relief then to just relax on Sunday. Among the things Rob wanted to do was call his mother. When he got through, she was delighted beyond words. Both Rob and Sarah talked with her. She wished them well and made a special point of welcoming her new daughter to the family. Sarah showed Rob tears as she hung up.

Their afternoon was spent quietly, and then that evening they watched the Bruins beat Toronto, 4-3. "Good game," Rob said. "Too bad Mike didn't come out in time to see it. He's a Leafs fan and would've enjoyed the game even if they did lose."

On Monday, Rob drove the two of them to Palmyra and they picked up both the license and the wedding band.

"Love the ring, sweetheart," Rob said.

"I do, too. It's elegant, and I like having our initials on the inside."

"Now, that's the last time you get to see it until sometime after four o'clock on Saturday afternoon."

Mike showed up at the cottage late in the day on Christmas Eve. Sarah put together a good dinner and there was chatter all through the meal. As might be expected, it was mostly about the upcoming wedding.

On Christmas morning, they exchanged gifts, had a full breakfast, showered, and then left for Worcester. It was an especially festive day and much of the talk centered on Saturday's events. It was a treat that Sarah's only living grandparent, Minnie Buchanan, was there to open gifts and to sit at Peg Stuart's table. She'd been a Rob Grant skeptic, and showed him a little of that before dinner.

"I haven't had much confidence in you, young man. You've had two divorces and then it's been two years that you've played around with Sarah. I hope this isn't a temporary thing. Sarah's too nice to be hurt."

Before Rob could organize a response, Sarah jumped in and came to Rob's defense. She very concisely summarized what had gone on in Rob's life and assured "Grandma" that they'd be fine. Rob showed Sarah a warm smile. "If she were an attorney, I'd hire her," he said.

"Well. Guess I better believe her. She's on your side. Not much doubt about that."

"We'll spend the rest of our days together—at least what's left of mine."

Gifts exchanged, and another delicious dinner served, Rob and Sarah collected the guys, said their good-byes, and got ready to start for Hampden Lake. Their parting words were, "See you on Saturday." It had been a delightful afternoon, and they went home filled with dinner and love for each other.

When they were in bed that night, Rob and Sarah loved for the last time as Rob Grant and Sarah Stuart. The following morning, she returned to her apartment in Palmyra and would spend the last three nights as a single woman in the company of her roommate, Amy Porter.

Early on Thursday evening, members of the wedding party assembled at the church for a rehearsal. The music was chosen and the good Reverend Gordon walked them through the sequence of steps to be followed during the ceremony. At the end of the rehearsal, Rob handed the pastor their marriage license. That formality completed, the various members of the party dispersed.

RD Borger, Rob's former boss at Sentry Oil, and close friend since April 1967, arrived early on Saturday afternoon to play his part as Rob's best man.

"RD, I'm *so* pleased you could make it. It's a real treat to have you here and to have you agree to be a member of the wedding party."

"Congratulations, Rob. I'm very, very happy for you. I'm just sorry I couldn't have been here for the rehearsal or let you know sooner what time I'd be able to show up. My travel schedule has been a nightmare, but I wouldn't have missed *this* day for anything."

It was only minutes later that friend, Derek Erwin, arrived. Rob introduced the two of them and then offered them a drink. "Suppose I could have one, too?" Rob asked.

RD, having been married twice, said, "Sure. I always have." The three of them shared a vigorous laugh.

Drinks poured, RD proposed a toast. "You've finally done it, Rob! The very best to both of you." Derek Erwin added his good wishes.

Then, at the church, the ceremonial moment was upon them.

Skip Rydell was in place and providing the music as guests arrived. Rob and RD came from the sacristy to a place before the altar. Moments later, Erik walked down the aisle with Sarah on his arm and left her at Rob's side. She looked absolutely divine.

Reverend Gordon began the ceremony with the familiar words, "Dearly beloved, we are gathered here today…. "

After Rob and Sarah had exchanged promises, and each said "I do", the pastor then said:

"For as much as Robin and Sarah have consented together in holy wedlock and have witnessed the same before God and man, and there to have pledged their faith each to the other, and have declared the same by joining hands, it is by the power vested in me by the Commonwealth of Massachusetts that I now pronounce that they are husband and wife together, in the name of the Father, and of the Son, and of the Holy Spirit.

"Robin. You may kiss the bride." And with deepest feeling, Robin Milo Grant did exactly that.

The music began again, and as Rob and Sarah Grant walked down the aisle to begin their new life together, Rob recalled a fragment of a Moliere quote. It was something to the effect that trees that are slow to grow bear the best fruit. But mostly what was going through his mind was, "Our being together feels *so* right. It *will* last!"

And it did. For nearly a half-century.

Epilogue

Although the persons who populate the Rob Grant trilogy are fictitious, readers may be interested in knowing how the author sees the future for each of his principal characters. They're listed here in the order of their appearance in the three books.

Book One – ***Deliberate Steps*** **(*****Along a Familiar Path*****)**

Rob Grant – Continued working in real estate, including his having had a New England Region management role with a national company. That was followed by a brief career with the largest privately held bank in Texas. In the mid-eighties, his lovable Sarah accepted a teaching position with an international school in Switzerland. Rob became a consultant and then later wrote a novel about his life and times that became a brisk seller. Well into the new millennium, they are now both retired and living in central Europe.

Mike Grant – Entered the Navy, but was discharged because of a pre-enlistment back injury. His taste for beer led to alcoholism. Finally, in his early thirties, he took the cure, married and had two sons of his own. Unable to work, he and his family lived on welfare for a number of years. Then to compound all their misery, they lost what few possessions they had when hurricane Katrina struck New Orleans in late August 2005, so there was no change. They continue to live off the State of Louisiana.

Greg Grant – Never really having gotten the drug monkey completely off his back, he regressed and was in and out of rehabilitation programs. Eventually moving to California, he became a highly skilled and twice-certified electronics technician. But because of his continuing abuse problems, he drifted from job to job. In his mid-forties, Greg suffered a paralyzing stroke. It so depressed him that he committed suicide.

RD Borger – An excellent manager and a brilliant writer, he authored several books on human resources management while serving as a vice president with major New York based companies. He and Marcia did finally marry, but later divorced. RD and Rob stayed in touch over the years until RD's untimely death in early 2003. He was seventy-eight.

Regina Grant – Moved back to Iowa a matter of weeks after Rob took Mike home with him to Hampden Lake, Massachusetts. She continued working for major daily newspapers, retired in late 1999, and then died suddenly of a heart attack two years later. Kyle and Denny remained in the Midwest, but since neither had any skills, they had ongoing job problems. Rob eventually lost touch with them after Regina died.

Kate Skowron – Vanished completely. In later years, Rob tried, but failed, to trace her through the University of Nevada–Las Vegas alumni affairs office.

Arlene Olsen – An alcoholic, she went AA after she moved back to the Toronto area. It served her well. She moved up in the CanAir organization and was reported to have married a 707 captain.

Alan Wilcox – Eventually sold all of his properties at Hampden Lake. He let the town take back for taxes due any that couldn't be built on. The big 1813 home he used as an office was also sold. Then the McCallum-Wilcox partnership was dissolved in the late 1970s and the Springfield office building was bought by an investment syndicate. The Wilcox share of the profit was substantial. After the seventy-three and seventy-four gas shortages eased, the Florida condos sold out quickly. By the mid 1990s, Wilcox had pulled out of Massachusetts completely and was said to be working in New York State for a major recreational projects developer.

Luisa Cappelletti – A woman of importance in the first two books, she considered that Rob was her "one great love of a lifetime". After she ended their affair in early December 1969, she was rarely seen in the company of a man. She spent her years building up her women's specialty shops business from the original store in Sheffield's redevelopment district to a dozen stores throughout the area. Rob once half jokingly said that he guessed Lu wanted to be Connecticut Woman of the Year. She achieved that honor in 1998 only months before she died quietly at age sixty-four.

Kim Rossi – The woman with whom Rob had his longest affair, and who is found in all three books, had a key support role throughout the most difficult period of Rob's life. But when he moved to New England in January 1972, and left her behind, she, in the words of an acquaintance, "was a good woman who went bad". She started drinking heavily, and then sleeping around trying to recapture what she and Rob had shared. She then eventually lost her job. Kim remarried, but it failed, had an affair for a couple of years that also failed. In the end, she lived alone until she died of cancer not long after her lifelong friend, Lu. Her sons, Chris and Ian, detested their mother, moved away, and didn't even come to her funeral.

Sharon Kerner – A favorite of Rob's, she became a fairly prominent artist beginning in the seventies and continues to live well. She finally divorced the husband who disappeared early in Sharon's only pregnancy, one which resulted in her bearing a daughter in 1970. She never remarried, but, aided by the fact the she kept her pretty face and trim figure, she had a string of affairs that continued well beyond age sixty.

Helen (Flynn) O'Brien – Close to Rob throughout his New York years, she served as his "partner" at IMMCorp, and his lover after he'd left the company—and she'd divorced Danny O'Brien. When Rob left Manhattan, permanently, she was heartbroken. But hearts mend and in the course of her duties, she handled the employee processing of a new legal department hire. They hit it off well. He'd lost his wife the year before (it reminded her of Rob and Marianne) and he soon asked her out. They eventually became close, married and had two children. They've been a devoted couple, but Helen often thought to herself over the years that there was never anyone like Rob Grant. To this day, he continues to occupy a very special place in her heart—and she in his.

Melanie Goldman – After their fling in Mexico City, and later on in New York, she went back to Kansas City for about a year. She returned to Manhattan, then met and married a clothing industry executive.

Book Two – ***It Isn't Easy Being a Lion***

Justine Siegel – A dear friend and splendid lover, she never married but rather chose to climb the corporate ladder at Kirchberg Publishing until she retired very comfortably, in June 2000. Troubled by arthritis, even at the time she and Rob were close, she now has some limitations on what she can and can't do. Justine's presence continues into book three, and she and Rob (and Sarah) remain friends.

Doug Newcombe – Continued in the executive search business until alcohol took its toll and he lost much of his client base. At about the time Rob left NAGE, Doug married a black woman with an unruly pre-teen son.

The marriage soon failed. Newcombe then closed down and was last reported living somewhere in coastal South Carolina.

Book Three – *Imprints* (*On a Healing Heart*)

Paul Lenard – Remained a good friend. In the late seventies, he bought a farm in New York and operated a very successful consulting business. Rob and Sarah stayed in close touch, even after they'd moved to Europe. Paul's health declined in the late 1990s, and he died suddenly at age seventy-six a few days before Thanksgiving Day 2004.

Sarah (Stuart) Grant – After spending thirteen years in the Massachusetts public school system, she accepted a post at a private school in south Texas. In 1986, Sarah was then offered a chance to become a founding staff member at a new school in Switzerland. Rob gave up his vice presidency at a local bank and became a consultant. Two years on, Sarah was offered a chance to teach in north central Europe at a far better salary. Rob continued his consultancy, and then into his seventies, he wrote a novel based *very* loosely on his life and career. As a footnote, by the time Rob proposed in early December 1973, he'd finishing sowing his wild oats and was faithful to his Sarah from that day on. The Grant's serene marriage has been the epitome of shared love and compassion.

Amy Porter – Remained friends with the Grants over the years. Amy got out of teaching and into other endeavors. She had a brief affair with a businessman, but he walked out of her life. She still carries the torch for Rob and elected not to married.

Peg Stuart – Finally had to admit that Sarah and Rob had a wonderful marriage, so she was a frequent visitor in Hampden Lake—often accompanied by Val and Erik Hansson. Peg retired, and though not well off, she enjoyed her leisure time until cancer took her only weeks before Rob and Sarah's twenty-first wedding anniversary.

Margaret Grant – Survived Sam Grant by twenty years and made the best of her life by remaining active in her church. "Margie" suffered a fall, and died just days later—on Rob's birthday in 1987. She was loved by many and scores of people, including children, came to her funeral.

Holly Kimball – Left to take her new assignment in Texas, and Rob never heard from her again. A very special woman, he hoped that life has treated her well.

Dawn Hylton – Remained friends with Rob until he returned to Massachusetts in early April 1974. As a going away gift, she gave him a Florida good luck piece: a sand dollar encased in a mushroom-like, plastic setting. Over the years, it has worked. Very effectively!

Acknowledgements

There are those who read some or all of the trilogy as it was taking shape over the two years it was in work, and I'd like to publicly express my thanks to them for their help, ideas, and suggestions.

My wife, Sandra. On the scene, day in and day out, she helped with every aspect of what's involved in putting together three books totaling over 1,100 pages. Her contributions included assisting with punctuation, omissions, transposed words, storyline ideas, phrasing, and proofreading. She read every word in the three books, all half-million of them, at least once. She's been an absolute gem!

Conrad Schiel. A retired 747 captain, he also read all three manuscripts and was able to find errors that we'd missed. I couldn't have done without his help, and I'm indebted to him for his interest and steadfast support.

Then there were four people who read excerpts. They each made comments that gave me food for thought. They are:

Bev Agolini
Robert Hall
Bette Ann Romaine
Wendy Thoren

Last. Thank you Google! From the start, I wanted to create an authentic period piece, and their well of information enabled me to do just that. I'd forgotten the numbers of certain New York subway trains, the completion details of the World Trade Center—which I watched "come out of the ground" in 1969 and 1970. Then there are references to music groups, vocal artists, sports events, movies of the time, the Apollo 11 lunar landing, the shootings at Kent State, Vietnam, the Nixon-Agnew finance committee, plus other well-known people and historical events dating from October 1968 through the end of 1973. There are many more examples, but you get the idea. I visited the Google site hundreds upon hundreds of times. Their links to an infinite number of sources allowed me to create a historically accurate background for all of the fictional characters who populated my three books.

Printed in the United States
76092LV00007B/49-66